A Knife in Darkness

The first in the Hippolyta Napier series

by

Lexie Conyngham

Lexie Conyngham

First published in 2016 by The Kellas Cat Press, Aberdeen.

ISBN: 978-1-910926-21-5

DEDICATION

To the people of the lovely town of Ballater, who despite fire and flood in 2015 are stalwart always.

Any apparent similarities between anyone in this book and anyone in real life are merely unhappy coincidences.

Dramatis Personae

Hippolyta Napier, newly moved from Edinburgh
Patrick Napier, a doctor gathering his practice
Mrs. Riach, a housekeeper with opinions
Ishbel, the maid, who keeps her opinions to herself

Dr. Durward, an established but retiring medical practitioner
Allan Strachan, unctuous merchant to the quality – or bad-tempered dinner guest?
Mrs. Strachan, his wife, very fashionable but not very forthcoming
Mrs. Kynoch, the late minister's widow, not at all fashionable
The Rev. Mr. Douglas and his wife Alison, of the Manse
Mr. Strong, notary public, and his worthy sisters
Davie Morrisson, the village constable, of debatable competence
Rab Lang, the night watchman, more observant
Dod Durris, the sheriff's officer, a man of mystery

At Dinnet House:
Colonel Verney, veteran of Waterloo
Basilia Verney, his niece
Thomas Forman, his batman
Tabitha, the maid

At Pannanich:
Julian Brown, a gentleman who needs mothering
Mr. Brookes, an invalid

Chapter One

Had she but known it, that small incident on the journey encapsulated much of what was to come. A staggering view, a medical case, a mystery, and an animal in the wrong place: if she had been able to read the signs, would she have done anything differently?

It had not been the smoothest of journeys. Exhausted by the whirlwind of post-wedding socialising in Edinburgh, Dr. and Mrs. Napier had waved goodbye to her friends and relations at Leith – some of her friends in tears at the firm belief they would never see her again, since after all she was travelling out of reach, beyond civilisation, where surely there were still wolves that would specifically eat not only pretty young newly-weds but also any letters or parcels of food directed to them. The little boat they had booked passage on, along with a quantity of luggage suitable for anyone moving home to somewhere beyond civilisation (and numbered efficiently in distinctive blue paint at the instance of her mother), turned out not to be the direct Aberdeen boat they had hoped it was, but instead called in to every port along the east coast of Scotland – and the definition of 'port' here was, as Patrick Napier remarked, a broad one. The sailors tossed other people's boxes and kists about with a joyous abandon that made Mrs. Napier's bridesmaid, Charlotte Moir, count over and double check the crate containing the new china at least twice an hour. On arrival in Aberdeen, as Patrick was ensuring the vehicles for their onward journey were in fact ready, Mrs. Napier and Charlotte oversaw with as firm expressions as a couple of nineteen year old ladies could muster the landing of their cargo, and were fairly satisfied – until Charlotte took a turn over a rope on the harbour's edge and, in a desperate swoop of skirts trying to avoid a dip in the filthy water, managed to turn herself without turning her foot and broke her ankle badly. Patrick, who had been in circular negotiations with the unco-operative carriage driver, dived to help and muddied his new coat in an assembly of decaying herring guts. The carriage driver had to be distracted from some concerns of his own over a crate on the dockside to take them immediately, and in Charlotte's case very painfully, to the relations in Aberdeen with whom they had hoped only to have dinner, where Charlotte was forced to arrange a prolonged stay. Patrick's coat had to be tied to the top of the cart of luggage, where the smell was less likely to frighten the horses, and next day the Napiers, without Charlotte, set forth along the smart new Union Street to the west, to begin their married life together.

Patrick Napier had spent most of the journey reading some new medical textbooks he had acquired in Edinburgh, while his wife pressed her face to the window, admiring at first ripe farmland in the summer sunshine, a scattering of ancient castles and their outbuildings, and neat slated cottages along the winding road. They soon left the luggage cart behind, making the most of the good road to set a healthy pace, only stopping at the tollbars along the way. Past a village Patrick briefly identified as Banchory, the countryside became wilder and more beautiful, she thought: the hills grew steeper and more rocky, the birch woods danced about the road, the rippling shallows of the silver and brown Dee twisted and turned down the valley back to Aberdeen. Already she longed to take out her paints – if she had the remotest idea in which box they had been packed.

At one of several tollhouses – Kincardine something, she thought? – they noticed that the cart with the luggage had fallen behind, and the postilion, whose heart had never really been in the journey, volunteered to walk back to meet it, so they left him there. Mrs. Napier looked back and noticed that he seemed to think the cart might be hiding in the village inn, but passed no comment.

At last, after several villages had raised her hopes, and after the tollgates themselves had ceased, Patrick bent to glance out at the surroundings.

'Nearly there,' he assured her, with a smile. 'Up ahead – that's the Pass of Tullich, where the road goes to the right of that great outcrop, Craigendarroch. But we'll turn left here.'

'Is the village on the river, then?'

'Spa town,' he corrected with a grin. 'Yes, it's in a bend of the river. The local laird liked it called a spa town. He didn't stoop to planning mere villages.'

She glimpsed the rock he pointed to before they passed into another of the same birch woods with all its delicacy, the road edges frilled with ferns. The carriage wheels grated as they left the fine surface of the commutation road and embarked on the side road for the village – spa town – then seemed suddenly to jump sideways. Her head was already halfway out of the window: she snatched at its frame with an exclamation, and tried to see further ahead. The carriage stopped.

'What on earth …?' cried Patrick Napier, a protective hand on her arm.

'Oh, I see!'

Her breath was snatched away. A stag, his antlers sprawling wide, had skipped into the way of the carriage, causing the horses to shy. The coachman swore loudly but indistinctly, threw up the reins and plummeted to the ground. Mrs. Napier grabbed the door handle and in a moment was down the steps, and the stag, regarding her for a moment with wide, thoughtful eyes, stalked away.

'Hippolyta! Do be careful!'

'The coachman has fallen down!'

Patrick was out of the carriage in an instant – she never saw him move as quickly as when someone was injured or ill – his medical bag in his hand, fair forehead wrinkled with sudden concentration. He hurried forward to the casualty, lithe limbs quick to bend to attend to him.

Knowing the coachman was in good hands, Hippolyta Napier stepped neatly around him and went to soothe the horses, which, despite having caused the incident with their fright at the stag, seemed to feel that the coachman's fall was an equal affront. The lead horse submitted to a degree of attention from her as if it were quite his due, and the others gradually concurred behind him. She kept a hand on his soft nose and looked about her again with delight. What a country to come to as a new wife! she thought. How could anything be more perfect? Used as she was to the smoky streets of Auld Reekie, a daughter of Edinburgh, she inhaled the fresh Deeside air and no longer wondered why anyone would come this far north for the good of their health.

A movement caught her eye in the woods to one side. She turned her head quickly – bonnets were a severe impediment to subtle glances – and saw a figure in a brown coat, moving away through the trees.

'Hello!' she called out. 'Hello?'

But the figure was heading away from them, stepping high over juniper and blaeberry. She had the distinct impression that he had been watching them – as indeed who would not watch an overweight coachman fall from his carriage? But he had not offered help, or even a greeting. Hippolyta was sure that such unfriendliness would not be typical of her new neighbours, yet she could not suppress a slight shiver as the figure shifted between pale tree trunks, and disappeared into the woodland shadows.

'Yes, dearest?' Patrick answered vaguely, slapping the coachman's face lightly to restore consciousness.

'No, not you, dear. There was a man in the woods there.'

'Was there? A local farmer, no doubt.'

'Could it have been a poacher, do you think?'

'Can you hear me? Wake up! Hippolyta, what was this fellow's name, do you remember?'

'Robert,' said Hippolyta definitely. 'Robert Wilson. He said he lived in Auchmill, I think the name was.'

'I doubt he'll be going home tonight,' Patrick murmured. 'Come along, Robert, that's it. Up you come.' He eased the befuddled coachman into a sitting position, and the horses stirred uneasily at the movement behind them. Hippolyta patted the lead horse encouragingly.

'What the bloody hell happened there?' demanded Robert, who seemed to have wasted no time returning to his usual grumpy mood.

'Sir, a lady is present!' warned Patrick. 'You fell from the carriage when the horses shied at a stag.'

'Bloody beasts, all over the road. If it's no stags it's sheep or the like. Bloody teuchters.'

'It's all right, Patrick, I'll avert my ears,' Hippolyta assured her husband. 'But Mr. Wilson, what's a teuchter?'

'It's a rustic person, my dear.'

'Oh!' Hippolyta wondered if the coachman would like all deer and sheep to adopt a more metropolitan way of life, and a scene flashed through her mind of a couple of stags discussing current affairs in a coffee house on the Lawnmarket, while perhaps the sheep were busy in the lawcourts. She smothered a little unladylike snort of laughter behind her generous bonnet, and paid close attention to the horses.

'No bones broken, Robert. Are you able to rise? You have a bump on your head that will no doubt swell monstrously.'

'Aye, I can rise well enough,' declared the coachman ungraciously, and indeed rose – and sat again very quickly. 'It's all ganging round and round,' he explained, not at all pleased with the effect.

'Do we have a drop of ale? And your smelling salts, my dear,' Patrick called gently to Hippolyta.

'Mr. Wilson's ale I can see up on his footrest,' said Hippolyta. 'My salts … I'm afraid I'm not very sure where they are. In fact, I think perhaps I gave them to Charlotte.'

'Oh, well: I'm sure the ale will help,' said Patrick, and reached up for a leather-covered flask. The coachman snatched it from his grasp and took a healthy draught, blinked, wiped his mouth with his sleeve, and considered the world through scrunched-up eyes.

'I dinna ken,' he remarked, obscurely.

'I'd like to get him into his bed,' Patrick said to Hippolyta. 'He needs some rest, and a cold compress, too, to take the swelling. There's an inn in the village …'

'But we should put him up, if we can,' protested Hippolyta. 'He was hurt bringing us here and he's in our employ: surely we can find a bed for him?'

Patrick pursed his lips, eyebrows high.

'I suppose so. I think there's room.'

'Perfect,' said Hippolyta. 'And then it will be easy for you to keep an eye on him, too.'

'The question is, though,' said Patrick, 'how do we get him there? He's not fit to climb up to his seat, let alone drive.'

'If we could manage to sit him into the carriage, do you think we could lead the horses along the road?'

Patrick was taken aback.

'Do you think they would go?'

'They might, if we asked them nicely.'

Patrick looked down at the befuddled coachman.

'It can't hurt to try, I suppose. And certainly neither of us can drive. In that case, my dear, could you possibly help?'

'Oh!' Hippolyta was not in the habit of manhandling strange men, but an image came into her mind of those friends at Leith Harbour and their dismayed gazes as she set off into the wilds. Her mouth formed a determined line. She had chosen the wilds, and she should face what came with them, even if it were nothing so out of the ordinary as a coachman with a bump on his head.

'Any hints, Robert?' Patrick asked the coachman as they settled him along the hard seat. The coachman tipped back, let out a wild groan and vomited over the floor. Hippolyta slapped her hands to her mouth. Robert slumped back on to the cushions, looking somewhat relieved.

'There's a bucket on the back of the carriage,' Hippolyta ventured, trying not to breathe in. Patrick cast about, then pointed off the road beside the birch wood.

'I believe there might be a stream there: I think I remember it rising in the winter.'

'Rising? Up here?'

'Oh, the Dee itself has been known to flood, you know! But there will be no danger at this little burn. Would you rather stay with Wilson, or fill the bucket? We cannot let him sit in this filth, I believe.'

'No, not at all. I'll go with the bucket, my dear,' said Hippolyta. She unhooked the bucket from the back of the carriage, adjusted her gloves, and set off.

She was only thirty yards or so from Patrick when she found the stream, but it felt much further. If she did not look back at the carriage, she could think herself alone in the Highlands, a situation akin to nothing she had felt before. Papa would never have let her so far from his sight, and Mother would not consider it quite proper: and her sisters would laugh indulgently and gather her up with their own bairns, as if she were still a baby. A little thrill ran through her.

She steadied herself at the side of the stream, and leaned to dip the bucket into the clear silver water. She could feel the chill rise from it even though she kept her hands dry and her elaborate skirts clear. Keeping the bucket at the best angle she could find to scoop the most water, she gently straightened – and nearly dropped the bucket. The shadowy man in the brown coat was watching her again, from within the wood.

'Hello!' she called again. He must be shy, she thought. 'Do you live around here?' Struck by a moment's anxiety, she added, 'Are these your fields?'

The man backed off into the woods again, and turned away. A light, sunny breeze gusted, and the birch leaves tossed like a great shrug: he was gone.

She could see Patrick watching her from the road.

'All well?' he called.

'Yes, yes!' She strode determinedly towards him with the bucket, trying to look as if she negotiated this kind of thing every day. When she was closer, she added, 'That man was watching again.'

'Well, I didn't imagine he would have gone far,' Patrick admitted, taking the bucket from her with one hand and helping her back on to the road with the other. He glanced at the woods, and quickly kissed her on the lips. 'There! Now he'll know there's no point admiring you from a distance: you are spoken for, ma'am.'

They laughed together, then remembered the task at hand. Robert Wilson was lying back with his feet across the carriage, and opening both doors Patrick sluiced the vomit away fairly expertly with the water from the bucket. Then they returned to the horses, and with a few persuasive words from Hippolyta they eased them forward, encouraging them as they again took the strain of the heavy carriage.

And so Hippolyta Napier entered for the first time the spa town that was to be her home, leading a carriage and four with her new husband, while the coachman snored loudly in the carriage itself.

'It's like the New Town of Edinburgh in miniature!' Hippolyta cried in delight.

'Well, it's very regularly planned, yes,' agreed her husband. 'This is the green, you see: and fortunately we have only to turn here …' Conversation paused as they tried to work out a way to turn into the narrow street at the edge of the green. The corner into the village had been tight enough. 'And here we are, at last!'

A cottage sat like an eager dog waiting for attention by the side of the road, two little dormer windows like anxious eyes above two ordinary windows downstairs, with the door in the centre. A little garden, full of summer flowers, softened its granite outline. Hippolyta beamed at it, and turned to smile a greeting at all the people – mostly small boys – who had gathered to see such an odd sight, and in gathering had helped them along from the foot of the village. The horses had been less keen on their welcome and had shied at several unusual noises, but they were now being led away to the inn's stables for food and water, and a couple of labourers had been encouraged to help Robert Wilson out of the back of the carriage and into the cottage.

The way was barred by a stout woman in dusty black, who stood in the doorway and glowered.

'Ah, Mrs. Riach! I'm back!' Patrick hurried up to her. 'May I present Mrs. Riach? Mrs. Riach, Mrs. Napier.'

'Aye, welcome, I'm sure,' said Mrs. Riach, with a slice of a curtsey that cut off Hippolyta's greeting like a carving knife. 'What's this fellow, though?'

'The coachman, Robert Wilson, has suffered an injury,' Patrick explained. 'He'll need a bed made up for him just now, Mrs. Riach.'

'That's all very fine, but what about your dinner? Will you be wanting it or not, for it's been ready these past two hours?'

Hippolyta stared at her. Her mother's housekeeper never spoke like that to her mother: Mrs. Riach must be very angry about the dinner being spoiled.

'I'm sure we could eat it just as soon as Mr. Wilson is settled, Mrs. Riach. After all, if it has been ready for two hours, perhaps it could keep just a little longer?'

She thought she was being sensible, but the look Mrs. Riach flashed upon her was to say the least dismissive.

'Mr. Wilson is not well and he needs to lie down, Mrs. Riach. I'm sure you don't want to keep these good people waiting in the street while we eat our dinner.'

Patrick's argument seemed to sway her more efficiently. Wilson was brought into the kitchen and propped on a settle until

Mrs. Riach and a maid had made up a rough bed in the attic, and the labourers then helped him up the stairs and laid him down on it. One of them even stayed and thoughtfully pulled off the coachman's boots. Then the labourers were tipped, the coachman settled on his side with a pail for any further vomiting and a cold compress on his head, and with the dust of the road still on her face Hippolyta sat down to dinner at what was intended to be her own table, with her husband at the head. The food was lukewarm, but they could hardly object: at least, so Hippolyta thought.

'The trouble is,' said Patrick softly when Mrs. Riach had departed with the maid for the kitchen, 'I only suggested a time we might arrive. I made her no promises, and she should know that travellers cannot be held to a particular time. I am sorry, my dear.'

'Oh! I see,' said Hippolyta. 'I did wonder how she could have known when we were supposed to eat. Still, the food is delicious, and a hot meal would have been heavy, no doubt, on a warm day like this.' She smiled at him. 'The house is charming! I look forward very much to exploring it and the village – oh! Spa town!'

'Spa town,' Patrick laughed with her. 'Well, let us go for a walk after dinner, and see who we see.'

At least, Hippolyta thought, she had the chance to change out of her dusty travelling clothes and into one of her new walking dresses, in her favourite blue floral print and with a deep layered skirt heavy with overstitching around the hem. It swung with gratifying elegance as she examined her appearance in the cheval glass: it was as well she had kept some clothes in the carriage with them, for who knew when the cart might arrive. Patrick smiled as she came downstairs and offered her his arm, and they set off down the little garden path and out on to the sunny green, where there was a surprising number of elegant people promenading.

'The summer's visitors,' said Patrick. 'We are growing fashionable! Some are ill, some fancy they are ill, and some simply enjoy the clear air. It will clear out quickly enough when the weather changes, but it is bringing quite a little prosperity to the town.'

Almost opposite their cottage was a tall, imposing church – a centrical church for three parishes, Patrick explained, and almost as large as any one might see in Edinburgh. Around it the little rows of houses were arranged just so, as the old laird had dictated. The streets were clean and neatly kept, with none of the middens and ashpits they had seen in the villages along their way.

'Old Farquharson of Monaltrie had seen to the buildings at the spa,' Patrick explained, 'but the place proved too popular.'

'Where is the spa?' Hippolyta asked, looking around for some Bath-like structure.

'Oh, over on the other side of the Dee, and downstream a mile or so, with a hotel which is also full at this time of year. But the land there is steep: he built Pannanich Lodge further upstream to accommodate more visitors, but even that proved insufficient, and so he came here to the nearest flat land and planned his village – spa town – here. Pannanich is the name of the wells, too, but this area was known as Ballater so he kept the name.'

'And is he still the laird?'

'No, he died last year. The place belongs to Farquharson of Invercauld, now: we'll see how things go with an absent landlord.'

'But you said there are still lots of visitors for the spa?' Hippolyta had a moment's anxiety: Patrick's practice was to be built – was being built – on the visiting patients and those who had taken up longer term residence to be near the healing waters.

'That's right: the spa and the fresh air really do seem to make people feel better.'

'That I can well imagine,' Hippolyta agreed, taking in a deep breath. She had just puffed it out with a laugh when someone called out from across the street,

'Dr. Napier! I'm delighted to see you back, sir!'

They both turned, and Patrick smiled and bowed a greeting. The man who had called out hurried across to them, arms out in welcome.

'Mrs. Napier! Napier, man, introduce me to your new wife at once!'

'My dear,' said Patrick, 'this is Dr. Durward, my mentor here. My wife, Dr. Durward.'

'Never mind 'mentor', Mrs. Napier, your husband is a much valued colleague. I don't know how I should manage all these people and their illnesses were it not for him. And I don't know when I was so delighted as when he told me he was to go to Edinburgh and bring back a wife!'

Hippolyta curtseyed very properly and smiled. This was more reassuring. Durward was a broad, florid man, handsome enough, not fat but heavy like a plough horse, with blue eyes of marked intelligence. He felt reliable, if loud.

'I have heard a great deal about you, Dr. Durward. I believe my husband has been very fortunate to find such a situation and such supportive friends.'

'Nonsense!' cried Durward, with a firm gesticulation of disagreement. 'Napier here is the kind who would find – and deserve – friendship and fortune everywhere he goes.'

Hippolyta decided that anyone who discerned such virtues in her lovely husband had to be a friend, and favoured him with a broader smile.

'And what do you think of your new home, Mrs. Napier?' the new friend asked.

'I think it's charming, Dr. Durward. I am sure I shall be very happy here.' She and Patrick exchanged glances in the manner of many newlyweds, which, she tried to remember, tended to have a nauseating effect on those around them. He was so handsome, though, it was difficult to control such glances: she watched him as he assured Dr. Durward of the books he had brought back for him from Edinburgh. He was as tall as Durward, though obviously not so wide, but his shoulders were broad and sat very well in his tailored coat. He was fair haired – so was she, but his was a warmer fair, with hints of reddish brown to it – and his eyes were deep blue of a shade she found particularly pleasing to gaze into. Her heart gave a little bounce as she thought again how lucky she was.

Durward was smiling indulgently at them, and she pulled herself together.

'Do you live nearby, Dr. Durward?' she asked.

'I have a little place next to the inn, by the river,' he said, with a gesture down the hill. 'But being a carefree bachelor – or that is not a phrase I should use in front of newlyweds, is it?' he laughed. 'Being a lonely bachelor, I spend a good deal of my time preying on others with better run establishments, seeking company, food and entertainment. A shameful existence, is it not?'

It was Hippolyta's turn to laugh, seeing that Patrick found Durward amusing, too.

'Perhaps you should find yourself a wife, too!' she teased.

'I have often said so, Dr. Durward,' Patrick supported her.

'Alas, I am too old for such romances,' said Durward, with a mock-tragic expression. 'I must simply make do with friends, and trust that I do not wear out their patience! And now I must go on, and leave you to your walk, I believe: I am off to call on the Strachans, and see if they will feed me a little supper later. Good day to you!'

'I hope I did not say anything out of place,' said Hippolyta when he was out of earshot. 'He seems to invite teasing and familiarity.'

'He does,' Patrick agreed. 'And he has been a good friend to me, so I should not want you to be cold to him. I do wonder, though, why he has not married. It cannot be for lack of funds, and he is a handsome man.'

'*Fairly* handsome,' said Hippolyta, her eyes on her husband's face again.

'Only fairly?' he asked, and the conversation subsided into one only really interesting to those taking part - though to them, delightful.

She did admit to a few darker clouds on the horizon, though, when she went to find Mrs. Riach later.

'Dinner was delicious, Mrs. Riach. I know we shall have to meet daily to plan meals and suchlike, but perhaps you already have intentions for tomorrow?'

The housekeeper muttered something incomprehensible.

'I beg your pardon?'

'Ah sed, how would Ah ken fit you'd be wanting afore you even cam here? Fit wye wud Ah ken a' that?'

Hippolyta found herself focussing hard on Mrs. Riach's lips, as if watching the shapes they made could give her a clue to her meaning. She jumped when she realised Mrs. Riach had stopped speaking and was waiting for her response.

'Well, we're here now. And you would know what Dr. Napier likes, anyway.'

Mrs. Riach grunted unattractively.

'When do you like to do your marketing?' Hippolyta asked, trying to be accommodating.

'Early on, a' course.'

'Of course. Shall we meet at seven tomorrow and discuss the day?'

'Aye, Ah suppose. Fit wye am Ah supposed to feed thon loon up the stair?'

Loon, thought Hippolyta – what on earth? Up the stair, though: she must mean Robert Wilson.

'You'd better ask Dr. Napier what he is allowed to eat,' she said quickly, relieved to pass on some responsibility. 'He's had a bang on the head and he's been sick, so perhaps he should not have anything heavy just yet.'

'Aye, right,' said Mrs. Riach. 'Did you want a'thin' else? For Ah'd best go and change his bucket the now.'

'Yes, yes,' agreed Hippolyta, relieved, 'off you go and do that, by all means.'

The housekeeper all but shoved past her, and disappeared up the stairs. Hippolyta leaned against the wall and sighed.

'But, my dear Charlotte,' she wrote later to her erstwhile bridesmaid back in Aberdeen, 'I fear that the close friendship I have always admired between my mother and Mrs. Stair will be harder to achieve with Mrs. Riach than I had hoped. But no doubt she had looked forward much to our arrival and to have it spoiled by our lateness and the incumbrance of the injured coachman must have disappointed her greatly. Once he is well and gone, and the slight over the dinner (which was perfectly good, if a little chilled) is forgotten, we shall get along very well, I am sure!'

Chapter Two

The next morning, Patrick Napier announced that he would have to go and see some of his patients, in the village and at the wells. Hippolyta waved him goodbye proudly, conscious of the pleasure she took in being a doctor's wife, then wondered what she was to do with her time until he reappeared for his dinner. She had already had her morning meeting with Mrs. Riach, during which she was informed in no uncertain terms that her new husband was fond of a piece of roast mutton but could not tolerate ham under any circumstances. Since Hippolyta had seen him tucking into ham with every appearance of enjoyment on several occasions, this puzzled her, but for the moment she let it lie.

It was another sunny morning with a delicate breeze breathing over it, and she was exploring the garden at the rear of the house when Mrs. Riach made her appearance at the kitchen door.

'Mrs. Strachan and Mrs. Kynoch have called, ma'am,' she announced with unwonted clarity.

'Mrs. Who and Mrs. Who?'

'Mrs. Strachan, she's the wife of Mr. Strachan that has the shop in the high street. And Mrs. Kynoch, she's the widow of the old minister. You'd best smarten yourself up,' she added, smacking her lips sharply together as she saw the damp and the leaves on Hippolyta's gown. Hippolyta flicked out her shawl and rearranged it, brushed down her skirt and followed Mrs. Riach indoors, trying not to be cross with her housekeeper.

'Mrs. Napier. Welcome to Ballater.'

Mrs. Kynoch, the widow, was small, fat, and beady-eyed. She wore an assortment of clothing which seemed to have been selected at random, and her voice was irritatingly squeaky, but her smile seemed welcoming enough. Mrs. Strachan, on the other hand, was tall and fair, with a wide bonnet straight from some very fashionable emporium, and a distant, kindly expression on her face. Her gaze hovered somewhere slightly above Hippolyta's eyebrows. Hippolyta, heart thumping, asked Mrs. Riach to bring in tea, and showed the ladies to seats – well, the lady and Mrs. Kynoch, anyway, she could not resist thinking.

'Was your journey a good one? I hear your coachman was injured!' Mrs. Kynoch bent forward eagerly in her chair.

'Yes, he has a concussion, but we hope he will be quite well soon.'

'How fortunate for him to be conveying a doctor at the time!'

'Well, perhaps. If the accident were to happen anyway, I suppose,' said Hippolyta.

'I'm sure nothing like that has happened to the regular coach for an age!' she shrilled.

'There's a regular coach?'

'There are two! The Aberdeen and Ballater Coach – that's the one that used to be the Telegraph Coach, only now it goes to Anderson's in the Castlegait, not to Dempster's – it goes on Tuesdays, Thursdays and Saturdays in the evening. The Royal Highlander, it goes to Dempster's now – Dempster's is in Union Street - it's much more convenient for it goes every day at a quarter to three, and you're into Aberdeen by nine at night. Not that I ever take either of them myself, nowadays … But then you'll need to know about the carrier, too. He goes on a Wednesday and comes back on a Thursday, and if you need friends to direct anything he lodges at Ross's in Little Belmont Street. Everything goes through Aberdeen, of course! But of course if you have an urgent message to send at any other time – or not quite urgent, but, you know, not that needs to wait for the carrier, Mr. Strachan frequently has carts going to and fro, doesn't he, Mrs. Strachan?'

'Oh, yes,' said Mrs. Strachan. 'I'm sure you would be very welcome to make use of any going in a convenient direction.' Hippolyta, head spinning with Mrs. Kynoch's information, had the impression that she and her parlour were a touch too low for the merchant's wife to connect with, and bridled a little. Was not her father a lawyer in Edinburgh? But Mrs. Strachan was so very elegant.

'You are very kind, ma'am,' she said dutifully.

'Are you settling in well?' Mrs. Kynoch bounced in again. 'Is there any other information you need? I know your dear husband is such an established member of the community here already, but gentlemen do not always know quite everything a lady needs to run her household!'

'I believe I am well enough informed at present, ma'am,' said Hippolyta.

'And you have travelled all the way from Edinburgh! We were all very excited when Dr. Napier told us the lovely news! Tell me, were you born in Edinburgh or had you come to stay there?'

'I was born there, and lived all my life there except for a few trips to England,' Hippolyta explained. 'My father is a lawyer. I have two older sisters who are already married with children of their own, and they live in Edinburgh, too.'

'Then it must be strange for you to come so far north!'

Hippolyta laughed, a little stiffly. She did not want to be thought of as some foreign traveller, anxious at every wild landscape.

'I believe I shall be very happy here!'

'I have heard, Mrs. Napier, that you paint exceeding well,' said Mrs. Strachan suddenly. Both the other ladies stared at her, surprised. Hippolyta cleared her throat.

'Someone has been very kind, ma'am, but it is true that I love to paint.'

'Are these two works your own, then?' Mrs. Strachan asked, rising to examine two watercolours on the wall behind Hippolyta. They were of the Hermitage at Braid, near Edinburgh. Hippolyta and Mrs. Kynoch rose, too.

'They are, ma'am. I have brought a few views with me, to remind me of my childhood home.'

Mrs. Strachan leaned delicately towards them, like a fine reed bending in the wind, the back of her dress with its low waist sitting so perfectly Hippolyta gave a little sigh of envious delight. Mrs. Kynoch eyed the nearer one briefly.

'I haven't an artistic bone in my body, Mrs. Napier, but I'll agree they're bonny! Mrs. Strachan, now, she has quite the eye, have you no?'

Mrs. Strachan made a small dismissive noise, and continued her close study in silence.

'Have you visited Edinburgh, Mrs. Kynoch?'

'Oh, aye, I was down for the General Assembly with my late husband once or twice. It's a gey noisy place, is it no?'

Hippolyta smiled kindly.

'It can be, until you grow used to it, I suppose.'

The tea arrived and Mrs. Strachan was persuaded to leave the paintings and return to her seat. Hippolyta noted that Mrs. Riach had produced some rather fine biscuits which she had not seen the previous day, and some good china. Evidently these guests were to be impressed. Mrs. Kynoch was, and chattered about biscuits and baking, and domestic affairs, and Hippolyta began to feel quite grown-up to be taking part in a conversation of this kind, even if she was learning more than talking. Mrs. Kynoch knew every tradesman in the three parishes, and was not slow to offer her opinion on them. Hippolyta wondered how far she was to be trusted in her opinions, with her silly voice and her faintly ridiculous clothes. Mrs. Strachan by contrast said very little, though Hippolyta and Mrs. Kynoch both tried to draw her out. At last they decided that it was time to leave, and both ladies rose.

'Mrs. Napier,' said Mrs. Strachan, 'I have been thinking about your lovely watercolours. I should so like to see how you paint this area. Perhaps you could make a study of the view to the Pass of Tullich, with the rock of Craigendarroch above it? I am sure you would depict it quite charmingly.'

'You are very kind, Mrs. Strachan!' exclaimed Hippolyta, as delighted as if she had received a royal commission. 'I shall certainly consider it!'

'Oh, aye, there's lots of bonny views round abouts, if that's your interest!' agreed Mrs. Kynoch. 'And then come the winter there's other things to do, like the soup kitchen for the schoolboys. I'm very pleased to have met you, Mrs. Napier!'

'And you too. Thank you for calling.'

Well, thought Hippolyta, that will be the start. From Mrs. Riach's attitude, it seemed that the principal females of local society had called, and if she had been found acceptable, no doubt the rest would follow.

She was not wrong. The rest of the morning was soon disposed of as the minister and his wife arrived, disappointed but not altogether surprised to find that she was not of their flock.

They were welcoming enough despite that, he a great countrified bear of a man and she a little mouse, whose face Hippolyta could barely remember if she turned away for more than a minute. They were followed, at a precise interval which made Hippolyta suspect they had been waiting around the corner, by a pair of elderly sisters whose brother was the local man of law: Mrs. Riach had evidently pegged them slightly further down the social scale, for the best biscuits were no longer to be seen. By the time they left, Hippolyta felt she was swimming in tea, and was delighted that no one else made an appearance.

'Why do they all come at once, Mrs. Riach? And yet not all together?'

'Aye, feels wi'in feels,' muttered the housekeeper obscurely. 'I'll put the rest of the good biscuits out for Dr. Napier with his wine. He needs fattening up.'

'I don't really think he does …'

But the housekeeper had gone.

An invitation arrived later in the day from Mrs. Strachan for Dr. and Mrs. Napier to come to dinner on Saturday evening. Hippolyta felt she had passed some kind of test, and excitedly told Patrick when he came back for his dinner.

'Mrs. Strachan? Well, the food should be good,' said her husband.

'Mr. Strachan is a merchant, isn't he? He must be in a good way of business.'

'Oh, yes, certainly. He's a general merchant: what he does not stock cannot be bought in the three parishes, I should think.'

'Mrs. Strachan is very smart.'

Patrick regarded her with a smile.

'Not as smart as you, my dearest! You need not be nervous.'

'Oh, I'm not nervous! I shall wear my brown silk gown. The blue one is still to arrive.'

'Along with a good deal of other luggage,' Patrick agreed. 'I hope the cart has not been upset somewhere along the road.'

Two days after their arrival, Hippolyta was relieved again to be able to say to Mrs. Riach that she and the doctor would be out for supper that very evening, neatly pre-empting the Strachans' invitation.

'Oh, aye?' was the housekeeper's suspicious response. 'And am I to be left in the house on my ain with yon loon up the stair?'

'You'll have Ishbel with you,' Hippolyta pointed out, though the maid looked about eight and was unlikely to be much help in a struggle to the death. 'And we'll only be at – oh, what is it called? At Dinnet House, with Colonel Verney. Not far away, should anything happen, which I'm quite sure it won't.' She tried to imitate her mother's brand of brisk sympathy, which had been applied over the years to servants and children alike: no one ran to Hippolyta's mother for a warm cuddle.

'At Colonel Verney's, aye? That'll be affa fine. You'll no need much in the way of dinner.'

'Is that so?'

'Aye, he feeds his own well enough – so I'm told,' she added, with a look of dark significance.

'Why should we be considered Colonel Verney's "own"?' Hippolyta asked her husband at breakfast. Patrick looked up from his book and blinked. The table wobbled dramatically, but he had promised to be rid of it when her own table came on the cart. She had been eyeing up the bare bachelor parlour for artistic improvement when the cart arrived. She dabbed her spilt hot chocolate with her napkin.

'I'm not sure. Who said it?'

'Mrs. Riach.'

'Are you settling in well with her?' Patrick asked, addressing himself to his plate of eggs with more focus. They had already gone cold while he had been distracted by his book.

'I'm not sure. She seems very nervous about having Robert Wilson still in the house.'

'I think he'll be fit to go home tomorrow,' said Patrick. 'I saw him this morning and he seemed very comfortable.'

The unworthy thought entered Hippolyta's mind that the coachman had indeed looked very comfortable when she had seen him, and was perhaps in no hurry to leave.

'Well, when he is gone we shall be able to start again. I should not like her to think she was in any danger in her own home.'

'I'm quite sure she's not,' said Patrick vaguely. Hippolyta

eyed his plate as he cleared it efficiently.

'Do you think we should keep some hens?' she asked.

'Hens?'

'It's just – I've never had such a garden before! There is every plant in it I could desire, and still room for more. And a run of hens would be a lovely thing to have, would it not? You could have fresh eggs every morning, instead of having Mrs. Riach treat for them in the village.'

Patrick regarded her over the book.

'Have you ever kept hens?' he asked mildly.

'Well, no. We had no room for such things in Edinburgh.'

'Hm. Well, see what might be involved and tell me again. Remember there will be foxes here, and possibly pine martens.'

Hippolyta was momentarily distracted by the charming thought of such animals in her garden, and that moment was enough for Patrick to lose himself once more in his medical texts. She smiled indulgently, and finished her chocolate, wondering who to ask about hens.

The day sparkled with heavy showers amongst the sunshine: any hope that they might do something to lift the heat turned out to be false. The heat did little for Mrs. Riach's temper, particularly as the cream turned sour even on the cool stone shelf in the pantry, and Hippolyta noticed that the housekeeper seemed to be limping quite badly. She mentioned it to Patrick as they were changing for supper.

'A limp? She hasn't said anything before,' said Patrick. 'I'll try to watch her tomorrow.'

'I hope she has not injured herself attending to Robert Wilson,' Hippolyta murmured, feeling guilty.

'Are you ready, my dear?'

'Almost!' She stood and fastened her cloak at her throat, and swirled to show him. Patrick beamed.

'I always liked that brown gown in Edinburgh: it's like greeting an old friend. An old and very elegant friend,' he added quickly, a hint of mischief in his eyes.

'It is not old at all!' Hippolyta told him firmly. 'And I beg you will say nothing of the sort this evening! I want to look smart for my new acquaintances, not make them think I care nothing for their invitation and turn up in any old thing.' She slapped him neatly on the arm with her gloves, and they laughed. 'Now, tell me about the Colonel.'

They set off arm in arm in the evening light - no sign of sunset yet in these northern parts, thought Hippolyta. Blossom in the hedgerows was richly scented after sun and rain.

'He's a Waterloo veteran, and lives with his niece and his old batman. He's housebound, pretty much, which is why our services are there.'

'Oh! He's Episcopalian?'

'That's right. I warned you there's no church nearer than Aberdeen, so a visiting clergyman comes and takes Communion in Dinnet House every second Sunday. There are a few residents now who join us, and often one or two of the visitors to the spa.'

'So he is a sociable gentleman?'

'Not really. I have been there a few times, but there are rarely other guests. He is my patient, and has been a very good one, often recommending me to other people at the spa.'

'Does that not make him unpopular with Dr. Durward?'

Patrick shrugged.

'Dr. Durward is not eager to acquire new patients. He enjoys a quiet practice, I believe, and has money of his own so he is not dependent on patients for his income.'

'An enviable position!'

'I'm not sure of that, certainly at my time of career,' said Patrick seriously. 'Because I have to take anyone who offers me an injured leg or a gall stone, I learn much more about my profession. Dr. Durward prefers to read books. And I do not believe I could ever turn away a patient in pain or distress.'

Hippolyta squeezed his arm.

'I am quite sure you could not, my dear. You are too good!'

'Too good for you?' he asked, teasing.

'Maybe!'

Dinnet House was a plain, even ugly, old building, severe in the evening light at the end of a short drive between roughly kept lawns. The manservant who answered the door to them fitted the house very well: he stood with military precision in the doorway, with a face like a fortification. However, he ushered them into the house without hesitation, and Hippolyta found that the interior was a good deal friendlier than the exterior. The hall was warm with Turkey rugs and well-polished old furniture, and the drawing room into which the manservant escorted them was of a piece with it, with a good fire to ward off the evening chills. Two people were already in the room: a young woman, about Hippolyta's age, stood as they entered, but the old man in the chair did not. Nevertheless, he cried out happily at their appearance.

'Dr. Napier! Very good of you to come!'

'Colonel Verney, may I present my wife?'

'Damn it, I should stand for such a fine girl coming into my house! Forgive me, Mrs. Napier, the old legs don't work as they used to. Here, take my hand in place of a bow.'

Smiling, Hippolyta approached and offered her hand, which he unexpectedly kissed. She curtseyed, a little confused.

'Well worth the journey to Edinburgh for this, eh, Dr. Napier? This is my niece, Basilia,' Colonel Verney waved, eyes still on Hippolyta. The two women curtseyed to each other, and Hippolyta was pleased to see Basilia's fashionable gown and hair. She had been nervous that she would stand out oddly in her Edinburgh styles, but clearly the Paris plates made it this far north, and not just for Mrs. Strachan. Basilia was yellow-haired and pretty, with a broad, pale face only lightly touched with powder, and large, dark eyes. She met Hippolyta's greeting with a very welcoming smile.

'I have been looking forward so much to having someone my age to be friends with!' she said at once. 'I was so pleased when Dr. Napier announced you were coming! And I understand you love drawing and painting?'

'Very much,' Hippolyta agreed. 'Which is fortunate, as I have no skills in anything else at all!'

'Ah, we have that in common, then!' said Basilia with a grin. 'But alas, if you will not play the piano either, it will be a quiet evening! But of course, Dr. Napier has always played beautifully for us when he comes here.'

'Has he? Oh, good!' Hippolyta wondered how often Patrick had visited the Verneys, for he had not, to her recollection, mentioned them to her before.

The manservant brought a tray of negus, and the company sat. Basilia and Hippolyta found a good deal to talk about: Basilia asked about Edinburgh and their journey, and described various pretty views about the area which were popular to paint. Patrick was being interrogated by the Colonel over news from Edinburgh, too, a city with which he seemed quite well acquainted. Time passed very easily until supper was served by the manservant, when the Colonel was wheeled through to a dining room with a small supper table, and the rest followed. They sat to salmagundi and cold roast ham and stewed cucumbers, all very well prepared.

'I know that this house is a picture of misery on the outside,' the Colonel said as Hippolyta filled her plate happily. 'So I try to make it as welcoming as possible inside, ably assisted by Basilia and old Forman here,' he waved at the manservant who impassively continued to serve the wine. 'I rented it when I had tried the wells for a few weeks and found much benefit: I wanted to be able to stay longer and be a part of the life of the village, as far as I could. Pannanich Lodge and the hotel are all very pleasant but they are full of sick people!'

'It is a charming house, Colonel,' said Hippolyta sincerely. 'Nothing could be more welcoming.'

'It's an old Jacobite bunker,' said the Colonel, with dismissive humour. 'The Jacobites were rife here, apparently. Glad I wasn't soldiering in those days.'

'There's a legend of a hoard of Jacobite silver!' said Basilia, eyes wide. 'It's supposed to be buried somewhere near the house.'

'Though improbably it's supposed to be six hundred silver pennies hidden in a boot,'

'That would be quite a boot,' Patrick remarked thoughtfully.

The Colonel laughed.

'My point exactly. But then there are legends of giants in these parts, too! And it's true that the locals are of unusually great average height – or is it that I only see them from a sitting position?' he asked with a smile at Hippolyta. She considered.

'I have not seen very many people so far, but it is true I feel a little smaller here than I did in Edinburgh,' she agreed. 'But are there truly giants?'

'More giants than kelpies or witches, as far as I can judge,' said Basilia. 'Everyone you ask seems to have known someone of extraordinary height – now dead, of course, and not able to be measured!'

'It must surely have put the Jacobites at an advantage, if they could recruit giants from these parts,' murmured Patrick. Jacobites were still a sensitive subject for Episcopalians, but they were amongst friends here.

'It didn't help them in the end, though. This house was besieged, they say, though it is not a place I should like to defend. There was a murder here, too.'

'A murder!' Hippolyta stared.

'Yes, though I have no idea if it was a Jacobite affair or not. No one will tell me anything in detail about it, so I suspect there is less to it than it sounds. The best I have is that two men were killed, which makes me think it was probably a fight that ended tragically and one side or the other has called it murder. In any case, I have found no ominous bloodstains on the floor, and no ghost seems to walk dissatisfied through the halls at night, Mrs. Napier, you may be assured!'

'Oh, but ghosts or no ghosts, the thought of living in a house where a murder has taken place is a little unnerving!'

Basilia smiled.

'But you agree there is no lingering feeling of unhappy spirits, is there, Mrs. Napier?'

'No,' admitted Hippolyta, 'none at all. Oh!'

For just at that moment something brushed against Hippolyta's skirts under the table, and she jumped. Patrick pushed the tablecloth aside, bent down, and rose again holding a bundle of white fluff.

'A kitten!' cried Hippolyta with delight, all nerves forgotten.

'Oh, I beg your pardon, ma'am.' Forman, the manservant, quickly scooped the kitten from Patrick's hand. He had blushed to the roots of his receding hair, and held the kitten in one large hand, stroking its head with a delicate finger. All sternness had vanished from his face.

'He has a tribe of them,' the Colonel declared indulgently. 'How many is it, Forman?'

'She had six, sir.'

'Six kittens and a cat. Forman was a quartermaster sergeant at Waterloo: organised food and drink for all his men, oversaw the wagon trains, fought off the Frenchies and got me seen to and set up when I was injured, but can he control seven cats? They have him run ragged, haven't they, Forman?'

'Yes, sir,' admitted Forman, still stroking the kitten which purred loudly in his arms. Hippolyta put out a hand and let the kitten sniff her fingers, before fondling its silky pink ears. 'Today one of them disappeared altogether, but I could hear it mewing. I was all through the kitchen trying to find it, then I discovered it had found a hole inside the windowseat and gone in under the floor – it's a wooden floor, ma'am,' he broke off to explain to Hippolyta. 'I had to take up five floorboards to find it.'

'And the mess under the floorboards was extraordinary!' added Basilia. 'I told him we'd better clear it out before he puts the boards back. Old bits of paper, rags, pieces of broken wood – I can only think they laid the wooden floor to make the kitchen warmer and then stuffed rubbish underneath to block the cold. It is a bitter room, isn't it, Forman?'

'It is, Miss,' Forman agreed. 'I'd best take this young gentleman back to his mother now, sir.' He bowed to the company and vanished into the servants' quarters.

The Colonel was eyeing Hippolyta, who watched the kitten wistfully.

'He'll be looking for homes for the kittens soon, I should imagine,' he said pointedly.

'Oh! Do you think he would let me have one? Patrick, my dear, could we have a kitten?'

Patrick considered.

'I should think so,' he decided.

'Then if it is possible – if Forman would allow it, and if he doesn't already have homes for them …'

'I shall speak to him,' said the Colonel with a smile. 'I'm sure something can be arranged. I know Forman would not want them to go to bad homes.'

'Such a delightful kitten, Charlotte!' Hippolyta wrote to Aberdeen the following day, adding to her original letter until the carrier on Wednesday. 'He is as lively as can be, and we have named him Snowball for he is pure white. This morning Patrick found him curled up asleep inside his hat when he went to put it on! But I must desist, or my entire letter will be kittenish. Basilia Verney seems a sensible, pretty girl of about our age, and I am sure she will grow to be a great friend: we already have much in common. But I wish you had not broken your ankle, silly girl, and then you would have been here with me to meet her – and the kitten!'

Chapter Three

The Strachans lived in a new house of three bays, at the top of the village, and as a sign of their increasing gentility it was at some distance from Mr. Strachan's commercial establishment. Though the evening was still light and fine, and would be for some hours yet, lamps had been lit in the windows and the hallway was warm and welcoming.

Mrs. Strachan greeted them with cool grace, and Dr. Napier presented Mr. Strachan to his new wife. Strachan was smart and sharp, with black hair and whiskers, and dressed as fashionably as his wife. His smile was welcoming but, Hippolyta felt, assessing: she thought she had been costed from cap to slippers.

Upstairs in the drawing room, Mrs. Kynoch was already in residence, in an evening gown in a shade of lemon Hippolyta did not feel she should have risked. A feather which almost matched peeped out of a red turban on her busy head. She greeted Hippolyta with a pleased expression on her silly face and offered her squeaky congratulations to Patrick.

'And I daresay you have already met Dr. Durward,' Mrs. Strachan gestured to the doctor, handsome in evening dress. Hippolyta curtseyed. 'We are a small party, as you see, Mrs. Napier: that tends to be what is preferred in Ballater.'

Hippolyta thought she caught the least twitch in Dr. Durward's eyebrow, but she was not sure what comment he was making.

Slim glasses of sherry were distributed, and Mrs. Kynoch leaned across to ask Hippolyta if she had met anyone else in the village yet.

'I have met the minister and his wife, and the Misses Strong were kind enough to call, too. Everyone has been extremely friendly,' she added politely.

'It's a friendly town,' Mrs. Kynoch agreed. 'Usually,' she added, as if to herself. Hippolyta glanced round at her: she seemed to be looking at her host, Mr. Strachan, who was listening to Dr. Durward tell some kind of amusing story.

'And last night Colonel Verney invited us for supper.'

'Did he?' Mrs. Kynoch turned to her in mild surprise. 'The Colonel does not entertain very often. Of course, you are fellow members of the English church, so I suppose that encouraged him to honour you.'

Dr. Durward's story ended, and Patrick and Mr. Strachan laughed with him, just as a servant entered to say that dinner was served. Mr. Strachan stepped across to offer Hippolyta his arm, while Dr. Durward led Mrs. Strachan without looking at her. Patrick was left with Mrs. Kynoch, which did not appear to disconcert him – though lemon, Hippolyta thought fondly, was definitely not his colour.

Dinner would not have disgraced any Edinburgh New Town table, and nor would the setting, where every piece of silver and glass and china was brand new and shiny.

'Did I hear you say that Colonel Verney had honoured you with a supper invitation?' asked Mr. Strachan in the course of conversation. Hippolyta was surprised he had heard her across the drawing room.

'Yes, indeed. We had a lovely evening.'

'Did you, indeed?' There was a slight edge to his voice.

'Yes: Miss Verney has a lovely voice, and performed very well.'

'I've never heard her,' said Mr. Strachan without interest.

'And we met the cats!' Hippolyta felt she was struggling with this conversation. 'His manservant has a white cat with six charming kittens.' She glanced at Mr. Strachan but there was no response. She turned a little to the rest of the table. 'It was most amusing, for they are very lively little things, and one of them had found a way under the floorboards in the kitchen! Forman had had to pull them up to rescue it – and then he very generously gave me the kitten! We have called it Snowball,' she added, with a self-deprecating smile.

'Lovely!' said Mrs. Kynoch. 'I adore kittens! And cats are so sensible and useful about the house. I have an ancient tabby, myself: he is tremendously good company.'

Hippolyta favoured Mrs. Kynoch with another smile, grateful that someone had responded. Mr. Strachan looked thoughtful.

'I once had a patient with a cat. Between them they were nearly the end of me,' said Dr. Durward, and launched smoothly into another amusing anecdote.

'Have you been to the Wells yet, Mrs. Napier?' Mrs. Strachan asked when they had all laughed.

'No, I have not! I hear the path is very picturesque, though.'

'Of course, you are a painter,' said Dr. Durward. 'No doubt you will find all kinds of picturesqueness in these parts that we have never dreamed of, coming in with a new and artistic eye.'

'I hope to paint a good deal, certainly,' Hippolyta agreed. 'The countryside is lovely: and Miss Verney has agreed to be my companion on occasion.'

'I shall take you to the Wells tomorrow, my love, if you wish,' said Patrick. 'I have a patient or two to see, but they should not take long and it is nothing very serious in either case.'

'Pannanich Lodge is worth a look as well, if it is not too busy,' put in Mr. Strachan. 'The old laird built it for visitors to the Wells, you know, but then when he built the bridge he was able to bring people down here instead. A very sensible man, the old laird. Telford himself designed the bridge, you know, and the laird spent five thousand pounds on it only ten years ago.'

'I understand he is much missed,' said Hippolyta dutifully.

'A laird who invests in his lands is much to be desired,' said Mr. Strachan. 'Commerce is life, you know.'

'Does Mr. Strachan think of nothing but trade?' Hippolyta asked Patrick the following morning, as they walked across the bridge over the Dee. To the right, on both sides of the glinting river, were rich agricultural lands grey green with barley. Ahead she could see only a steep hillside facing them, delicate with birchwoods and juniper. She stopped to note a splash of foxgloves, just going over, in a shaft of sunlight. Her paints were calling to her.

'I'm not entirely sure,' said Patrick. 'I have rarely heard him speak of anything else. Except for the Burns Mortification, and I suppose that is money, too.'

'The Burns Mortification?'

'Yes: a native of these parts, who made money in the West Indies, set up a mortification to give bursaries to boys at the school here who want to go to one of the universities. Strachan is one of the trustees, along with Dr. Durward, and, I think, the minister and old Mr. Strong, the lawyer.'

'Only four trustees?' asked Hippolyta, daughter of a lawyer herself.

'Does that seem few? I'm not sure. But I think they are hoping to change that, anyway. I'm a little vague about these things, my dear.'

'Hm. What a pretty road! I love the way the woods are so busy on this side, then the land drops away to the river to our left.'

'Broad enough for a decent sheep pasture, anyway,' agreed Patrick, who was a countryman by birth. 'And of course for Pannanich Lodge. That's it, just up ahead.'

Between the road and the river stood a large, squareset building, not more than half a century old, poised confidently over the waters. Beyond it, trees thickly in leaf caught the morning light off the river, and lawns spread to catch the sun. Several people, one or two wrapped warmly in blankets like invalids, sat outside and watched them, having little else to watch. 'And this is for patients at the Wells?' she asked.

'That's right: a woman runs it, rented from the estate. It's decent accommodation: families can stay there very respectably. Some still stay nearer the wells themselves, though: apart from the big hotel there are others, usually poorer types, who lodge in a couple of the cottages there, and cannot afford to travel back and forth to the Wells each day.'

'I'm very glad to see it, having heard so much about it.'

Patrick squeezed her arm contentedly.

'I'm pleased when you take an interest in my work.'

'But of course I do!'

It was a public sort of place for an embrace, so they smiled at each other and walked on, not a moment too soon as a man pushed a handcart almost into them.

'Beg pardon, Doctor!' he called out. The cart was full of empty jars and bottles.

'Strachan has been sending goods up to the Lodge and the hotel, then,' said Patrick, 'and those are the empties going to be refilled. He makes good business from the visitors.'

They were closer to the lodge now, and as they passed it one of the men on the lawns called out to them.

'Napier! Mrs. Napier!'

They turned, and recognised Dr. Durward coming towards them, smiling cheerfully. He brought with him a young man who did not appear that willing to be brought.

'This is Brown,' said Dr. Durward. 'Dr. Napier, Mrs. Napier, Brown. He's been taking the waters.'

Hippolyta wondered if they had done him much good. He was a helpless looking fellow, his hair standing all on end and a look of incompetent neglect about him that made her want him to take him in hand and tidy him up. His clothes were fashionable but unloved. He bowed anxiously.

'You're a patient of mine in a quiet way, aren't you, Brown?' asked Durward encouragingly. 'But he doesn't need much attention, so I come up and play a few hands of cards with him now and again, just to stave off the boredom.'

'Lots of, of sick people,' said Brown in a snuffly voice. 'Not much to do. Glad enough to see Dr. Durward, thank you sir, thank you sir.'

'A ringing endorsement!' laughed Durward. 'But I'll let you get on: going up to see the Wells, Mrs. Napier?'

'That's right.'

'Well, I wish you joy of them! Some of the water is very good indeed – and some is quite foul!'

It was not then much further to the Wells themselves, the source of Ballater's unexpected prosperity. The first sign was a long, narrow modern building of two storeys, up a steep little slope by the side of the road: the Pannanich Hotel. Like the Lodge, it had a look of fashionable elegance which Hippolyta had not at all expected to find outside Edinburgh. At its front door Hippolyta looked back to see the fine view across the Dee valley, all jagged rocks and softening birchwoods and the river calmly glittering over its shallow, curving bed. This would be a view to paint, too: she hoped the weather would hold until she could at least satisfy some of her longing to paint. She hoped too she had enough in the way of materials – then she considered that Mr. Strachan would probably be able to supply her with all she needed, for a price. He had probably furnished the three or four lady artists she could see across the road, painting the same view.

'One of my patients is in here,' Patrick explained at the door. 'It will be a simple thing to see him, but would you like to wait in a private parlour? You could take tea, or sample the waters if you dare!'

'I shall sample them some time, but I should love a cup of tea!' Hippolyta confessed. 'I had no idea it would be such fine weather this far north! I am quite fading.'

'You don't look it! But oh! Here is my patient, in any case. He is a source of deep gratification for me,' he added, murmuring in her ear, 'for he asked for me by name, rather than Dr. Durward!'

Hippolyta beamed, ready to love the patient on sight. They had reached a public parlour open to the passage to the right of the main door, and a few guests were seated there reading or writing. One of them, a painfully thin man with a yellow face, glanced up from his place on a chaise longue, a blanket over his legs, and greeted Patrick with a slow nod.

'Dr. Napier, good to see you.'

'And you, Mr. Brookes. Shall I ask your man to take you back to your room for your consultation?'

'Not at all, Doctor: there is little to be done for me today, I think. But is this lady Mrs. Napier?'

Patrick introduced them.

'Like many in these parts, Mr. Brookes has worked in the West Indies,' he added.

'And broken my health in the process,' Mr. Brookes put in with a wry smile. 'I have come home in an attempt to recover, or at least to die in a healthy climate.'

'I am very sorry to hear it, sir,' said Hippolyta, though having seen his complexion she was not the least surprised. There was something familiar about him, she thought, but she could not place where she might have seen him before. His accent was not local:

perhaps he hailed originally from Edinburgh and she had seen him there. Patrick was discreetly taking his patient's pulse, and listening to his chest. No one else in the parlour took the least notice: most here would have some kind of complaint and medical visits were common.

'All as usual,' said Patrick at last.

'No better?' asked Brookes.

'Well, at least no worse,' said Patrick kindly. Brookes grinned.

'What a thing to have a positive medical man! Dr. Napier makes me feel better each time he visits,' he told Hippolyta, 'and without the least drug or powder. He is worth paying just for his company.'

'Are you still taking the waters, sir?' Patrick asked.

'Faithfully.' Brookes made a face, twisting his loose yellow skin alarmingly. 'Have you tried it yourself? You should!'

'I've taken it a few times,' Patrick admitted. 'It's … refreshing.'

'That's a word for it.' Brookes laughed, and Hippolyta decided she liked the man. They stayed and chatted with him for half an hour or so, when he appeared to grow tired. Patrick rearranged the cushions under his head and pulled his blanket up to his chin, and Mr. Brookes settled, with a grin of thanks, to sleep.

'You're excused church tomorrow,' said Patrick with a smile, 'as far as I can excuse you.'

'You? You're a fancy Episcopalian. You're in no position to excuse a good kirk man,' Brookes chuckled drowsily, and wriggled himself comfortable.

The other patients Patrick wanted to see were both lodging in cottages, and Hippolyta waited outside perched on a dry rock, planning her paintings. There was a great deal of coming and going around the wells, where stone basins had been set up to make them accessible to those who could not move easily, or indeed those in fine clothes. Ballater was very far from the wilderness her friends had expected, she thought. Yet when she looked out from the hillside, there was very little civilisation to see. Could there still be dangers here, amongst such fashionable people? Could there be wolves?

After Pannanich, Patrick was finished with patients for the day, and as the weather continued very fine, Hippolyta was easily able to charm him into escorting her to a suitable site for taking some preliminary sketches of the rocky headland known as Craigendarroch, the view with which the charming Mrs. Strachan had challenged her. They wandered about at the top of the town for an hour or so, trying to find an angle that pleased, wondering if another time of day would make the cliff seem more or less imposing, present an aspect that was more or less romantic. The debate pleased them, and the sketches went well: at home, after dinner, she tried a little colour in them, experimenting with the effects, while Patrick played some of his favourite music from Oswald and the Earl of Kellie. In between they chatted idly, and Hippolyta felt at the end of the evening that if all married life could continue this way, the world would be a pleasant place indeed.

A young man with close-cropped hair, shiny elbows to his coat and telltale white bands at his collar was handing his horse to a servant as Patrick and Hippolyta arrived at Dinnet House the following morning. He started as he realised they were close behind him, and removed his hat quickly, allowing them to precede him into the house. Forman stood at the open door, and gestured them towards the parlour, where a table had been made ready with a fair white cloth, seats arranged facing it. The man they had met at the door hurried forward, bowed to Colonel Verney who sat in the front row, and laid a small case on a side table. He drew from it a communion chalice and patten and arranged them on the main table, then hurried out again with the case clutched half-open to his chest.

'Good morning, good morning! Good to see you both!' called Colonel Verney, and they went to greet him. 'Plenty of room – come and sit here with me! Basilia's fussing somewhere. This is Mr. and Mrs. Whitstone, from – where did you say you were from? So sorry: head like a sieve these days.'

'From Barnstaple,' said Mr. Whitstone, 'in Devonshire.'

'Here for the waters, too,' Colonel Verney put in.

'That's a very long way to travel,' said Patrick politely. 'Have you found the waters efficacious?'

'Indeed, indeed, sir! I am a new person, as you see!' said Mr. Whitstone buoyantly.

'Dr. Napier is a medical man, and this lovely young lady is his new wife,' explained the Colonel. Murmured congratulations followed, and Mr. Whitstone generously made free of information concerning his symptoms to Patrick, who listened gravely, nodding. A couple of village families came in, children washed and groomed and warned into best behaviour in a gentleman's house. They sat at the back and adopted an attitude of prayer on the hassocks that had been provided. Hippolyta felt awkward that she was not doing the same: it was like church and not like church, standing in someone's parlour: one could not help but be sociable, but when would one be expected to go and kneel as usual? At least in Edinburgh they could go to St. George's with nice Mr. Shannon with his soft Irish accent and his love of church music: here she could see no musical instrument at all, and wondered if they would even sing a hymn.

However, she need not have worried. In a moment Basilia came in, gave her a great smile in greeting, and pulled the cover off a neat parlour organ in a polished mahogany case. She sat herself down at the keyboard and quietly began a little voluntary, as a few more people arrived. Hippolyta and Patrick sat where they had been directed in the front row, then knelt in prayer. After a moment or two, Basilia's fingers found new, livelier chords, and the little congregation rose to their feet as the young man they had seen earlier strode in, this time covered in a crumpled white surplice and with a long green stole dangling around his neck.

The clergyman led the service briskly, and although they did indeed sing two hymns, a psalm and a canticle, they were all short ones. The clergyman beat the time on the edge of the communion table, not allowing Basilia to lag behind. He preached for six minutes precisely (Hippolyta had developed a bad habit in her childhood of timing sermons), without bothering to exchange his surplice for a Geneva gown, and seemed to feel that the strength of his piety could be judged by the depth of his Oxford accent, for it grew thicker as the service grew more solemn.

All present except the children partook of Communion, and knelt again for the prayers following. At last they stood for the final hymn, and the clergyman shot out, surplice and stole flying, and the congregation compliantly followed to shake his hand in the hall. Patrick and Hippolyta, along with Basilia who had played to the end, were the last out, and the clergyman had barely touched their hands when he was off into a side room, already pulling his surplice over his head as he went.

'He has already taken a service in Aboyne this morning,' Basilia explained, 'and he has to ride back now to Kincardine o'Neil to take one there. He's very busy in the summer.'

'Heavens,' Hippolyta remarked. 'He must have a strong horse.'

'Well, if he is not on the road you are most likely to find him at a horse fair,' said Basilia with a smile. The clergyman dashed out of the side room with his black case, one thumb holding it slightly open, and darted back into the parlour. They could see him gathering up the communion vessels and accoutrements and packing them with practised speed and a muttered prayer into the case. Then he turned, bowed to Colonel Verney, and strode back past them with a nod and vanished through the front door. Forman, stern looking as ever, shut the door gently behind him, then crossed the hall towards them.

'Excuse me for addressing you, ma'am, but may I ask how the kitten is settling in?' he said to Hippolyta.

'Of course! He is a delight. We have named him Snowball, you know. Please come and see him any time you wish, for I am sure he would be glad to see you. He is such an affectionate little thing!'

Forman's grim face lightened.

'You are very kind, ma'am. I might just find the time to slip down and see how he is. Not that I have any doubts of your care for him, ma'am.'

'Of course. You need to see for yourself, I understand!'

'Thank you, ma'am.' He bowed, and passed them to go back into the parlour. In a moment he returned, pushing Colonel Verney in his chair. The Colonel beamed at them all.

'Off for my constitutional!' he exclaimed. 'Will you join me as you return to the village? I shan't be long: Forman is very quick to haul me on to my cart!'

'I'll come too, shall I, Uncle? I'll just fetch my bonnet and shawl.' Basilia skipped off up the stairs and Forman pushed Colonel Verney over to the front door. Patrick hurried to hold it open as Forman manoeuvred the chair outside, where a neat little dog cart was waiting, with a toy-sized grey pony between the shafts. Hippolyta could not resist going to greet it.

'Watch him, he nips!' cried the Colonel, as Forman swung him across from the chair to the cart. The pony, however, was not going to be a slave to his own reputation, and nosed Hippolyta affectionately. Forman turned in surprise.

'Do be careful, ma'am – though truly he seems quite happy,' he admitted. 'Comfortable, sir? Then I'll take his head,' he added, coming forward to the pony. The pony dutifully nipped his sleeve, and Forman batted him away gently.

Basilia came out, bonnet and shawl in place, and the party set off, with the Napiers and Basilia walking level with the Colonel under his rugs.

'Always do this on a Sunday after the service,' he explained. 'Works up an appetite for my dinner, and I can see if anything is going on in the village without my knowing about it. Doesn't often happen, mind you! Old Verney keeps an eye on things, even when I'm stuck at home most of the time! Reconnaisance always pays, whatever battle you might be fighting. Wellington knows that, you know.'

'And what kinds of things do you find that you haven't known, sir?' Hippolyta asked. 'What things do the villagers hide from you?'

'Oh, anything and everything, my dear! A tree cut down, a new house built, a field left fallow: all these things which are none of my business whatsoever and yet so interest me when I am accustomed to being at home all day. My spies here,' he gestured to Basilia and Forman, 'bring me much of the news, but they cannot remember everything.'

Chapter Four

By the time they reached the village green, the adherents of the established church of the three parishes were beginning to emerge from their own morning service, the hunched minister standing by the door to bid them good day with uncertain nods and shrugs. The sun shone blessedly on them, and the church looked quite splendid: the congregation were bright in summer clothes, and in no hurry to return to their homes in the warm sunlight.

'What are the other two parishes?' Hippolyta asked. 'Ballater and?'

'Not Ballater at all,' said Patrick with a laugh. 'Glenmuick, Tullich and Glengairn. It's quite extensive, but not, as you can imagine, very densely populated. There's Dr. Durward.' He waved.

'And there's Mrs. Strachan - and Mrs. Kynoch,' said Hippolyta, seeing them in the distance. It was hard to miss Mrs. Strachan: her willowy form was tall amongst her fellow parishioners, and her fashionable elegance stood out: she had a crisply starched pelerine that emphasised the broad slope of her sleeves over her shoulders, and the flower print over her green dress was echoed in her purple kid gloves: she would not have looked out of place at an Edinburgh New Town assembly. Mrs. Kynoch, by her side, was dressed in mismatched colours like an over-used paint palette. Hippolyta wondered if she realised how much worse she looked by contrast, or if she even cared. She could hear her grating voice already, and sighed.

Dr. Durward, handsome and heavy, was approaching to meet them, and they were nearing the bulk of the crowd anyway.

'Good day to you, Colonel Verney!' said Dr. Durward. 'Good to see you out and about. How do you do?'

'Very well, I thank you,' said the Colonel. 'Your young colleague keeps me ticking along like an ancient clock, so that I can be a constant source of irritation to my relatives and my neighbours.'

'Splendid!' said the doctor. 'Being a source of irritation is an encouragement to survival amongst many of my patients, too.' They chatted in a friendly fashion as Mrs. Kynoch spotted Hippolyta and hurried over.

'Good day to you, Mrs. Napier! You'll have been to the English service, no doubt?'

'Yes,' said Hippolyta with a curtsey and a stiff smile. 'Colonel Verney is most hospitable to let it be held in his home.' She noticed Mrs. Strachan hovering a little distance away, waiting for her friend, but not approaching. Could she have offended her in some way?

'Rather different from your experience in Edinburgh, I daresay,' said Mrs. Kynoch sympathetically. 'I remember there are at least two English congregations there, are there not? It must be strange to worship in someone's drawing room, when you are not used to it.'

'I found it very pleasant: quite refreshing,' said Hippolyta. She did not want to be thought of as some arrogant tounser, looking down on how things were done in the country. Mrs. Kynoch smiled and looked about anxiously for Mrs. Strachan, saw that she was not approaching and turned back to nod goodbye to Hippolyta before she went to rejoin her friend.

Other worshippers from the parish church were around them now, and conversations ebbed and flowed. She saw Dr. Durward out of the corner of her eye, approaching her.

'Mrs. Napier, I hope you are settling in well?' he asked. She admitted she probably was. 'You'll have plenty of acquaintances already, I'm sure, if Mrs. Strachan has called on you.'

'That's right: on Wednesday nearly everyone in the village called!'

'Not all together, though, I'm quite sure! Do you like a challenge, Mrs. Napier?'

'A challenge?' She turned to meet his eye, but was pleased to see him smiling. He spoke quietly.

'Yes: Mrs. Strachan is a leader in our little society. To my knowledge, she has never attended a doctor in the village, but I understand – such are the rumours in a little place – that she has recently taken to ordering a quantity of patent medicines from Aberdeen to be brought in with her husband's stocks. Do you think you could build up your acquaintance so that she naturally turns to Dr. Napier when the time comes that she acknowledges she needs proper medical attention?'

'Well, yes, I suppose I could …' She was dubious: Mrs. Strachan did not seem that willing to be a friend to her. 'But why not to you, Dr. Durward?'

The doctor smiled again, a little self-consciously.

'Your husband is building up his practice, while I am allowing mine to decline gently. And Dr. Napier is much more *au fait* with all the current fashions in medicine than I am: partly, no doubt, thanks to his travels to see you in Edinburgh! But it has been to his professional advantage, too. It would be much more desirable for all that she should approach him if she wants a doctor.'

'And you consider this to be a challenge, Dr. Durward?' She smiled back, not wanting to look as unsure of herself as she felt.

'Well, she is not what anyone could call approachable, is she?' Durward asked, dropping his voice even further. 'But if she is his patient, and happy to be so, anyone else who is anyone else in the three parishes will follow.' He nodded, sure that she had accepted, and moved off to talk to someone else. Hippolyta looked about her: there was the minister with his wife, and there were the two elderly sisters who had visited her – what was their name? Strong, that was it: and that must be their brother, the lawyer, who looked over seventy himself. Contrary to their surname, all three must be quite frail. She noticed that none of the parties was talking with any of the others, just as her visitors had arrived separately. What was it Mrs. Riach had said? 'Feels wi'in feels'? She tinkered with the odd vowels sounds in her head. Fools within fools? Oh, of course: wheels within wheels. She was not used to the odd way the people up here turned their *wh* sounds into *f*s. But what wheels did the housekeeper mean?

'Nevertheless, you are a stranger to this town and all that is to do with it, and I shall strongly oppose any appointment that might be made concerning you!'

The words, spoken softly but with an edge that sent shivers

down her spine, made her turn quickly. Who had said that?

Colonel Verney was sitting calmly in his donkey cart as the home-going crowd ebbed around him. Leaning over him, tall and wiry, and as fierce as a man could look, was Mr. Strachan.

'Well, Mr. Strachan,' said the Colonel quite as though he were not being towered over, 'it is the decision of all the trustees together, as I understand it, so you will no doubt have the chance to have your say. I am not pushing myself forward, you understand: I was requested to make myself available.'

'By whom? By that fool of a minister we have?'

Again, Mr. Strachan, formal in his fashionable blue coat, managed to sharpen his words like knives. She glanced around for Patrick, anxious in case Strachan should attack the Colonel: it seemed improbable, but something in Mr. Strachan's manner made her feel afraid. Instead, she saw Basilia, who had been speaking to some acquaintance, and came back to join her.

'Dear Mrs. Napier,' she said at once, 'I have been meaning to ask you something, and I quite forgot.'

'A moment, though,' said Hippolyta, 'for I think Colonel Verney may need help.' They turned to look over at Basilia's uncle, but to Hippolyta's surprise he was gossiping amicably with the minister, and Mr. Strachan was nowhere to be seen.

'What's the matter? Was he looking ill again?' asked Basilia anxiously. 'Sometimes he takes a little turn, but he has not had one for so long I began to believe the waters here had truly cured him.'

'No, no, he was quite healthy … There was a man speaking with him, Mr. Strachan.'

'Oh, yes: a tall, thin man, with very black hair?'

'That is the one! He seemed to be quarrelling with Colonel Verney.'

'Oh, I'm sure he could not have been,' said Basilia, cheerful now she was sure her uncle was in no danger. 'Mr. Strachan is quite genteel. But anything you might ever want to buy you will find in Strachan's warehouse. He even runs a small servants' agency, for the benefit of those who have decided, like my uncle, to take up residence here for a while, for the waters.'

'Is that how you found Forman?'

'No! No, Forman has been with my uncle since they fought together in the Peninsula – but for pity's sake do not ask my uncle about that, or we shall have the whole war over again in narrative form!'

'I see! I shall try to remember,' Hippolyta laughed. 'Well, what were you going to ask me, then?'

'To ask you? Oh! I am so forgetful!' Basilia Verney struck herself on the wrist with her fan in irritation. 'I am planning a little painting expedition tomorrow morning, early, if the weather holds, which I believe it will. I had thought to walk across to the Pannanich road and paint the village from the river: the view is quite pretty and the river is delightful. Would you care to join me?'

'I should love to,' Hippolyta answered delightedly. 'I have been itching to bring out my paints since I arrived, and was only able to start yesterday. I noticed that view when my husband and I walked to the Wells yesterday: it is charming. What time do you plan to start?'

'Would eight be too early? The light on the water is delightful then.'

'If it is for the sake of good light, I don't think it is too early.' It would allow her time for her daily meeting with Mrs. Riach, anyway, which she was determined every day to improve. She tried to remember where she had put her painting stool after yesterday's expedition: Patrick had joked that she had asked him along only to carry her furniture, like a Highland pony.

'If you have anything heavy,' Basilia was saying, 'Forman can bring it for you, and then return to my uncle. We shall be quite safe and comfortable, you can be assured.'

'Then I shall be very happy to join you.'

'Dr. Durward has challenged me!' she told Patrick late that evening.

'Challenged you, my dearest? In what way?' Patrick blinked, one hand still fingering the notes of the little box piano. They had been singing hymns together.

'To secure you Mrs. Strachan as a patient. He fears she is not well, but wants to make sure that it is to you she turns.'

'Good gracious! I had no idea Dr. Durward observed his fellow villagers so keenly. But I should certainly welcome her as a patient, should she have need of me.'

'I shouldn't like her to be ill,' agreed Hippolyta. 'But he says she is ordering patent medicines from Aberdeen.'

'I wonder what for?' Patrick mused, playing a soft arpeggio. 'But certainly, if she were to consult me it would help my practice enormously.'

'She is so beautiful that it is possible others would contract illnesses simply to follow her to your door!'

Patrick grinned.

'Well, perhaps: but even the fees I could charge her would assist us. I should like some day to provide you with a rather more suitable home, my dear, at the very least: but at present, as you know, we shall have to make do with this one.'

'I love it: and I especially love the garden. And now we have a kitten, it feels like a family home!'

The peaceful moment was shaken almost at once by a clatter at the door, and the skipping footsteps of Ishbel going to answer it. Patrick let the piano alone to listen, and in a moment Ishbel was at the parlour door with a note. He took it.

'I'm sorry, my dear, I have to go to someone taken ill – at the inn, Ishbel? Is that where the message came from?'

'Aye, sir, it's the lad from the inn that's brought it.'

'Fetch my hat and gloves, then, please. Hippolyta, my love, I must desert you!'

In a minute he had gone, leaving her now picking out odd notes on the keyboard. He was the player, not she, and she sighed, failing once again to do justice to both hands of an air of Thomas Moore's. The kitten, roused from a tiny swirl of slumber by Patrick's departure, stretched and yawned, and began to wash as if it were quite a grown-up cat. Laughing, Hippolyta reached for her sketch book, and began to draw him.

The kitten, Snowball, seemed not in the least disconcerted by his move to more humble surroundings, and had taken charge of the household at once. He regarded his human companions as something between staircases and bedwarmers, nestled in the most unlikely places, and had a purr as loud as a steam engine, all of which combined, despite the scratchmarks on the furniture, to charm Hippolyta's heart and even to encourage Patrick to tickle him behind the ears. The following morning at breakfast Snowball presented Hippolyta with a bird, which on inspection seemed to have been dead for some time. He sat back, immensely proud of himself.

'Oh, silly cat!' cried Hippolyta, tapping him on his pink nose with a severe finger. The poor bird was shedding feathers in a pattern of red and gold across the floorboards. 'Don't kill pretty birds! Or bring in other cats' leavings, either! I hope Mrs. Riach is feeding you enough. Do you see what he has brought in, Patrick?'

'I'm still in a quandary about last night,' said Patrick, with an absent frown at the kitten. 'I hope I have not abandoned a patient.'

'Tell me again what happened?' Hippolyta recovered a discarded paper from the firebasket and scooped up the dead bird, placing it on the bookcase temporarily out of Snowball's reach. Snowball looked deeply disappointed. 'I had been asleep by the time you came home.'

'Yes: I was sorry to waken you. I went down to the inn with the inn boy, but no one there knew of anyone taken ill. I asked the boy who had sent for me, and he said it had been a Mr. Jenkins who has been there this last week. I found Mr. Jenkins and he said a lady in a nightgown and shawl had stopped him in the corridor, all urgency, and begged him to send for a doctor. He did not know the lady, and as he had acquired a jar of Glenlivet in order to sample local produce on his stay, and had indeed been sampling it, he was not sure he would be able to identify her again. The innkeeper could think of only two women staying in the inn who might match Mr. Jenkins' very hazy description, and neither of them admits to running about the corridors in her nightgown – though one is elderly and very respectable, and might not admit to it even had it happened. I just hope there is no sick person there still wondering why a doctor has not come to their aid.'

'I'm sure if there is, they will soon send again,' Hippolyta assured him reasonably.

'If it is not too late.'

There was a crash from the bookcase. Kitten, dead bird and a rather ugly old pen pot had descended precipitately to the floor.

'Oh, Snowball! I'm definitely going to talk to Mrs. Riach about your rations, silly kitten!'

'But it's a cat,' said Mrs. Riach later, slowly, as if Hippolyta might have made some mistake in identifying the animal. 'It's supposed to work for a living.'

'Not killing birds,' Hippolyta objected. 'It was a goldfinch. A very pretty little thing.'

'Well, I dinna see how you could train a cat no to kill.'

'You could make sure he has a decent breakfast and supper, as I said. If he isn't hungry, he won't want to kill birds.'

'He'll no want to kill mice either, and killing mice would be gey useful around here in the autumn.'

'Well, it's not the autumn yet,' said Hippolyta, putting off in her mind the thought of dead mice at the breakfast table. 'Oh, Mrs. Riach, have you ever kept hens?'

The housekeeper pursed her lips and sighed, considering.

'Aye, I had a couple hens when I was wee.'

'I should like to keep some hens in the garden,' said Hippolyta, trying to sound as if she had always done so.

'Oh, aye?'

'I shall be making some enquiries as to where I can buy some,' she went on, undeterred by the housekeeper's tone.

'Aye, well,' was Mrs. Riach's response, by which she appeared to mean that as long as no one blamed her when it all went wrong, she had no specific objections. 'Is yon loon away home the day?' she asked, changing the subject to one dear to her heart.

'Robert Wilson is quite well enough to leave now, yes. He will be taking his carriage and horses back today, as I understand it.'

'Well, that's something, onywye.'

'And I shall be out for the rest of the morning,' Hippolyta added, with a glance at the mantel clock. The housekeeper, deciding she was therefore dismissed, left before Hippolyta had had the chance to confirm what was to be for dinner. She sighed: how did one train a cat - or indeed a housekeeper?

The front door was half-open as she reached Dinnet House at five to eight, and she paused, wondering if she should go in straight away, as she had heard sometimes happened in the countryside, or rattle the risp. In the end she rattled at it, and waited. After a few minutes she rattled it again. There was a scraping sound, and a window opened above her head. She backed on to the drive and looked up.

'Oh! What time is it?' cried Basilia, who was wrapped in a light dressing gown.

'Just gone eight,' said Hippolyta. 'Listen – there's the church bell.'

'Goodness! I am sorry. Why did nobody waken me?' Her head disappeared for a moment, and then suddenly popped out again. 'Has no one come to the door?'

'No, but it's half-open,' Hippolyta explained.

'Then for goodness' sake come in and I shall be down directly!'

The window descended, and Hippolyta, with a grin, pushed open the door and entered the hall.

The hallway was dim after the bright morning sunshine outside, and she had to pause for her eyes to adjust. As the colours came to life, she heard footsteps at the top of the stairs, then noticed that Colonel Verney was sitting with his back to her in his wheeled chair at the door to the servants' quarters, waiting, presumably, for Forman to help him.

'Colonel Verney!' she called out in greeting.

'Uncle!' called Basilia at the same moment from the top of the stairs. 'Tabitha did not wake me, and here is Mrs. Napier all ready to go and I not even dressed nor breakfasted!'

'Colonel Verney?' repeated Hippolyta, suddenly nervous. He had not moved. She found herself walking towards him, far too fast, yet as if her legs were wound about with heavy fleeces, twice their normal weight. She reached him just as Basilia finally stopped talking, and came down the stairs.

'Uncle?' she said again. Hippolyta put out a hand to the Colonel's shoulder, then snatched it back as his head sank abruptly on to his chest. She darted around the chair. The Colonel was slumped in it, his dark coat collar standing proud of his own neck, and his shirt front almost as black – but with blood.

'No, dear, don't –' she said quickly to Basilia, but Basilia fought past her, then slapped her hand across her own mouth. It did not stop the scream.

'Uncle!' she cried, then sagged to the floor, her pretty dressing gown spilling round her.

Chapter Five

Quite clearly Colonel Verney would benefit from no urgent attention: his hand, when Hippolyta flung off her gloves and tentatively felt it, was stone cold. She turned instead to Basilia, knelt beside her and rubbed her hands hard. Basilia began to show signs of revival. Hippolyta looked about her for a bell pull, saw none, and raised her voice.

'Forman! Forman! You are needed quickly!'

She listened for the manservant's footsteps, but all she heard was a muffled thumping from somewhere nearby: the parlour? Basilia sat up with a weighty groan, and Hippolyta helped her to her feet.

'Who else should be here?' she asked.

'Forman, of course,' whispered Basilia, 'and my maid.'

'No cook?'

'Forman cooks: Uncle has always had it that way. A woman from the village comes in each day to help him with things.'

'Where is Forman, then? And where is your maid?'

Basilia's legs wobbled, and Hippolyta helped her to a hard hall chair.

'Did – did someone attack Uncle?' she asked, her voice quivering.

'I think so. We need help here. Let me leave you for a moment and see if I can find Forman. And what is that noise?'

'Oh, do be careful, Mrs. Napier!' Basilia snatched at her hand. 'If someone attacked him, they might still be in the house!'

'But then I don't think they would be thumping and banging like that to try to attract our attention, do you?' Hippolyta hoped she was right. She opened the parlour door, her own hand shaking, and looked about the room. Nothing looked amiss, but the banging grew louder. Across the room was another door, with a key turned on the outside: it looked like a press built into the depth of the wall. Glancing behind her, Hippolyta hurried over to the door and was about to turn the key when better sense prevailed. She leaned close to it.

'Who is in there?'

'Who's that?' The voice was small and undoubtedly female.

'It's Mrs. Napier, the doctor's wife,' said Hippolyta, and for the first time she said it without that little heartskip. Her heart was too busy beating fast anyway. 'Who are you?'

'Tabitha, ma'am, Miss Verney's maid. Please will you let me out? I've been here all night!'

'Good heavens!' Hippolyta turned the key at once, and the door practically fell open with the force of the little maid's eagerness to be free. 'What on earth were you doing in there?'

The cupboard was shallow: the maid had not had much room to manoeuvre. She was dishevelled, and in a great hurry.

'Excuse me, ma'am!' she cried, and ran from the room.

'What on earth?' Hippolyta followed her back into the hall, but she had already crossed it and run past Colonel Verney in his chair, then through the door to the servants' quarters. Hippolyta hurried after her. Just the other side of the door she caught sight of a side door slamming shut, and a great sigh of relief came from beyond it. Hippolyta's mouth formed an O which was almost amused, in the circumstances: being locked in a cupboard all night had many disadvantages.

She paused in the plain stone corridor, and a white kitten emerged from an open doorway, mewing at her plaintively.

'Hello! Are you Snowball's brother? Or sister, perhaps. Tell me, kitten, where is your Mr. Forman, then?'

She heard the door to the hallway open again behind her. Basilia had followed her, but stopped there, obviously reluctant to leave her uncle unattended.

'Do you think Forman could have done this?' she asked. 'Could that be why he is not here?'

Hippolyta swallowed, not sure what to say. The kitten mewed again, staring up at her as if willing her to do something – feed it, probably.

The door of the privy opened and the maid reappeared,

blushing bright red.

'Sorry, miss, sorry, ma'am,' she said hastily. 'I'd been in there all night.' Her accent was soft rural English, Hippolyta thought: perhaps from the West Country, though she was not sure. She had been to Bath once. The maid was rounded and comfortable looking, a woman who enjoyed her food.

'You must be hungry, too,' said Hippolyta. 'But how did you come to be locked in the cupboard?'

The maid's face turned from red to white at speed.

'Have we been burgled, miss?'

Basilia frowned.

'Could that be it? A burglar?'

'I had just come down from seeing to you, miss,' Tabitha explained, 'and I peeped into the hall and saw that all the candles were out. Well, I thought Mr. Forman couldn't have deliberately put them out yet, so I went to light one. Then someone grabbed me from behind – right round my waist, miss! And a hand over my mouth, and he pushed me quick as lightning in to the parlour and into the cupboard, and shut the door fast!'

'Did he say anything?' asked Basilia. 'Did he ask you where the valuables were?'

'No, miss. He didn't say a word.'

Hippolyta picked up the kitten, stroking it thoughtfully.

'Did you notice anything about him?' she asked. In her mind's eye she was trying to picture the scene. 'Did you see his hands? Are you sure it was indeed a he?'

The maid looked at her, and through her as she considered.

'It all happened so fast, and it was dark,' she explained. 'All I can say is he must have been a big man, to lift me away like that!'

'And so fast,' agreed Hippolyta. Forman was a big man, but why would he need to lock the maid in the cupboard? So that she did not see him murder his master? Whoever the killer, that must have been the reason.

'Should we go and see if there is anything missing?' asked Basilia. She was starting to shake, and Hippolyta pulled herself together.

'Miss Verney, do go and sit down again. Tabitha, help your mistress over to that chair, then fetch her a rug. I'll go to the kitchen – this way, I take it? – and bring some tea and food for both of you, and then Tabitha, I think you should run to the village and fetch … what do you have here? A constable?'

'There's Mr. Morrisson,' said Basilia doubtfully, but she allowed herself to be eased back to the seat. Hippolyta turned with the kitten and made for the open door.

The kitchen was cold: the fire was out. Two more kittens and the mother cat wriggled off an old blanket on a window seat and came to wind themselves into her skirts, purring heavily.

'More hungry mouths, eh?' asked Hippolyta. 'Where is Forman, then, mother cat?'

To her left she could see a pantry, with a meat safe. She found some cold beef, and laid the plate on the floor, where the cats immediately huddled round it. Then she considered the fire: Basilia needed a hot drink of some kind, but how long would it take to get the fire started? She wondered if the kettle were even warm, and stepped round the central firwood table to find out.

Forman was lying face down on the floor just in front of the stone fireplace.

An upturned pan lay before him, and a pool of blood had spread around him, soaking dark into the floorboards – presumably, Hippolyta found the random thought in her mind, the floorboards he had had to pull up to find his stray kitten. She could see where the boards had been lifted, to the left of the fireplace: some of the edges were a little splintered, showing white against the dusty colour of the old boards. The blood was as black as Colonel Verney's: that must mean that they had both been dead for some time. She swallowed hard, and made herself bend down and feel Forman's rough hand: as she had expected, it too was cold.

Her head swam a little as she straightened, but she told herself firmly – though it was her mother's voice she heard - that it would be of no practical value whatsoever to faint. She saw the outside door through a little hallway at the back of the kitchen, and tried it: it was locked, with the key on the inside. She returned to the stone corridor and tried one of the presses with which it was lined: as she had hoped, it contained bedlinen. She took two sheets, returned with one to the kitchen to lay it over Forman, picked up the small kettle by the fireplace, returned to the pantry, the cats once more at her heels, to collect a tea loaf she had seen there, added a clean knife from the table to her burden, and edged back towards the hallway. The cats followed.

'The fire's out,' she explained briefly. 'The parlour one will be quicker to light, no doubt. Tabitha, can you go and set this kettle over it? There's water in it. Right, Miss Verney, here is some tea bread – oh, Tabitha? Here's a slice for you, too. Now, let me just …' She spread the sheet out over Colonel Verney. Tabitha was hovering in the parlour doorway.

'I didn't realise, ma'am, not until just now. I thought he was just sitting in his chair. I'd never have run past him like that if I'd known. I wouldn't.'

'Of course you wouldn't, Tabitha,' said Basilia. The maid paused for a second, still troubled, then went to heat the kettle.

'I'll leave Tabitha here with you,' Hippolyta decided, 'and I'll go for the constable. Morrisson, yes? And I'll just go and fetch cups and saucers and sugar – I'm not sure there's any milk. But Miss Verney,' she knelt at Basilia's feet and quickly took her hands, 'I pray you not to go into the kitchen. There has been another incident.'

Basilia's dark eyes widened dramatically.

'Forman?'

Hippolyta nodded.

'It seems clear that he was not guilty of your uncle's attack, at any rate. But he may have disturbed the attacker, and lost his life in the same way.' She watched Basilia for a moment, checking that she was not about to faint again, then picked up her gloves and bade her farewell for now. It was clear they needed someone in authority, and quickly.

Outside the sun was still shining, the morning as beautiful as it had been when she arrived. It seemed wrong. She strode quickly along the drive towards the village, a tumble of emotions in her head: horror, fear, concern for her new friend, sorrow at the deaths of two men she had liked, and at the same time a little machine ticked away, a machine she had only seen working before in her mother. Had she done everything she should have? Had she tended to those who needed it, asked the questions she ought to ask? She was fairly sure her mother had never met with a murder but she was a woman of remarkable competence, the one to whom everybody turned when a charity bazaar needed to be organised, or a soup kitchen established, or a female school inspected. For years Hippolyta had watched all this activity from a distance: more of her mother's methods seemed to have sunk in than she had thought.

She asked the first person she met where Mr. Morrisson lived, and was directed to a very small cottage at the lower end of the village, near the river. She would be passing her own front door to reach it, and decided that if there was the least chance that Patrick was in, she wanted to fetch him – to hand the matter over to him? She considered that as she hastened up her own front path. A lady should no doubt defer such a matter to her husband. But a quick reflection told her again that her mother had never done so: she would not hurry to relinquish her responsibilities, either.

'Mrs. Riach! Mrs. Riach, is Dr. Napier at home?'

The little maid, Ishbel, appeared, curtseying almost as she hurried up.

'Mrs. Riach's taking her nap, ma'am,' she whispered.

'Her nap?' Hippolyta's eyebrows rose. 'Is the doctor at home?'

'No, ma'am, he's gone to Pannanich Wells to see a patient.'

Hippolyta thought quickly. Regardless of her husband's company, which she would have dearly loved, she knew that a doctor would need to look at the two bodies – or that was what would happen in Edinburgh, for she had seen such accounts of court cases in the papers. But should she send for Patrick, or for Dr. Durward, who might be closer? Well, Colonel Verney had been Patrick's patient: she hoped that was a good enough reason, and quickly told Ishbel to fetch her master from the Wells as soon as possible and ask him to go to Dinnet House.

'Has there been an accident, ma'am?' Ishbel's eyes held a flash of excitement.

'No, not at all: Colonel Verney has need of him urgently, that is all.' After all, it had not been an accident. 'Hurry, now, please.'

'Yes, ma'am.' Ishbel scurried through the front door and Hippolyta, overcoming an unworthy temptation to rush noisily into the kitchen and rouse Mrs. Riach from her slumbers just for the sake of it, left to find Mr. Morrisson.

Mr. Morrisson's cottage was so small Hippolyta had to stoop to rap on the door. The rapping was met with silence from within, but a man passing by with a handcart leaned towards her.

'Ma'am, if you're looking for Davie Morrisson, he's out on his rounds.'

'Of course – he's the constable, is he?'

'Aye, ma'am, I suppose,' was the uninspiring reply. 'This time of the morn you'll likely find him down at the bridge – observing the traffic,' he added, in a voice layered with sarcasm.

'Thank you.' Hippolyta hurried on towards the bridge which crossed the Dee river: Patrick would already have gone that way this morning to reach the Wells. It was a fine, stone, five-arched structure, low lying, and built (as everyone announced proudly, by Thomas Telford, only ten years since) to withstand the sudden surges that could sweep down the Dee from the hills in wet weather. At the Wells end, the bridge road turned left amongst pretty birch woodland: at the village end of the bridge, where the inn was surrounded by rather elegant flower gardens overlooking the river, it was adorned with a number of elderly men sitting about a pump and warming their bones in the sunshine. Hippolyta regarded them with suspicion. One of them was wearing a dark greatcoat and a three-cornered hat, both indicating a rather dusty authority. She approached.

'Mr. Morrisson?'

The greatcoated man straightened himself and removed his hat politely.

'Aye, ma'am, that's my name.'

'You're the constable here?'

'Aye, ma'am.' He straightened still further, but it did not render him any more impressive. He would have been in his seventies, thought Hippolyta with all the alarm of youth at such a prospect. 'Have ye a complaint, ma'am? Has there been a disturbance?' he asked slowly.

'There has been a disturbance, yes,' Hippolyta replied, deeply aware of all Morrisson's cronies angling their ears towards the conversation. 'Will you please come with me?'

'Aye, ma'am, if you say so.' Morrisson took up a battered walking stick and bade good bye to his companions, replaced his hat, and began to follow Hippolyta. She had to keep stopping to wait for him to catch up, and at last slowed her pace considerably to walk with him.

'What seems to be the matter, then, ma'am?' he asked

'You're needed at Dinnet House, Mr. Morrisson. There have been two deaths.'

Morrisson stopped dead.

'Deaths! Michty!' he exclaimed squeakily.

'Deaths?' came an echo from behind her. Hippolyta spun round. Mrs. Kynoch was there, her mouth open, wearing a strange kind of bonnet that resembled a stook of corn. Hippolyta hid a sigh.

'Yes, ma'am.'

'At Dinnet House, did you say?' Mrs. Kynoch examined Hippolyta's face briefly. 'But of course you do not wish the world to know just yet,' she went on more quietly, glancing around to see if anyone else had heard. 'But is it poor Colonel Verney?'

'Yes, and Forman, the manservant.' Hippolyta resigned herself to a slow walk with both Mr. Morrisson and Mrs. Kynoch, who seemed determined to follow them.

'Both of them? Good heavens: then was it a fever? They both seemed perfectly well yesterday.'

'No, it was not a fever. Mrs. Kynoch, I have some disturbing news to tell you. They seem to have been attacked.' She waited for Mrs. Kynoch to shriek, or faint.

'Attacked?' Mrs. Kynoch did not react as Hippolyta expected her to at all. Instead she looked rather thoughtful. 'Is Miss Verney safe?'

'She is there with her maid. She did not want to leave her uncle.'

'Then perhaps – as Mr. Morrisson no doubt knows exactly where Dinnet House is – perhaps we should hurry ahead and see that they are both safe?'

'Of course.' Hippolyta was cross with herself for not thinking of it. 'And I have sent someone to fetch my husband from the Wells to see the – the injuries,' she added, defending herself in front of Mrs. Kynoch who, after all, she thought was a silly woman.

Mrs. Kynoch set a cracking pace back up through the village and out to Dinnet House, leaving poor Morrisson gasping some distance behind. Mrs. Kynoch herself was breathing hard, but she did not slacken until she had reached the front door. Inside, the sheet-covered chair and Basilia, white and slumped still on the seat where Hippolyta had left her, told their own story. Mrs. Kynoch did not hesitate.

'Miss Verney, where is your maid?'

'I'm here, ma'am.' Tabitha slipped out of the parlour. Beyond her Hippolyta could see that the fire was still unlit. 'I can't get it to draw, ma'am,' Tabitha explained.

'I'll see to that. Take your mistress upstairs and see that she dresses in something warm, and come back down for her tea. Is there brandy?' she added.

'Mr. Forman keeps it in the dining room, ma'am,' said Tabitha.

'Is it locked? Good, then fetch it on your way and give Miss Verney a good glass of it. Mrs. Napier, stay here, please, with the Colonel, while I see to that fire. I take it the kitchen fire is out?'

'That's right, and Mr. Forman is in there.'

'Well, we shan't disturb him, and we have nobody to sit with him just yet. Will you be all right here on your own? I shall just be in the parlour.'

'Yes, yes, I shall be perfectly all right,' said Hippolyta.

'Then you can be here when Mr. Morrisson finally arrives, and show him what he needs to see. My! What a day!' She rolled away into the parlour on her chubby feet, leaving Hippolyta sinking breathlessly on to the hall chair. She should have seen to the fire herself before she had left to fetch Morrisson, she supposed. Her mother's voice reprimanded her. Still, Mrs. Kynoch had not had to look at two dead bodies, and all that blood! Thank goodness she had not fainted.

She stared across at the covered form of Colonel Verney, and felt a tear well in her eye. She had liked him, and more to the point, the Colonel had been kind to Patrick, promoting his practice. She hoped Patrick would suffer no harm from this. And poor Forman, with his beloved cats – who would look after them now?

She had her handkerchief out and was crying in earnest when Mrs. Kynoch came back out of the parlour and handed her a hot cup of tea.

'You've had a shock, my dear,' she murmured. 'I'll take this up to Miss Verney, then come back to keep you company.'

The hot black syrupy tea scalded her tongue, but soon dried

her tears. She finished it, set the cup down and blew her nose. A step on the gravel outside helped her to recover: Mr. Morrisson, presumably, at last.

But it was not Mr. Morrisson: it was Patrick. She jumped up and flew into his arms.

'What on earth has been going on here?' Patrick demanded. 'Ishbel said Colonel Verney needed me urgently.' He gently pushed her back to examine her face. 'You've been crying, dearest!'

'I didn't want to tell Ishbel what had really happened,' Hippolyta explained, 'but I have some very bad news for you. Colonel Verney is dead.' She told Patrick the events of the morning.

Patrick's grip tightened a little on her elbows, eyes turning to the covered chair beside the stairs.

'Is that him?'

'Yes, dearest. And Forman, poor man, is all alone in the kitchen. With the cats, though,' she added.

Patrick crossed to the covered chair and went behind it to lift the sheet so that she could not again see the terrible bloody corpse. He studied it carefully, and at last reached out to touch the Colonel's throat gently, tipping his head back to the upright position. Hippolyta watched him, not able to see the Colonel's face, but observing how intently Patrick studied his patient, even in death.

'Perhaps I should ask Dr. Durward to confirm my findings, obvious though they are,' he murmured, half to himself. 'No doubt this will end up in a court of law.'

'If they find the man who did it,' Hippolyta added. Patrick looked up at her in surprise.

'You do not seem very upset, my dear,' he said, more puzzled than reprimanding.

'I am truly sorry for Colonel Verney, and for Forman,' said Hippolyta. 'And it has been a terrible shock. But somehow … you remember you used to tell me all about your medical jurisprudence lectures? I found them so interesting. And Mamma – well, Mamma would not throw a fit of hysterics at something like this.'

'No, not at all,' Patrick agreed drily.

'But what could have happened? Do you think it could have

been a burglar?'

'It's possible. But you didn't mention whether Miss Verney had noticed anything missing.'

'No, she has not yet said. But perhaps a burglar, who had once killed two people and imprisoned another to raid a house, would not have missed going upstairs and making sure that Miss Verney did not see him, either? And would have stolen whatever there was to be stolen from her, and she would have already noticed it?'

'Perhaps.' Patrick drew out his spectacles and tapped them on his hand. It was a habit of his she had begun to notice. 'I had better go and see poor Forman.'

'Do you want me to show you where he is?'

'No: I shall find him easily enough from your description. You had better stay here in case Morrisson arrives: I passed him on the way not realising we were going to the same place, so he cannot be much longer.'

Hippolyta crossed the hall to stand near him, speaking quietly.

'Is he any … any use?' she asked, listening for anyone at the door.

'Any use? As a constable, you mean?'

'Yes: he seemed awfully feeble.'

'He is. And he is growing a little deaf and confused, and he was never perhaps very sharp in the first place. But he's the only constable we have, so we must try to assist him as best we can.'

'Of course, Patrick.'

He clasped her arms again and kissed her on the forehead, smiled into her eyes and vanished through the servants' door. Hippolyta sighed and paced the hall a little, swinging her arms to get the blood running and tapping her boots on the wooden boards, then she remembered she was supposed to be guarding a corpse, and went to sit down primly again on the hard wooden hall chair. It was not really a chair designed to be sat on for long: she thought that Colonel Verney looked more comfortable than she felt.

If it had been a burglar, why had he come to Ballater to burgle? If he were a local man, or if he were there for the purpose, might he not break into other houses, and commit who knew what violence? She shivered, picturing her neat little cottage.

If it were not a burglar, then who could it have been? She wondered about that, staring at the open doorway and listening for

Morrisson's slow footsteps. She barely knew the Colonel, but he seemed a respectable enough man, well known in the community. The guests, or congregation, at the service yesterday had seemed to like him well enough, and appreciate his hospitality. But then she remembered what had occurred afterwards in the village, outside the church. The merchant, Strachan: he had had some quarrel with Verney, certainly. What had he said?

She was struggling to recall Strachan's words, and what Verney had said in reply, when there came a wheezing and coughing at the door, and Morrisson arrived.

Chapter Six

Morrisson was breathing so heavily that Hippolyta jumped up and led him over to the chair, feeling guilty at dragging the old man this far from his seat by the bridge. It was some minutes before he could even speak, and then it was through gasps for breath and wet lips that made his speech close to incomprehensible. Hippolyta left him where he was and hurried through to the servants' quarters, where Patrick was standing by Forman's corpse, looking about the room. The pantry had had a barrel no doubt containing ale: she drew off a cupful.

'Mr. Morrisson has arrived,' she explained, 'but I am afraid he might pass out.'

'Good heavens,' said Patrick, and went after her with all speed. Morrisson was not a good colour as they returned to the hall, but he brightened considerably at the sight of the cup, and downed the drink lustily.

'Thank you, ma'am, thank you,' he said more clearly, settling back on the chair. 'You're gey quick on your feet, ma'am. You left me far anent ye!'

'Yes, I'm sorry about that, but Mrs. Kynoch and I were anxious about Miss Verney'

'Aye, aye, I understand. Now, what seems to be the problem here? A break-in? For the night watchman rarely comes all this way out of the village, ken.'

'There's a night watchman?' Hippolyta was relieved. Surely he would have seen something suspicious, even if he had not been this far out. Perhaps this matter would soon be resolved, after all.

'Aye, but he's asleep the now, ye ken, ma'am.'

'Of course.'

'So,' Morrisson went on with slow patience, 'what was there that was taken awa'?'

'We don't know yet. Miss Verney is very shocked, you understand.'

'I think perhaps,' Patrick put in gently, 'it might be as well if you saw the bodies, for they will have to be moved soon, no doubt.'

'The bodies?' Morrisson's faded eyes sprang wide.

'I'm sure I said there had been two deaths, Mr. Morrisson,' said Hippolyta a little sharply. This was not boding well. 'Colonel Verney and his manservant Forman have been – well, murdered, I suppose.'

'Definitely murdered,' agreed Patrick. 'Their throats have been slit.'

Hippolyta swallowed: she had not thought too closely about where all that blood had come from. Morrisson tutted.

'Their throats slit, eh? That's gey, gey bad, that is.'

'Yes, it is,' agreed Hippolyta. 'Hadn't you better look at the bodies?'

'Och, there's no call for that!' said Morrisson, quickly shaking his head. 'If the Doctor here says their throats was slit, then I'll take it that that's what happened. I've never,' he said, leaning forward confidentially, 'much cared for the sight of blood, to tell you the honest truth, Mrs. Napier.'

Patrick and Hippolyta glanced at one another. Hippolyta thought she detected a warning look in Patrick's eye: she was growing cross, and should consider holding her tongue. She sighed sharply, then heard a step on the stairs.

Basilia Verney, still pallid, her dark eyes like coal, descended the stairs in a black gown, followed solemnly by Mrs. Kynoch. Mrs. Kynoch's gaze flickered over to the covered chair, but Basilia's did not waver, gazing at the elderly constable.

'Miss Verney, I am sorry for your loss,' said Patrick, and she turned and put out a hand to him, touching his gracefully. Morrisson, clutching his three-cornered hat, bowed.

'I'll need to ask you one or two questions, Miss, if you are quite well. If not no doubt I can come back any time that's convenient to you.'

'I should rather answer them now, Morrisson,' said Basilia in a low voice. 'Mrs. Kynoch, would you mind staying with – with my uncle? Mrs. Napier, if you and Dr. Napier would be so good as to bear me company.'

'Of course, my dear,' said Hippolyta at once. Basilia led the way at a pace that would not have challenged Morrisson into the parlour, and seated herself in a chair, as if she feared she might break. Hippolyta sat next to her and impulsively took her hand. Basilia squeezed it.

'Is that your uncle, Colonel Verney, that's dead?' Morrisson asked.

'Yes, it is,' said Basilia, in the same low voice.

'And I hear his manservant's dead and all, Mr. Forman?'

'So Mrs. Napier tells me.'

'He's in the kitchen, Morrisson,' Patrick put in.

'There'll be a blade nearby, no doubt,' said Morrisson.

'I couldn't see one,' said Patrick. 'I did look.'

'Och, it'll be there. You ken what's happened: Forman's slit his master's throat –' there was a little gasp from Basilia – 'and then in remorse slit his own. I've heard tell it happens,' he added, confidently.

'As I say, I could find no blade,' said Patrick, dubiously. 'Perhaps it is under him.'

'Forman was devoted to my uncle!' Basilia was suddenly emphatic. 'He would never do such a thing!'

'He was a soldier, was he no? And used to killing, then,' said Morrisson.

'Not my uncle,' said Basilia stubbornly.

'He'll have been drinking, mebbe. When would you say it happened, Doctor?' he asked Patrick.

'Both bodies are cold,' said Patrick, 'and neither smells of alcohol.'

'And Colonel Verney was wearing evening clothes,' added Hippolyta suddenly. 'It must have been yesterday evening, before they even retired for the night.'

'That's when Tabitha says she was locked in the cupboard!' added Basilia. 'There: it cannot have been Forman. He was very fond of Tabitha, and he would no more have locked her in the cupboard for the night than he would have killed my uncle.'

'If he was fond of her,' said Morrisson obstinately, 'that'll be why he locked her in the cupboard, and didna kill her.'

'We'll look for a blade when Forman is moved,' said Patrick. 'Until then, it's hard to be sure either way.'

Morrisson, satisfied at his morning's work, set off down the hill to the village soon afterwards. Basilia burst into tears.

'How could he think that poor Forman could have killed Uncle?' she sobbed.

'Come and stay with us until this is sorted out,' said Hippolyta. 'You can't stay here on your own, and so upset.'

'But what about Uncle? I cannot leave him here!'

'Well …' Hippolyta glanced around at Patrick, who was blinking rapidly at her. At that moment Mrs. Kynoch popped her head round the door.

'Miss Verney! The daily woman is here. Shall I send her down to the village for the woman to lay out your uncle, and Mr. Forman?'

'Oh! Yes, please, Mrs. Kynoch,' said Basilia, and Hippolyta wished she had thought if it.

'Then I'll stay here with her for tonight, if you wish,' Mrs. Kynoch went on. 'I don't suppose you'll want to be here on your own – or not at all. Perhaps there's a room free at Pannanich Lodge?' She glanced at Hippolyta, who was delighted to be able to say,

'There! Now you can come and stay with us after all.' Out of the corner of her eye she noted a little satisfied nod from Mrs. Kynoch.

'Thank you, Mrs. Kynoch,' said Basilia. 'I shall be staying at Dr. Napier's house.'

In the end, they took the cats, too.

The woman from the village was not at all keen on cats, and white ones made her quite jumpy. It was enough to be spending the night in a house with two murder victims, they discovered, so while Tabitha packed clothes for Miss Verney and herself, Hippolyta found a large basket and, lining it with their own blanket, tempted first the kittens and then the mother cat into it with small pieces of the cold beef from the meat safe. She had the impression that the cats would have gone into the basket anyway, but wanted to see how much beef she was prepared to give them. Struck by a sudden idea, she went to find the stables and the pony, and called Patrick to help her bring out the little cart: between them they managed to harness the one to the other, for she was not at all sure that Miss Verney could manage to walk to the village on her own in her current state, and it would then be a simple matter to load the two little trunks on to the dickey at the back, and she herself could sit with Basilia with the cat basket on her lap. However, the pony was used to being led rather than driven, and drew the line emphatically at being led by either Patrick or Tabitha. Hippolyta had to manoeuvre herself out of the cart again and go to the pony, while Tabitha sat herself into the cart to hold the cats.

'I don't want to be left to take that animal back, Miss: it was only ever Mr. Forman that could handle it,' Hippolyta overheard Tabitha muttering to her mistress. She sighed: no doubt she could walk the pony back herself. It seemed that living in the countryside required a good deal of walking unbiddable animals here and there, while looking like a travelling circus.

The travelling circus image was clearly crossing Mrs. Riach's mind, too, when she opened the door to them.

'Is that party all coming in here?' she demanded rather loudly, eyes wide.

'Miss Verney and her maid have come to stay. There has been an attack at Dinnet House and both Colonel Verney and Forman are dead,' said Hippolyta succinctly.

'And I suppose they'll want dinner?'

'I imagine they will!' said Hippolyta. 'How good of you to think of it, Mrs. Riach. I know you'll do your best to satisfy everyone.'

Mrs. Riach snorted very slightly, then saw Tabitha hand Patrick the cat basket.

'Fit's in thon thing?'

'Snowball's mother and the rest of her kittens.'

'Are they coming in and all?'

'They are, yes.' Hippolyta was firm.

'How many?'

'Five kittens, I believe. Not counting Snowball.'

Mrs. Riach breathed out heavily, staring ahead.

'Ye dinna need to wyte me if the hale household gangs wud. Ah'm near skaikent wi' yon erst cat already and his eesage, the things he brings intil the kitchen has to be seen.' With further incomprehensible mutterings, she turned and stalked into the depths of the house, her limp pronouncedly worse than Hippolyta remembered it being in the morning. Struck by guilt at not at least having warned her housekeeper, Hippolyta took the cat basket herself from Patrick and let the cats out in the parlour, with the door shut. She returned carefully to the front garden to find Patrick handing Basilia out of the pony cart, and her favouring him with a sad smile.

'Come, Miss Verney,' she said at the gate, 'welcome. I could wish the circumstances happier.'

'Hallo! Moving in?'

Dr. Durward's cheerful voice came along the path in front of him. Hippolyta was about to leave Patrick to explain, but Basilia leaned heavily on his arm and with a glance at Hippolyta, Patrick led their unexpected guest indoors. Hippolyta, going to the pony, could hear him calling Mrs. Riach to bring tea. She hoped Mrs. Riach would oblige.

'There has been a terrible incident, Dr. Durward,' she explained as he stopped by the gate. 'Colonel Verney and his manservant have been murdered.'

'Murdered!' Dr. Durward's fine eyebrows shot skywards, and his jaw dropped. 'How on earth?'

'It is not yet known,' said Hippolyta solemnly. 'It happened late last night. We have yet to find out what the night watchman might have seen. I don't suppose you yourself were out last night, Dr. Durward?' she asked suddenly.

'Dear me, Mrs. Napier! I hope you are not suggesting I might have a penchant for murder!'

She laughed a little.

'Not at all, of course! I wondered only if you might have seen anything.'

'Well, I was out last night, as it happens, but quite the other end of the village – in fact, I was up at Pannanich Lodge, playing cards with that Mr. Brown I introduced to you. To be frank, Mrs. Napier, his problems are less physical and more a question of melancholia. Keeping him company and keeping him cheerful are the best medicine I can provide.'

'And you saw nothing on your way home? I do feel so sorry for poor Miss Verney: to lose her uncle so tragically is one thing, but not to know who did it or why, or if they might strike again, is quite another.'

'I see your reasoning, Mrs. Napier. But I still cannot help you: I went to the Lodge for dinner yesterday, then I regret to say we played cards all night. I came back over the bridge in the dawn. There! You have wrenched a confession of me of my dissolute life! But I should not be frivolous, I know. The matter is far too serious. A murder in Ballater!'

'I'm afraid so. And now you must excuse me, Dr. Durward, for I should attend to my guest.'

'Of course. Be good enough to give her my condolences, if you would: and if I can be of any assistance at all she is only to let me know.'

He raised his hat and bowed, and carried on up the path. Hippolyta turned, and found that two kittens had already escaped from the parlour and meandered into the front garden, sniffing their new environment. She scooped them up and carried them back into the house, kicking the door quickly shut behind her. The parlour door was shut, she was pleased to see, and she managed to open it with one-handed caution and deter any further escapes with her skirts. Basilia was reclining on the chaise longue while Patrick sat beside her attentively.

'Dr. Napier has been so kind, dear Mrs. Napier!' said Basilia.

'Is Mrs. Riach bringing tea?' Hippolyta asked.

'I believe so,' said Patrick. 'I did ask her.'

The door was thrust aside as if it had caused some offence, and one of the kittens did its best to trip Mrs. Riach as she entered with the tea tray. Hippolyta dragged it out of the way, and closed the door gently behind the housekeeper. Mrs. Riach distributed the tea things forcefully on to the parlour table, curtseyed like a blow, and marched out again, this time almost staggering. Again, Hippolyta eased the door closed behind her.

'You're right,' said Patrick thoughtfully, 'she has a terrible limp. I must talk to her about it.'

'Unfortunately the pain makes her a little, ah, distracted,' said Hippolyta, who wondered if that was in fact so. She had never suffered much in the way of pain herself, but she knew that when her oldest sister had a headache, everyone suffered.

'Oh, Mrs. Napier! You have left your painting things at Dinnet House!' Basilia exclaimed suddenly.

'No,' said Patrick proudly. 'I noticed them in the hall and brought them out to the cart. They should be here.'

'Thank you, my dearest!' cried Hippolyta. 'I must fetch them in.'

She hurried back to the hall, where her box and stool had been abandoned by Mrs. Riach by the hall table. She brought them back into the parlour.

'Mrs. Strachan,' she said with some pride, 'has asked me to make a painting of – is it Craigendarroch? The peak beside the Pass of Tullich.'

'Oh, yes, a popular view,' Basilia agreed. 'Though there are many around.'

'I so look forward to starting again here.' It seemed to be a subject that could distract Miss Verney a little from her tragedy. Hippolyta, who could talk effortlessly about art, found herself wondering what Basilia would do now: presumably it depended on how Colonel Verney had left her. She was of marriageable age. Did she have any other relatives to go to?

Patrick finished his tea, removed a cat from his lap, and rose.

'I fear I should return to my patients, if you ladies will excuse me,' he said.

'And I should take the pony cart back,' said Hippolyta, 'for I don't know that anyone else wants to!'

'Then I shall walk with you, my dear,' said Patrick. 'I don't want you going up there alone.'

'I think I shall take a little nap here, if that is all right,' said Miss Verney. 'I cannot say when I have felt so exhausted. Thank you both so much for taking such care of me!'

The pony was waiting outside, availing itself of the happy opportunity to take occasional nips at passing lads. Hippolyta gathered up the reins and began to lead the cart in a circuit of the green, to avoid having to turn in the narrow path. Then a thought struck her.

'There will be no one at Dinnet House to see to the pony. Should we take it down to the inn, instead?'

The pony, listening, was evidently unimpressed, and did its best to buck in the shafts. The cart tipped backwards, and the pony twisted hard, trying to shake it off. Hippolyta took a closer grip on the reins and hushed the pony, stroking its nose firmly. The pony calmed, the cart stopped rocking, and they set off side by side with the pony now on its best behaviour.

'I had no idea how useful you would be about the place, my dear!' said Patrick. 'All the local inhabitants will be coming to you about their difficult animals!'

Hippolyta smiled in pleasure, but she had other concerns.

'Do you know where the night watchman lives?'

'I believe he's in one of the cottages just down from the church. Why do you want to know?'

'It seems to me we need to ask him if he saw anything last night, any strangers about the town around dinner time. Do you think,' she added, swallowing a little, 'that a person who cut two throats would be very bloody?'

'It depends,' said Patrick automatically. 'But my dear, you are not going to ask questions of the night watchman! That is the constable's job, and no business of yours!'

'But Patrick, you saw the constable! He can barely walk, let alone chase a murderer! And he would have poor Forman the murderer, when Miss Verney says he would never have done such a thing. And you said you could see no blade with Forman, so how could he have killed himself and then hidden the blade? Surely he would have died very quickly?'

'Oh, very quickly, yes. But I'm sure, if we find no blade under Forman's body, there will be no question even in Morrisson's mind that there is a murderer still to find. And he will talk to the night watchman. It is no business of yours.'

Hippolyta was silent. She had not noticed before that Patrick was really quite like her dear father. Papa put his foot down on things, too, sometimes. She tucked that thought into a drawer at the back of her mind, and changed the subject.

'Do you think that Mrs. Riach's leg is causing her a great deal of pain?'

'It looks like it,' said Patrick. 'I must indeed ask her if she has had an accident to it, or if it is perhaps rheumatic.'

'Patrick,' Hippolyta went on, following a related theme, 'do you like ham?'

'Ham? Yes, of course: I am very fond of it, if it is not too fatty.'

That must be it, Hippolyta thought: perhaps Mrs. Riach had presented Patrick with a fatty piece of ham, and he had expressed dissatisfaction that she had misinterpreted. Well, that would help: ham, beef, mutton, and their variants would no doubt see them through the weeks, with perhaps an occasional chicken if she could keep the hens she wanted. Peas were fresh at the moment, and the fruit was well in: Mrs. Riach had made strawberry jam before they had arrived, and was planning gooseberry jam this week, and the raspberry canes looked, even to her untutored eye, very promising. It did seem that Mrs. Riach was a reasonable housekeeper: Hippolyta had to do her best to make her life a happier one so that she would stay. Perhaps another maid to help her, along with Ishbel? Hippolyta had hopes that Ishbel might be a little more of an upstairs maid, so a kitchen maid might be useful. Oh, if only her mother had had a little more time to teach her housekeeping! Her sisters had been well taught and their houses appeared to run like clockwork: Hippolyta, coming along last and late, had missed the lessons while her mother busied herself with prison visiting and soup kitchens. She sighed: she did not want to let Patrick down.

'The stables are up this end,' Patrick was saying, guiding her so that she would guide the pony. The stable yard was fresh and swept, and a familiar equine nose jerked out over a stall door to watch them as they arrived.

'Isn't that one of the horses from Robert Wilson's carriage?' Hippolyta asked. The stable lad had hurried forward to greet them.

'That's right, ma'am,' he said. 'They've been here a few days the now.'

'I know – but I thought he was going today?' Hippolyta turned to Patrick.

'Ah, yes. But he was a little worse this morning, my dear. He had another dizzy spell. I thought it best to let him rest for another day, anyway.'

'Oh! I did not know.' That could be another reason for poor Mrs. Riach's mood: the two attics contained her and Wilson, the two main bedrooms contained herself and Patrick in one and now Miss Verney and Tabitha in the other, while Ishbel bedded down, she believed, in a press in the kitchen. It was a full house, particularly if you added the cats. It was perhaps best that their own luggage cart had not yet arrived: where would they fit everything?

They saw the pony and little cart settled in the stables, and Patrick tipped the stable lad quite generously while warning him about the pony's habits. With a squeeze of the hand, he left her outside the inn and headed for the bridge and Pannanich, while she walked thoughtfully back to the centre of the village. There was the church, stern admonishment on the green, reminding her to obey her husband – but it was not her church, she reminded herself obliquely. The cottages below the church were small and neat, and only one of them had its shutters closed, as if, perhaps, someone were still asleep within. She took a breath, straightened her shoulders, and knocked on the door.

After a moment a head in a night cap appeared round the door, bleary-eyed.

'Sorry to disturb you,' Hippolyta began, 'but is this the home of the night watchman?'

'Oh! Aye,' said the woman, rubbing her eyes. 'That's my Rab. He's sleeping. Fa's wanting him?'

'There's been a murder in the night, and I want to know if he saw anything odd.'

'He's no being blamed for a'thing?' asked the woman suspiciously, too sleepy to be shocked at the news.

'Not at all,' said Hippolyta in surprise: she had not considered the possibility. Now, of course, she wondered if the night watchman were not perhaps the best placed person to commit night time crimes. However, the woman had disappeared, and in a moment the door swung open. Stooping, Hippolyta entered the cottage, and immediately stopped, unable to see anything in the darkness until her eyes had adjusted from the sunshine outside. The woman shoved open a shutter, which also let in a little fresh air: the one room was heavy with the stale odour of night time bodies. A box bed stood open, and a thin man sat on the edge of it with a bewildered look on his face, while his wife hastened to wrap a blanket around his bare legs. Hippolyta looked away until he was presentable, hoping the darkness would hide her blush.

'Mr. – oh, I'm sorry, I don't know your name,' she began.

'Ah, Lang, ma'am.'

'Mr. Lang, very good. I'm Mrs. Napier, the doctor's wife.'

'Aye, I ken fine, ma'am,' said Lang, slowly coming to himself.

'I'm sorry to waken you, Mr. Lang, but there's been a murder – two murders, in fact. Colonel Verney at Dinnet House and his manservant Forman were murdered before they went to bed last night, and Miss Verney's maid was locked in a cupboard.'

'Oh, aye?' To do him justice, even just wakened Lang looked much more alert than the constable Morrisson. Hippolyta drew courage.

'Were you on your rounds by then?' she asked.

'What time would that have been?'

'Around eleven last night, apparently, or a little earlier.' Basilia had confirmed that that was roughly when her maid had gone downstairs.

'Aye, I would have been, true enough.'

'And do your rounds take you out as far as Dinnet House?'

'Times they do,' Lang nodded slowly, thinking. 'I would have been past the gate last night the back of one, mebbe? I saw nothing strange or startling: shone my lantern in the gateway but there was nothing there.'

Well, by one presumably Colonel Verney and Forman were already dead, Hippolyta thought.

'What about earlier in the evening – where would you have been nearer eleven?'

'Eleven … I'm finishing going about the village streets and heading a wee bitty up the hill. I'd have been nearing Mr. Strachan's new house, I suppose. Eleven … Aye, that'd be about right.'

'Was the town quiet by then?' Hippolyta asked. 'With all the visitors it feels almost like the city during the day.'

'No, it's quiet enough at night,' said Lang. 'Whiles there'll be some gentleman drunk from the inn, or a young couple forgetting the time. Whiles the visitors here for their health will be taking the odd walk about to help them sleep. There was a fellow last night nearby the Strachans' house – all their windows were dark, so he must have been out on his ain for a walk. I've seen him up at Pannanich Hotel afore now, but there he was, out to stretch his legs round the village.'

'Who was that, then? Do you know his name?' Hippolyta asked.

'I canna call to mind – oh, aye, I can! It's a Mr. Brookes, that's who it was. I dinna think he saw me, for the light wasna good, and he's likely no so used to it as I am.'

Mr. Brookes – surely that was Patrick's patient, that she had met only a few days ago, thin and frail. Could he really have walked all the way down to the village? And if so, why?

Chapter Seven

Pondering this mystery, Hippolyta left the cottage and went back to pass the church and cross the green. She had not walked more than a few steps when two busy voices hailed her.

'Mrs. Napier! Oh, Mrs. Napier, such terrible news! And you only new to the village!'

'You mean Colonel Verney and his man? I know: isn't it awful?'

It was the Strong sisters, the elderly pair who had visited her the other day. They could be mistaken for nothing but sisters, for they were exceedingly alike: both broad-jawed, sensible-looking women with wiry grey hair and surprised, faded brown eyes. In character, however, they were at variance.

'And you were really there?' asked the younger, Miss Ada Strong. 'What was it like? Was there,' she lowered her voice, 'a very great deal of blood?'

'Ada!' admonished her sister. 'I am sure that if Mrs. Napier was indeed there the memory is far too upsetting for a genteel girl like her to wish to relive it!'

Hippolyta, who had had her mouth open to tell Miss Ada all the details, shut it again sharply.

'But Mrs. Napier is married to the handsome Dr. Napier: she must know about such things as blood!'

'There was a certain quantity of blood,' said Hippolyta, with what she hoped was a genteel expression of distaste on her face. 'It was all very distressing.'

'And Dr. Napier went to attend to the bodies, no doubt?' Miss Ada went on. Her eyes, Hippolyta noticed suddenly, took on an expression when she mentioned Patrick's name that she had not thought to look for in one so old.

'Ada!' snapped Miss Strong. 'You have taken Miss Verney under your wing, I believe, Mrs. Napier? Very good of you.'

'Naturally she had no wish to stay in the house, and as others had kindly offered to sit with the Colonel and his man, and she had had a very grave shock which required my husband's attention, it was thought sensible to bring her back to our house.'

'Well, and a distraction for her, too,' said Miss Ada, 'though not perhaps a very timely one,' she added quickly, as though she had said something out of place. Her sister, Hippolyta noticed, elbowed her sharply.

'We shall of course call to pay our respects,' Miss Strong said firmly.

'Aye, and it'd be lovely to see the young doctor, too!' Miss Ada added with an expansive wink that left Hippolyta quite speechless.

The sisters bade her good day and passed on, and she had just about recovered her breath when she met, by the church, appropriately enough, the minister and his wife. She struggled briefly to remember their name: oh, yes, Douglas.

'Mrs. Douglas!' She curtseyed.

'We have just heard the most distressing news,' said the minister in his low voice. 'Colonel Verney …'

'Yes, indeed,' said Hippolyta. Really, news seemed to travel on wings around here. 'It is more than sad.'

'A murder!' Mrs. Douglas' mousy treble trembled. 'In our little town! Such a thing has never been heard of!'

'It is very distressing,' agreed her husband. 'Their throats slit, I understand?'

'Um,' said Hippolyta, anxious not to be thought ungenteel again, 'yes, I'm afraid so.'

Mrs. Douglas turned quite white.

'My dear,' she said, 'I wish to go home! If two strong men can be killed in such a terrible way –'

'In their own home, though, Alison,' said the minister, with clumsy assurance. 'You'd be better out here, I think.' Seeing her begin to flutter her hands in agitation, he tried again to soothe her. 'Alison, Alison, keep in mind, dearie: there are people in a worse state than ourselves for whom we should be strong.'

Hippolyta could not quite imagine little Mrs. Douglas being strong. A thought struck her.

'I imagine there is a kirkyard near the town? For I see there is none around the church here.'

The minister, his wife's tiny hand in his bear-like paw, turned his attention back to her.

'Oh, aye, there's a place where the Tullich kirk used to be before the laird had this one built,' he said, with a jerk of his shoulder at the church. 'It's out bye, no far away.'

'And are Episcopalians buried there along with – with your flock?' she asked: a goose had walked over her grave, for the thought came to her suddenly that it might well be where she would be buried herself, when the time came.

'Aye, aye, but by their own – your own – ministers, ken?'

'Of course. I must see if Miss Verney has considered that,' she added, half to herself. If the clergyman only came from Banchory once a week at a gallop, where did that leave funerals?

The rest of the day passed in a kind of suspension: Hippolyta sat and drew with Miss Verney, hoping by that to keep their minds from the worst of the horrors they had seen. Miss Verney, in addition, wrote to the bishop in Aberdeen asking for a clergyman to come and bury her uncle and Forman, and Hippolyta went out once again to send it with the coach at the inn. On the way back she met Patrick, returning from Pannanich, and walked with him, arms linked, back home.

'How is Mr. Brookes?' she asked, aiming for an innocent tone.

'Mr. Brookes? Oh, he is quite well. He mentioned you.'

'Did he?' she asked vaguely. 'When you say he is quite well, how ill is he, actually? Can he get up and walk around the place – for a constitutional, that is – at all?'

Patrick laughed a little.

'No, no: he is quite bedridden. He has a servant who carries him down to that public parlour where we met him each day, when he feels well enough. He had yellow fever, I believe, and made a recovery, but his strength is quite broken and he has not walked for some years, he tells me.'

'Poor man.'

'Indeed.'

Basilia brightened when they returned, and ate a little dinner with them, then rested. After supper, when Patrick had been playing the piano a little, and toying with Moore's "Oft in the Stilly Night" to please Hippolyta, Basilia asked,

'Dr. Napier, will you be so good as to play the plaintive from "The Almond"?'

Patrick, always happy to play Oswald's songs, obliged immediately with a simple setting for the piano. The mournful air rose and fell in the little parlour, where the late sunlight stretched dim up the walls, patterned with leaves lifted by the evening breeze. Basilia listened a little as Patrick sang the words, then turned to Hippolyta, beside her on the sofa, fell into her arms, and cried her eyes out.

'How long are they staying, then?' demanded Mrs. Riach the next morning.

'I have no idea, I'm afraid,' said Hippolyta. 'And I am sorry that Robert Wilson has had a relapse.'

'Aye,' said Mrs. Riach lugubriously. It was hard to tell whether she was convinced by Wilson's state or not. 'What am I to feed you all on the day?'

'I heard Mr. Strachan had some nice hams in.'

'I tellt ye,' said Mrs. Riach sharply, 'that Dr. Napier disna like ham. He willna countenance it.'

'Then perhaps a hodge podge? We could use yesterday's mutton.'

'Aye, mebbe,' said Mrs. Riach, consoled by Hippolyta's tone. She gave one of her brutal curtseys – unaffected, it seemed, by any pain in her hip – and vanished from the parlour. Struck by a sudden thought a moment later, Hippolyta followed her through the door at the back of the hall: she had meant to ask her to find a little fish for the mother cat.

Through the door the house looked more complicated than she had expected. A set of stairs turned up to her left, and an unlooked-for passage headed to her right, as well as the short one ahead to the kitchen. She listened. There was silence. She turned right, and was surprised when a cupboard door in the passage shut quickly at her approach. She tried it, but the door would not budge.

She stepped back and looked at it sternly. There was nothing out of the ordinary about it: it was a plain panelled fir door. Had she imagined that it had moved at all?

After a moment, she turned and went back to the kitchen, which was where she expected it to be. Mrs. Riach was at the fire with her feet up, while Ishbel peeled vegetables.

'I meant to ask if you could find some fish when you were out, please.'

'There's speldings in the pantry,' said Mrs. Riach, drawing herself reluctantly to her feet.

'It's for the mother cat. She's called Bella.'

'Aye,' said Mrs. Riach, in that flat way she seemed to have perfected. Hippolyta glanced at Ishbel, who was concentrating hard on her vegetables, then left the room.

'I must go and sit with my uncle today,' said Basilia, pale as a lily, as they sat at breakfast.

'Of course: would you like me to come with you?' Hippolyta asked. She had thought to put on black this morning, so would not have to change.

'Oh, would you? You are so kind, Mrs. Napier!'

'Not at all. I could not see you go on your own.'

So after breakfast they took their sewing and walked up to Dinnet House, which managed to look even more forbidding despite the sunshine.

Mrs. Kynoch, roused apparently from a doze by their arrival, greeted them with due solemnity and no hint of the awkwardness involved in welcoming Basilia to her own home in such difficult circumstances. She showed them to the dining room on the ground floor, where she and the woman from the village had laid out both Colonel Verney and Forman.

'We thought it not inappropriate,' she explained, keeping her squeaky voice down to a gentle croak, 'for Colonel Verney had, I believe, fought alongside Mr. Forman and in other circumstances their lying in the same place would not have been thought out of place, even though one was an officer and one a common soldier. And with only two of us to watch them … I hope you will feel we did right, Miss Verney.'

'Yes, yes of course,' said Basilia quickly, but her eyes were on her uncle. They had laid him out in clothes they must have found in his rooms, a neckcloth high around his neck and another around Forman's, hiding, as Hippolyta had hoped, the awful gashes at their throats. She could not quite believe now that she had been so calm the previous day. Both men were that waxy, yellow colour in the candlelight that Hippolyta had seen before in the dead. Basilia bent over her uncle and kissed his brow. 'I have written to the Bishop for someone to come and take the funeral services.'

'Of course.' Mrs. Kynoch, who was wearing the same odd assortment of clothes she had been wearing yesterday, stood with her head bowed at the doorway.

'Mrs. Kynoch,' said Hippolyta, 'perhaps you would like to go home and rest? We'll be here for a while, no doubt.'

'Are you sure, Mrs. Napier? That would be most kind.'

'Not at all: you have been so kind in arranging everything.' She walked with Mrs. Kynoch back towards the hallway. However silly a woman, she thought, Mrs. Kynoch had behaved very practically and generously in this instance.

'We have done our best to clean up the hall and the kitchen,' Mrs. Kynoch added to Hippolyta when they were out of Basilia's hearing. 'She won't want to be troubled with such things just now, but later it will be less upsetting for her that they are done. The woman who cleans came to help in the afternoon.'

'Good: I'm sure it was hard work,' said Hippolyta. She pictured the darkened floorboards in the kitchen, and swallowed. 'I know she will be grateful when she is a little recovered. Tell me, though, Mrs. Kynoch: was there any sign of a blade of any kind, when you moved Mr. Forman's body?'

'A blade, dear?' Mrs. Kynoch frowned for a second, and then realised what Hippolyta meant. 'No, there was not. There was no sign at all that Mr Forman made away with himself.'

'Patrick thought there wouldn't be,' Hippolyta murmured, half to herself. 'They were both killed. At least Miss Verney won't have to think that poor Forman murdered her uncle.'

Mrs. Kynoch put a hand out and touched Hippolyta's sleeve.

'She is fortunate to have found a friend like you at the right time,' she said, smiling. 'She has always seemed a little lonely, without much female company.'

'Then I hope to continue to remedy that, at least until she knows what her future must be.'

Mrs. Kynoch nodded approval, and took up her bonnet from the hall table. She departed down the drive, and Hippolyta returned to the darkened dead room to keep her new friend company.

The next few hours passed uneventfully. Basilia sat close to her uncle's corpse, with occasional glances at Forman, and wept periodically. Hippolyta sat in the window seat, stitching her first shirt for Patrick as neatly as she knew how. There was more light than she had expected, for the shutters were as old as the house and did not quite meet. At dinner time, however, she was delighted to see the man himself appear at the end of the driveway, carrying a large wicker basket. She hurried to meet him at the door.

'I bring you dinner!' said Patrick, waving the basket with some difficulty. 'Mrs. Riach said you had come here, and Miss Verney, too. I'm sure you would both benefit from some food.'

'Indeed I'm famished!' Hippolyta agreed, kissing him almost as much for the food as for his own self. 'Will you come in? There is only the two of us here: the village woman –I don't yet know her name – has gone home for now, and Mrs. Kynoch is off for a rest.'

'I have brought enough for three!' said Patrick, 'though it is a solemn enough place for a picnic.'

They took the basket to the kitchen and served the food on to plates, added a bottle of wine to the collection and some glasses, and carried all on trays back along the passage to the dining room. They set everything on one end of the dining table, and encouraged Basilia to leave the bodies far enough to come and eat.

'Your physician insists,' said Patrick with mock sternness. 'You will do no one any good by fainting from hunger, however unhungry you might feel.'

'Then of course I must do my best,' said Basilia, though she still moved as if in a dream. She managed a moderate quantity of food before sighing and excusing herself to return to her uncle's side. Patrick and Hippolyta finished what they could, then took all back to the kitchen to tidy away.

'It is strange to have a wooden floor in a kitchen,' Hippolyta remarked, trying not to picture Forman's body lying on it.

'There's an extra step from the passage into the room,' said Patrick. 'I think perhaps once the floor was stone just like most kitchens, but it was covered over, perhaps because it was damp, or unusually cold.'

'The whole house is a cold one,' said Hippolyta, with a shiver. Patrick's arms slipped round her and she leaned back on him, wanting his warmth as well as his comfort.

'I think it best if Miss Verney stays with us again tonight,' he said. 'Such a cold place after such a shock: I should worry about her taking a fever.'

'Yes, indeed. But presumably Robert Wilson will be away tomorrow?'

'Ah, not quite,' said Patrick, dropping his arms from her waist. 'He's still very giddy.'

'Oh.'

'I hope you don't mind: the thought of someone not quite well handling a team of strong horses like that: it seemed to me very unwise.'

'Of course: no, I don't mind at all, not at all.' But what would Mrs. Riach say, she thought. Then she remembered her confusion in the servants' quarters at home. 'Patrick, how did you come by Mrs. Riach?'

'Come by her?'

'I mean, was she recommended? Or did you find her through an agency?'

'Oh, I see! Well, neither, really. She came with the house.'

'Really?'

'Yes – I told you I rented the house from Dr. Durward, didn't I? Well, he insisted on it, really. He was living there, and when I came here – pretty much at his invitation, that is – he said he wanted to move into somewhere smaller, and would I mind taking on the house as he had no wish to sell it, and he was concerned that any tenant might be worried by people turning up on their doorstep looking for the doctor. Of course I was quite happy to take it on: the rent is low, for it is not a convenient house except in terms of its situation. But if you don't like it, my dearest, if there is anywhere else we can afford …'

'It's a charming house!' cried Hippolyta, and meant it. 'But sometimes I do wonder … So Mrs. Riach was Dr. Durward's housekeeper?'

'I suppose so: I don't imagine she simply moved in after he left.'

'No, I don't suppose so.' She frowned. It was not so much

Mrs. Riach, nor indeed Ishbel, who seemed a very promising young girl. But what had it been that had disappeared into that locked cupboard?

Well, whatever it was, she had no time to attend to it now. Miss Verney needed her. The pair of them returned in silence to the dead room, to find that Dr. Durward himself was sitting quietly with Basilia, paying his respects to the corpses. He stood when they entered.

'Good day to you both,' he whispered, a shadow of his usual ebullient self in the presence of the dead. Hippolyta curtseyed, pleased to see him. She was grateful to Dr. Durward, or for his laziness: many doctors, she supposed, would cling on to their practice to the very end, and not have the sense to hand it over gradually to a younger man, as Dr. Durward seemed happy to do. His financial good fortune should therefore also be theirs. She wondered, as she settled again at the window seat, that a gentleman of money should have become a physician: or perhaps he had come from a mercantile background, and an ambitious father had pushed him towards medicine. She liked to speculate on people. Mrs. Strachan, for example, she thought, her mind wandering. She seemed very genteel for a merchant's wife. Who were her family? Had Mr. Strachan made an advantageous match, a good business deal?

Dr. Durward was rising to go, murmuring something about having just dropped in between patients. Patrick walked out to the hall with him, talking in low tones. They left the door ajar, and Hippolyta crossed to close it against the draught, but caught a little of their conversation.

'Yes, I saw both wounds,' her husband was saying, and her ears sharpened. 'A narrow blade, I should say, extremely well honed, and a slash from left to right, perhaps from behind – that would be more likely than a left-handed assailant.'

'I'll bow to your learning in medical jurisprudence,' she heard Durward reply seriously. 'From behind, eh? Well, it would be easy for almost anyone to reach Verney, seated in his chair, but Forman was a tall fellow. Are we looking for someone equally tall? Or was he, too, seated?'

'Not seated, I'd have said, from the way he fell. But his assailant could have stood on the chair, perhaps.'

An assailant standing on a chair? thought Hippolyta, as their voices faded. That sounded extremely unlikely. What excuse would you give for suddenly climbing on to a chair with a sharp blade, then asking your victim to come closer? And presumably Forman already knew that Colonel Verney had been attacked, so he would not have been likely to trust someone near him. A tall person, acting quickly, was much easier to picture. And, she thought, doing so, any blood would probably have flown forward and Forman's body would have shielded the attacker from being covered in the stuff. Oh, dear: she blinked. That would be a hard image to shift from her head. She wished she had not overheard. She shut the door firmly, and returned to her window seat just before Patrick came back into the room.

Patrick left not long afterwards, to go back to his work. Two hours or so later Mrs. Kynoch returned, with the village woman – Martha, her name was, though Hippolyta could get no surname from her – and urged Hippolyta to go home for the night, and take Miss Verney with her. Basilia was reluctant to leave her vigil, but as the sun gradually dimmed she lost her nerve, and followed Hippolyta reluctantly back to the house on the green. Mrs. Riach had broth waiting, a sensible touch, for Miss Verney was shivering despite wearing not only her own shawl and spencer, but Hippolyta's shawl, too. Patrick, who had been sitting reading by the light of a single candle, hurried to light more and the parlour fire as Hippolyta settled Basilia on the sofa with the broth. He rose to take Basilia's pulse and touched her forehead with the back of his hand.

'Early to bed for you, Miss Verney, and Hippolyta, my dearest, if you would call her maid to fetch warm bricks before she goes up and make sure the fire is lit in that room.'

'Of course, Patrick.' She hurried off to issue instructions and Tabitha, looking concerned, became busy in the kitchen. Hippolyta returned more slowly to the parlour. Could it have been Tabitha who had hidden in the cupboard that morning? She had forgotten that the maid was in the house. But surely a cupboard would be the last place she would have hidden, after her recent experience. And why would she hide at all?

'A message from Aberdeen,' Patrick was saying as Hippolyta

returned to the parlour. She eased a sleeping pair of kittens from a chair at the table, and sat down, arranging them on her lap. Basilia was reading a brief letter.

'The Bishop says that Mr. Downes will arrive in the morning to take the funeral at noon, if all can be ready,' she said, dazedly. Hippolyta and Patrick exchanged surprised glances, but Patrick was professionally calm.

'I'm sure it can be ready, if you are ready for it,' he said kindly. 'If you like I can send to the beadle now so that he can have the graves prepared, and to the carpenter for the coffins.'

'It seems so sudden,' said Basilia. 'It was only yesterday …'

'In general I believe we are a little quicker at such things than is the practice in England,' said Patrick. 'It is simply the custom.'

She looked up at him for reassurance, and he smiled. Uncertainly, Basilia smiled back.

'It would probably be best, then,' Hippolyta put in, eager to support her husband. 'You will feel better when everything is properly arranged. Is there any relative you need to tell? Anyone living nearby?'

Basilia blinked at her.

'No, there is no one. No one at all.'

'Then there is no reason to wait. We can write some cards now to some of the people in the village – spa town – and as Patrick says he can send to the beadle and the carpenter.'

Patrick sat down at the table and sorted out cards and paper and pens and ink, and he and Hippolyta busied themselves constructing a list of things to do and people to contact. When the list was completed in consultation with her, Basilia retired to her warmed bed, and Hippolyta sat up writing until her hand ached and all the invitations and instructions were completed. The carpenter had been warned, the beadle instructed, Mrs. Riach consulted and food ordered, and even bearers had been selected and requested to attend. By the time it was all done, Hippolyta was drowsy and ready for her bed.

At some point in the night, she woke to the sound of footsteps coming from somewhere on the first floor, to her left, she thought. What was there? Patrick was beside her, and Basilia's room was to her right. She listened hard, but the sound had stopped. A trick of an old building, perhaps: she had no sooner come to this comforting conclusion, than she was already asleep again.

Chapter Eight

By the time the coffins departed the following day, all Hippolyta wanted to do was to flop on to a sofa and sleep.

Organising the funeral seemed to have required a monumental effort, particularly at short notice. The parlour at Dinnet House had been cleaned and tidied by the mysterious Martha from the village as soon as it was light, and a troop of Mr. Strachan's best messenger boys had arrived bearing trays of food from the shop, silently jostling each other in the kitchen to see if they could see the bloodstains. Hippolyta chased them out like hens, and began to arrange the food as elegantly as she could on the ashets from the press. It was one part of housekeeping at least at which she could rely on herself: Martha was acting pretty much without direction, except when Mrs. Kynoch arrived and made her do the window glass again with vinegar and brown paper. At ten the pony cart, retrieved from the inn, arrived with Basilia, Tabitha and Mrs. Riach's contributions to the food: Hippolyta had to admit she had done a good and plentiful job, and her pastries were noticeably better than the village baker's. Mourners began to arrive at eleven, and amongst the first of them was Mr. Downes, not the same clergyman as the one the previous Sunday but an older man, who explained that he was the incumbent of a church near Peterhead who had happened to be in Aberdeen, and had been directed by the bishop to come out for the funeral. Basilia thanked him very prettily, and he seemed at once ready to serve her to the very best of his abilities, treating her to a broad smile which he reined in to a sorrowful sympathy when he remembered the nature of the occasion.

The villagers who made their way from the front door to the dining room to pay their respects, then into the parlour to settle for refreshments, seemed for the most part very sorry to have to lose both Colonel Verney and Mr. Forman, even if they had not been in the village for very long. Mr. Douglas, the minister of the established church, who had arrived alone, made some particularly generous remarks to Basilia along the lines of having valued Colonel Verney's advice and counsel greatly. Hippolyta, who was sitting beside Miss Verney to support her, wondered what advice the minister had sought, but Basilia leaned over almost immediately to solve the little mystery.

'Mr. Douglas had done my uncle the honour of asking him to become a trustee of the Burns Mortification – a dreadful sounding thing, is it not? But apparently it is a fund to help poor scholars in Ballater attend the university.'

Hippolyta nodded, frowning a little. That was the mortification, then, that Patrick had told her about. She had been surprised, she remembered, that there had been only four trustees, and Patrick had thought that was about to change. Well, if Colonel Verney had been the only new prospective trustee, then they would be stuck with four for now. Who were the others? She tried to remember. Dr. Durward, and Mr. Strachan, that was it, and the minister, and of course Mr. Strong the man of law. She smiled at herself, as the Strongs had just that moment entered the room and come to greet them. It was really not a big village at all.

It was the first time she had met Mr. Strong: her impression, having seen him before only from a distance, was that he was a very frail old man. Now, close to, she realised that he was far from frail, and was indeed endued with a wiry strength that made him appear much younger, though his face was still feathery with wrinkles. He had the same faded brown eyes that his sisters had, but despite their dim colour the expression in them was as sharp as one of Patrick's scalpels. By the time Basilia had introduced her, Hippolyta felt she had been gutted and turned inside out, all her secrets revealed to the world. It was not at all a pleasant feeling, and she was relieved to turn to the Misses Strong and have to deal only with Miss Ada's curious remarks and Miss Strong's constant reproofs of her sister.

Hippolyta had not been to many funerals in her nineteen years, she was happy to say. She was not, therefore, sure how typical this one was. Conversation was awkward and stiff, and the little groups that formed about the room seemed rigid and unchanging. She was heartily relieved when Patrick arrived, for Miss Verney was of course not disposed to be chatty herself. Both ladies turned to him at once.

'Miss Verney, I hope you are not over-taxing yourself,' he said, examining her face over his glasses, then removing them absent-mindedly. Hippolyta was pleased: he was much more handsome without them. He tapped them on his hand.

'I have done nothing but sit and be attended to, Dr. Napier, I assure you,' said Basilia with a grateful smile. 'Everybody has been so kind.'

'And so they should be, on such a day,' he replied. 'You must not think to decline the least offer of assistance. You need to rest and recuperate from the shock, or you will not be strong enough to sustain yourself in the days to come. Grief can be a very powerful force.'

'I'll do all you say, Dr. Napier,' Miss Verney assured him, her great dark blue eyes wide and serious. Hippolyta smiled, delighted that people treated her husband with such respect for his medical authority.

The Strachans arrived, Mr. Strachan with a keen eye to see how well his groceries were being consumed. Once he had checked that, and greeted Basilia without noticeable warmth, he led his wife off to stand with the Strongs. The minister nodded to both of them as they passed, and Mrs. Strachan seemed to try to respond, but Hippolyta, watching her irresistibly, thought she was tugged on past by her husband. He seemed a hot-tempered man, Mr. Strachan: she remembered seeing him on Sunday, leaning over Colonel Verney in his pony cart, positively ranting.

Ranting … Her blood stopped suddenly, and she tipped a little off balance. Patrick caught her elbow.

'Are you all right, my dear? Too hot?'

'No, no, not at all. Just a sudden – I think I must be a little tired.' It was not the place to discuss what she had remembered. But surely she had remembered correctly, all the same: Mr. Strachan had been threatening Colonel Verney. She glanced over at the merchant, standing proudly over little Mr. Strong and his sisters, only occasionally deigning to stoop to catch some word or other. Mrs. Strachan, she thought, did not look so self-assured, bending her graceful head to talk with the Misses Strong – or at least, to listen to them, for Hippolyta did not see her speak at all. She looked weary, though it did not affect her beauty.

'My wife sends her apologies.' The minister, Mr. Douglas, interrupted her thoughts. 'Her nerves, you know,' he added, as if he were not quite sure himself. He stood there waiting uncertainly for a response, and it came to Hippolyta suddenly that he was not, unlike many clergy, much at home in drawing rooms and in the better sort of company. Mr. Downes, the Episcopal minister, held his delicate negus glass and conversed easily quite as if he had been trained from birth. Mr. Douglas, by contrast, clutched a pastry as if he expected it to crumble over him at any moment, and slurped uneasily at a glass of wine. She smiled at him.

'I am very sorry to hear it: I hope she will be quite well soon. The duties of a parish minister's wife are no doubt very taxing,' she added, repeating something she had heard her mother say. It seemed to work. Mr. Douglas snatched gratefully at a familiar topic and talked at some length about parish work, and all Hippolyta had to do was to nod and shake her head every now and again.

It seemed an age, though, until Mr. Downes set down his negus glass and touched a napkin to his lips, then called everyone's attention. Basilia was by his side as they led the way across the hall to the dining room, gathered about the two coffins, and prayed. The carpenter who had made the coffins was at hand and slipped the lids into place at the end of the prayers, and then the bearers, hastily arranged, hoisted the coffins and tidied the mortcloths over them. Mr. Downes led the way outside, waited for the bearers and mourners to form up, and set off at a steady, respectful pace to walk to the kirkyard. Patrick gave Hippolyta's hand a quick squeeze and joined in, along with Dr. Durward. Hippolyta found another handkerchief to offer Basilia, whose tears streamed endlessly down her pallid cheeks, then put an arm about her and led her back into the house with the other women, to wait for the men's return. She cast a final glance down the drive at the retreating cortege, and noticed a movement in the trees at the bottom of the drive. A figure, waiting there, joined the mourners discreetly near the back of the line: as far as she could see, it was Dr. Durward's patient, the shilpit Julian Brown. It was good of him to trouble to attend a stranger's funeral, she thought, and followed Basilia through the front door.

The women had all retired once again to the parlour, and at Mrs. Kynoch's suggestion Basilia had just rung for fresh tea, when they heard the rattle of the risp at the front door.

'Someone must have forgotten something,' Basilia said dully.

'But what?' Hippolyta asked, and despite her fatigue she found herself back in the hallway. Tabitha, who looked a little unravelled herself, was just opening the door to a large, dark haired man with an inoffensive expression on his bespectacled face.

'I'm looking for, er, Miss Verney?' he began, with an expectant glance at Hippolyta, then he noticed her cap and her wedding ring.

'Who shall I say, sir?' Tabitha's face was dubious: it was not quite clear whether this man should have been going to the back door. There was something slightly ambiguous about him. Hippolyta decided to intervene.

'It's not a very good time, I'm afraid,' she said firmly. 'Miss Verney is in mourning –indeed, you have arrived just after the departure of the coffins.'

The man's eyebrows rose in surprise.

'The funerals are already taking place? So soon?'

'Yes, this morning. May I ask who you are, sir, and the nature of your business?'

'I'm – my name's Durris, ma'am, and I've been sent by the sheriff to see what the business is here.' He paused, thoughtful. There would be no men to talk to until the interments were over, but clearly he wished to waste no time. 'Two murders, wasn't it? And no obvious killer?'

'That's right: Colonel Verney and his man both had their throats cut while Miss Verney was alone upstairs asleep, and Tabitha here was locked in a press.'

'Oh, aye?' He regarded Tabitha with interested concern. 'I take it you didna see the fellow's face, then?'

'He grabbed me from behind, in the dark,' said Tabitha uneasily. 'I din't see nothing at all.'

'I see.' Durris contemplated the hallway, apparently waiting for them to make the next move.

'Well, you'd better come in, then,' said Hippolyta at last. 'I can show you where the bodies were found, at the very least,' she added briskly, 'then there's no need to disturb Miss Verney just yet.'

'But I cannot see the bodies themselves, then?' Durris confirmed, stepping carefully into the hallway. 'They are kisted and away?'

'Two doctors saw them, and will no doubt be able to tell you much. Well, one definitely saw them, and I think the other did,' she corrected herself, wondering how much Dr. Durward had actually looked at them.

'Was the one that looked properly at them Dr. Napier, by any chance?' Durris asked. Hippolyta managed not to beam.

'That's right: my husband, Dr. Napier, examined both bodies.'

'You're Mrs. Napier! Oh, that's splendid! Splendid indeed. I did hear the doctor was to go away to marry, but I hadn't heard tell it had happened yet.' He glanced shyly at Hippolyta again. 'Dr. Napier has been kind enough to advise me on several medical matters in connexion with my work for the Sheriff. I've always been very grateful for his intervention, ma'am.'

'I'm very glad to hear it, Mr. Durris.'

'I did wonder at your connexion with all this, ma'am.'

'Well, I also found both the bodies,' Hippolyta explained with perhaps misplaced pride.

Durris' broad face grew concerned again.

'Did you, ma'am? That must have been very distressing for you.'

'It was not pleasant,' she agreed. 'Tabitha, run along, will you, and see to the tea for the ladies in the parlour? And if Miss Verney asks – but not unless she asks, do not disturb her – I am giving some information to the sheriff's man.'

Tabitha, who had been showing some signs of agitation at the repeated mention of bodies, was glad enough to skip away. Hippolyta led Durris further into the hallway, indicated where Colonel Verney's chair had been, and explained how she had found him.

'And you say he was quite cold?' Durris walked softly for a large man, paying attention to what she was saying while he subjected the hall to a detailed scrutiny.

'That's right. I – I touched him because he was sitting in the chair as if he had fallen asleep in it. I had to make sure …'

'Of course. I'll ask Miss Verney, too, but was there any sign that anything had been taken, at all?'

'There was nothing that I saw, but I had only been in the house twice before.'

'Oh, aye, that makes sense.' He drew out a notebook and pencil, and began to make a few notes and, as far as Hippolyta could see, sketches. She was unexpectedly impressed. 'Now, what about the manservant?'

'Mr. Forman,' Hippolyta acknowledged. She led him through the servants' door and along the passage. He moved slowly, taking in the details, so that she had to wait for him at the kitchen door. Martha, the woman from the village, was helping Tabitha load trays to take to the parlour. Hippolyta waited until they had gone back past Durris and along the passage to the hall.

She indicated the place on the floor where she had found Forman lying.

'My husband said,' she began thoughtfully, 'that both he and Colonel Verney had had their throats cut from left to right, and that that meant it could have been a left-handed assailant in front of them or, more likely, a right-handed one behind them.'

'He told you that, did he?' Durris asked in surprise. Hippolyta chose not to correct him.

'But Forman was tall, and he would have needed someone tall to do that to him. My husband suggested that someone could have stood on a chair, but that seems unlikely to me, do you not think?' She had not been able to voice such a doubt to Basilia, and she did not want Patrick to know she had overheard his conversation with Dr. Durward. It was quite a relief to be able to air her thoughts.

'It's hard to picture,' said Durris, and Hippolyta favoured him with a happy smile.

'My very thought.'

'But it could have happened,' Durris went on. 'The question is, what order were they killed in? Forgive me, ma'am, talking so freely, but –'

'But I started it?' she finished when he paused. He gave a little shrug.

'Say that someone broke into the house to burgle it, and found that the residents were still awake. Colonel Verney is in the hall, maybe, while Forman goes to fetch something from the kitchen. I met the Colonel maybe twa three times: he was always in that chair, was he no?'

'He was, I believe. Forman moved him about the place: I don't think he could convey himself on his own.'

'Then the burglar – wait, though, did a'body hear him cry out? Colonel Verney, I mean.'

'No one has mentioned it. But if it was dark, perhaps he didn't see the burglar?'

'Was it dark? Why were there no lamps?'

Hippolyta thought about it.

'It was a light evening, but that hallway always seems to be dark. But the maid, Tabitha, she said she came down from settling Miss Verney for the night, and found the hallway in darkness. It was when she went to find a light that she was grabbed from behind, dragged into the parlour and locked in the press.'

'Was the parlour dark, too?'

'I don't know: we could ask her.'

'For if it was, and the burglar had blown out all the lights in the hall to hide himself before Colonel Verney appeared, then Colonel Verney could not have been coming from the parlour. Where else could he have been?'

'In the dining room? In the servants' quarters here? There's at least one other door in the hall: it might be his library, or anything.'

'Well: we'll have to find that out.' Durris made himself another note. 'We'll need to see what order things happened in.'

'Why?' Hippolyta was puzzled. Surely it was enough that both men were dead on the same evening?

'Well, so that we can work out how everything happened, ma'am. Did – Forman, wasn't it? – did Forman disturb the burglar who then chased him into the kitchen and attacked him – in which case yes, he would need to be tall – or did the burglar decide to attack Forman first, since he was the more dangerous of the two? He could have climbed on a chair and lain in wait, if that makes sense, in a darkened kitchen, killed Forman and then returned to dispose of Colonel Verney, too, knowing he could do nothing to defend himself.'

'That is an unpleasant thought.'

'My apologies, ma'am.'

'Not at all: the whole business is unpleasant.'

There was silence as Durris made his little sketches of the kitchen, floorboards creaking under his feet despite his soft tread.

'There are no other relatives, ma'am, I believe?'

'That's my belief, too. There's certainly no one else living here.'

'But you're by way of being a friend of Miss Verney?'

'That's right,' she said, 'though of course we have not known each other long. Miss Verney has been staying with us since the murders were discovered.'

'Aye, I see. Would you be so good as to come with me then to look at whatever other rooms are off the hall?'

'Of course,' said Hippolyta, belatedly considering that she should probably mention such a thing to Basilia. But she was curious, too: did Colonel Verney sleep downstairs? What were his private quarters like? How did a gentleman who could not climb stairs arrange his life?

There were two other doors off the hallway, both at the back in the even dimmer recesses under the landing gallery. The first was, as Hippolyta had surmised, a kind of library, where Colonel Verney must have done his business. There were not many books, and those there were were of an age to have been on their shelves for many years. One or two newer ones were military histories, and a couple of novels of the type Hippolyta had never been allowed to read. There were, however, two or three deedboxes lying open and empty on the floor, papers in orderly piles on the broad desk, an elaborate inkwell and a couple of much-used pens, and more papers folded into long strips and bound in bundles with string, again all very neat. Each bundle, Hippolyta saw, was labelled in a black, sloping hand.

'Outgoings, 1827 – 1828' was the nearest. 'Vouchers, 1821 – 1822'. She stifled a yawn.

'Did he do much business?' asked Durris, fingering the papers. He slipped one out from a bundle, and unfolded it carefully. '"The Burns Mortification" – what's that?'

'Oh, I've heard of that! It's a local trust for scholars – bursaries for university. Miss Verney said that the minister had asked Colonel Verney to become a trustee.'

‘It looks as if he was giving the papers a good going-over first,’ Durris remarked. ‘I wonder if there was anything here worth stealing?’

‘Nothing looks disturbed,’ said Hippolyta.

‘True.’ Durris refolded the paper along its original lines, and slid it precisely back into its bundle, then straightened the papers and returned the bundle to its place. If Durris had stolen anything, Hippolyta thought, he would have left no trace at all. ‘I wonder where the papers are usually kept? Was someone taking a chance when they were, maybe, not locked in the parish safe?’

‘Maybe he had found an irregularity in the trust, and someone was trying to hide it!’ Hippolyta’s father had occasionally mentioned irregularities in trusts: it was always a stressful subject.

‘Who were the other trustees, then?’ Durris asked reasonably.

‘Ah, the minister, Dr. Durward, Mr. Strachan, who’s a merchant, and the man of law, Mr. Strong.’

‘Oh, aye. Maybe not the most likely suspects for slitting people’s throats,’ he added, ‘with respect.’

Hippolyta felt herself blush, and was cross.

‘Well, Mr. Strachan was threatening Colonel Verney only last Sunday!’

‘Was he, indeed?’ Durris looked directly at her for once, narrowing his eyes. They were grey, she saw, with a sense of calm that stopped her irritation at once.

‘Well, that’s what I thought it was. He was certainly very cross.’

‘Where was this? What did he say? – did you see this yourself?’

‘Yes, yes I did. It was outside the kirk. Our service had finished and Colonel Verney had taken his constitutional in his pony cart down to the village as we walked back ourselves, and we met everyone coming out of the kirk. I didn’t see him approach, but I suddenly heard him – and he was saying something about opposing any appointment that was made, meaning that Colonel Verney would be appointed to something, I thought. That would make sense, if he didn’t want the Colonel to join the trustees. He said the Colonel was an outsider and it was none of his business.’

‘Well,’ said Durris, making a note, ‘it might be the mortification, it might be something else. Did a’body else hear him say this?'

'I don't know: I didn't notice anyone else paying particular attention.'

'And what did the Colonel say?'

'He was quite calm about it, said he hadn't – what was it? He hadn't pushed himself forward, he had been approached. And then Mr. Strachan said the minister was a fool, or something to that effect.'

Durris put away his notebook again, and made a gesture at the paperwork around them.

'I'll have to gang through this more carefully soon, in case there's other business here that could point to a murderer. Shall we look at the other room?'

They returned to the hall, and tried the next door. It led, via a little antechamber, into a bedroom. Hippolyta backed out hastily, but curiosity drove her to watch from the doorway. The room was not large, though there was space for the Colonel's chair to be manoeuvred about from dressing table – which had the look of a campaign piece – to window to bed. A smallish wardrobe stood against the near wall, and a trunk that again had probably seen many a baggage train was at the foot of the bed. Durris opened it and glanced inside, murmured 'Blankets,' and felt around them, apparently, to his satisfaction. He opened the wardrobe but Hippolyta could see nothing of the interior: there was a cheval mirror on the other side of the room pointing in roughly the right direction, but Durris' bulk blocked all the view.

'Clothes,' he said again. 'Little drawers, too, with collars and so on. You're no missing much, ma'am.'

She pulled back, blushing again. It was easy to be too curious.

'Aye,' he said, sliding back the last of several drawers and shutting the wardrobe softly, 'time to go and speak to Miss Verney, if you'll let me.'

Hippolyta sighed, hoping he would be kind to Basilia.

'Where do you think best to talk with her? I should say that the dining room has been arranged for the coffins, so that might not be a good place.'

'She's in the parlour, is she no? With all the women from the funeral, no doubt?'

'That's right.'

‘Then I might as well go in there, eh? Talk to them all at once.’

Goodness, thought Hippolyta: she was still not sure whether this sheriff’s man ought to be at the front door or the back door.

Chapter Nine

'Ladies, this is Mr. Durris, the sheriff's man.'

Hippolyta abandoned him quickly at the parlour door and went to sit with Basilia, taking her hand. Durris was unperturbed. His eyes took in the room: the occupants, the elderly furniture, the cloth-covered box of the parlour organ, even, Hippolyta was sure, the door of the wall press where Tabitha had been imprisoned.

'Good day to you, ladies,' he said after a moment. 'I'm sorry to intrude at such a time, but I was unaware that the funerals would be taking place so soon. You'll ken that I need to ask some questions if we are to understand what happened and find the miscreant that did these terrible things.'

Hippolyta glanced around the room discreetly. Mrs. Strachan's beautiful face displayed a very proper mixture of anxiety and sorrow, which Hippolyta immediately tried to imitate. Mrs. Kynoch seemed to be aiming for the same, but her teeth gave her the look of a concerned rabbit. The Strongs were excited.

'But nobody knows who did them,' said Basilia. Durris regarded her kindly.

'I'm sure we'll find that one person here might know one fact, and one person there might know another, miss, and eventually we'll put all the facts together and discover the truth.'

He put it so simply, but with a confidence that made Hippolyta, at least, believe him completely.

'Mr. Durris, is the sheriff aware of any miscreants in the area?' Mrs. Kynoch asked squeakily. 'Has anything like this happened nearby?'

'Oh, Mrs. Kynoch, surely we would have heard of it!' exclaimed Miss Strong. 'Such a shocking thing!'

'Unless the sheriff had decided to hide it, for reasons of his own,' added Miss Ada with dark relish.

'The sheriff is not much in the habit of concealment,' said Durris reassuringly. 'And no, we don't know either of any other events like this, nor of anyone in the area likely to carry out such an attack.'

'Is it hamesucken, do you think?' Hippolyta asked suddenly, remembering her father's work. The Misses Strong, evidently similarly educated by having a lawman for a brother, raised their thick eyebrows at her in eerie union.

'It could be hamesucken, it could be burglary with violence,' said Durris.

'What?' asked Basilia in bewilderment.

'Hamesucken is the offence of entering a person's house with the intent of attacking him. The intent has to be there, of course,' Durris added to Hippolyta, 'for it might have been that a burglar entered the house and happened upon the Colonel, and panicked.'

'Either is quite dreadful,' said Mrs. Strachan suddenly, in her soft voice, and everyone turned to look at her. She blushed prettily.

'Aye, but the motives are different,' said Durris. 'Now, the sheriff doesna ken of anybody suspicious nearby. Did any of you see anything odd, or anyone acting strangely?'

'There are so many strangers in the town these days,' said Mrs. Kynoch. 'With the wells being so successful. It's very hard to keep track of who's here, and who's staying where.'

'Are they not mostly up at the Wells and at Pannanich Lodge?' asked Durris. Hippolyta wondered where he was from – clearly not Ballater.

'No, lots of visitors lodge in the village, particularly in the summer. Anyone with an extra room can find someone to stay in it,' Mrs. Kynoch explained to him.

'Well …' said Durris, adjusting his glasses. 'In that case let us work from the other end. Miss Verney,' his gaze lighted on Basilia, 'do you know of any reason why someone would wish to attack your uncle?'

Basilia swallowed hard, and edged forward on the sofa, as if preparing herself for some kind of challenge.

'It is not easy to think of such a thing,' she said stiffly, and Hippolyta squeezed her hand. She found herself torn between wanting to protect Basilia and eagerness to hear any information she might have. Basilia glanced at her gratefully, great eyes wide, then dropped her gaze to the carpet, evidently searching her memory.

'My uncle was a soldier, of course,' she said. 'Most of what he spoke of was his memories of soldiering. He had fought at Waterloo and received a sabre slash across his legs, which rendered him unable to walk for the rest of his days. He talked a great deal of his fellow soldiers and his travels in those days, but I do not recall any mention of anyone that he considered a personal enemy: I doubt any agent of Bonaparte would have troubled to seek him out especially to take their revenge. I don't think he would have stood out that much on the battlefield.' She gave a little fond smile.

'What about family? Has he relatives besides yourself, Miss?'

'He never married, and his parents and his brother and sister are all dead,' said Basilia. Something in this response caused Durris to take out his notebook and write something carefully.

'When did you come to be living with him?' he asked.

'I joined him in Bath about five years ago, when my mother died. My father, his brother, had died some years before that.'

Durris noted that as well, and gave Basilia a rather assessing look, as if trying to gauge her age. Hippolyta reckoned Basilia would have been about fifteen, then, when she joined her uncle.

'And when did you move up here?'

'We came up here first the following summer – that would have been in '25. He had felt no good effect from the waters in Bath, and the social season he regarded as oppressive. Someone had mentioned the wells here and he thought he would try them. We came up for the summer and stayed in the Lodge, and when we returned to Bath for the winter he found he missed the air here – Bath can be so stuffy, whether cold or hot. He made enquiries for somewhere to stay more permanently, and we finally found this place – not ideal, he admitted, but roomy enough – and we moved here in the wintertime, in January of '27. It was bitter, that first winter! But my uncle loved it.' Again that fond smile.

'Since you have been living with your uncle – or in anything he referred to about the time between his leaving the army and your joining him – have you been aware of anything he might have done that might have caused someone to attack him like this? Or anything he owned that someone might have gone to such an effort to break in and steal?'

'Goodness, no! He was well enough off, but he had no great treasures!'

'Oh, treasure!'

Miss Ada had perked up suddenly, and everyone stared at her.

'Have you remembered something? Miss Strong, is it not?'

'Aye, you'll have met our brother,' said Miss Ada dismissively. 'The Jacobite treasure! That's supposed to be buried somewhere at Dinnet House, is it not?'

'That's a legend, you silly goose,' said her sister firmly.

'But what if it wasn't?' She looked about the room, seeking support. 'You've all heard the story, have you no? A boot full of silver, buried somewhere in the grounds.'

'Which no doubt someone came back and collected years ago,' said Miss Strong.

'No, the fellow that buried it was hanged in Edinburgh! That was the story.'

'Aye, story,' Miss Strong reinforced. 'That's all it was.'

Durris stood in silence, waiting for them to stop, and no one else interrupted.

'Ladies,' he said at last, when they had ground to a halt, 'you may be right and you may be wrong, but we canna tell at the present moment. Has anybody else heard tell of anybody looking for Jacobite treasure hereabouts?'

They all shook their heads, though Hippolyta suddenly remembered the night watchman's supposed sighting of Mr. Brookes, up and walking, near the Strachans' house. Could that have been what he was seeking? But he was nowhere near Dinnet House. Should she tell Durris about him? She decided that now was not the time, anyway. Nor, with Mrs. Strachan sitting so elegantly across the room, was it the moment to mention publicly her husband's apparent attack on Colonel Verney on Sunday. Durris, however, evidently remembered what she had said.

'Is there a Mrs. Strachan in the company?' he asked.

'Here,' said Mrs. Kynoch, waving to her right. Mrs. Strachan paled, and straightened up, not quite meeting Durris' even gaze.

'I believe – is it your husband? – is a merchant in the village?'

'That's right.' There was a modest quaver in Mrs. Strachan's voice, and she was hard to hear. Durris nodded encouragingly.

'So Colonel Verney would have been – or his household would have been – one of his customers?'

'Yes, that's right,' she said again. 'Most of the larger households in the village are.' She sounded more apologetic than boastful, as if she regretted complicating the case. Hippolyta wondered at her lack of assurance.

'Did your husband have any other connexion with the Colonel? A business matter, perhaps?'

Mrs. Strachan shook her head slowly.

'I don't think so. My husband does not generally discuss business matters with me, but there is constantly business in the house and I think I would know.'

'Thank you, ma'am. Miss Strong, may I put the same question to you? What connexions did your family have with Colonel Verney?'

'I know my brother had meetings with him, but my brother is a very discreet man,' said Miss Strong, her prim face indicating that she would co-operate as far as was proper, and precisely no further. 'He would never say what the matter of the meetings were.'

'No matter how much I asked,' sighed Miss Ada, and received another of those sharp nudges from her sister.

'Does anybody here have any idea why Colonel Verney might have been killed?'

'There's one person, I suppose,' said Basilia sadly.

'Who's that, then, miss?'

'Well, Forman. Forman was his servant before Waterloo: no one knew him better, I should think. He attended him constantly for years.'

'Aye, and may have died defending him, and all,' suggested Miss Ada soulfully.

'No one alive, then,' Durris specified exactly.

They exchanged glances around the room. The others who had not contributed more than nods and sighs, the visitors who had attended the service on Sunday, the villagers who had not been so closely acquainted, shrugged politely, but no ideas were forthcoming. Durris adjusted his glasses, and made another note in his pocketbook.

There was a scuffling noise and voices in the hallway, and Durris turned and opened the parlour door. The men had returned from the interment. Hippolyta looked anxiously until she saw Patrick, who came to join her on the sofa. Mr. Strachan went to his own wife and the minister and Mr. Strong hovered in the middle of the room, apparently not noticing Durris behind the door. Mr. Strong cleared his throat to still the sudden surge of conversation.

'Miss Verney and, ah, Dr. Napier: may I see you in Colonel Verney's study?'

'Me?' asked Patrick in surprise.

'Yes, Dr. Napier, if you'd be so good,' said Mr. Strong.

'May I come?' asked Hippolyta. 'I think Miss Verney is in need of female company at present.'

Mr. Strong regarded her sternly over the tops of his narrow glasses.

'You may,' he said, 'but you must remember to treat anything you hear as confidential.'

'Of course!' Hippolyta was affronted.

Durris cleared his throat.

'If this is to do with the death of Colonel Verney, then I must also insist …' he said gently. Mr. Strong turned to see him.

'Durris! I had no idea you were here, man. Of course: of course you may attend. But no one else!' he added sharply, as if he expected the whole crowd might sweep in after him. He led the way, authoritative though short, out of the parlour and unerringly across the hall to the study Hippolyta and Durris had seen earlier: he had obviously visited it on many occasions, and went to take his seat in front of Colonel Verney's desk: there was no chair behind it, of course, as Colonel Verney would have remained in his wheeled chair there. Mr. Strong reached over the desk, took a fold of paper, and waited until they had all settled, Miss Verney and Hippolyta on an old wooden-backed long chair, Patrick against a bookcase, and Durris with his back to the door. Mr. Strong eyed them each in turn, then opened the fold of paper.

'As you might expect, I am able now to tell you the contents of the late Colonel Verney's last will and testament – his testament testamentar,' he added, 'which he asked me to draw up for him about four weeks ago.'

'He changed his will? So recently?' asked Basilia, sitting up.

Hippolyta glanced round at her: she had turned a little pale.

'He did, miss.'

'He did not mention such a thing.'

'No. I have the impression that he was not an expansive man, when it came to discussing his own affairs.' Mr. Strong nodded a little, as if in approval. 'The contents are for the most part quite simple, and not, one would think, particularly contentious or unusual. Of course there is a generous bequest to Thomas Forman. I have no record of a will made by Forman, and if there is one or if an inventory is raised to settle any debts he may have left, there may be some difficulties unless we can establish whether Colonel Verney or Forman died first: but we shall deal with that as matters arise. I don't suppose you, Miss Verney, know anything about any relatives Forman might have had?'

Basilia was taken aback.

'I'm afraid I don't remember his mentioning any relatives at all.'

'Mm-hm. Very well,' said Mr. Strong. 'We shall speak again. The bulk of the estate, which consists of some small properties in parts of London and Edinburgh, bought chiefly as investments, and some bonds, as well as the contents of this house not belonging to the landlord here, are now left to you, Miss Verney.'

She nodded in acknowledgement, clearly unsurprised.

'Your cousin, of course, is no longer mentioned: Colonel Verney removed all reference to him when he changed his will four weeks ago.'

'You had a cousin?' Hippolyta asked.

'We heard that he had died. We were not close,' Basilia said quickly.

'Still: very sad,' murmured Hippolyta.

'Nevertheless,' Mr. Strong said pointedly, expecting their full attention, 'there is one other major bequest which must be deducted from the estate before the remainder goes to you, Miss Verney. Colonel Verney was particularly grateful for the medical attention he had received since his arrival in Ballater, and for the companionship of the physician in question. He therefore, Dr. Napier, left you one thousand pounds.'

'A thousand pounds!' Hippolyta could not help exclaiming. Patrick was blushing.

'He mentioned there was something, but that is more than generous,' he muttered. Basilia was regarding him in a very curious manner. 'Miss Verney, I trust you will find there is plenty in the rest of the estate: otherwise I shall of course make the sum over to you.'

'There is plenty, as I understand it,' Mr. Strong reassured him with a disapproving squint over his glasses. 'Colonel Verney's wishes were very clearly expressed, and generally one abides by the wishes of the deceased as expressed in their will.'

'Of course,' Basilia and Patrick chorused, then smiled uneasily at each other. Durris, half-forgotten by the door, was scribbling quickly in his pocketbook.

'May I ask,' he said, 'how much was the bequest to Thomas Forman?'

'Five hundred pounds,' said Mr. Strong, consulting the document in front of him. Durris pursed his lips silently, and wrote it down.

'And were there any other bequests?'

'Another five hundred pounds to his church in Bath, and yet another five hundred to the Diocese of Aberdeen, with the wish that it should be used in future to help fund the building of an Episcopal chapel in Ballater.'

'Very proper,' Durris conceded, still writing. 'And all these can easily be met out of the estate?'

'Certainly,' said the lawyer.

'And … the cousin,' Durris went on. 'What were the previous arrangements?'

'Well,' said Mr. Strong, 'I have not the facts to hand, but as I remember them Dr. Napier was of course not mentioned – the will was about ten years old, and they would not have been acquainted – and apart from the legacies to Forman and the churches, the estate was divided equally between Miss Verney and her cousin.'

'Do you have a copy?'

'It is doubtless in here, unless he has destroyed it,' said Mr. Strong, with a controlled gesture intended to take in the whole study.

'Uncle always destroyed old papers,' Basilia said quickly. 'It would be pointless to search for it, I should think.'

'May I have your permission to look, all the same, miss?'

Durris asked politely.

'Of course: I shall happily help you.' She turned a smile on the sheriff's man, eyes wide. It was the first proper smile Hippolyta had seen her give since the bodies had been found, and she was delighted to see it.

'But you will not need to start that today,' Patrick put in. 'You will be very much fatigued after the funeral and all the arrangements: this place can be locked up tonight and you will come home with us again to rest.'

'If you say so, Dr. Napier,' said Basilia immediately, dutiful as ever. 'Would tomorrow be useful to you, Mr. Durris?'

'That would be perfect, Miss Verney,' Durris said blandly. 'Is there a key to the study door?'

'I have one,' said Basilia, and handed Durris a bunch of keys from her reticule. 'My uncle had another: I believe it's on his bedside table now.'

They rose and began to leave the room, as Basilia arranged another meeting with the lawyer to deal with her uncle's lease on Dinnet House. Durris waited for them all to pass through the study door, then locked it, and handed the bunch of keys ceremonially back to Basilia. She replaced them in her reticule.

Back in the parlour, the mourners were ready to leave and awaited only Miss Verney so that they could bid her goodbye. In a few minutes, the only people left were the Napiers, Miss Verney and Durris. A moment later, Tabitha joined them from the servants' quarters, bringing coats with her.

'We're going back to the Napiers, Tabitha.'

'Oh, thank goodness, miss!' Tabitha exclaimed, then blushed at her outburst. 'I never want to spend a night in this house again, miss!'

'Nor do I.' Basilia sighed. 'We shall have to consider our future, Tabitha.'

'Well, you are most welcome to stay with us for as long as you need us,' said Hippolyta at once. She linked arms with Basilia and walked with her through the front door of Dinnet House.

'There is one thing, though, Mrs. Napier, that I would ask, if it is not too much trouble,' Basilia said in a low voice.

'Of course: what is it?'

'Is there any other room for Tabitha? It was good to have her on the couch with me for the last two nights, but now that we are settled – in truth, Mrs. Napier, she snores!'

'Oh! Well, no doubt we can find another space for her. There is a corridor I only found the day before yesterday and if I find a habitable room along that, she is more than welcome to it.'

'It is an odd little rambling house, is it not?' said Basilia. 'Charming, of course!' she added. 'I love it dearly. But it is not perhaps what you expected, coming from the rational buildings of Edinburgh, for all I have seen of them?'

Hippolyta laughed.

'It is not like my parents' house, but I loved it from the first moment I saw it!'

'Then I shall say no more! And if you can find space for Tabitha, I shall love it even better.'

When they returned to the odd little rambling house on the green, Hippolyta excused herself and went to the servants' quarters to see what could be done about a separate room for the snoring Tabitha. Mrs. Riach was for once busy preparing dinner, with Ishbel dutifully attending to the peeling and chopping and taking away of the scraps, which she did with considerable nimbleness. She stopped and curtseyed when she saw Hippolyta in the kitchen doorway.

'Mrs. Riach, what accommodation do we have here?'

'Accommodation?' queried Mrs. Riach. 'It's a house, that's what it is.'

'Yes, I know,' said Hipplyta, drawing on what she hoped were her reserves of patience. 'But how many rooms are there? In the servants' quarters, that is.'

'There's enough to go round,' replied Mrs. Riach, turning back to pounding spices in a mortar. There was some emphasis in the pounding that unnerved Hippolyta a little.

'Would there be enough to go round to Tabitha, Miss Verney's maid? Miss Verney has asked if she can be accommodated elsewhere in the house.'

Mrs. Riach stopped pounding again and sniffed, considering.

'There might be space enough,' she conceded. 'Send the woman through here and we'll see what we can do.'

'You're very kind, Mrs. Riach. Thank you,' said Hippolyta.

Delighted that the negotiations had gone unexpectedly well, she made her way back towards the main hall but again, the doorway to the unknown side passage was open. She was sure it had not been when she had gone to the kitchen. She paused, listening. The passage seemed completely empty. Should she explore? she wondered, then took a grip on herself. She was mistress of this house, after all: Patrick had never said to her that there was anywhere she could not or should not go, so she could explore if she wanted to.

But she discovered, when she ventured along the passage, that there was not much to explore. On the right hand wall, which must, she realised, back on to the dining room behind Patrick's study, there was a line of built-in presses, all their doors firmly shut. It was one of these that she had seen close that day, and had then been unable to open. This time they all opened readily at her touch, or readily enough, for some creaked and one stuck a little. They contained, as was only reasonable, sheets, towels and blankets, all the linen a small household desired, along with, in one case, a jar of something scented. She sniffed: it was dried orange peel, rosemary, lavender, cloves and peppercorns, intended, she presumed, to deter moths. The presses were quite deep: it would have been easy enough for someone to stand in any of them between the shelves and the closed door, just like the one where Tabitha had been locked in Dinnet House. However, today there was no one in evidence. Could Tabitha have hidden herself that day in alarm at her approach? It seemed a strange thing to do.

At the far end of the passage was a little window set quite high in the wall, and though it was open a little way it was clear it could open no further. If the mysterious person had been an intruder, they had not entered the house this way.

The other side of the passage had two closed doors, which opened inwards, and were therefore not likely to be more presses. Hippolyta tried the first one, the one further from the main passage. It opened smoothly, to show her a very small bed chamber, scarcely large enough to contain the two narrow beds it held. A window with a thin curtain to it showed the garden beyond, at the back of the house. Neither bed was made up, but both had blankets folded in a square on the ticking mattress. A chamber pot was set neatly under each one, and an open press in the passage wall held four hooks for clothes. The final adornment was a jug and basin under the window, with a very small mirror behind it. It all looked perfectly suitable for Tabitha's accommodation away from her mistress.

Hippolyta closed the door again and moved on to the other door. It too opened easily, and the room within was very similar to the first one. There were the same two beds, the same jug and basin under the window, the same chamber pots, the same open press with its hooks. Here, however, both beds were made up, two cloaks were hanging in the press, and a servants' box was at the end of each bed. Hippolyta stopped and thought. Two servants? Was Mrs. Riach sleeping down here? It had been Hippolyta's belief that the housekeeper slept in the attic, and that Ishbel the maid slept in the kitchen, but that was before she knew of this accommodation. Perhaps Mrs. Riach had moved downstairs because she did not wish to share the attic with Robert Wilson – surely he would be moving out soon! – but on the other hand, given the difficulties they had had in carrying Robert Wilson up the narrow stairs, surely it would have been more sensible to bring him through to this passage and put him in the empty room, and then, if there were any question of unsuitability, both Ishbel and Mrs. Riach could have slept in the attic. It would have been much more practical.

She glanced at the cloaks. One was relatively new, the other very ragged and old, with many patches. She could not imagine Mrs. Riach wearing it, but at the same time she hoped it was not Ishbel's. Surely she would have left home in a better garment than that? She would try, perhaps, to make discreet enquiries, and see if something better could be done for her.

She closed the door gently, and glanced about the passage. There was nothing more on this side: back in the main passage was the door to the pantry, next to the kitchen, and between it and the main hallway was the foot of the tiny stair that led up to the other floors: the front stair in the main hallway only went to the first floor, and it had been, as she remembered, very awkward to push and pull Robert Wilson the rest of the way. She must ask Patrick when the coachman was going. And where was the rest of their luggage? It was as if, she thought fancifully, Robert Wilson was part of a clockwork weather vane, and the luggage cart could not arrive until he had left Ballater. In that case, she wished he would go with all speed.

She sighed, and returned to her proper territory at the front of the house, to wait with their guest for dinner.

Chapter Ten

The dining room was possibly Hippolyta's least favourite part of her new home. It was inserted behind the front room on the side of the house opposite the parlour – in front, she now knew, of that row of presses in the side passage - and had only convenience of situation in its favour, being halfway between the parlour and the kitchen. It was dark by nature, with a window only to the side of the house which looked out on the wall of the neighbouring house and little else. It would not matter in the winter, Hippolyta considered, when one dined after dark, but in the summer it was rather depressing, and required almost as many candles as a winter evening would. The inside walls were a hard white, which even the yellowing of age had not rendered warm. The table was long and narrow which should have been practical, but seemed instead to indicate a general meanness in the room, and its proportions made lighting the little fire difficult, if not dangerous. The carpet on the floor was mostly grey, and the only decoration on the walls was a couple of insipid landscapes of unknown origin, which Hippolyta's painting fingers itched to replace, and three miserable religious prints that seemed unlikely ever to have inspired good behaviour – or good digestion - in anyone. Hippolyta wondered who had chosen them: they did not suit what she knew of Dr. Durward at all, nor indeed Patrick. She looked forward to finding some bright curtains when their furniture arrived to frame the gloomy view. Only some decent silverware, which Patrick had inherited from his mother, cheered the mood: that, and eventually Mrs. Riach's asparagus soup. At the first mouthful, the Napiers cheered somewhat, and even Miss Verney took on a healthier colour.

'Dr. Napier, do you remember poor dear Forman's asparagus soup last summer?' she asked with a smile. 'How much of it did we have to eat! Goodness, I thought I should turn green and stringy before we ever saw the end of it!'

'There was a great deal of it, certainly,' Patrick agreed, smiling in turn. 'Poor Forman had discovered an asparagus bed in the gardens at Dinnet House, and he was keen to use as much of it as he could.'

'We never bothered very much with the gardens,' said Basilia, in reminiscent mood. 'Uncle could not go out into them anyway, and it hardly seemed worth his employing a gardener just for me to wander around, or for Forman to have vegetables when we could buy better in the village. But we did manage a few evenings in the spring, last year and this, didn't we? Before things became overgrown in the summer.'

Patrick nodded, finishing his soup absently. Basilia finished hers and sat back.

'Oh, yes, very pleasant evenings. Do you remember when we discovered the old summer house? And the fountain?'

'I find old gardens like that rather melancholic,' said Hippolyta. 'Now, the garden here is very pleasant, and always something interesting growing in it. Did I tell you I have a plan to buy some hens?'

'There must have been hens at Dinnet House, too, I should think,' Basilia went on. 'It was quite expansive in its day: kitchen gardens, hens, an orchard and a pleasure garden with the summer house, all within the tall stone walls. Really, those walls seemed to trap the warmth. Those spring evenings were positively balmy, weren't they, Dr. Napier?'

'It sounds delightful,' said Hippolyta, trying not to sound ungracious. 'Tell me about the summer house, then.'

'Well, it was very dilapidated, of course. Dr. Napier thought we ought not to go in, but I felt brave and with a little adjustment of parts of the roof – well, we could just stoop underneath and inside there was a seat which was almost good enough to sit on. From there one could sit and watch the birds in the roses outside, and smell the beautiful scent, and listen to the wind in the trees – oh! It was charming, was it not?'

'It was a hazard, certainly,' said Patrick. He let Ishbel clear his soup plate, and waited for Mrs. Riach to present him with the beef for carving. 'I think there might even have been badgers underneath it: something had been digging around it over the years.'

'Perhaps someone hunting for the Jacobite silver!' said Hippolyta lightly. Mrs. Riach dropped a dish of potatoes heavily on to the table, and limped back to the narrow sideboard for the peas. Patrick frowned at his housekeeper's hips, assessing them. Full skirts and the old-fashioned high waist of Mrs. Riach's gown no doubt made casual diagnosis much harder, Hippolyta thought. Patrick carved the beef, and Mrs. Riach returned to distribute it to the ladies, then vanished for the kitchen. 'Mrs. Riach has been mentioning that Dinnet House has always had a reputation,' Hippolyta went on, then hesitated. After all it had been Basilia's home for several years.

'A reputation?' Miss Verney's eyebrows rose smoothly up her high forehead.

'I mean for – ah, for odd goings-on. Nothing unrespectable, if that's the word,' said Hippolyta hastily.

'I suppose she meant the old murder. Or the Jacobite silver, indeed,' said Basilia lightly. 'Uncle was always telling those stories, wasn't he, Dr. Napier?' She sighed. 'I shall miss his old tales now, though I confess I often found them terribly dull. I wish I could hear them once again!' She sniffed once, and the tears began to trickle.

'My dear Miss Verney,' said Hippolyta at once, passing her a handkerchief.

'I am so sorry! One thinks one has cried all one can, and then off one goes again!'

'I believe it comes in waves,' said Hippolyta, remembering something her mother had said. 'It is only a few days, after all: though time will no doubt help, it is too soon to be completely recovered, surely. You would be too unfeeling.'

Basilia dabbed at her huge eyes and nodded.

'You are quite right. It is too soon – too soon to decide, too, what to do now. I tried to think about it this afternoon, but my mind simply will not turn to the question. Will you forgive me?'

'Forgive you, Miss Verney? Why, you must simply stay here for as long as you need to. Such decisions cannot be rushed,' said Patrick.

'Thank you, Dr. Napier, you are both so kind!' Miss Verney

sniffed again, then blew her nose delicately. Her eyes were still lustrously moist, Hippolyta thought, watching Basilia's gaze lingering on Patrick. It was something to be proud of, the way people obviously liked and depended upon her husband, she told herself. Quite something.

After dinner, Patrick excused himself to deal with some letters he had been unable to answer in the morning, busy as they had been with the funeral. Miss Verney and Hippolyta retired to the parlour and their sewing, not saying much. When the door was knocked, they both jumped, and listened hard for Mrs. Riach's steady steps (no limp just now, thought Hippolyta, trying to gather information for Patrick's diagnosis) to answer it.

In a moment, the parlour door opened, and Mrs. Riach, with a puzzled look, announced Mr. Durris. Clearly she, too, was not sure whether he should be allowed in the parlour or not. Hippolyta rose to greet him, and showed him to a seat at the table with them.

'Is the doctor at home?' he asked, looking about as if Patrick might be hiding behind the curtains. One of the cats tested his knee with a contemplative claw, then leapt on to his lap. He began automatically to stroke it, and Hippolyta gave a tiny nod of approval.

'Mrs. Riach, will you tell Dr. Napier, please? Will you take some tea, Mr. Durris?'

'Thank you, no: I've just had a cup or three,' said Durris mildly.

Mrs. Riach gave a stiff curtsey, and after a few minutes Patrick came in, greeting Durris without surprise.

'I hope that if I speak to all of you at once,' said Durris, managing to stand and sit again without annoying the cat, 'it will save a bit of time. There's a good deal to do in such a case, as you can no doubt imagine, when there is no clear suspect. I've been to talk with the constable you called in, Mrs. Napier, and I'll go to see the night watchman in the village when he's likely to be up and about, and I already have a few thoughts in my mind, but I need to make sure I've covered everything, of course.'

'Of course.' Patrick nodded.

'Now, Miss Verney,' Durris turned a little towards her, but again not too far so as not to disturb the cat. It purred loudly. 'I'd like you to tell me about last Sunday evening. Not just around the time the attack must have occurred, but earlier – say from dinner time?'

'Of course.' Basilia was white as chalk, but she sat up and laid down her sewing, folding her hands on the table top. 'We had dinner around our usual time for a Sunday – around four, that is, rather early. Uncle always liked rather to have a substantial supper on a Sunday, sometimes with guests there, and though there were none last Sunday it is a habit we had fallen into. So we had dinner early, and I suppose then Tabitha and Forman had theirs in the kitchen. I played the parlour organ for my uncle, hymns, you know, which we sang together, and some Bach: I think I played the toccata and fugue in D minor, which was a particular favourite of his. He used to beat the rhythm along with me on the arm of his chair with great hilarity.' Her voice broke, and she pulled out again Hippolyta's handkerchief, applying it to those great eyes, which she then turned on Durris. He blinked. 'I am sorry, Mr. Durris. This is altogether upsetting, and yet I know you must have our help if you are to find my uncle's killer.'

'Just go steady, Miss Verney, if you please,' said Durris with solemn kindness. 'Any detail might help.'

'Of course.' Basilia settled her breathing, gazing down at the tablecloth, and went on. 'Forman brought in the supper around half past eight, and we ate it in the parlour. There was cold beef, I remember, and an artichoke pie. Forman was a very good cook.' She caught her breath again. 'We finished eating – a large bowl of raspberries and cream – and then I said I should not stay up much longer for I find Sundays quite tiring, on account of all the playing. Oh, where shall we have our services now?' she asked suddenly.

'We'll find somewhere,' said Patrick comfortingly.

'Services?' asked Durris.

'Our Episcopalian services: we have been in the habit of having them at Dinnet House on a Sunday morning,' Patrick explained. 'And Miss Verney has kindly played the parlour organ for our hymns.'

'I see,' said Durris. 'Of course: the English church,' he murmured. 'Were there many at the service last Sunday?'

Basilia listed the people who had attended, and Durris wrote down the names.

'Is it a – a peaceable congregation?'

'It is, for the most part,' said Patrick. 'Our main bone of contention is the provision of a church building, though the need for one is something on which the congregation is united – that is why Colonel Verney's legacy will be most welcome, though the circumstances are deplorable.'

'I see,' said Durris again. 'Is there other money saved?'

'I have no idea. The Bishop in Aberdeen will know, no doubt. As far as I know there are no definite plans of any kind as yet.'

'The Bishop … very well,' said Durris, quite as if he spoke to bishops at least once a week. For all Hippolyta knew, he did. He was a most ambiguous man, she thought. He nodded to Basilia to continue.

'So he read a sermon to me, and we had our prayers, and I bade him good night and rang for Tabitha. It would have been about ten o'clock, I suppose.'

'Did she come straightaway?'

'Yes, I believe so,' said Basilia after a moment's thought. 'She usually does, and I don't remember anything different. I met her upstairs in my room, of course, and she helped me prepare for bed.'

'How did she seem? Did anything strike you as strange about her?'

Basilia flashed him a look of alarm.

'Why would she seem strange? Nothing had happened by that point, surely? Not when she came upstairs: it was when she went downstairs that she was seized.'

'Aye, so she says,' Durris agreed. 'We only have her word for it, you ken. She could have gone downstairs and let someone in, for example.'

'She has been with me for eight years!' Basilia exclaimed, affronted. 'I cannot imagine her ever doing such a thing! Besides, she would have no need to at that time of night: the doors were never locked until my uncle went to bed.'

Durris nodded slowly, making another note.

'Very well, Miss Verney,' he said, though Hippolyta thought he had not necessarily abandoned that line of enquiry in his mind. For herself, she hoped they were not harbouring an accomplice to murder in the house: she might have to do something about securing the doors at night. 'So Tabitha helped you get ready for bed. And … er, how long might that take?'

'Oh!' Basilia thought. 'Well, she brought me a chocolate, and it was very hot, so eventually when I was in bed I sat and drank that while she put my things away, and so on, and then she took the cup away and said good night, so I suppose perhaps the whole thing took around half an hour? Perhaps even three quarters. I believe the clock on the mantelpiece said eleven, or ten to eleven, just before I blew the candle out.'

'And Tabitha would just have gone downstairs then?'

'That's right. Well, she left me, anyway.'

'With the chocolate cup and saucer?'

'Yes.'

'I found it on a shelf by the back stairs,' said Durris thoughtfully.

Basilia frowned across to Hippolyta and back to Durris, as if Hippolyta could explain the sheriff's man's thoughts, or stop him suspecting Tabitha.

'So once you had said goodnight to her, and blown out your candle, then what happened?'

'What happened? I fell asleep, Mr. Durris. As I say, I find Sundays tiring, and I had arranged with Mrs. Napier here to meet her to go painting in the morning, so I settled down at once and fell asleep. I knew nothing more until I woke at the sound of the front door in the morning, and opened the window to find Mrs. Napier outside. I was puzzled why Tabitha had not woken me, and why no one had answered the door, and I came to the top of the stairs to greet Mrs. Napier but she had just found my uncle – my uncle's body - in the hall.'

'I see,' said Durris once again, making another careful note. Hippolyta wondered how important something had to be before he wrote it down. 'Now, when would your uncle usually have gone to bed?'

'Oh, around midnight, usually,' said Miss Verney. 'He and Forman kept late hours, and I believe that sometimes, after I had retired, they would sit together and reminisce about their army days over a brandy or two. They were better friends than many I've known.'

'And do you know what Colonel Verney's night time rituals

were?' Durris asked modestly.

'I believe Forman would come and take him across the hall to his bedroom and help him to bed, blowing out the lights in the parlour before they left it.'

'So the lamps would be lit in the hallway?'

'It's candles in sconces,' Basilia corrected him. 'It's still rather old-fashioned. Yes, they would still be lit until Forman had settled my uncle, and had locked up the house for the night. Then I believe he would blow out the candles and retire to the servants' quarters.'

'He slept near the kitchen?'

'That's right, so as to be on the same floor as my uncle in case he rang or called out in the night. Tabitha, of course, slept in the attic.'

'Of course.'

Of course, Hippolyta thought, unlike her own topsy-turvy establishment.

'Yet Tabitha says she came downstairs and found the hallway in darkness, and when she was dragged into the parlour it, too, was in darkness,' said Durris. 'A situation which would normally only occur when the household had retired completely, yet Colonel Verney and Mr. Forman were still fully clothed.' He stopped, and let them consider this strange contradiction for a moment, while the cat rearranged itself on his lap. 'Hm,' he remarked, as if he himself were not sure what to make of it all. His dark eyebrows twitched in confusion. 'Now,' he went on, 'you'll see that I have to work out where a number of other people were that night, between ten and eleven o'clock, and maybe even a little later: because the hallway was dark, of course, Tabitha would not be able to tell us if Colonel Verney was there at that stage or not. Fortunately it's not so long ago that people will have forgotten where they were. You, for example, Dr. Napier: you'll know what you were doing on Sunday evening?'

'Of course,' said Patrick, though he looked puzzled. 'I was …'

'You told me you were here all evening,' said Miss Verney suddenly. 'Don't you remember saying so?'

'Oh!' said Patrick, appearing no less confused. 'Then if I said so, presumably I was. I was here all evening, then, Durris, with my wife.' He glanced proudly at Hippolyta. She smiled back, and squeezed his hand, pleased he had worked it out. She had not been sure they had been at home, but if he said so then that must have been the case. She remembered something.

'Dr. Durward told me he was at Pannanich Lodge all night, playing cards with a patient of his: a Mr. Brown,' she said. 'At least, that's what he told me! I'm sure he's right.' She glanced at Basilia, and was surprised to see her frown.

'Do you know of anybody else, by chance? Don't worry if you're not sure: I shall check everyone anyway.'

'You'll never check everyone in the town,' said Patrick with a smile. 'We're far too crowded these days!'

'So people keep telling me,' said Durris, 'but I have to start somewhere. Thank you all very much for your time – and Miss Verney, is it still suitable to go through Colonel Verney's papers tomorrow?'

'Of course,' said Basilia. 'I shall go to Dinnet House around nine, if that will suit you? And I shall remember to bring my keys, of course!'

'Thank you, miss: that will certainly make matters easier. Now, young fellow, where shall I put you?' he said to the cat, which ignored him. He picked it up gently and handed it into Hippolyta's arms as they all rose to bid him goodnight. The cat, unperturbed, purred quite as if such a move had been its intention from the start. He bowed and left.

They heard the front door close, and sat down again.

'Oh!' said Hippolyta, 'I should have mentioned Mr. Brookes!'

'Mr. Brookes? At Pannanich Lodge?' Patrick was surprised.

'That's right. Um, someone told me – I'm not sure now who it was,' she added carefully, remembering just in time that Patrick had told her not to question the night watchman, 'that they had seen Mr. Brookes in the village, on Sunday evening.'

'Had his man brought him in?' Patrick asked, as Basilia looked from one to the other of them. 'Mr. Brookes is one of my patients, a crippled man staying at the hotel at Pannanich Wells,' Patrick explained.

'That's just it,' said Hippolyta. 'He didn't seem to be crippled. He was seen walking about on his own.'

'Then whoever told you that must be mistaken,' said Patrick.

'If you're sure, then I suppose they must have been,' said

Hippolyta, with a confidence she did not quite feel. It was not that she did not trust her husband's analysis of his patient: it was that the night watchman had been so sure: and it was, after all, part of his job to identify anyone acting oddly after dark. But then how well could he know Brookes, who was only a visitor and not even staying in the village?

Basilia looked thoughtful.

'Have you met Mr. Brookes?' Hippolyta asked her.

'No – no, certainly not.' Basilia seemed less sure than her words would indicate.

'Now, I must finish those letters before supper,' said Patrick, rising reluctantly again. 'Supper … I don't suppose you could persuade Mrs. Riach to find us some ham, some time soon?'

'Oh, yes, you've always been so fond of ham, haven't you?' added Basilia. 'Forman knew how to boil a ham: I wonder if his recipe is in the kitchen? You always enjoyed it, Dr. Napier.'

'Ham: of course, my dear. I'll do my best,' said Hippolyta, and wondered how.

It was dark when Hippolyta woke with a jump. What was that noise?

She sighed. She really had to become used to the creaks and groans of an old house at night.

She turned on to her back, and despite herself listened hard again. Silence: there, she had been mistaken anyway. But then she heard a footstep.

Where was the sound coming from? She thought it might be from the back of the house, from the servants' quarters. But then she heard it again, and this time it seemed to be from somewhere at the front of the house – Miss Verney's room, perhaps? Or was Robert Wilson moving about upstairs in the attic? She listened hard. Why would Robert Wilson be moving about in the middle of the night – now that he was, she was quite sure, fully recovered. What was he up to?

Then she heard another step, and this time she was sure it was from the servants' quarters. Tabitha? Was Durris right: could Tabitha have let someone into Dinnet House to murder Colonel Verney? But then Basilia had said that there would have been no need to let anyone in, as the doors would still have been unlocked.

To guide someone, then: to show them perhaps where Colonel Verney's study was? She listened: the steps were definitely in the servants' quarters, though if anyone had asked she would have said they sounded rather light for the solidly built Tabitha. She sat up slowly, unwilling to disturb Patrick over a servant perhaps only fetching a drink of water.

Then there was a little flurry of footsteps, and they were definitely from the front of the house. Again, they seemed too light for Robert Wilson, or even for Mrs. Riach, and try as she might she could detect no hint of a limp. She eased herself carefully off the bed, slipped a shawl over her shoulders and wrapped it tight, and headed for the bedroom door: then she stopped, turned to the fireplace, picked up the poker, and left the room, telling herself she was being completely melodramatic.

The landing was empty, and she could hear nothing. She tiptoed, in bare feet, over to the door that led to the back stairs, and swung it open as quietly as she could, straining her ears to listen for any sound on the attic floor. There was nothing. What next? Perhaps Basilia had asked Tabitha to come up to her room for some reason: perhaps she was unwell. Hippolyta thought about that: Basilia would not hesitate to send Tabitha to waken Patrick, if that were the case. But could there be some other problem? Should she go and see? Or should she go downstairs to the servants' quarters and find out what was going on down there? That could be Tabitha, fetching something for Basilia: would she need help?

Indecision was not going to help, she thought, and nor was standing in the middle of the landing clutching a poker. She crossed the landing with determination, and knocked briskly on Basilia's door. There was no answer. She tried again.

'Miss Verney? Miss Verney, is everything all right?'

'What's going on?' Patrick had surfaced, and was standing in their bedroom doorway, scratching his head.

'I heard a noise up here, and footsteps in the servants' quarters. I was anxious that she might be ill.'

'And she's not answering her door?'

'That's right.'

'Then we had better check, I suppose.' He rubbed his face. 'Well, you'd better check. I don't think she would appreciate a strange man blundering into her bedchamber.'

Hippolyta bit her lips together, and turned back to the door. She knocked once more, and at no response, she turned the handle and opened it.

'Miss Verney?' Now that she was in the bedchamber, it seemed reasonable to speak softly. But there was no need: Miss Verney's bed was empty, and there was no sign of her in the room.

Chapter Eleven

'Oh, she has been murdered! Murdered!'

Tabitha had not taken her mistress' disappearance calmly. She had to all appearances been asleep when Hippolyta and Patrick had gone downstairs to fetch her, settled in one of the beds in the far room that Hippolyta had discovered earlier. Her kist was open at the end of the bed, and her clothes and belongings had been distributed about the little room in the manner of one planning to stay. Roused by the news that Miss Verney was missing, she had stood in the middle of the little room, her bedclothes in a tangle about her legs, and waved her hands in the air as if she had scalded her fingers.

'There is no evidence that she has been murdered, Tabitha!' said Patrick, trying to find smelling salts in his doctor's bag.

'In fact, she seems to have gone out dressed and with her bonnet and cloak,' Hippolyta added, who had carried out a cursory search in her guest's room. 'Did she say anything to you about going out?'

'No! No, she never did! Of course she didn't! Where would she go in the middle of the night? Oh, she has been lured away and murdered! The whole household is cursed – when will he come for me?'

'If he'd wanted to kill you he had ample opportunity, instead of locking you in a cupboard,' said Hippolyta shortly. Patrick passed her the smelling salts and she waved them under Tabitha's nose: the maid jerked backwards in shock, and sat hard on the bed.

'Has she ever wandered in her sleep before?' Patrick asked, a little more gently. Tabitha shook her head, blinking.

'She didn't mention having to meet someone? Or go somewhere?'

'No, ma'am.' Tabitha was beginning to gather her wits. 'She didn't say anything like that. And she said she would get herself ready for bed: she was very kind. She said I'd had a tiring few days and could benefit from an early night, so I made sure she had hot water and a chocolate as usual, and left her. She said she was going to read for a little.'

'Perhaps she has not left the house,' said Hippolyta suddenly. 'We should look in the parlour.'

She took her candle and hurried back into the passage, and noticed the door to the room next to Tabitha's shut suddenly and silently. Oh, well, no doubt Ishbel did not wish to be disturbed in the middle of the night if she was not needed. She pushed back through the door into the main hall, and crossed to the open parlour door. Shadowy cats wove around her nightdress hem, but there was no sign of Miss Verney. Patrick with his own candlestick caught up with her, with Tabitha tagging along behind, tying her shawl in an absently complex knot.

'No sign?'

'None.'

'The dining room?'

Hippolyta could not imagine why anyone would willingly spend unnecessary time in there, but she followed Patrick who opened that door and looked inside. He walked right round the table, while Hippolyta ridiculously crouched to peer under the table. Miss Verney was not there.

'Your study?'

Patrick frowned, but closed the dining room door and opened the study door, the front room on that side of the house. It was not a large room, and made to seem smaller by the shelves of books around the walls: Miss Verney, however, was not to be seen. They returned to the hall.

'Then it seems she has left the house,' Patrick said.

'Unless she climbed to the attic – or went to the kitchen?'

'The kitchen door was open as we passed, and I didn't see her,' said Tabitha helpfully. 'Though I suppose she could have been under the table there …'

Hippolyta frowned at her, and she fell silent.

'Then perhaps we should try –' Patrick was in the middle of saying, when the front door opened in front of them, the candle flames lurched, and in walked Basilia.

'Miss Verney!' Hippolyta exclaimed, as Tabitha cried 'Miss!'

Basilia jumped backwards and staggered, slammed against the doorpost and slid slowly down it to the ground in a faint. Patrick swept down beside her, patting her cheeks, while Hippolyta handed back the smelling salts. Basilia gasped, and her eyes opened.

'Where – where on earth am I?' she asked in a shocked whisper.

'You're on our front door step,' said Patrick. 'Where have you been? Are you quite well?'

'Been? What do you mean?'

'You've been out, out of the house somewhere. We were anxious,' he explained.

'But … I have no idea. I … the last thing I remember I was reading in my room. I mean in my room here, of course.'

'It will be all the alarm and emotion,' said Patrick with professional concern. 'It has been a more than strenuous day. Have you had any history of walking in your sleep?'

'Walking in my sleep? No! Well, not for years,' she amended. 'When I was a little girl …'

'Then that will be it,' said Patrick firmly. 'The strain of the last few days will have taken its course, and you have had a wander. I do not think you can have been out for long.'

'Thank goodness you came to no harm,' Hippolyta put in. 'You could have been lost, or walked into the river, or anything! Would it be best if she went to bed properly now, my dear?'

'Yes, yes, that would undoubtedly be best. Tabitha, will you see your mistress safely to bed?'

'Of course. Come along now, miss: and I'll fetch you another chocolate, so you'll feel it's just your ordinary bed time.'

Tabitha looked heartily relieved to have her mistress back in one piece, and no further evidence of a household curse. She helped Basilia quickly up the stairs, and Patrick and Hippolyta waited for them to disappear before Patrick locked the front door carefully, and took Hippolyta in his arms.

'Clever wife!' he said fondly. 'Thank goodness you heard the noises, or we might never have known! Now we can do things to prevent her wandering too far if she walks again – like taking this key away.' He slipped the front door key out of the lock, and tucked it above the moulding around the door. 'Now I think we may leave them to their own devices, and return to our own bed.'

But long after Patrick had fallen asleep, Hippolyta lay wakeful, listening for footsteps – for there had certainly been two sets. And moreover, whatever Miss Verney claimed about a history of sleepwalking, Hippolyta was not altogether sure her new friend had been speaking the truth. She had seen Basilia's eyes when she first came through the front door, and there had been an instant – she was sure of it, however the candle flames had swooped – when Miss Verney had made the decision to stagger back and slump on the floor. Why should she do that?

Nevertheless, Hippolyta was young and managed to rouse herself at the usual time the next morning – Thursday morning, she thought, though it took her a moment to work it out. When she ventured into the kitchen after breakfast to ask Mrs. Riach to come and discuss the day's business, she was surprised to find Robert Wilson sitting, quite at home (as no doubt he felt by now, she thought uncharitably) at the table, eating a dish of eggs and fresh bread.

'Mr. Wilson! I am glad to see you up and about,' she said, as he pulled himself reluctantly to his feet.

'Aye, ma'am. I'm feeling much improved, thanks to you and your household – and Dr. Napier, of course.'

'I'm very pleased to hear it.' Mrs. Riach caught her glance past Wilson's back, and rolled her eyes. 'Can we assume that you'll be able to resume your duties soon?' Hippolyta asked him, trying not to sound too inhospitable.

'Aye, ma'am: I've only to finish these eggs and I'll be off. I hear the horses and the carriage are down at the inn.'

'That's right: safe and sound, I'm sure.'

'I've – ah, I've washed a shirt for the loon,' said Mrs. Riach, 'to see him on his way.'

'That was very kind of you, Mrs. Riach,' said Hippolyta in surprise. Was Mrs. Riach developing a fondness for her unwelcome guest?

'Well, I got the lass to do it. I wasna going to do it mysel'.'

'Ah. Of course.' So much for that notion. 'Well, Mrs. Riach, when you're ready, please come to the parlour.'

'Aye, ma'am.' Hippolyta was dismissed, and left.

In the hallway she found Patrick, on his way out to his patients at Pannanich. He beamed at her.

'Good news!' he said. 'The luggage cart has arrived!'

'It has? Good heavens – and all safe?'

'I trust so. Apparently they had two mishaps: a wheel was lost at Inchmarlo, and the axle sheared, which held them back more than a day for the local cartwright had hurt his hand, and then they missed the turning to Ballater and found themselves up the Linn of Dee which is much further on. When they realised, they turned back, but they seem to have tried every turning to the south that they could along the way. They sound most repentant.'

'How did you find out?'

'One of the carters came to the back door. Ishbel came to tell me ten minutes ago. I thought you were still upstairs.'

'I was ten minutes ago – since then I've been in the kitchen, where I met Robert Wilson. He says he's to leave today. So is the cart outside?'

'No, it's down at the inn: they arrived very late last night, and today wanted to make sure they had the right directions this time before venturing up to the house.'

'Well, they are welcome any time they appear!' cried Hippolyta. 'I have almost forgotten what is on it, it has taken so long!'

'I sent that message back with him. They should be here within the hour.' He kissed Hippolyta goodbye, and set off. She went to the parlour and straight to the window, hoping she might already see the cart approaching: it would be too wide, she thought, to go to the back of the house. There was no sign yet but she stayed there, admiring the sunlight in the pretty front garden, and wondering if today she might be able to paint even just a little. She had still not managed to do much with the painting of Craigendarroch, the great crag over the town that Mrs. Strachan had asked her to paint.

Strachan … what had Mr. Brookes, if it had been he, been doing lingering around the Strachans' house late at night, the night that Colonel Verney had been killed? Patrick was so definite that Mr. Brookes was incapable of such a venture on foot. Was that really true? Patrick could be – well, he was such a nice man. Sometimes she thought that his patients took advantage of his good nature. And if he was wrong, and Mr. Brookes was capable of wandering about the town at night, what was he up to, and why had he taken advantage of Patrick to deceive him? It argued no good motive, certainly. Could he have killed Colonel Verney and poor Forman? But surely he was a stranger to the town: could he have known the Colonel before? Patrick said Mr. Brookes had been in the West Indies. Could the Colonel have travelled there with his regiment? Basilia would probably know, since her uncle had talked so much about his military days. It would be easy to ask her: not so easy, though, to ask Mr. Brookes or Mr. Strachan what their association might be. But Mr. Strachan had seemed to threaten the Colonel … oh, she wished she knew what Durris the sheriff's man thought. She had the impression that there was a good deal going on in his sensible head.

The door opened, and Mrs. Riach entered with a solid curtsey. Hippolyta gestured her to sit at the table, and sat opposite her. The morning's duel had begun.

Apart from further complaints regarding the hunting prowess of the tribe of white cats (now named Franklin, Snowball, Arctic, Parry, Polar and, ironically, Spot, with their mother Bella), the duel did not go badly and Hippolyta was just nursing her wounds when Basilia appeared, a little tired looking but already in bonnet and gloves.

'I must go to Dinnet House and meet the sheriff's man to look over my uncle's study,' she said. 'I wonder, would you be kind enough to accompany me? I cannot say that I feel up to facing the task alone, yet I am already so indebted to you and Dr. Napier.'

'Oh, not at all!' Hippolyta sprang up. 'I should be happy to come with you. Just let me fetch my bonnet.'

The day was already warm and heavy, and the hedgerows, as they left the squareset village behind, clotted with meadowsweet and with a scent as thick as toffee. The first few spots of rain struck them like small pebbles, and as they hurried under a tree the heavens opened and rain dashed at the ground as if punishing it for some terrible wrong.

'So many of these showers this summer!' said Hippolyta,

trying to hold her skirts clear of the bouncing drops.

'I keep expecting the air to lighten after them, but it never does,' agreed Basilia.

'At least they tend to be short.'

Already the torrent was easing, and a few brave individuals were venturing out into the last of the drops.

'It will wash down the drains, I suppose,' remarked Basilia practically, as they edged back out from their shelter and continued on their way.

'I've rarely known such a wet summer, though.'

At the gate to Dinnet House, they met Mr. Durris, who bowed in greeting.

'I was coming to see if you were nearby,' he explained.

'I hope we haven't kept you waiting,' said Basilia, with a sad smile. 'I'm afraid I had a rather disrupted night. Not, of course, the fault of my hosts!' she added, gesturing prettily to Hippolyta.

'Oh, are you coming in, too?' Durris asked, surprised when Hippolyta started up the driveway.

'Miss Verney asked me to keep her company – to be at hand if she needed me,' Hippolyta said. 'I hope that is all right?'

'Of course, of course,' said Durris, 'that's quite proper. I didn't mean …' He tailed off, with a little frown on his broad face. Hippolyta chose to ignore it, and set off for the front door.

Basilia undid it with her keys, and crossed the hall to the study, unlocking that door, too. She pushed it open.

There was nothing much to show, but somehow it was clear that someone had been in the room since the previous evening. Durris darted forward, then stopped, turning on his heel.

'Everything's been moved, hasn't it?' he asked.

'It looks like it,' Hippolyta agreed.

'I don't think I could say for sure,' said Basilia, frowning.

'Look,' said Hippolyta, 'that row of papers. I saw it twice yesterday, and I'm sure it was right at the edge of the desk. Now it's much nearer the middle.'

'Would someone have come in to clean, miss?' Durris asked.

'No, no,' said Basilia. 'I told her not to. And anyway, she wouldn't have a key.'

'Would you know if anything was missing?'

Basilia sighed, and sank into a hard armchair.

'I wouldn't have the least idea.'

Durris breathed out sharply through his nose, considering.

'Well, there's nothing we can do about it, I suppose. But look, the window has been forced: there's a fresh chip off the frame.'

Hippolyta came to look – Basilia stayed where she was – and saw a clean, sharp slice off the wood of the frame, lying on the sill outside.

'Who would do such a thing? Surely if the murderer wanted to steal something, he would do it at the time, not come back later.'

'Unless he was disturbed that night,' suggested Durris.

'But by whom? He was disturbed by Tabitha, yes, but he locked her in the cupboard. Perhaps he was even disturbed by the Colonel and Mr. Forman, but he killed them. Why should anything else stop him?'

Durris looked at her for a long moment.

'Quite right, Mrs. Napier,' he said at last, 'quite right.'

'But that means,' said Hippolyta, thinking it through, 'that someone else came here last night, not the murderer, and broke in to look at these papers.'

'Yes, it does.'

'Someone else?' Basilia's question was rather shrill. 'Is this place never to be at peace again?' Hippolyta turned back to her, and thought for a moment she saw Basilia slip something – a long piece of paper – into her reticule. But Basilia quickly drew out her handkerchief, and Hippolyta thought she must have been mistaken.

'It may be someone who simply knew the place was empty after the funeral, miss, and came to chance their luck,' said Durris, clearly intending to soothe.

'Well,' said Basilia, 'there is a strongbox over there. As far as I can see from here, it has not been tampered with.'

Durris turned and saw the box, and stepped over to look.

'You're quite right, miss: the lock is still in place. Would you have the key?'

'No, but it'll be upstairs on my dressing table, with the spare key for the study. A moment, Mr. Durris!'

She rose with the least sigh, and left the room. They heard her footsteps light on the wooden stairs.

'Mr. Durris,' said Hippolyta, 'may I say that you don't seem over-concerned that the papers have been disturbed?'

'Do I not, Mrs. Napier? Yet I am not at all happy that someone has broken into the house and rifled around in here.'

'Hm. I –'

'Mrs. Napier, may I ask you something? You agreed with Dr. Napier – and indeed Miss Verney – that your husband was at home on Sunday evening. Yet the night watchman claims to have seen him on the green, around half past ten. How do you account for that?'

'The night watchman must be mistaken, I suppose,' said Hippolyta slowly. And if the night watchman could not identify Patrick reliably, could he identify Mr. Brookes, who would be even less familiar?

'He seemed very sure of himself,' said Durris quietly. 'And he seems a steady, sensible sort of man.'

As did Durris, Hippolyta thought. But could he be right? Had Patrick really been out on Sunday evening? He and Basilia had been so sure, that she had not examined her own memory.

'Is there something wrong?' Basilia asked, coming suddenly back into the room.

'No, not at all, miss. Have you that key?'

Basilia handed him a small set of keys, about four in all. The strongbox key was the smallest, and Durris quickly applied it to the lock. The strongbox lid was heavy, but opened smoothly in Durris' large hands.

Hippolyta did not want to seem nosey, but the contents seemed orderly.

'Does this look right to you, miss?' Durris asked. Basilia considered.

'Yes, I think so: some jewellery of his mother's that I think is intended for me, and that box contains a silver clock. He won it in some horse race in the Peninsula, and he was very proud of it but found it extremely ugly.'

Durris flicked over the catch on the box and opened it. A silver clock was revealed, of unpleasing proportions and decorated with heads of what were presumably supposed to be noble steeds but instead appeared as mules with evil expressions. The movement lurched into a tinny tick as the clock was moved. They considered it for a moment, then Durris slid it back into its case and latched it.

'Some bonds here,' he went on, 'actually quite a few. And some gold sovereigns.'

'For emergencies, he always said,' said Basilia. 'I think that's all I should expect to see there. He had only the one watch, and he was wearing it on his waistcoat. And he had his Sunday pin in his neckcloth: his everyday ones would be on his dressing table, no doubt. They were not of particular value, though he was fond of them. He liked to look smart, the more so, he said, because he was crippled.'

'Well,' said Durris, closing the strongbox, 'let us look at the papers.'

Hippolyta settled herself in a chair at the window, distancing herself from the examination of the late Colonel Verney's business. Basilia seemed at a loss but Durris was methodical, showing her each pile of papers and going through the headings with her. Those on the desk belonged almost entirely to the Burns Mortification trustees, but there were more in a press which, Hippolyta understood though she tried not to listen too much, derived from the Colonel's business and property interests around the country. Correspondence concerned those and various military friends and charitable concerns relating mostly to Waterloo veterans. The Colonel seemed to have been a generous donor to his fellow soldiers.

'And he didn't keep many personal letters, anyway,' Basilia explained at one point. 'Once he had replied, he generally burned them.'

'That certainly simplifies things,' said Durris solemnly. 'And these are all very straightforward. I have not found any threats or hints of scandal.'

'Are the trust's papers all right?' Hippolyta asked suddenly. 'I'm sorry, I didn't mean to interrupt. But it's struck me before that he might have found something there. My father is a lawyer, you see, and such things have happened before.'

'Did Colonel Verney mention anything about the trust's papers, Miss Verney?'

Basilia considered.

'I don't think so. He didn't say very much about it at all: just that the minister had asked him if he would become a trustee. Then all the papers arrived in deedboxes, and he spent hours going through them.'

'Hm,' said Durris. Hippolyta was surprised he did not make a note. The notebook had not even appeared for him to list the contents of the strongbox. He surveyed the room, and examined one or two deedboxes, making sure they were empty. Their interiors gleamed dully, reflecting nothing. 'Well,' he said at last, 'perhaps we should tour the rest of the house, and see if anything is obviously missing or different.'

Basilia turned quickly to Hippolyta.

'Oh, my dear!' This was clearly what she had been dreading: probably her uncle's study was less familiar to her and therefore less distressing to contemplate. Hippolyta jumped up to take her arm, and they led Durris out of the study. He locked the door behind them and solemnly again handed the keys to Miss Verney.

'The window is not secure,' he remarked, 'but I should be surprised if someone should try it again – and besides, with this door locked they could go no further than the study. Shall we start with the parlour, miss?'

They crossed the hall, and Basilia subjected the parlour to an emotional scrutiny. Durris examined the press where Tabitha had been locked, shaking his head a little, and checking the lock and key. Basilia declared that she could find nothing missing, and they moved on.

It was much the same around the rest of the house. Colonel Verney's tie pins were all present and correct in his bedchamber, and some odd coins were in a shallow dish on his dressing table, as if he had taken them from his pockets when he changed for dinner: they amounted to a pound or so, an easy prey to a casual burglar. The kitchen quarters were unremarkable: Forman's bedchamber was military in its bare precision, his weekday clothes folded and laid exactly on the shelves in the press, his washstand spotless, only white cat hairs on his grey blankets indicating anything about the man who had slept there. Durris fingered the hairs, and glanced at Hippolyta.

'He had given me a kitten a few days ago,' Hippolyta said. 'It seemed sensible, when the house was to be empty, to adopt the mother and the other kittens.'

'Ah, the cat in your parlour?'

'That's one of the kittens, yes,' said Hippolyta with a smile.

Durris' mouth twitched, but he did not smile back. He seemed, Hippolyta thought, more distant now than he had been when they had first met, the previous day. Could he really believe that Patrick was hiding something? That she was hiding something about Patrick? Had he really been out on Sunday evening? She had to think.

Chapter Twelve

The house was too distracting, though: she needed to concentrate on that, first. Upstairs there were four generous bedchambers, though three were frigidly bare, with only dustsheets ghostly over a few pieces of old furniture. Basilia's room was the fourth, set over the front door, and had been painted in fresh, clean white with floral patterns on the bed hangings, and warm rugs. The fireplace showed recent signs of a decent blaze, and there was a shelf of well-handled books and a sewing table. It was a friendly room, one Hippolyta would have liked for herself, certainly. On the night table, beside a Bible and a candlestick, were a few objects, which Basilia claimed quickly.

'Best not to leave these here, I suppose. I left my uncle's keys here,' she held them up, 'and this is his watch.' She picked it up, a fat gold circle, and slipped it into her reticule. 'And his Sunday tie pin.' She showed it to Durris, a flash of bright enamel, and then it disappeared with the watch and chain. She glanced around, though she must have looked before. 'There is nothing missing here: my jewellery, such as it is, is in its case at Dr. Napier's house. Shall we go up to the attic? I have to say that there are parts of the attics I have not explored, and I should not know if there was anything taken or left there at all. We only use the best bedroom there for Tabitha: the rest is locked. No doubt she would have mentioned it if she had found any of her own things gone.'

'Then if you have no idea about the rest there is little point in looking,' said Durris easily. They left Basilia's bedchamber and headed again for the stairs to the ground floor. 'There is one thing that has struck me: do you know anything about the kitchen floor? I noticed that it looked at one place as if someone had been pulling up the floorboards: and it is an odd thing, surely, to have floorboards in a kitchen?'

'Yes, they were there when we moved in, of course. But pulled up … why would that be?'

'Forman was looking for the kitten,' Hippolyta reminded her.

'Oh, yes! Of course: I had forgotten. One of Forman's kittens got into the windowseat and found a way down under the floorboards, and Forman was concerned that it would not be able to find its way back. He pulled the boards up to rescue it, then put them back down again, I suppose. He was prodigiously fond of those kittens.'

'He said it was a terrific guddle underneath, didn't he?'

'A guddle?' She looked briefly confused at Hippolyta's unaccustomed Scots. 'Oh, yes! So he did. So the floorboards must have been down for years.'

'My husband said it may have been a means for raising the floor above some damp,' said Hippolyta, as they reached the hall. Durris descended the last stair and blinked slowly at her.

'Did he, then?' he asked. Hippolyta felt suddenly uncomfortable. Basilia, roused from her own thoughts, studied her intently, then looked at Durris, puzzled. The sheriff's man was untroubled. 'Well, I think we've done all we can here today, miss, thank you very much. I hope I have not taken up too much of your time.'

'Not at all,' said Miss Verney graciously. 'And if I can do anything more to help, please let me know: we have to find who did this. My poor uncle …'

'Of course. And you, Mrs. Napier: thank you for your assistance.' He met her eye with his calm grey spectacled gaze, and that uncomfortable feeling surfaced again. It was difficult to guess what might be going through his mind. Of what did he suspect her?

'We'd better be going,' she said, and hoped he would not notice the slight wobble in her voice. 'It will be dinner time soon.'

He said nothing more, but stood in the hall, a little aside from the place where Colonel Verney had died, and bowed as they left. Outside the house, Basilia paused and looked back, as though bidding the ugly old place farewell.

'I confess,' she said softly, 'I don't know what to do. It disconcerts me that I am easy about leaving the house with only a complete stranger in it, but I feel a deep aversion to the place – I suppose that is natural, though I was never very fond of it.' She turned away, and set off down the drive, her black skirts clearing the dusty pathway by a few fashionable inches. Hippolyta, admiring the cut of the gown, caught up hurriedly. 'I don't want to stay here, in this house, so I suppose I should give up the lease. But where shall I go? I know you have been very kind about me staying with you, but I mean in the long term. How strange it feels, to have no family left in the world!'

'It must be, indeed,' Hippolyta agreed, trying to imagine a sudden extermination of her parents and all her sisters. Even then she would be left with quite a regiment of cousins. She could not conjure up the image of a world entirely empty of them: it would require something in the nature of a battle to remove all of them at once, and even then she was quite sure her mother and sisters would probably win. She pulled her mind back from this thought to Basilia's problems. 'Well, you have time to consider. And at least for this afternoon, let us retire to the garden at home and paint. I don't think I can survive much longer without taking out my paints!'

'Of course, dear Mrs. Napier,' Basilia touched her lightly on the arm. 'You have been so kind attending to my concerns that I have dragged you away from your own. Please, indeed, let us be artists!'

'No baggage cart yet!' sang out Patrick as he arrived home for dinner. 'We have another little problem. Apparently something has been stolen from it.'

'Stolen!' Hippolyta, hurrying out to greet him as usual, stopped short. The kitten on her shoulder swayed dangerously and ran down her back. 'Ouch. What? When?'

'Apparently when it was in the inn last night,' Patrick answered the latter question first, allowing her to help him with his coat before he took her hand in his long cool one. 'A largish crate, I'm told, right in the centre of the near side? Does that sound familiar?'

'It could be the parlour table,' said Hippolyta hesitantly, 'but why steal that? There were things packed around it, of course, in the crate, but it was a hotch potch: and nothing of particular value,

I think.' She frowned, trying to remember. 'A fish slice? And perhaps a pair of salt dishes? I'm not sure.' No doubt her mother had lists of what was in every box and basket, but she did not. Or if she did, they were packed in the boxes and baskets themselves.

Basilia had emerged from the parlour at the sound of their confusion, and joined in the conversation at once.

'It's not very nice to think that it might have been stolen here, where people know you, is it?' she put in. 'If it had been along the road, you could almost understand, but right in Ballater …'

'Yes, indeed,' said Hippolyta, who had not thought of that. 'Someone who knows us …'

'Oh, here they come now.' Patrick had heard the heavy wheels outside, and reopened the front door to look. 'They'll have to bring it through here.'

'But dinner's nearly ready,' said Hippolyta, thinking of Mrs. Riach.

'But the carters are already delayed,' said Patrick, 'and I don't think the cart will fit down the lane to the back gate. I think we're going to have to get the things indoors, anyway. We can sort it out later.'

'And what about the missing box?'

'The constable knows.'

'Morrisson?'

'I know,' said Patrick with a smile, 'but surely even he could manage to trace a simple stolen crate. Particularly one that size.'

'Where do you want these, then, sir?' The carters were already bringing the first baskets along the garden path, and in a moment the main hallway, small though it was, was packed with familiar luggage, all marked with the odd powdery blue paint her mother had chosen to distinguish it. The cart had evidently met a few of those thundery showers on its journey: some of the paint had slithered down on to the cart itself.

'But that's the parlour table!' Hippolyta exclaimed, peering into a large wooden box.

'Oh, aye, Mrs. Napier, are you thinking about the missing kist?' asked the older carter. 'It was a bigger yin than that, about yon height,' he waved a hand near his own shoulder, 'and powerful heavy.'

Hippolyta frowned.

'I cannot think what that could be,' she said.

'Fitever it was, they left the crate behind,' muttered the younger carter, for whom life appeared not to be happy. 'All in bits, too, so we canna use it again. Fit for would he do a thing like that?'

'All in bits? Have you the bits with you?' Hippolyta asked. The younger carter looked at her as if she was showing signs of dangerous lunacy, but that that was only to be expected in his line of work.

'Aye, they're in the back of the cart. They're no good for a'thing but the fire. I didna think you would want them.'

'I just want to see them.' She followed him out to the cart, which was nearly empty. Tucked up against the board was a heap of broken fir wood planks, yellow on one side where the weather had not seasoned it, and greyish on the other. She lifted the planks one by one, examining them.

'That wasn't our crate,' she said at last.

'It wasna?' The carter looked at her in blank surprise.

'No. My mother marked each crate with a number in blue paint, and there's nothing on this.'

'Maybe we lost a bit.'

'I'll make sure.' She darted back into the house, and returned in a few minutes. 'No, all the numbers are there, I'm positive. This was not our crate.'

'Then fit wye did we lug it all the way fae Aberdeen?' demanded the carter. 'I near put my back out lifting yon thing!'

'It wasna yours, ma'am?' asked the older carter, joining them. 'Well, that's – that's sort of good.'

'It's good for us, but have you inadvertently taken someone else's crate from the harbour, and lost it?' Hippolyta asked him gently.

'Oh. Aye, well, that wouldna be so good. But I'd swear it was with all your boxes fae the start. We're careful, see.'

'Aye,' added the younger carter, 'and we dinna gang roond the harbour picking up the heaviest crates we can find just for the fun of it, like.'

'If it was really heavy,' she continued, 'maybe that's why it was broken up. So that whoever stole it could take the contents bit by bit: I assume it vanished last night?'

'That's the way of it. We was sound asleep over the stables.'

'Well, you weren't woken by anyone bringing in, say, another cart?'

The older carter shook his head, but the younger one scowled.

'Wait there a mintie,' he said. 'There was no cart, that's a fact, but I did hear something in the middle of the night. Something rolling, I thought.'

'That'll be barrels going into the inn,' said his companion.

'Well, if it was, it was only the one. And fit wye would they be doing that in the middle of the night? And onywye,' he added, screwing up his face even more horribly as he struggled to remember, 'it was ganging aff.'

'Ganging aff?' Hippolyta repeated with precision.

'Aye: I mean the racket was ganging oot the stableyard, no towards the inn.'

'Well,' said Hippolyta, 'I think you have part of your solution. Either there was something heavy inside the crate and they brought something like a handcart to remove it, or whatever was in the crate could itself be rolled, and they rolled it away.'

'Michty,' remarked the older carter flatly. 'Fit'll we dae?'

'I have no idea,' said Hippolyta. 'You could try telling Mr. Morrisson, the constable.'

'Aye, right,' said the younger carter, equally flat.

'Or Mr. Durris, the sheriff's man. He's in the town, too.'

'Oh, aye?' The older carter brightened. He exchanged looks with the younger man. 'We'll do that, then, I reckon. Though why someone should come and steal the very thing from your cart that you didna put on it …'

'Maybe that's it,' said Hippolyta, suddenly struck by a thought. 'Someone set it with our things at the harbour, and collected it here. They didn't have to pay carriage or bring it themselves.'

'Och, that's no right!' grumbled the younger man.

'But it fits, doesn't it? Now, gentlemen, I'm afraid my dinner is waiting. Go round to the back and the housekeeper will find you some ale and bread and cheese.'

'Ale, aye. Thank you, ma'am.'

'It's all very peculiar. Why our cart?' Patrick asked when she explained what had happened, and her deductions. Gratifyingly, neither he nor Basilia could find fault with them.

'It may have been the only one going to Ballater,' Hippolyta suggested.

'And where, then, did the contents go?' asked Basilia.

'That's no longer our concern, I suppose,' said Patrick. 'And you've seen that all your mother's numbers are on the boxes and baskets we have?'

'Yes, fortunately. My mother is a very organised woman,' she explained to Basilia, with a crooked smile.

'That is very fortunate indeed,' said Basilia. 'I must remember that trick when I come to move our – my – belongings from Dinnet House.'

'My dear,' said Patrick to his wife, 'if Miss Verney doesn't mind, I was thinking that we ought to invite some people to dinner soon.'

'Of course! I had quite forgotten. Miss Verney, would you mind? So soon after your loss?'

'Not at all,' Basilia smiled weakly, which made Hippolyta feel instantly guilty for asking. 'It would cheer things tremendously, and after all, it's not as if it's a ball, is it?'

'Well, no: that would stretch the house considerably,' said Hippolyta, briefly terrified at the thought of hosting a ball. 'Well, if you're quite sure … We need to ask the Strachans at the very least, and perhaps Dr. Durward and the Strongs?'

'And Mrs. Kynoch,' added Patrick.

'Oh, yes. And should we ask the minister and his wife?'

'Perhaps we should, yes. All the usual conventions have been turned over a little, haven't they?'

'Well, it isn't Edinburgh,' Hippolyta conceded kindly. 'That would be, um, ten altogether. Do you think … er, well, I'd better talk to Mrs. Riach about it.'

'We have ten chairs in the dining room. Well, we have a dozen.'

'Yes, but it's not just a matter of chairs,' Hippolyta murmured. At least now their good china had arrived: she would need to check that none of it was broken before any invitations were issued, though. 'I'll talk to Mrs. Riach when she's had her rest.'

'Her rest?' Patrick looked surprised.

‘She always has a rest after dinner, didn’t you know?’ Hippolyta had been warned off disturbing the housekeeper during this sacred time.

‘I had no idea. Her hip must be very bad.’

‘Of course if you felt we should look for another housekeeper –’ said Hippolyta, filled with sudden hope.

‘Oh no, not at all. Not unless she feels the household is taxing her too far,’ said Patrick, his handsome face filled with kind anxiety.

‘She has not said so, but perhaps she is trying not to inconvenience us,’ said Hippolyta carefully.

‘You should ask her – but try not to make her feel she should leave! I don’t want her to feel offended,’ said Patrick. Hippolyta sighed.

‘I’ll do my best.’

The weather was so lovely that she managed to quell her eagerness to arrange all the cart’s exciting contents until later in the evening, and took Basilia outside at least to fit in an hour’s drawing and painting. It was delightful under an archaic apple tree in the leafy shade, and even in that one hour Basilia produced a series of sketches of kittens and flowers, and Hippolyta made good progress with her Craigendarroch study. At the end of it, tea was required, and she popped her head into the kitchen to ask Mrs. Riach to bring some. The housekeeper was by the fire, her plump body settled into a wooden armchair with a cushion, her feet up on a creepie stool on another cushion, an expression of bliss across her features. She was snoring with a sound of waves crashing on a windy day. Reluctant to spoil this picture of domestic comfort, Hippolyta tiptoed over to her, and became aware of a miasma of brandy about the woman. She picked up the teacup she saw on the floor and sniffed it. If there had been any tea in it, it had been heavily diluted. She blinked. Best, she thought, to let Mrs. Riach sleep off her excesses. She padded out again as quietly as she could, and found Ishbel scrubbing vegetables in the scullery.

‘Could you bring some tea, please, for Miss Verney and me in the parlour? Mrs. Riach seems to be asleep.’

‘Aye, ma’am.’ Ishbel curtseyed, then remembered to put down the cabbage she was holding.

'Um, Ishbel.'

'Aye, ma'am?'

'Do you know where Mrs. Riach's brandy came from?'

'Oh, ma'am, she didn't take it from the pantry, if that's what you mean!' Ishbel's eyes were wide.

'All right. So it was her own?'

'Robert Wilson bringed it her, ma'am. Before he left for Aberdeen.'

'He brought her brandy? As a thank you, you mean?'

'I suppose so, ma'am. But I think she paid him for it.'

'I see.' Hippolyta hesitated, then asked, 'What did it come in?'

'Come in? I dinna ken fit you mean …'

'I mean did he bring it in a bottle? In a flask? What?'

'Oh, no, ma'am. She gived him one of the jugs from the kitchen and he bringed it back full.'

'Yes, and now she's full,' Hippolyta murmured. 'Thank you, Ishbel. Very interesting.'

Mrs. Riach seemed mostly recovered by supper time, and Hippolyta took the chance to consult her on the matter of the dinner. She had had the chance to check the china, and it seemed all to be sound: it was now in a pretty dresser in the dining room, and brightened the room very slightly.

'Dinner, eh? Well, I suppose.'

'Would you prefer to have ten at dinner, or several smaller parties?' Hippolyta asked her, hoping to make the whole idea more appealing.

'Och, bring on the ten. Who did you say? The Strachans, the Strongs, the minister and his wife …'

'Dr. Durward. And Mrs. Kynoch.'

'Oh, aye. That'll be grand.' A little smile that Hippolyta did not quite like played around the housekeeper's thin mouth. 'All in together. That'll be some evening!'

'Well, thank you very much, Mrs. Riach. I know you'll rise to the occasion. I thought of Saturday?'

'Aye, aye, I can make a start the morrow.'

'Very good. I'll look forward to it.' It had all seemed to go well: Mrs. Riach retreated with an uncharacteristic chuckle and no hint of a limp, and yet Hippolyta had a niggling feeling that it had gone altogether too well, and that she had missed something very important.

Supper passed peacefully and afterwards Patrick played the piano softly while Basilia and Hippolyta put finishing touches to their afternoon's painting. After the disruption of the previous night, they were ready to retire earlier than usual, and it was only when she and Patrick were alone together that Hippolyta thought to broach the subject of Mrs. Riach's brandy supplies with her husband.

'She was drunk?' Patrick asked, astonished.

'Well, she was asleep, but she smelled very strongly of brandy. And apparently Robert Wilson had brought it for her, in one of our own jugs!'

'Robert Wilson? The coachman?'

'Yes … I wonder, do you think he has left already?'

'I believe so.'

'And he was quite well?'

'He was, I should say. Quite recovered.'

'Patrick, is there another inn in the village besides the main one by the bridge? A howff, perhaps, some less respectable place.'

'I don't think so. Mr. Douglas the minister would not encourage it.'

'Hmm.' Hippolyta considered. For her theory to be correct, Robert Wilson had had to have somewhere to dispose of the rest of his brandy, and the carters had heard something being rolled out of the stableyard, not towards the inn. And of the many things in the world that could be rolled, a barrel of brandy somehow came readily to mind.

She came awake suddenly to darkness, and aware that she had again heard a noise, she sat straight up, concentrating hard. Yes, it was a footstep again. Was Miss Verney on another of her night time perambulations? Well, with the front door key up on the ledge, she was surely safe: she would not be able to wander outside again. She listened: the footsteps were sounding softly in Basilia's room across the landing, just as before, but there seemed to be no indication that she was heading further afield. Absently, Hippolyta slipped out from under the covers and stepped over to the bedroom window, where the shutters had been left open. She gazed outside, seeing the massive church across the silent green, the shadowy hills beyond. Closer, below, the front garden was busy with the pale blurs of flowers amongst the bushes, the path a light strip bare from the door to the gate.

Except that it was not bare.

Her heart leapt in alarm. There was a dark figure there, on the path, a man, though further than that was hard to say at this awkward angle, in the dark. The man's face was turned up and shimmered slightly in her eyes as she tried to focus on it, but all too quickly the man looked away, and moved silently to the gate. She could hear, very faintly, its low squeak as he opened it, passed through and shut it again softly behind him. His shadowy form slipped away, down the hill to the left, towards the main street, the inn, the road to Aberdeen, the bridge over the river. Who could it have been?

Taking a shawl she tiptoed out of the bedroom and paused on the landing. There was no sound now coming from Basilia's room, and none from the rest of the house. She remembered the figure moving about in the servants' quarters, seemingly hiding from her. Could it have been Robert Wilson, about some dark business to do with a keg of brandy? But no: surely that figure had been too short for Robert Wilson: and besides, if her theory was correct, Robert Wilson would have had no need to move from his room in the attic until their baggage cart had arrived from Aberdeen. There were too many things going on here, she thought with sudden anger, about which she was being told nothing. It was her house now, she was mistress of it, and whatever happened under this roof was her business. She caught herself just about to stamp her bare foot on the landing carpet, and stopped just in time, laughing briefly at herself. But it was very annoying.

She paced slowly down the stairs, avoiding ones she had already noticed that creaked, listening as she went. Still nothing moving. She felt her toes connect with the rough warmth of the hall carpet, and paused again, before stepping slowly forward. It was quite dim in the hallway, but her senses were all alert, and it was her feet again that gave her the clue. She touched something cold and slightly damp with her toes, bent down and picked up something moist and crumbly. She sniffed it. A fresh, earthy smell filled her nostrils: it was, in fact, earth. She went to the front door: it was firmly locked, and the key, when she reached up, was just where Patrick had left it when he secured the door that evening, just where he had placed it the previous night. Had Miss Verney been watching that evening? Could such a memory be retained as she sleepwalked? Or had she been asleep at all? And if not, was the man outside on the path the reason for her wanderings, or was he in fact waiting to attack her in her vulnerable state?

It was only as she returned to bed, easing under the covers so as not to wake Patrick, that another question assailed her.

Could the night-wandering man outside have been the mysteriously mobile Mr. Brookes?

Chapter Thirteen

Friday morning, when Hippolyta woke full of energy to prepare for her dinner guests on the following evening, dawned damp and misty. It was the first time she had seen Ballater in anything but sunshine or a downpour, and the effect, though not displeasing to her artistic sensibilities, left her a little listless.

'I had hoped we might paint again today,' said Miss Verney in the parlour after breakfast, 'but the light is very unsympathetic.'

'Isn't it?' Hippolyta put aside the sketch she had been making of the church spire in the mist, and instead contemplated the pictures from the baggage cart which she had moved into the parlour, but had not yet arranged. 'Did you sleep well last night?' she asked. 'Or better than the night before, at least?'

'I slept very well, thank you,' said Basilia smoothly.

'Oh, that's good. I woke and thought I heard footsteps, but it must have been from the servants' quarters.' She shrugged, outwardly dismissing it, then jumped as she heard again the low creak of the front garden gate. She glanced quickly out of the window, and sprang up.

'Oh, it's Mr. Durris again!' she exclaimed.

'I wonder what he can want with me this time?' Basilia asked, a little tremor in her voice. They paused and listened as Ishbel's little feet padded along the hall and the front door opened. Durris' voice was low but indistinct from here, and they both turned to look at the parlour door, expecting it to open at any moment. But instead, Hippolyta heard the study door open across the hallway, and Patrick's voice raised in what she could not help noticing was a slightly uneasy greeting. Durris' voice murmured back, and then the study door shut. Ishbel's footsteps pattered back towards the kitchen.

'No need to worry, then,' said Hippolyta lightly. 'It's not you he wants to talk to.' But what did he want to say to Patrick? she wondered. He had given her such suspicious looks yesterday – and then he had said that someone had seen Patrick out in the village on the Sunday night, the night that Colonel Verney was murdered. She had been so quick to say that the person had been wrong – Lang, the night watchman, that was who it had been – that she had almost not allowed herself to take in the possibility that he could have been right. And had she not herself been impressed by the night watchman's apparent efficiency, his air of reliability?

But if she thought about it, and did not just blindly accept what Patrick had said, had he indeed been out on the Sunday evening? Her stomach churned a little just thinking about the possibility, and she tried to concentrate on the arrangement of the paintings. After a moment in which neither she nor Basilia said a word, Hippolyta tapped her foot sharply on the floor and declared,

'You know, I believe there are altogether too many paintings here, and several of them simply will not suit this room. Perhaps the hall would be better for – for this one, for example.' She snatched up a dark oil painting depicting what her family had always thought to be an Italian prospect in a thunderstorm (and had, she suspected, never much liked), and went out into the hallway. The white walls were bare, and she spent some minutes holding the heavily framed painting up in one space or another, tilting her head and considering the light on it, all the while straining her ears to listen for any voices she might hear coming from the study. Why would they not speak louder? It was really most unfair. She crossed the hall and tried the painting against the walls on either side of the study door, then nearly dropped it as the door opened suddenly and Durris backed out right beside her. He was still speaking.

'As I say, Dr. Napier, I'm giving you fair warning. If you can think of what you might have been doing, then – oh, Mrs. Napier, good day to you.' He stopped backing, turned and bowed, his face bland.

'Oh, Mr. Durris! I had no idea you were here. Will you stay for some tea?' she asked, as innocently as she could manage on the spot. Durris gestured with his hat.

'I thank you, no. I had to see Dr. Napier on business, but I must carry on. Good day to you,' he said again, this time in farewell. She saw him to the door, then went back to the study. Aware of the fact that the parlour door was still ajar, and as alert as all eavesdroppers are to the possibility of being overheard, she closed the study door gently and went to Patrick at his desk, taking his hand. He looked deeply concerned, his pale brow wrinkled.

'My dearest,' she said softly, 'is something the matter?'

'The matter? No, not really,' said Patrick unconvincingly. She cleared her throat a little.

'Is it perchance that Mr. Durris thinks you might have been out in the village the night that – that everything happened at Dinnet House?'

He started, and stared up at her.

'How – why should you think that?'

'He mentioned something yesterday – just in passing. It was only afterwards that I thought – what with the Colonel's will, as well – that maybe he thought that you had – had something to do with the Colonel's death.'

Patrick was even more shocked.

'I'm not at all sure that such thoughts are appropriate in a wife!' he cried, and then after a moment a colder note entered his voice, one that she did not care for. 'And do you think I had something to do with it?'

'Of course not!' she exclaimed. 'How could you think such a thing? And you yourself said you were here, at home, on Sunday evening, and Miss Verney agreed with you. It never even occurred to me to think about it until now!'

'I did say I was in on Sunday evening,' said Patrick, flatly. 'I told him that, for what with Miss Verney saying so I thought I must have been. But now I think I was mistaken. Don't you remember? A messenger came from the inn, to call me to a patient, whom I then could not find? Remember?'

'Was that Sunday?'

'I believe it was: we were out on Saturday night at Colonel Verney's, anyway, and of course by Monday night everything had – happened. When I think about it I feel sure that we had been to the service in the morning, and we were singing hymns, I think, when the messenger came. Something like that, anyway. But because I've told him one thing, and then another, I believe Durris is suspicious of me – and of course, there was no patient.'

'But others in the inn will know you were there!'

'Well, I hope so,' said Patrick, although he did not look hopeful. 'I cannot believe I muddled my nights like that. It was very foolish.'

'It could happen to anyone,' she said, soothing him like a nervous horse. 'And I should have remembered, too: but then I'm always terribly muddled.' She knelt down beside him, both his hands in hers, and bowed her head against him. He kissed her hair, and they sat in silence for a long moment, their breathing matched, drawing comfort from simple touch, until a little too soon he shifted away.

Hippolyta barely noticed, though: her unruly mind was skipping on: who did he say he actually had seen at the inn? Would they remember? Should she go and see them? It would not please him to know that she was going to question strange travellers and inn servants, but then, he did not need to know. And it was for his own benefit, after all – and hers. She did not like the looks Durris had given her, all the more because she believed that Durris was a good man, possibly an intelligent man. He needed to know that Patrick was innocent of all harm, and if she had to prove that herself, she would.

She returned to the parlour in a thoughtful mood. It would require some good excuse for her to leave the house this morning in this damp mist, and instead she took up her sewing and applied her mind to her problems. Durris seemed to think that Patrick might have had something to do with the Colonel's murder. She did not believe that he had. Therefore, someone else had done the deed – or deeds – and then, another person had broken into Dinnet House afterwards, too. It was just possible, she thought now, that they had been the same person. What if the murderer had taken something, but afterwards found it was the wrong thing? She stabbed sharply at the cloth. No use pursuing that idea for the moment, when they had no idea even if anything was missing, or when it might have gone.

Durris would have to have the minister, or Mr. Strong, or Dr. Durward, or Mr. Strachan, or all four, go through the mortification papers and see if there was anything amiss. But then, if there were something amiss, presumably one of them already knew about it: she had heard of no one else who had a concern in the trust, or a right to see the papers. The four trustees were the only men who would notice something wrong, and the only four presumably who would have had the chance to make something wrong. She stabbed again, and wondered if her father would like to pay his youngest and favourite daughter a visit and give her a little advice. But if Durris had any sense, he would find some other local lawyer to look through the trust papers and see if anything was wrong with them. In any case, he would probably not accept the word of the father-in-law of his chief suspect. How could she persuade Durris that Patrick could not be responsible for Colonel Verney's death?

The obvious way to do it would be to show Durris who had, in fact, carried out the killings. That would be tricky: it was not exactly a job for the respectable new wife of the local physician, particularly one who was not well acquainted with the town. But then, it seemed likely that the miscreant was someone known to Colonel Verney, as they had not been a common burglar, so there was a high chance that she had already met, or heard of, the murderer in the few days she had been here. Belatedly, a chill ran up her spine. In her anxiety over Patrick and for Basilia's well-being, it had not occurred to her that the murderer was likely to be someone she knew.

If there was indeed something wrong with the trust, then the four chief suspects, she thought, trying to be orderly, were the four existing trustees. It would be a matter of working out which of them might have done something wrong, and how they might have tried to hush it up. Mr. Strong the lawyer, Dr. Durward the physician, Mr. Strachan the merchant, and Mr. Douglas the minister: Mr. Douglas seemed wary and clumsy, Mr. Strachan bad-tempered and probably against Colonel Verney's appointment as trustee, Dr. Durward seemed careless of anything serious, and Mr. Strong had been incisive and a little fierce. He clearly knew his way about Dinnet House and Colonel Verney's study: he might well have been familiar with the Colonel's night time routine. She suddenly spoke out loud, as if she had been carrying on an audible conversation.

'Miss Verney, was Mr. Strong a frequent visitor at Dinnet House?'

Basilia, not unreasonably, raised her fine eyebrows in surprise.

'Mr. Strong? Ah, yes, I suppose so. My uncle's man of business is in London, of course, but Mr. Strong advised him, I believe, when he wanted to have a more general conversation about business. Or for anything Scotch, for I gather that your Scotch law is different from English law.'

'Yes …' Hippolyta frowned, trying to remember what else she had planned to ask Basilia. 'Oh, yes: another question. Was the Colonel ever posted to the West Indies?'

'The West Indies? I don't believe so. And I think he told me, or I heard him tell others, every detail of his military service from his first commission onwards, so I should be surprised to find that he had been there and I did not know. Why do you ask? And why did you ask about Mr. Strong? The Misses Strong used to call, too: my uncle found them very amusing, though he thought the elder might have marriage in mind!'

'Oh, I thought it was the younger who was on the hunt for a husband!' They laughed a little, pleased to have happened upon a lighter moment, and Basilia seemed to forget Hippolyta's odd questions. Hippolyta rang for tea and then paced the room a little. Basilia eyed her.

'You are not happy to be kept indoors like this by the weather, are you, Mrs. Napier?'

'Not at all,' Hippolyta agreed. 'I have grown too used to all that lovely sunshine. But I must decide on these paintings, for Mrs. Riach said she could bring a man in tomorrow morning to hang them if I can decide where they are to go.'

She had placed a few more of them before the tea arrived, and afterwards, with Basilia's help, arranged the rest in a flurry of swaps and swoops. By the time their guests arrived tomorrow evening, the Napiers' house would look much less like bachelor accommodation and much more like a home – complete with seven cats. But instead of calming her, all the activity had made Hippolyta even more impatient to be doing something useful. She snatched up her most water resistant bonnet and her darkest gloves, and made for the door.

'Miss Verney, I shall not ask you to accompany me, for you are not yet well, I fear. But you must excuse me for at least half an hour, or I shall simply faint with impatience!'

Basilia laughed at her.

'I should be delighted to accompany you, if you have no objection! I feel I need some fresh air myself. This – ' She made a gesture at the low ceiling of the parlour and then stopped suddenly, apparently catching herself in the act of making some negative remark about the house again. 'This is very comfortable, but in the summer surely we should not be held prisoner in our houses!'

Hippolyta bit her lip, glancing up at the ceiling when Miss Verney had passed her. There was nothing wrong with it, as far as she could see. It was just a ceiling, slightly low, yes, not as grand as those in Dinnet House, perhaps, but a perfectly serviceable ceiling. Her eyebrows twitched. She liked her new home. If Miss Verney wished for something better, she could go back to her own house.

But in the moment it took Basilia to run upstairs for her own bonnet, Hippolyta's mood had recovered, and they set out into the misty air arm in arm.

'Where did you think to walk?' Miss Verney asked.

'Um, I had thought to go to Strachan's shop, first of all,' said Hippolyta, thinking on her feet, 'and then I had an enquiry to make down at the inn.'

'At the inn?'

'Yes, so I am glad you have come with me, to add respectability to my venture!' Hippolyta grinned, so that Miss Verney had to smile back, puzzled though she seemed to be. 'But first, Strachan's. It's up past the church, isn't it?'

'That's right: you'll have passed it a few times, I should think.'

They set off up the green, quiet today with most of the town's visitors staying indoors, and the sounds of the people going about their business muted by the damp air. No one lingered to chat as they met, and men's hats were pulled low and women's shawls bound tight. Though no rain actually fell, the trees they passed were lined with silver droplets amongst the leaves, and the ground underfoot had lost its summer dustiness.

Strachan's merchant house was on the left not far up from the green, a low building with a coomb-ceiled upper floor, but much less restricted in width and depth. Strachan had evidently taken over the shops to left and right of his original site, and perhaps built back, too, for the shop within was dark and cavernous, smelling of spices and paper and cured meats and sharp cheeses, of soap and wool and polish. Not a speck of dust could be seen anywhere, though it must have taken a team of boys to dust the endless shelves and racks, and to sweep the smooth wooden floors to a sheen like the flank of a well-groomed thoroughbred. Hippolyta looked about with curiosity and some delight, an expression on her face which Mr. Strachan had no doubt interpreted as he hurried forward to greet his customers.

'Mrs. Napier! Delighted to see you in my shop! And Miss Verney, too: I trust you are both quite well?'

He was a different man from the sharp, angry character Hippolyta had met or seen before, and it was almost a moment before she could persuade herself that he did not have a twin brother he kept in the shop.

'Thank you, yes, Mr. Strachan. And you and Mrs. Strachan?'

'Oh, yes, indeed: we are to dine with you tomorrow night, I believe? Very much looking forward to it! Very much. Please, come and take a seat and make yourselves comfortable, ladies. Is there anything I can show you today? We have some very fine gros de Naples just in from the Glasgow warehouses, Mrs. Napier, in l'Eau de Tiber: if you'll forgive me I am quite sure that the effect that shade would have with your appearance would no doubt be very pleasing for a husband! And Miss Verney: some Norwich crape? It is the very thing worn at Court when the late Duke of York was so sorely missed.'

'Actually,' said Hippolyta, used to this almost-impudence from certain Edinburgh shopkeepers but surprised to find it here, 'I was hoping to see what hams you have.'

'But of course! Immediately. Alexander!' A senior shopboy was summoned, and directed very particularly by Mr. Strachan in the samples of ham he was to fetch. In a moment he was back with two plates, two forks and napkins, and offered the plates to Hippolyta and Basilia so that they might try the tiny cubes of pink arranged on them.

'Oh, heavens, they are all quite delicious!' said Hippolyta after a few minutes. 'How am I to choose?'

'Will it be contributing to tomorrow evening's feast, Mrs. Napier?'

'I hope so.'

'Then may I be so bold as to suggest this one?' Strachan gracefully indicated one that Hippolyta had indeed especially liked. 'Dr. Napier has always enjoyed it at our own table, I believe.'

'Then that is the very one,' said Hippolyta. Now all she would have to do would be to persuade Mrs. Riach to serve it. It struck her that if it was delivered to the kitchens, Mrs. Riach was quite capable of 'losing' it before it ever reached the table. She added quickly, 'I know it is a little unconventional, but I should like to take it with me now.'

'But of course.' Mr. Strachan did not bat an eyelid, but hurried the shopboy off to wrap the desired weight of ham. Hippolyta hoped she had estimated the weight correctly, but at least the merchants had not blinked at that, either.

'You have a very fine business here, Mr. Strachan,' she commented. 'Has it been here for long? It has the air of an establishment of many years' stability – though of course entirely up to date.'

Mr. Strachan purred a little, she thought.

'My father started the business, Mrs. Napier, but I was lucky enough to be able to expand it considerably. We take a pride in being able to supply anything our customers desire at very little notice: I have built up connexions very extensively, which of course is of benefit when we have so many visitors in the town, with tastes which perhaps are less familiar to us so far north.'

'Of course: how very fortunate. Do you often receive unusual requests?'

'Oh, I could not possibly say!' Mr. Strachan replied with alarming archness.

'Of course not: the soul of discretion. Oh: before I forget, my husband asked me to find out if you had by chance some good brandy in stock? He particularly wanted to have some before tomorrow night.'

'Brandy?' Mr. Strachan coughed suddenly. 'Ah … I shall have to investigate the cellars. Brandy …' he murmured, as though she had asked for something much more obscure. He frowned. 'If it please you, Mrs. Napier, I shall send a boy round to tell you if we are able to provide it.'

'Very good: but I should like to know today, in case my husband wishes to make other plans.'

'Of course, of course.'

'Then that is all for now, I believe. Miss Verney?'

'Yes, I am quite content,' said Basilia, and they both rose to go.

'Oh, Miss Verney,' said Strachan suddenly, 'perhaps we could have a little word some time about your lease? No hurry, no hurry at all: just when it might be convenient for you.'

'Oh, yes, of course, Mr. Strachan.'

They left the shop and turned back towards the green, Mr. Strachan seeing them off personally at the door, Hippolyta carrying a brown paper parcel full of admittedly delicious ham. A dog which had been sheltering in a doorway sniffed, and watched them wistfully.

'Is Mr. Strachan your landlord?' Hippolyta asked, trying not to sound too surprised.

'Yes, yes, he owns Dinnet House.'

'A grand sort of house, for a merchant, if he has his new house, too.'

'Yes, but then, Dinnet House was never his own, if you see what I mean,' said Basilia. 'It came to him through Mrs. Strachan, I believe.'

'Through Mrs. Strachan?'

'Yes: it was her family home.'

Well, thought Hippolyta, perhaps that was the simple answer to the question of where Strachan's money had come from to expand his father's modest business. He had not embezzled it from the Burns Mortification: he had simply married it.

The rain was a little more like rain as they descended the gentle hill of the main street towards the bridge. The inn sat looking out over the river, a picturesque spot, Hippolyta thought, tucked into its corner by the bridge and adorned, for the benefit of visitors, with its pretty gardens. They found the inn's messenger boy quickly enough, as he sat by the door playing with a puppy.

'Aye, I remember the doctor last Sunday,' he agreed, as the puppy abandoned him for the attractions of Hippolyta's parcel. 'I fetched him here an' all.'

'Do you remember who he was supposed to see?' Hippolyta asked, holding the parcel higher.

'A wummin. I dinna ken fit wummin, ken. There was a Mr. Jenkins biding here the time, but he's awa' on up to … dinna ken fa. Caithness, mebbe? Onywyes, he was the one sent me off to fetch a doctor, for he said there was a wummin sick in the passage. Well, I dinna want to see a wummin sick. Bleeding, aye, that has somethin' to it: you see some good injuries in an inn, times. There was a fella once cut off all his fingers wi' a scythe, I seen him. But sick: there's aye too much of that kind of thing. So I lit aff and fetched the doctor, and I brung him back. But by then Mr. Jenkins, he had a jug of whisky, and he wouldna have kent the wummin if she'd been his ain mother. Which I doubt she was, the age he was, an' all. So that was that.'

'Can you remember what time Dr. Napier left here?'

'Time?' The question puzzled the boy. 'I dinna ken. It was night time.'

'Is the innkeeper about?' asked Hippolyta. The puppy was jumping to rather an impressive height, and its paws were muddy: she was doing her best to keep her skirts clean, but it was not likely to last.

'You could try yonder,' said the boy.

'Why don't you go and fetch him for me?' asked Hippolyta with a smile and a small coin. The boy obligingly went, and the puppy, torn between his master and the tantalising parcel, sat in bewilderment and in a moment, with the quick exhaustion of the young, fell asleep. Hippolyta let her arm down in relief.

But the innkeeper knew nothing of Patrick's departure time, either. He remembered the occasion well enough, and the search for a sick woman, but try as he might he had no clear idea of when Patrick had set out for home, just up the hill. It could have been nine, he thought, or it could have been eleven.

Hippolyta could have wept in frustration, but she tried hard not to let it show in front of Basilia. There was Patrick's whole story confirmed, but she was no nearer to proving he had not left the inn, walked up the hill and killed Colonel Forman and his manservant.

Chapter Fourteen

Though she heard no strange footsteps in the middle of the night, and saw no wandering strangers in the front garden, Hippolyta did not sleep well that night. There must be some way, she was determined, that she could prove to Mr. Durris that Patrick was entirely innocent of the deaths of Colonel Verney and Forman.

She lay staring up at the darkened ceiling, trying to think the problem through, but her mind in its agitated state leapt from fact to fact and from fancy to fancy. It was night time: perhaps she should slip quietly out of the house and go to find Lang, the night watchman, and ask him where he had seen Patrick – or thought he had seen Patrick – last Sunday night. But even as her rational mind told her that prowling around Ballater at night was probably not wise, particularly with a murderer in town, her more romantic nature admonished her. Surely she could trust Patrick, her beloved new husband? What did it say about her that only weeks after their marriage and their strenuous journey here and the beginning of their new life together, she was ready to suspect him of cold-blooded murder? She felt herself blush with shame, and not just at the thought of being caught wandering about the village in her nightgown. But if Lang, the night watchman, could simply put her mind at rest, then where was the harm?

But what if he did not put her mind at rest?

What if he told her he had definitely seen Patrick, not somewhere innocently between home and the inn, but between home and Dinnet House? She swallowed hard. No, she should trust Patrick, whatever anyone said.

But, said another small voice in her crowded head, but she had not actually known Patrick that long, had she?

That was ridiculous, she told herself firmly. It was true that they had not perhaps known each other well for very long: they had met three years ago, when Patrick had come to Edinburgh to take some medical courses not covered at Marischal College, his university in Aberdeen. He had visited their house with other medical students, a little older than them, a little quieter and more studious, and she had taken to him almost immediately – he was, she fully admitted, extremely handsome. A year of social exchanges: a few moments at a dance, or a picnic, and they had an understanding. Then correspondence, and a visit to speak to her father, who was saddened, more than anything, to be losing his youngest and dearest daughter. Patrick's elder brother, a comfortably-off farmer by Longside, had then met with Hippolyta's father: Patrick's own father was long dead. Negotiations continued on which her father reported faithfully to her, but she remembered no doubt at all entertained as to Patrick's character. He had a reference, as was proper, from the Episcopalian minister in his home town to the Rev. Mr. Shannon in Edinburgh, and no one questioned it. He was no scoundrel, surely. But, said the little voice again, murder was not embezzlement. Murder was not theft and reset. Her father had said to her, à propos of one of his cases, that murder was an odd crime, and rarely habitual. What if Patrick had killed Verney because he knew Verney had named him in his will? What if he thought he needed the money to keep her in a house suitable for her status? She gulped again: how awful if he had murdered for her sake, but quite against her will! A dreadful thought!

The pillow was hot, wherever she laid her head, and she slipped out from under the covers, poured herself a glass of water from the carafe by the bed, and went to stand again by the window. The night time garden was dark and damp, and silent. She sipped the lukewarm water, and rubbed her eyes, then glanced back at the bed, at the long shape of Patrick's body lying peacefully, turned away, under the blankets. She was more awake now, and much more rational, she told herself. Patrick would no more have murdered his old friend Verney than she herself would. She was being completely ridiculous. There was no need to see Lang, for Lang had no doubt – no doubt at all – seen Patrick somewhere between here and the inn, and that was that.

A vast yawn snatched her suddenly, and she stretched, a wave of sleepiness hitting her hard. She set the glass down and tucked herself back into bed, turned the pillow over, and almost immediately fell sound asleep.

The morning dawned cloudy but more dry than not, the air less stifling than it had been all week. Hippolyta's morning meeting with Mrs. Riach went uncharacteristically smoothly: Mrs. Riach was absorbed in preparations for the dinner that night, accepted the ham with only a passing complaint ('The Doctor will no eat it, a' course, but the guests might think it fine enough.'), and listed proudly all the other things she was in the midst of baking and cooking. Hippolyta's mouth was watering already. As a compromise, they agreed that the ham should feature in the shape of a raised pie, for which Mrs. Riach explained she had a very fine mould, and her hot water pastry was never kent to fail. Puddings and fools followed in the list, until Hippolyta wondered if there would be any room on the table for the guests' own plates, or money left in the housekeeping for the rest of the year. But at least Mrs. Riach seemed happy: she spoke the King's English as clear as glass, and left the room with no trace of a limp. Had she simply felt that Hippolyta would not allow her talents their full scope? Hippolyta shrugged: she had a dozen theories to explain the general phenomenon of Mrs. Riach, but no proof of any of them.

At breakfast, they heard the door and Ishbel's rush to answer it. In a moment she came into the parlour to present a note to Miss Verney, who sat back in surprise.

'Will you excuse me?' she said. 'I see it was directed to Dinnet House but to be redirected if necessary … Oh! It is from our clergyman – the one that you met last Sunday. He would like to know if he can hold the service here tomorrow, knowing that I have moved out of Dinnet House.'

'I thought you said he came once a fortnight?' Hippolyta asked.

'Usually, yes. Summers are unpredictable, though – winters even more so!'

'Could we hold it in here?' Patrick queried, glancing about the not particularly large parlour.

'If we moved the furniture back, and took the table out for the time,' Hippolyta suggested. 'We could use the hall table for the communion table, for at least it is rectangular and not round like this one. And we could bring in a few of the dining chairs … Do you think?' she asked her husband. He frowned.

'If it is not held here, where could we have it?' he asked. 'The inn would not perhaps be entirely proper. But perhaps Pannanich Lodge? Or the hotel there?'

'It would be somewhat further for the clergyman to ride,' Miss Verney said slowly. 'But if you think one of those places would be better …'

'It would be very cramped here,' said Patrick.

'But how much more friendly to have it in someone's house, as is usual here, than to be in a hotel!' said Hippolyta, who had the whole thing planned in her mind's eye. 'And we have your piano: I'm sure you could play beautifully for it.'

'Or I could – if you wish,' said Basilia modestly. Hippolyta smiled briefly at her. She knew they would have a poor showing if she herself played, so the matter was out of her hands.

'I see I am defeated,' said Patrick, with a grin and a sigh. 'Please tell the clergyman he may come here if he wishes – but he will have to leave his horse at the inn.'

'I'm sure that will be acceptable!' said Basilia, already scribbling a note for Ishbel to take back to the waiting messenger. 'Thank you so much, Dr. Napier!'

'It will be to our advantage, too,' said Hippolyta lightly. 'Think of it: we have only to come downstairs and we shall be at church!'

'We had better have breakfast cleared quickly,' said Patrick. 'And I take it you are going to warn Mrs. Riach?'

Hippolyta's face fell. The thought had not occurred to her.

'Yes, of course I shall,' she agreed, trying to sound unconcerned. 'In fact, I might tell her now, while she is in a good mood.'

She contrived to put the problem out of her mind, however, unwilling to annoy Mrs. Riach at this delicate time. It would be her first dinner, and she very much wanted everything to go right, particularly as Mrs. Strachan would be there. She remembered Dr. Durward's challenge to her, to win Mrs. Strachan over as a patient: she had not done much towards that in the last week, but no doubt he had had no expectations that it would happen straightaway. These things had to be taken gently, she thought. There might be an opportunity that evening to drop a few words into the conversation about Patrick's success with other patients, his popularity with the visitors to the Wells, his growing practice – but she would have to be subtle. There should be other conversation, too: for example, perhaps there would be some way to find out from Mr. Strachan whether or not he knew that Mr. Brookes had been seen outside his house? Or to probe into the most likely of the trustees to have done something untoward with the funds of the Burns Mortification? No doubt, even with Miss Verney there, the murder would be spoken of: could she watch her guests to see if any of them gave anything away?

She shivered suddenly: here she was, expecting to find out secrets from her guests, as if she were fully content that one of them should be a murderer. But what a thing to think! But then she had already considered the possibility that the murderer might be someone she had already met: and these were the chief people she had met since her arrival, and the chief people of Colonel Verney's acquaintance.

Unbidden, the thought came into her head that of all the men, only Mr. Strong was too small to have been able to kill Forman easily: and there was always the possibility that he had used a chair, though she still found it hard to imagine. Even Mrs. Strachan would have been tall enough, she thought, then dashed the idea away: the very notion was abhorrent. Mrs. Kynoch, Mrs. Douglas and the Misses Strong were all far too small. She gave an involuntary chuckle at the thought of the Misses Strong conspiring in the act, one waiting on the chair and the other distracting Forman so that he would perhaps back into position – and then she remembered that she had liked Forman very much, and he had loved his cats, and she felt thoroughly ashamed.

Yet there was no doubt but that someone had murdered Forman and Colonel Verney, and someone would have to find out who that murderer was. Mr. Durris seemed very trustworthy, but the thought that he might suspect Patrick returned to haunt her, without all the baggage that had accompanied it in the dark of the night. What would Mr. Durris be doing today? Should she have invited him to dinner, too? It would have been a good opportunity to find out how his mind was working – was he the kind of person one invites to dinner? Again, it was hard to tell. He seemed equally at home in the kitchen and the parlour.

She jumped: she had glanced out through the trees of the front garden at the green, and there was Mr. Durris, heading unmistakably for the church. Was he about to pray for divine assistance? Or no: of course, he would be going to ask the minister, Mr. Douglas, for more information about the Burns Mortification. Before she had even considered what to do, she found herself walking swiftly – just short of an unladylike gallop – across the green, gloves tucked in her hand, fastening her bonnet strings as she went, and into the church.

Inside, she had to pause. What was she doing? She had never been into the building before, and had no idea where to go. If it was a typical kirk, it was probably fairly bare inside. Though she had slipped through the outer door, there was an inner door, too, double like the outer one. No one was about, and she put her eye to the crack between the two sides of the door. There was the minister, stooped and puzzled-looking, and Mr. Durris, gesturing to a nearby pew, perhaps intending that they should make themselves more comfortable for a little talk. She looked up above them. A gallery! Of course. She backed away from the door, and saw to her left the bottom of the staircase that must lead up to the gallery seating. Tiptoeing as softly as she could, holding her skirts to stop them rustling and turned sideways so that her sleeves did not slither against the wood panelled walls, she hurried upstairs.

In the gallery, she found herself most horribly exposed at a low railing, and quickly ducked down between the railing and the front pew. There were more steps in front of her, leading up to the back rows, and at the foot of them she saw a soft grey cloth and a brush. Evidently someone had been interrupted in the midst of their Saturday church-cleaning. She took the brush and began to sweep the pew gently, trying not to attract attention but hoping that if anyone saw her they might simply think she was there to help. Sure she had done her best to blend in, she cautiously peeped over the railing. Below was the thinning pate of the minister, Mr. Douglas, and his round shoulders straining the worn black of his coat, and Durris' thick dark hair. He had laid his hat beside him on the pew, and she could see one white corner of his precious notebook. She paused in her sweeping, and strained her ears to listen.

'… Burns Mortification?' came Durris' voice.

'What do you need to know?' Mr. Douglas asked in return. 'I'm happy to give you all the help I can, though I doubt it's much, all the same.'

'Well, when was it set up? How? Who are the trustees?'

'Och, it was set up before my time here. Mr. Strong and Mr. Strachan could mebbe tell you more about it all. My position as trustee sort of goes with the job here.'

'So you didn't know Burns himself?'

'No, no. Mr. Strong and Mr. Strachan did, I think, years ago, before the gentleman left the country. He made his fortune abroad, you see, and being a generous gentleman with, I imagine, no family of his own, he wanted to use some of it to help others from his old school and parish. It's no an uncommon thing, I believe: there are plenty of bursaries and so on if you're at the universities, boys helped by all kinds of wee sums here and there left by grateful predecessors.'

'Aye, I'm well aware. So this Mr. Burns is dead?'

The minister's breath hissed dubiously through pursed lips.

'I dinna ken about that. This here's a mortification: I think for that you'd need something like a trust disposition and settlement – but I'm no lawyer, ken. You'd need to ask Mr. Strong about that.'

'Where are the papers normally kept?'

'They're usually in their deedboxes in the session room.'

'I see: and that would be locked?'

'Oh, aye, locked up good and tight, normally. The registers is in there, d'you see?'

'Of course, aye. So it was unusual for them to be so, well, insecurely kept?'

'I suppose so.' Mr. Douglas did not seem to think that a point of much interest.

'And the trust is healthy? Do you administer a great deal of funds?'

Hippolyta, glancing again over the railing, saw the minister's great round shoulders shrug.

'I believe so. Mr. Strachan's always saying it's a generous fund, aye. But he's the one for the numbers: he keeps his eye on all that.'

'So Mr. Strachan does the accounts? And the money is presumably invested?'

'I suppose so.'

'And Mr. Strong does the legal side.'

'Aye, well, he would. Not that I think he's had much to do, since he set the whole business up on Mr. Burns' instructions.'

'And you …?'

'Me? Oh, what do I do, do you mean? Well, my predecessor was a trustee so it was simply assumed, after he died and I was called here, that I would just sit in in the same way.'

'I see.' Hippolyta was sure she could hear the tiniest scratch of a pencil on paper. 'So if something was wrong with the trust, would you be likely to know?' Now she could hear instead Durris straining not to accuse the minister of downright stupid neglect.

'Something wrong? But what could be wrong? It's only the four of us, and Mr. Strachan's awful handy with the money. You can tell that by looking at him: he's gey prosperous, wouldn't you say?'

'Oh, yes, a clever businessman,' Durris agreed wryly. He was probably wondering, Hippolyta thought, how clever Strachan was to be so prosperous. Had Strachan not wanted Colonel Verney amongst the trustees in case he spotted Strachan's fiddling with the money? She hoped Durris remembered what she had told him about Strachan's threatening behaviour to Verney. 'I believe it was yourself asked Colonel Verney to join the trustees? Why was that?'

'Och, aye, well, it was almost an act of politeness, really. The man was part of the community now, and he seemed a decent sort of gentleman with some experience of the world. Mr. Strong thought we ought to have a couple more trustees in case anything happened to any of us. The only name we could come up with, though, was Colonel Verney. Dr. Durward thought Dr. Napier was a wee bit young yet, and we all agreed. Though now, maybe, we should ask him.'

Hippolyta's ears felt as if they were stretching to the length of hares', but she could hear no reaction from Durris. Surely if he thought Patrick was guilty, he would say something to the minister about not allowing him to be a trustee, but there was no sound at all. Then she heard a creak, as he changed his position on the pew.

'You know your parishes as well as anyone,' Durris began, thoughtfully. 'Who would you say might have killed the Colonel and his man?'

'Aye, now, there's a question,' Mr. Douglas conceded. 'Mrs. Douglas, now, she reckons it's an agent of Bonaparte's, come back to take revenge for Waterloo – for you ken, the Colonel talked a good deal of Waterloo, as old soldiers will do. I myself think that's unlikely,' he went on, 'but I do wonder if he was robbed. It's a grand big house up there, and he might have had more money than he was letting on.'

'I don't believe he was robbed,' said Durris mildly. 'There seems to be nothing missing from the house.'

'Of course there's talk in the village about the house being unchancy,' said the minister with caution: it was not perhaps a fit subject for a man of the cloth. 'What with there having been a murder there before – but that was before my time, too.'

'And how long have you been here, Mr. Douglas?'

'Five years,' said Douglas, as if it were half a lifetime. 'Five years.'

Hippolyta poked randomly with the brush, frowning. She had forgotten the mention of an earlier murder: could it have something to do with the present murders? Presumably it was some incident during the Jacobite times, perhaps related to the cache of silver coins in the boot. She grinned, remembering Colonel Verney and his tales of Dinnet House's history. It had been a happy evening.

'Aye, it's easy seen you've no done that too many times afore, quine,' came a voice from above her, and she dropped the brush with a clatter. On the step next to her was an old woman, dressed in dusty black and apparently constructed of wire and leather. 'Oh, it's the young doctor's wife, excuse me!' It was Martha, who had helped to clean Dinnet House.

'Ah, yes, sorry, I've just remembered I have to …' Hippolyta scrambled to her feet in a heap of petticoats, and set the brush and the cloth neatly back on the pew. 'Good day to you,' she added, and scurried back down the narrow staircase, nipping out of the church before Durris might appear after her. In her ears she could still hear Martha's voice: 'It's the young doctor's wife!', and for the life of her she could not judge whether it had been loud enough for Durris to hear. If it had, she had no wish to meet him.

She let herself back into the house, and breathed a sigh of relief. Then she looked about. Basilia and Patrick were in the parlour, the door half-closed, and she was playing her violin, her back to the hall door and apparently oblivious to Hippolyta. Further along the hall, the dining room door was open, and Ishbel was polishing the sideboard with some concentration – and a good deal more skill than Hippolyta had just been demonstrating in the church gallery, despite the kitten which was trying to catch the end of her cloth. Hippolyta slipped through the door to the servants' quarters and into the kitchen, hot from the cooking fire. The back door was open to let in some heavily damp air, in the hope of cooling down the room: it was not working, and as another of those heavy showers began that moment it felt as though the door had been slammed shut again. Mrs. Riach was in the pantry, her back to Hippolyta, and turned just as she approached.

'Oh, Mrs. Napier, the ham's gone! It's those cursed cats, ma'am!'

'All that lovely ham? Oh, no!'

'Aye, all of it. I had it on an ashet here in the meat safe.' She showed the wire-fronted cupboard to Hippolyta: the door had a sturdy wooden latch. It was closed tight. Inside was a plate of cold beef: the rest of the cupboard was empty.

'The safe was latched?' Hippolyta asked, trying not to sound too suspicious.

'Aye, it was. It must have been … maybe it wasn't?'

'But it's latched now,' Hippolyta pointed out.

'Aye …' Mrs. Riach was biting her lips ferociously.

'While I could see a clever cat working out how to push that open,' Hippolyta said with clarity, 'I'm not entirely sure, Mrs. Riach, why the cat would latch the door closed again afterwards. To stop the beef from escaping?'

'Maybe it fell shut,' said Mrs. Riach, a little helplessly.

'And,' said Hippolyta, almost reluctant to push on, 'two further questions, Mrs. Riach. If the cats took the ham, why did they not take the beef? And if they took the ham, what have they done with the ashet? Or have they taken cutlery and napkins, too?'

She gave Mrs. Riach a moment to digest the image, while she tried quite hard to stop herself acting the part of her mother. Then she felt the need to give the matter a final poke.

'Perhaps you would go to Mr. Strachan's shop and buy some more ham for the dinner just now? Thank you so much, Mrs. Riach.'

She turned and left the kitchen, and as she did so she heard a heavy flump behind her, as if Mrs. Riach's legs had given way and she had sunk heavily on to her chair. She was on her way back to the hall when something pale caught her eye, something in the corridor she had found. She stopped, and looked more closely. On the floor, outside the door to the first little bedchamber, was a blue and white china ashet, just big enough to hold the ham she had bought. Needless to say, it was empty. In a flash, she was along the corridor and trying the bedchamber door. It was firmly locked.

Chapter Fifteen

But there were more urgent things to think about before the guests arrived for dinner: she had to change, for one, for which she would require Ishbel's help, and before that she had to make sure that the Craigendarroch painting, which was just about dry, was arranged in its temporary frame and hung on the wall in the parlour, where it would appear to its best advantage. She had already removed one of her old Edinburgh scenes to leave room: in fact, she thought, she would take the ones to each side down as well, so as to leave an expanse of bare wall to frame her new work. She fetched it from the upstairs landing, where she had managed to find room to leave it safe, and pattered back downstairs and into the parlour. Basilia and Patrick were still playing – or had been, though now they seemed rather to be talking. They jumped as Hippolyta bustled in. Hippolyta noticed that his flute was out on the table, too.

'My dear, could you possibly put the flute away just now?' she asked, 'for the guests will not be long in arriving, and I'm trying to have this room ready to receive them.'

'They will not mind a flute on the table, surely?' Patrick asked.

'Maybe not in itself,' said Hippolyta, 'but it seems to signal that we are not quite prepared for them.'

'Surely not!' Miss Verney put in. 'A musical instrument is an adornment for any room, is it not? And seems to me to indicate a readiness to entertain one's guests.'

'Oh!' Hippolyta turned from her pictures to look at them. 'Oh, very well, then. Now, how does this look?'

'Oh, there's one of the kittens,' said Patrick, jumping up from the piano stool. The kitten was pawing plaintively at the outside of the parlour window. He left the room, and they could hear him going to open the front door to let it in. There was a shout, and a scramble from the hall.

'What on earth?' Miss Verney set her violin down comfortably close to Patrick's flute, and ran out into the hall after Hippolyta. Patrick was standing at the open door, a kitten in his arms.

'I opened the door to this one, and one of the others ran in past it. I think it has a blackbird,' he explained.

'Where has it gone? Alive or dead?' Hippolyta demanded.

'I have no idea. I think it went into the dining room.'

'I cannot abide birds in the house!' squeaked Miss Verney.

'Then why don't you go and get changed, Miss Verney, and we'll deal with this?' said Hippolyta breathlessly. She took one step towards the dining room, but at that moment there came a cry from Ishbel, still polishing, and the cat shot back out again and sprinted across the hall, dropping the occasional black feather in its path. Miss Verney instantly made a dash for the stairs. The cat, a look of determination on its little white face, made for the parlour. Hippolyta raced in after it.

'I'll stay here to chase it out the front door,' said Patrick, 'if it's still chaseable.'

'Right,' said Hippolyta, her eyes on the cat. Franklin, she reckoned, the second best hunter in the litter. They would have no birds left in the three parishes at this rate. Franklin had retreated under the parlour table and stopped to examine his prize, which was flapping its wings frantically. 'It's still alive, anyway. I'll see if I can get it away from him.'

She knelt beside the table, and gradually eased away the nearest chair. The cat glared at her, grabbed the bird more securely with his teeth, and backed towards the corner. Hippolyta, impeded by her skirts, slithered forward, hoping that she could at least alarm the cat into running for the parlour door where Patrick could shoo him back outside. The cat, however, elected to run the other way, weaving between the other chair legs and making a dive for another corner of the room, behind a sofa.

'Let it go, Franklin!' she called, and grabbing her skirts in a bundle she jumped up and perched to peer over the back of the sofa. Franklin glowered up at her but she was able to reach down with one hand and grab the scruff of his neck. The cat let out a growl of complaint which must have loosened his hold on the bird. The blackbird, shedding feathers, gave a squawk and darted upwards, battered briefly against Hippolyta's hair, and wobbled up to perch on the curtain rail. There it settled, head deep down into its shoulders, feathers unnaturally spiky, and glared down at cat and human. 'Oh, bother!'

'What's the matter?' Patrick poked his head in through the door. Hippolyta was brushing fluffy feathers out of her hair.

'It's up there.' She pointed. At least she had not already done her hair for dinner, she thought.

'Hm. What would you like to do about that?' Patrick asked. She expected him to start helping her with brushing herself off in the appreciative manner of a fond husband, but for some reason he found watching the bird more interesting.

'I have to go and change – so do you. Could we …' She pondered for a moment, watching Franklin settle down on the sofa to wash himself after his partial triumph. 'Could we just leave it there? It's not doing any harm: it probably needs time to sort itself out, comb its feathers, that kind of thing.'

'Recover from the shock,' Patrick agreed. 'Do you think it will stay peacefully up there? Should we open the window?'

'It is mild, certainly. I had intended to close the shutters and light the lamps, but perhaps we could take advantage of the evening air, if the fire is lit.'

'And perhaps, too,' added Patrick thoughtfully, 'we should gently deter anyone from standing or sitting directly beneath it?'

'Good idea!' said Hippolyta, and giggled. 'But close the front door, my dear, in case little Franklin decides he needs to replace it with a new prize!'

She opened the window to a blackbird-sized gap, checked to see that her painting was straight and set off to the best of advantages, picked up the Edinburgh pictures, glanced around to see that all else was in order – despite the musical instruments on the table – summoned Ishbel from the dining room, and went upstairs with her husband to change.

Hippolyta gazed down her first dinner table with moderate satisfaction. The numbers were not even, of course, thanks to the two Misses Strong, Miss Verney and Mrs. Kynoch, squawking away at Patrick in her usual disastrous garments. By contrast, Mrs. Strachan on his other side looked tense, but beautiful. Dr. Durward and Miss Ada kept conversation lively in the middle of the long table, even making little Mrs. Douglas smile nervously, pale in an old-fashioned gown of cloudy muslin, high-waisted as if she had had it as her dinner gown all the days of her marriage. Mr. Douglas sat on one side of Hippolyta herself, and Mr. Strong on the other, a solemn enough pair but both out determined enough to enjoy themselves. Basilia sat between Mr. Strong and Dr. Durward, who were both kindly to her in their own ways, and Miss Ada was the one Hippolyta had elected to sit between the minister and Mr. Strachan as she was more than capable of keeping them separate. Low, shallow plates of white soup had just been cleared away, with the tureens, and Mrs. Riach had proudly arranged the dishes for the main course around the table, helped by Ishbel with an expression of deep concentration. Amongst them, Hippolyta noted with satisfaction, were four ashets of Mr. Strachan's finest York ham, and Patrick lighted upon his nearest one as soon as his guests would let him. She gave herself a little nod. Mrs. Strachan, she saw, put very little food on her own plate, and Mr. Strachan who was seated in the middle of the table glanced in that direction more than once, though Hippolyta could not quite see his face. She turned to offer some boiled onions to Dr. Durward, and found that he, too, was gazing down the table at Mrs. Strachan: Hippolyta waited a long moment before he realised that she had spoken to him. Was he worried again about those patent medicines, she wondered? Mrs. Strachan certainly looked rather pale, and perhaps, now she herself came to study her elegant guest, the dark circles under her eyes were rather more pronounced than they had been on the day of the funeral.

The minister leaned past Hippolyta with a polite nod and said to Dr. Durward:

'I had that sheriff's officer, Dod Durris, in the kirk today asking about the Burns Mortification. Has he been to see you, Doctor?'

'My maid said he called, but I wasn't in,' said Dr. Durward.

'What about yourself, Mr. Strong?'

'Aye,' said the lawyer after a pause. 'He's been.'

'And was he asking you about the Burns Mortification? I tellt him I kenned very little about the whole business, to be honest with you,' said the minister, looking anxious.

'Well, that's the truth.' Mr. Strachan had perhaps intended to mutter these words only to himself, but everyone stopped and looked at him. 'Well, it is,' he insisted. 'Mr. Douglas has no head for business, he'd be the first to admit it.'

'I would,' agreed the minister sadly.

'So why he took it upon himself to invite another trustee on to the trust I have no idea,' Strachan went on.

'We needed another man,' said Mr. Strong, his lips pursed.

'And the Colonel was a very sensible choice,' said Dr. Durward reasonably. 'You saw the business-like way he took all the papers off for examination. I'd have thought you would have approved of that, Strachan.'

'Aye, but –'

'May I ask, Mr. Strachan,' Hippolyta began bravely, and the men fell silent. 'May I ask why you thought Colonel Verney would not be a good trustee? I know nothing of these things, of course, but I did wonder what made a good trustee, in your view, and what a bad one?'

Strachan stared at her for a long moment, his dark eyes cold. He clearly had a manner for the shop, she thought, trying to hold his gaze steadily, and a manner – or lack of manners – for his social life.

'He had no notion of the business. Not of the trust, nor of the scholars, nor of the school, nor even of Scots law,' he said at last. 'I told him so myself,' he added, still holding her gaze, and she wondered if he guessed that she had heard him threaten Colonel Verney.

'Dod Durris mentioned irregularities,' said the minister helplessly, as if he knew he had lit a fuse.

'Irregularities?' said Dr. Durward and Strachan at once, though in rather different tones. Durward looked baffled. Strachan looked as if he were about to explode.

'He has no right,' Strachan added, almost spitting.

'He has every right,' said Strong precisely.

'If he thinks maybe somebody made a mistake, and maybe Colonel Verney found it out …' said the minister, trying to placate his fellow trustees.

'A mistake?' Strachan demanded. 'And if the Colonel found it out, then what? Whoever made the *mistake* murdered him?'

'My dear fellow,' began Dr. Durward, and Miss Strong grabbed Mr. Strachan's arm in firm fingers.

'Remember where you are, Mr. Strachan,' she said firmly, with the least nod at Basilia. Strachan flung up his hands to flick her off, and upended his beef, rich in gravy, over the table cloth. Hippolyta stifled a little gasp of dismay, and looked about for Mrs. Riach. The housekeeper was standing by the sideboard with a little grin of delight on her face. Hippolyta had to nudge her to call her to her senses.

'Cloths, Mrs. Riach, please,' she hissed, and the housekeeper pulled herself together and trotted out of the room.

It took a few minutes to sort everything out, while the Misses Strong involved themselves on each side of him in cleaning Mr. Strachan down and talking incessantly around him, so that he had no space into which to speak any more angry words. When he was settled again at the table with a clean napkin and a fresh plate of beef, Mrs. Kynoch addressed Patrick in her high voice, loudly enough to involve the whole table in the conversation just in case they were tempted to revert to the previous subject.

'Dr. Napier, I hope your marriage has not prevented you from playing in company! Will we be lucky enough to hear you this evening?'

'If no one else wishes to play, then perhaps,' said Patrick, with a smile.

'Does Mrs. Napier play?' asked Miss Ada, with a mischievous look at Hippolyta.

'Not well enough, I fear!' said Hippolyta. 'I am his most appreciative audience, though.' She glanced at Patrick, but his attention was on his plate.

'I remember some lovely duets – and indeed trios, weren't there? – with Miss Verney, do I not?' asked the minister. Mrs. Kynoch shot him a look across the table.

'Oh, yes: I believe I did hear you both play together once or twice,' she said.

'More than once or twice, I'm sure!' Mr. Douglas went on. 'I remember you played beautifully together.'

Hippolyta looked across at Basilia. She was blushing prettily.

'We are fortunate to enjoy the same style of music,' she remarked.

'Mm,' said Hippolyta. Fortunate indeed: she had tried quite hard to enjoy Patrick's favourite old music, but Oswald and the Earl of Kellie sounded very dated to her ears. She preferred something like Thomas Moore, with which, to be fair, Patrick often indulged her.

'We might play a little this evening,' Basilia offered, meeting Patrick's eye down the table. Her voice, Hippolyta suddenly noticed, was rather lower than usual, with something in it that made her feel just a little uncomfortable. 'That piece we played through earlier was coming along very well.'

'Oh! You are still playing together?' Mrs. Kynoch was surprised.

'Well, since I am staying here, Mrs. Kynoch, and I must practise, Dr. Napier was kind enough to accompany me, weren't you, Dr. Napier?' This time her voice carried a distinct purr. Hippolyta assumed what she hoped was a bland expression: she did not like the idea of her new friend trying to flirt with her husband at Hippolyta's own dinner table. That was definitely taking advantage of someone else's hospitality.

'No doubt you will both delight us after dinner,' she said firmly. 'Mrs. Strachan, I am sure you play beautifully?'

'I? No, no, not at all,' said Mrs. Strachan, flustered. 'Miss Strong is a very accomplished player, though.'

'Then Miss Strong, perhaps you will also perform for us?' Hippolyta asked.

'I'd be delighted,' said Miss Strong briskly. 'It's always a pleasure to be allowed to play on Dr. Napier's piano. Our own is good, but Dr. Napier's is a superior instrument, by far.'

'I was fortunate to inherit it from my parents,' Patrick explained with a smile. 'My brother has no interest in music, and I have no sisters, so I laid claim to it as swiftly as was proper.'

'No sisters!' Miss Ada sighed enviously, with a laughing glance at her own sister.

'Ada!' warned her sister.

'Ach, I was only pulling your leg,' said Ada. 'You've this place looking bonny, Mrs. Napier,' she went on. 'Your things all arrived on the cart all right in the end, then?'

'Yes, in the end,' said Hippolyta. It was true: the candlesticks and fresh paintings, the pretty épergne and bright floral curtains, all made a difference to the horrid old dining room, and in the candlelight even the mean, narrow table looked more like something designed to allow them all to join in the conversation. The parlour had been looking lovely too, she thought: she just hoped that the poor battered blackbird had escaped quietly through the window, without leaving more than a couple of feathers behind.

'I heard that something more arrived, more that just your baggage?' Dr. Durward raised his eyebrows.

'Well, we think so,' said Patrick. 'A large crate disappeared from the cart during the night, or its contents did. The crate was left broken up. But it was not our crate, nor our contents.'

'And no one knows who took it?' asked Miss Strong, though Hippolyta thought she probably had enough of an ear to local gossip to know exactly who was suspected of what.

'I think I might have an idea,' she said, 'but it would not be quite right to say, without proof.'

Mr. Strong nodded approvingly.

'I think you said your father was a lawyer, Mrs. Napier?' he asked.

'That's right.'

'Aye, aye.' He nodded again.

'But what do you think was in the crate?' demanded Miss Ada. 'Surely you could tell us that?'

'Well,' said Hippolyta, 'I think it might have been a barrel of brandy.'

She glanced about the table. The minister looked sorrowful, and his wife disapproving; the Misses Strong were excited at the mystery. Mrs. Kynoch was less excited and more interested, but she was watching Mrs. Strachan, who had only toyed with her main course. Dr. Durward laughed at the idea of a wandering brandy barrel, and Mr. Strachan looked furious.

'I suppose it had come into Aberdeen and the duty had not been paid on it,' Dr. Durward suggested, when he had stopped laughing.

'I suppose so, if I am right. Whatever it was, it seems to have joined our baggage at Aberdeen harbour, anyway.'

'Ha! In my limited experience, it is much more likely to lose baggage at the harbour, rather than gain it! A shame it escaped again before you had the chance to claim it, Mrs. Napier!'

'The daughter of an Edinburgh lawyer would have done nothing so dishonest, I am sure,' said Mr. Strong, just stopping short of wagging a finger at Dr. Durward. The doctor laughed again.

'I am teasing Mrs. Napier, as I am sure she is well aware, Mr. Strong! Taking the liberty of an old acquaintance with your husband, my dear Mrs. Napier. I hope you don't mind.' He made a little bow, quite aware, Hippolyta thought, of his own good looks.

'Not at all, Dr. Durward. Ah, pudding! Thank you, Mrs. Riach.'

Mrs. Riach had made the most of the garden's soft fruits, and had even managed to obtain some ice. Whatever her shortcomings, or at least the difficulties in dealing with her, she was certainly a very accomplished cook, Hippolyta thought. And to have produced all this, with only Ishbel for help, in such a short time in a small, old-fashioned kitchen: she probably deserved her occasional indulgence in brandy.

With appreciative noises, the guests finished their various fools and flummeries. Hippolyta was waiting for a suitable gap in the conversation to catch the eye of Mrs. Kynoch or Mrs. Strachan and invite the ladies to leave with her for the parlour, when Mrs. Strachan herself cleared her throat and asked,

'Mrs. Napier, have you had any chance at all, I wonder, to try a drawing of Craigendarroch? Mrs. Napier is a skilled artist, my dear,' she said to her husband. Hippolyta thought there was a very slight quiver in her voice.

'Indeed I have made a first, poor attempt, which you are very welcome to examine, Mrs. Strachan, since it was at your kind suggestion. Ladies, shall we rise?' It was the first time she had done more than follow her mother or some other hostess, and she hoped she had timed it correctly, but Patrick nodded slightly to her with the ghost of a smile to support her. The gentlemen rose as Mrs. Riach set brandy and port on the table. 'The painting is in the parlour, Mrs. Strachan: please come this way.'

The guests had not spent long in the parlour before dinner: the blackbird had surveyed them morosely from the curtain rail, unnoticed by the company, and the intending bird-murderer, Franklin, had rolled on the sofa cushions and been made much of by Mrs. Kynoch. He had now absented himself, and the ladies were free to arrange themselves on the seats without having to consult a cat. Hippolyta glanced up discreetly: the curtain rail was bare of wounded birds. Relieved, she closed the window and rang for tea. Miss Verney picked up her violin and took it over to the piano in a proprietorial manner that Hippolyta found herself not quite liking, and the Misses Strong enveloped little Mrs. Douglas – who was not really little, Hippolyta realised, but seemed so as she was so self-effacing, and took her to the sofa to discuss the poor of the parish. Mrs. Kynoch settled Mrs. Strachan on another sofa, and was turning to find herself a seat nearby when Hippolyta leaned towards her. Basilia had begun to play the piano softly, and it was possible to exchange a few private words.

'Is Mrs. Strachan quite well? Is there anything I can fetch for her?'

'I believe she is quite well, thank you, Mrs. Napier. She has not been sleeping very well, and her appetite is not good.'

'Yes … is there anything my husband could do for her?'

'No, no! I'm sure she has no wish to see a physician! Begging your pardon, Mrs. Napier, of course, with two physicians here in the house, but I believe she has no medical complaint.'

'I shall make sure Mrs. Riach hurries with the tea, in any case,' said Hippolyta anxiously, and went to find out what Mrs. Riach was doing. She slipped through the door at the back of the hall and into the kitchen, where she found Ishbel propped against the workbench, thin arms folded across her chest, and Mrs. Riach sitting on the edge of her usual seat by the fire, knees wide and hands on her thighs, roaring with laughter. Even though she saw Hippolyta immediately, it took her a moment or two to recover and make some attempt to stand.

'You'll be wanting your tea,' she announced, gasping a little.

'Yes, when you're quite ready, Mrs. Riach,' Hippolyta said, a little tartly. 'I am glad to see you enjoying your evening so much.'

'Och, well, if you must invite the four men that dislike each other most in the whole village, ma'am, you have to laugh or else you'd just go and hide the good china. Ishbel, is the water hot there?'

Hippolyta had no idea what to say to that, so she left the kitchen with a glare at the housekeeper which did nothing for either of them. She prayed that Patrick was keeping the peace in the dining room, and paused for a moment at the closed door, listening for raised voices. There was nothing but what she thought sounded like amicable murmuring from within. She took a deep breath, and checked her appearance again in the hall mirror: the elaborate hairstyle with which she had experimented seemed at least to be staying in place, and the candlelight flattered her gold hair and pale skin. She grinned, trying to give herself a little more confidence. Should she really show the painting to Mrs. Strachan now, when Mrs. Strachan did not seem well? She wanted her to be in a properly appreciative mood, to be impressed enough to want to be better acquainted with the artist, and even, if such a thing were possible, then to turn to the artist's husband in any time of medical need, not to spend her money on patent medicines from Aberdeen. It was as if Dr. Durward's challenge had become, in her mind, the gateway to Ballater society: if she could not meet it, she would never fit in. Ridiculous, she told herself, and turned to the parlour door. She would see how things went: the painting would keep for another time.

Basilia was still playing when she went in, and the Strongs had moved on to discussion of a project to mend the parish's mortcloths and other fabrics before they fell apart, according to Miss Strong. Mrs. Strachan looked up at her entrance.

'Now, Mrs. Napier, may I see your painting? I have so looked forward to seeing it.'

'Of course!' Hippolyta turned. 'Here it is!'

She gestured to the clean white space between the other paintings, dusted and spotless so nothing would detract from her delicate watercolour of birch-laden headland and cloud-light sky. The ladies turned to look, and there was a collective gasp. Hippolyta stared.

The painting was still there, but directly beside it was a strange shape on the clean white wall. She frowned. It was red and black, with other colours she could not quite identify.

'What …?'

'Looks like a bird's got in,' suggested Miss Ada helpfully.

'Oh, no!'

That was why Franklin was nowhere to be seen. The blackbird must have made a bid for freedom, gone for the door instead of the window, and smashed into the wall. On the floorboards at the foot of the wall, in a pathetic heap, was the remains of the bird, well chewed. It had left only blood and feathers beside her picture.

There was a snort behind her. Hippolyta spun round, to find Mrs. Strachan clutching her hand to her mouth, eyes wide. She was laughing – more elegantly than Mrs. Riach, it was true, but laughing nonetheless.

'Oh, I am so sorry, Mrs. Napier! And the poor bird!' she cried. 'But I am so grateful: I have not laughed for days!' She dissolved again for a moment, and then recovered. 'I have been so worried about all this murder business at Dinnet House I have not been able to sleep or think straight, and you have given me a moment of sanity! Thank you, Mrs. Napier!'

Chapter Sixteen

'It is a charming painting, Mrs. Napier: I look forward to seeing much more of your work,' said Mrs. Strachan, a little stiff with embarrassment, as Ishbel cleared away what was left of the bird. When she had gone, Mrs. Strachan continued, while Hippolyta poured tea for everyone. The after dinner cup was taken with more than usual enthusiasm. 'It seems only fair that both you and Miss Verney here should know what - what we all know, I think?' She looked about her anxiously: the Misses Strong and Mrs. Kynoch nodded, and Mrs. Douglas considered, eyes wide, before nodding, too.

'I think I ken what you're talking of, though it was before our time here,' she whispered, and Mrs. Kynoch patted her hand.

'I'm sure you've heard about it.'

'But what?' asked Hippolyta. 'What is it?'

Mrs. Strachan smoothed her beautiful skirts, her perfect posture consorting oddly with her nervous expression, and glanced at Mrs. Kynoch for support. Mrs. Kynoch nodded to her, encouraging her to go on. Mrs. Strachan took a deep breath.

'Twenty years ago – very nearly exactly twenty years ago – Dinnet House was my home. It had been my family's home for many years. I lived there with my father, and we had a small household, just a maid and a manservant. Very much like you, Miss Verney, I believe.'

'It sounds almost exactly the same,' breathed Basilia. Her face was set, frowning in concentration.

'My mother died when I was very young,' Mrs. Strachan, 'and I scarcely remember her, but my father and I were close, and it was a happy household. I would have been about your age, too, I think, Miss Verney: I had just marked my twentieth birthday.

'You'll no doubt have heard some of the stories about Dinnet House: the hidden Jacobite silver, for example.' She gave a little half-smile as Miss Ada nodded enthusiastically. 'I never found it! Though as children, several of us, my friends and I, would poke sticks into holes in the garden, hoping that something might clink and shine! There were tales of giants, too.'

'And a murder,' added Basilia, who was sitting on the very edge of the piano stool, gripping it tightly. Her toes in their little evening slippers pressed hard into the carpet.

'We never told stories of a murder,' said Mrs. Strachan clearly, 'because then it had not happened.'

Hippolyta found she was holding her breath. She set her cup back in her saucer, trying not to let it clatter, and set it on the table, for fear of dropping it. Mrs. Strachan's cup had been laid aside, and her hands were closely clasped in her lap, the fine cloth of her evening gloves twisted around her fingers. She seemed to need another moment to prepare herself: when she spoke again, her low voice shook a little.

'One night, I had gone to bed early, feeling a little chilly. My maid helped me to change, and left me. I slept very deeply, but in the morning I woke to the sound of a terrible scream. I shall never forget that sound, or the way it seemed to echo against the windows, around the house. For a second I thought I had dreamed it, or that my dream had somehow transformed the cry of a bird, or a fox, into something awful, but I knew it was not true. I seized my shawl, and ran out on to the landing. The maid was standing in the hall below me, shrieking, her arms in the air, calling, I at last understood, for help. I could see nothing amiss: I hurried down the stairs and slapped her face, thinking she was having a fit of hysterics. In a way she was, but with good reason. She had risen and gone downstairs into the kitchen as usual, and found my father's manservant dead on the floor – stabbed.'

Basilia gasped, and in Hippolyta's mind all she could see was Forman, lying sprawled on the kitchen floor in his own blackened blood.

'I called out for my father, but there was no reply. I ran upstairs to knock on his bedroom door – I remember how the panels shook as I hammered them - then ran inside, but his bed had not been slept in. When I came back downstairs I found the kitchen door was open, and when I ran out into the garden, there was my father – all silvered with dew – dead on the path. I knelt by him and took his hand in mine: it was cold, and he was stiff. He must have been lying there all night.'

She was dry-eyed, focusing on her memories, but Basilia started to sob.

'But did they find out who murdered them?' Hippolyta asked, and regretted immediately that her voice sounded quite so hard and business-like. Miss Ada bounced on the sofa, eager to speak, but her sister pressed hard on her arm. Mrs. Strachan drew herself back from the past, and gave a little shake of her head, half-denial, half flinging off the memories.

'There was a great deal of hunting done at the time: the sheriff himself took up residence in the inn for a month, I believe. My father was a wealthy and influential man. Of course I was only a girl, and they told me very little. They questioned me, gently, to find if anything was missing from the house, and they asked me if my father and the manservant could have had some kind of falling out, but it seemed to me very unlikely for they were two quiet and kindly men, and as far as I could understand it, the knife that was used was never found. But I must tell you, for it may explain a little about his manners in the last week, that my husband was, I believe, the sheriff's prime candidate for the murderer.'

She looked down at her lap, biting her lip. Hippolyta found herself biting her own, too.

'Forgive me,' she said, 'for this is all so strange to me. You were not married at the time?'

'No, we were not: and there were rumours that my father had objected to Allan's suit, which would give him a reason to murder him. But that was not the case: Allan had not declared himself,' she gave a little shudder, as if it hurt her to be so open. 'But his intentions, his wishes, were, ah, fairly clear, and my father would certainly have received him very happily as a son-in-law. He had said so to me in private. And I am glad he had, for it felt as if we had his blessing when we did marry, a year later.'

Hippolyta considered a moment, trying to phrase her next question in a way that did not imply her own suspicions.

'No doubt,' she began carefully, 'Mr. Strachan had some good reason to show for his not having been near Dinnet House on the night of the murders? For if the sheriff was suspicious, even when Mr. Strachan was innocent, he would need a good defence.'

She swallowed, not sure if she had gauged it correctly. Mrs. Strachan paused, and Mrs. Kynoch shot Hippolyta a sharp glance which Hippolyta could not quite read, out of the corner of her eye.

'Allan and his friend Dr. Durward had been drinking in his father's cellars. It was not a good reason not to be near Dinnet House, but it was a fortunate one. They were found unconscious in the cellar the next morning together, much the worse for drink, when everyone was looking for Allan, thinking he had murdered my father and absconded in shame.'

'They were young men,' Mrs. Kynoch broke in gently. 'Every young man has his daft moments: this one was just very well timed.'

'Yes, of course,' said Mrs. Strachan. She lifted her teacup with a rattle, and took a long reviving sip. Hippolyta reached out a hand to take and refill it.

'But they never found the person who really carried out the crimes?' she asked again, trying to grasp the parallels in her head. Mrs. Strachan shook her head.

'Never. I moved into the manse with dear Mrs. Kynoch to take care of me, and in a year I married Allan, and we put the house up for rent. Uneventfully, as it happens, until the recent terrible events.' She looked round at Basilia, who was white as a sheet, eyes startling red.

'I don't understand!' whispered Basilia. 'What has happened here? Was my uncle killed for something he did, or just because he was in the wrong place? And what does it have to do with something that happened twenty years ago?'

'We've all been wondering that,' said Miss Ada, with only the least hint of macabre glee. 'Would it be the same mannie striking again?'

'Ada!' snapped her sister.

The gentlemen joined them soon afterwards, and Hippolyta was alert enough to note an expression of intense relief on her husband's face. Clearly the gentlemen had been continuing their heated discussions on the Burns Mortification, and while Dr. Durward was as serene and entertaining as usual, the minister had a look of baffled discomfort and headed straight to sit by his wife, taking his hand in hers as much for his own consolation as hers. Strachan scowled furiously in a general manner around the room, and Hippolyta could well see how any self-respecting sheriff would like to investigate him for any murder in the vicinity. He must have been an uncomfortable person to live with, she thought, comparing him unfavourably with her lovely, peaceable Patrick: in society Strachan seemed generally to look as if throat-cutting would be the only thing that could relieve his feelings.

'Shall we have some music?' Patrick asked. 'Who would like to play?'

'There is no room to dance, though!' Hippolyta spread her hands to indicate the size of the room. 'But Miss Strong, I should be delighted if you would oblige us.'

Miss Strong was perfectly willing to oblige: the days must be gone, Hippolyta thought, when her skills might be helpful in attracting her a husband, and so presumably she played only for the love of it. She played a few Scottish and Irish airs with skill but without pretensions, and in one Mrs. Kynoch and Miss Ada sang with her, Miss Ada taking the alto and Mrs. Kynoch squeaking the soprano line with surprising accuracy but limited artistic effect. Nevertheless, the audience clapped appreciatively.

'Now, Miss Verney,' said Hippolyta generously. Basilia did not hesitate, but seized her violin and caught Patrick's eye.

'Dr. Napier?'

'Of course,' he said, snatching up his flute. Mrs. Kynoch took the piano part, to Hippolyta's surprise, and the effect was really very pretty, if relentlessly old-fashioned. Basilia kept her gaze firmly on Patrick, presumably for the rhythm, though how anyone could catch the right rhythm from a flautist had always been a mystery to Hippolyta. She watched as Patrick put the flute to his lips, considered, dropped it again, blew silently into it, shook it and rubbed it between his hands, and all the while Basilia watched him closely, eyes fixed on his face and hands, and for a miracle they came in united on their notes as if they had been playing together all their lives. When they finished, and Patrick bowed to the two ladies, Basilia curtseyed prettily and beamed all over her flushed face, eyes sparkling, and it was as much as Hippolyta could do to applaud and praise with the rest, and with a good grace. How long would it be until Miss Verney found herself somewhere to go? Hippolyta decided that she might try to assist her, and soon.

The guests did not stay very late, as it was a Saturday night: Mrs. Strachan in any case looked exhausted, though somehow easier in herself than Hippolyta had previously seen her. There were no carriages: the manse was next door, Mrs. Kynoch five minutes' walk away up the hill, the Strachans further up again, the Strongs across the green and Dr. Durward down by the river, so that they would all be in their own houses in less than a quarter of an hour. Hippolyta, used to a queue of chairs and carriages taking guests across Edinburgh, thought it very relaxed and pleasant, and hardly like the end of a dinner party at all.

Back in the parlour, they talked over the evening in a desultory way: Hippolyta described the incident with the dead blackbird and the painting, and Patrick told them how the debate on the management of the Burns Mortification had taken over the gentlemen's conversation again, but only in a circular, irritable, useless fashion that had succeeded in annoying everyone except the minister, who was simply baffled by the whole thing. Franklin the kitten wandered in, looking superior, with a couple of his siblings, and gradually the atmosphere in the house seemed to lose the tension of hospitality and revelations and quarrels, and Hippolyta rang for tea. It was only after it had arrived and Patrick had settled at the table, a cat on his lap, and Basilia had pulled out her sewing and curled into the arm of the daybed, and Hippolyta had pulled out her sketchpad and begun a drawing of the window with its pattern of leaves outside in the evening light, that she had found herself able to tell Patrick what they had discovered about the murders of twenty years ago – and even then she made sure to glance over at Basilia now and again, to see that she confirmed the story and was not made more anxious by it than she had been already.

'But what an outlandish thing to have happened!' said Patrick, when they had done their best to explain it. 'To have an unsolved pair of murders happen once, in such a fashion, is strange enough: but to find then that the very same thing had happened twenty years before, in the same house, in the same way, and also to a manservant and his master, is more than extraordinary!'

'You never found its match in any of your medical jurisprudence lectures?' Hippolyta asked hopefully.

'Good heavens, no, never. It was not the kind of thing we looked at, in any case. Twenty years ago … Well, I was a child, and you two were barely thought of! No wonder we did not know of it. I had heard stories that a murder had been committed at Dinnet House, of course: your uncle frequently mentioned it, but I never realised that the murder had been within living memory.'

'I'm not even sure my uncle did: I don't know that I should have cared to live in the house if I had known.' Basilia shivered.

'But for it to be so similar …' Hippolyta still found it inexplicable. 'Do you think it means that the same murderer who carried out the first attacks also killed Colonel Verney and Forman? Or is it someone who was well aware of the story, and copied the method?'

Patrick shrugged.

'Impossible to tell, until we find the person who did it.'

'But what could possibly be the reason?'

They all stared at each other, but no suggestions were forthcoming. Hippolyta could only think to herself that if the murderer turned out to be the same person that had committed the crimes long ago, Durris could not possibly suspect Patrick. That was one crumb of comfort.

She lay awake thinking about the matter long into the night, alone, for Patrick had announced that he needed to finish some work in the study. If the murderer were indeed the same person, now and in 1809, did that rule anyone out besides the three of them? Strachan, Dr. Durward, Mr. Strong – they had all been here then, but not Mr. Douglas, the minister. Strachan and Dr. Durward were tall enough, but Mr. Strong would have had to stand on that kitchen chair, the action she found so improbable. She found it even more unlikely it was the serious, severe Mr. Strong that she tried to picture, suddenly leaping up on a chair and asking Forman on some odd pretext to stand with his back to him: could he have pretended fear of a mouse? The thought made her smile, but at the same time it seemed more unlikely than ever. Strachan had, of course, proof that he was somewhere else during the first murders – and so, then, did Dr. Durward, who had produced proof for the second murders, too. The thought struck her that Mrs. Strachan, with her willowy elegance, was also tall enough to have attacked Forman without the aid of the chair, but the mere idea was abhorrent – but she had been in the house when the first murders had been committed, and who knew what quarrel she might have had with her father? She shook her head briskly. The idea was ridiculous. Mrs. Strachan was not a killer, and Mrs. Kynoch and the Misses Strong – either of them, she thought, could slip strong poison into a cup of tea if they felt the situation required it – were all too small and again, the chair would have to come into play. She tutted to herself.

Who else could have been here twenty years ago, of the people she knew? Of the people she had been thinking about? If anyone had been acting suspiciously in the village, Mr. Brookes came top of the list, but he was a newcomer: unless he made a habit of visiting Ballater and carrying out a couple of violent murders, then disappearing again for twenty years, then returning to do it again, he seemed an unlikely candidate.

An idea struck her: had Colonel Verney had any previous connexion with Ballater, or with Dinnet House? Basilia had said that he had come to the place for the wells, after finding Bath unpalatable, but how had he heard of the place? It was not on everyone's map. What was her reasoning here: was it that Colonel Verney might have been known to the murderer all along, or that Colonel Verney, who would have been an active, fit army officer in 1809, might have carried out the first murders and the second ones were some kind of revenge? She wondered if Basilia knew anything (though she could hardly suggest to her that her much-missed uncle had been a murderer), or perhaps Mrs. Strachan might know. What had Mrs. Strachan's name been when she had lived at Dinnet House? Would Colonel Verney have mentioned it ever? She must ask Basilia.

Her mind wandered into a side street. Basilia … It was all very well that Basilia had been used to playing duets with Patrick, and no doubt at all played them much better than Hippolyta ever would, but that did not give her any rights to ogle him like that across the dinner table, or indeed along her violin. Hippolyta had been pleased to find a friend of her own age in Ballater, but not so pleased that she could not give her up if Basilia continued to behave in quite such a possessive way. Hippolyta scowled into the darkness, and wondered if Basilia was sleeping well – or was dreaming, perhaps, of Patrick! Furious, she sat up sharply – and just as she did so, she heard the click of the front door shutting.

She flung back the covers and marched across to the window. Yes, there on the path outside, complete with bonnet and, as far as she could see, gloves, was Basilia Verney. Hippolyta had to restrain herself from stamping her foot. She would swear to it that Miss Verney had never suffered from sleepwalking in her life. Miss Verney reached the gate, and paused: some instinct made Hippolyta duck quickly behind the shutter, and peep round. Basilia looked back at the house carefully. Was she bidding it farewell? The hope jumped into Hippolyta's heart, but then she dismissed it. Basilia's close examination of the front of the house had been much more in the nature of someone checking to see she was not being followed. Well, if a follower was what Basilia Verney did not want, then a follower was exactly what Basilia Verney would get.

She was down the stairs and in the hallway before she wondered if she should think better of her idea. It was hardly the act of a respectable married woman, hurrying off into the night on her own: on the other hand, it was something she had always longed to be able to do, and here, in quiet Ballater, she might be less likely to be caught than she would have been in busy Edinburgh. Her cloak and bonnet were in the hall press, taken off in a hurry earlier, and there was an old pair of boots there, too. She was still wondering as her feet seemed to find their own way into the boots, and the cloak slipped eagerly around her shoulders and the bonnet seemed to fall directly on to her head: it felt odd sitting loose there when her hair was down, but she tied the strings tight and hoped it would not slip sideways. Then she tried the front door in one gentle hand: it was, as she had expected, unlocked. She pulled it open, slipped through as soon as she could, and eased it shut behind her. Then she trotted quickly down the path to the gate, and surveyed the open green in front of her.

It was a clear night, after the hammerstrike showers of the day. The moon was a mere sliver, but there was still a pallor in the sky from the day, deep grey blue above shading to a film of yellow in the western horizon. The shapes of things were easy to see: the white roses in the garden, and their petals pummelled to the ground by the rain, stood out almost glowing, but further away the details were hazy and colours indistinct. It was a movement, however, that caught her eye: to her left, downhill from the gate, she saw Basilia in her bonnet, heading for the main street down to the river, the bridge, the inn, and the road to Aberdeen. What was her goal?

Hippolyta tried to judge the best moment to leave the shelter of the gate, not too soon that Basilia would turn and see her, nor yet too late that she might lose her. When Basilia disappeared around the corner of the first house on the street, Hippolyta darted after her at last, feeling a blissful freedom not to be weighed down by bustling skirts. She was almost silent as she ran, but she kept an eye open, nevertheless, for the night watchman, in case she was spotted.

At the corner, she paused and peered round it. For a moment she could not see her target, then Basilia stepped out of the shadow of a building, making steady progress down the street. Hippolyta hurried into the same shadow, using it to hide herself while she watched Basilia approach the turn in the road that led off to Aberdeen. Basilia passed it, not even glancing to her left. Next there was the inn, rising up like a confused heap of crates beyond the road, a few windows still lit this late. It seemed quiet, though, and Basilia again passed without giving it more than half a look. She had to be heading for the bridge, the broad stone bridge that would take her over the Dee to Pannanich.

There would be no hiding places on the bridge, but on the other hand Basilia could hardly change direction on it, either. The only thing she could do would be to haul herself on to the parapet and fling herself into the Dee, and Hippolyta could not quite see Basilia doing that, certainly not in her bonnet and gloves. She edged after her, taking shelter where she could, keeping her eyes close on Basilia as she emerged from the shadows and began to cross the bridge. Hippolyta tiptoed to the end of the parapet, ready to duck down behind it if Basilia – or anyone else – happened to look in her direction.

Basilia was walking more slowly now, meandering from side to side, admiring, Hippolyta thought, the broad river in the reflected hues of the sky. Then another movement caught Hippolyta's eye: there was another night time wanderer, this time heading towards them, towards the town, over the bridge from Pannanich. Who was it? She strained to see.

It was a man, no doubt about it: a man in a tall hat, pale breeches and, as far as Hippolyta could make out, a brown coat. She watched closely. The man neared Basilia, removed his hat politely, and then swept Basilia into a passionate embrace. For a moment, Hippolyta considered running to her friend's rescue – but only briefly. It was immediately clear that she welcomed the embrace completely.

A brown coat, walking in from Pannanich at night: perhaps now she knew what he had been up to wandering around the village so secretively. It had to be Brookes.

Chapter Seventeen

Hippolyta, tired though she was, was shocked awake on Sunday morning by the sudden alarming recollection that church, that morning, was coming to them, rather than the more usual other way around.

A fear that by some mischance Miss Verney should return to the house first, from her secret assignation on the bridge to Pannanich, and lock the front door again to cover the traces of her night-time expedition, had left Hippolyta scuttling back almost as soon as she had observed the couple meet. Her head was full of faintly exciting visions of having to climb in through a window of her own house – exciting, but not entirely desirable, and tricky to explain to Mrs. Riach, should she find out. Or indeed to Patrick – if he ever noticed.

It was early when Hippolyta woke, though Patrick was evidently already up and about. She decided to dress before breakfast, and not to ring for Ishbel: she and Mrs. Riach would be busy enough this morning, besides having their own parish church to attend. Hippolyta wrestled bad-temperedly with her stays, and slumped, as much as they would let her, at the dressing table to try to arrange her own hair. She did not feel it was a great success, but gave up in the end with a style a little too plain for Edinburgh salons but still, she hoped, more interesting than Miss Verney's pale blonde locks.

Hm, she thought sharply, Miss Verney. Flirting with Patrick and meeting Mr. Brookes at the same time: what kind of a person was she? And Mr. Brookes must be old enough to be her father, and sickly besides. But at least that would mean that Basilia's attentions were not wholly focussed on Patrick. And Patrick's attentions?

She glared at herself in the mirror, the mirror she had sat before in her Edinburgh home since she was a child, the mirror her maid had smiled and wept at her in, the morning of her wedding. Had those tears been a bad sign? Had she made a mistake? Was Patrick not the man she had thought he was?

Well, she decided, even if he was not, she was certainly not going to go running back to Edinburgh. This was her home now, and Patrick was her husband, and whatever was wrong would just have to be sorted out, and that was that.

She gave herself a firm nod, poked her hair once more, and abandoned the mirror to go and see Mrs. Riach.

Mrs. Riach's good mood of the previous night was lingering still, and even Hippolyta's suggestion that the cats be kept out of the parlour after breakfast earned her nothing more than a dark, throaty chuckle.

'Aye, that'd be for the best,' she agreed. No doubt Ishbel had told her of the unfortunate blackbird.

'Indeed. By the way, Mrs. Riach, the ham last night was delicious. Dr. Napier particularly remarked on it.'

'Aye,' said Mrs. Riach with deep satisfaction, 'he's never liked ham.'

Before Hippolyta could comment, she curtseyed stiffly and left, with Hippolyta gaping after her.

At that moment, Basilia came into the parlour, yawning prettily, and Hippolyta shut her own mouth.

'Dear Miss Verney,' she heard herself saying brightly, 'I hope you slept well?'

'Very well indeed, thank you, Mrs. Napier! I always do in this house. And congratulations again on the success of yesterday's dinner: despite everything, I think it went splendidly.'

'I'm so glad you enjoyed it.' They exchanged glowing smiles, while Hippolyta thought, '"Despite everything"?' so crossly she was afraid she had repeated it out loud.

Patrick slipped into this happy moment, and cast an anxious glance at the parlour table, and at Hippolyta.

'Shouldn't we be having breakfast? This room will have to be rearranged, will it not?'

'Yes, of course. Breakfast will only be a moment.' She looked at her husband: he seemed dishevelled, though he was in his Sunday coat and had shaved. His honey-fair hair that she loved so much was all on end. She longed to smooth it then and there, but the presence of Basilia was more than inhibiting. She bit her lip, and went to the window instead, aware that Basilia was watching her.

'Not a very welcoming day for the poor clergyman, nor for the congregation,' she said, touching the glass. The window was cold, a steady grey rain falling outside.

'They'll come nevertheless,' said Patrick seriously.

'We'd better make sure we have plenty of room for wet hats and umbrellas and so on.' Hippolyta sighed, turning back as Mrs. Riach entered the parlour with the breakfast things. 'Can we do that, please, Mrs. Riach? Perhaps they could go into the side passage in the servants' quarters.'

'I'll see.' Mrs. Riach's few hours of co-operation seemed to be at an end. She landed the dishes on the table with more force than style. She left the room, and they sat to eat.

'Will it be the same clergyman?' Hippolyta asked Basilia.

'Probably: he said last week he would see us soon,' said Basilia, then her lip wobbled a little. 'So much has happened in a week! I cannot believe it.' She took refuge in her handkerchief, an impractical little scribble of lace. Patrick gallantly handed her his rather more efficient linen square, and Hippolyta gritted her teeth rather too hard on a piece of toast. She brushed crumbs from her sleeves, trying not to show her irritation.

'What will the clergyman require? A room to robe in – the dining room, perhaps? A communion table, a white cloth …'

'This table won't do, of course,' said Patrick, who was eating much faster than usual, evidently unsettled by the whole thing.

'Of course not: whoever saw a round communion table? But I thought perhaps the hall table would be a suitable size.' She had said so before, but she refrained from mentioning it.

Basilia and Patrick nodded, eating.

'Does he bring his own communion set?'

'Yes: he has a travelling one, in a case.'

'And wine? And bread?'

'He'll bring that.'

'Good.' Hippolyta thought through a service as best she could.

'Who chooses the hymns?'

'Oh, we've already done that,' said Basilia innocently, with a look at Patrick. 'We had a little think about it yesterday morning. You were out, I think.'

'And who will play?' Hippolyta asked, trying to focus on the practicalities and not her sudden deep desire to slap Basilia's broad, white face.

'Oh, I shall,' said Patrick. 'I shall just play the piano.'

'And we can bring through the chairs from the dining room, or as many as we think we'll need,' said Hippolyta briskly.

'As soon as we've finished breakfast,' Patrick agreed. She smiled at him, pleased to have established some kind of connexion. He wiped his mouth with his napkin, and met her eye without expression. 'Shall we start?'

Mrs. Riach and Ishbel, summoned by the bell, removed the breakfast things, and then Ishbel helped shift furniture and arrange a clean white linen cloth on the hall table, which they set against the fireplace, having no need for a fire despite the rain. The chairs were arranged in rough rows, while Mrs. Riach watched, arms folded, lips pursed disapprovingly. Patrick brought out the large Bible that lived in the parlour, and set it on the table, opened the piano, and shuffled some sheet music absently as he surveyed the room. Then he nodded.

'I think we're maybe ready.'

'Then we'll be off, Dr. Napier,' said Mrs. Riach grimly, with the air of leaving them to their fate. 'We have the kirk to go till.' She seized Ishbel by the shoulder and marched her off towards the kitchen, and when Hippolyta glanced through the parlour window a few minutes later she saw them, bonneted and cloaked against the rain, marching across the green to the centrical church.

Not a moment later, their own congregation began to arrive, one or two in polite bewilderment, trying to find a place that was new to them, and others grasping Miss Verney by the hand, telling her again how sorry they were for her loss. Miss Verney sat in the front row of the chairs, while Patrick waited in the hall for the clergyman: gradually the parlour filled with the smell of wet cloth, and Hippolyta, hovering at the parlour door to fend off the occasional cat, found herself torn between hostess and worshipper as she greeted newcomers. Most she had seen the previous Sunday, and some again at Colonel Verney's funeral. One or two were new to her, strangers staying in the town who had been directed to them for an English service. The clergyman arrived in a hurry, just as last week, and shot off without question into the dining room to change. While they were waiting for him, there was another quiet knock at the door and Patrick opened it again. Outside, his black coat drenched, was the young man Dr. Durward had introduced to them, Julian Brown.

'Room for another one?' he asked sheepishly, in a quiet voice, as if he feared the service might already have started.

'Of course!' Patrick bowed, and ushered him in. 'May I take your hat and gloves? We are not quite used to hosting the service yet, and our servants have gone to the parish church.'

'Oh, yes, yes.' Julian looked blank, but at Patrick's outstretched hand he snatched off his hat and gloves, and adjusted his soaking coat. 'I hope I don't ruin … anything, Mrs. Napier,' he said, with a shilpit grin.

'Not at all, Mr. Brown. Would you rather take off your coat and borrow a shawl? I should hate to think of you catching cold, and there is no fire, you see.'

'No fire? Oh, yes, of course there wouldn't be. August already, eh? August already, and look at it. The river's rolling along like sixpence,' he added obscurely, and wandered in to the parlour. He perched on the edge of a hard chair near the back, and as an afterthought bent his head in prayer.

The clergyman shot out of the dining room like a pigeon from a dovecot, all flapping surplice, surveyed the parlour professionally, and raised his eyebrows at Patrick. Patrick edged his way past the congregation to the piano, and played a rousing chord, and everyone rose to sing. Hippolyta paused, chose to leave the front door open for latecomers, and joined in at the back.

The clergyman announced that the service would be Morning Prayer instead of Holy Communion, as he had left his communion set in Aboyne, so the congregation stayed at their places throughout rather than joining in the polite, silent parade to the front to receive bread and wine. The clergyman made up for the loss with a twelve minute sermon instead of a six minute one, and a particularly passionate blessing and dismissal at the end. Then he swept to the parlour door to bid them all good day, while Patrick played a soft voluntary in the background. Basilia, acting the part of leading worshipper, paused a moment and then turned from the front pew to follow the clergyman out, glanced in Hippolyta's direction, and sank to the floor in a faint.

'Oh, good heavens!' Hippolyta hurried forward, and managed to clear a space around Miss Verney. Most of the congregation sensibly started to leave the room, and someone seated near it opened the window a little to clear the air. Patrick left off playing and came to kneel and take Basilia's pulse.

'Just a faint,' he said. 'Her heartbeat is quite regular.' He did not quite meet Hippolyta's eye.

'She has not been sleeping well, I think,' said Hippolyta.

'Oh? She told me she was sleeping very well,' he replied. Hippolyta opened her mouth to tell him that Miss Verney might not be absolutely honest, when Miss Verney stirred and tried to sit up. 'One moment, Miss Verney: sit up slowly, please. You have had a little faint.'

'Have I? Oh no!' Basilia put her hand to her forehead. 'I have caused you so much trouble, haven't I? I am so sorry!'

'Not at all, not at all, Miss Verney. Here, let me help you up on to this chair.' He slipped a hand under Basilia's arm while Hippolyta copied him on the other side, though he could no doubt have lifted her himself. Basilia sighed, and glanced about the room.

'And it was such a lovely service, too,' she added, though Hippolyta was sure she was looking for someone, someone specific. Had she been expecting Mr. Brookes? But then why would she pretend to faint? For she was sure that a woman who pretended to faint once was pretending to faint the next time, too, however unfair that might have seemed.

'All well?' asked the clergyman briskly, reappearing at the door as the last of the congregation, presumably reunited with their cloaks and hats, departed into the drizzle.

'Oh, yes, yes, quite well, thank you!' Basilia rose slowly and put out a hand to him, and he began the usual condolences, adding remarks about his gratitude to Colonel Verney for his accommodation of the Episcopalian services over the last couple of years.

'Though of course, this has been very well arranged, too,' he added, with a half-bow to Hippolyta and Patrick. 'May we impose on you again next Sunday week?'

'Of course!' Hippolyta smiled, though she felt Patrick twitch a little beside her. She refused to look at him. 'An honour, and no trouble at all. Can I offer you a glass of wine, or some tea? I'm sure you are in a great rush, as usual, but the rain is perhaps easing, and if you give it a few minutes more you might have a drier ride.'

The clergyman leaned back and took a look out through the front door.

'If I may, a glass of wine would fend off the weather very nicely, Mrs. Napier. I'll just go and remove these robes again – is the dining room still suitable?' He bustled off, and Patrick quickly helped Hippolyta rearranged some of the chairs, taking the table, now bare, back into the hall, desanctifying the room to make wine and tea seem more in place there. As if they knew, a couple of the cats reappeared and settled on a sofa, washing off rainwater with steady pink tongues. Hippolyta hurried to the servants' quarters to find wine, remembering that Mrs. Riach and Ishbel would not have returned yet.

The clergyman did not stay long, hurrying out with the wine almost still on his lips to retrieve his horse from the inn stables and head back down Deeside to his next service. When they had waved him off, Basilia gave another of her delicate little yawns.

'I think I must excuse myself, dear Mrs. Napier, and go and rest for a little. I fear I must not have rested as well as I thought I had.'

'You should certainly lie down for an hour or so, Miss Verney,' said Patrick solemnly. 'It is early days yet: you still don't have your full strength.'

Basilia sighed and retreated to the stairs, as if reluctant to admit to her own weakness. Hippolyta went back into the parlour and began to sort out the chairs, setting the heavy dining chairs to one side to be returned to the dining room. Patrick, in silence, took them one by one across the hall to their place. Both of them jumped when there came another knock on the front door.

'Surely not someone late for the service?' Hippolyta joked, though it fell rather flat. Patrick merely glanced at her, and went to open the door. On the doorstep, with that strangely humble sense of entitlement that seemed to characterise him, was the sheriff's man, Durris.

'Good day to you,' he said, lifting his hat a little, blinking behind rain-smeared glasses. 'I apologise for disturbing you on the Sabbath, but you'll know that we want to make some progress with this case.'

'I understand,' said Patrick, stepping back to let him in, though Hippolyta thought she detected some reluctance in his tone. She felt her spine stiffen: she could not allow Mr. Durris to drag Patrick off to his study again, all on his own. She had to deflect the attack, if attack it was going to be.

'Please come in, Mr. Durris: we were just tidying the parlour after our morning service. Will you join us for some tea?' She was sure she had heard the back door, so with any good fortune Mrs. Riach was back and she would not have to go and see to things on her own, leaving Patrick defenceless. Durris blinked at her.

'Some tea would be most welcome, Mrs. Napier,' he said after a moment. 'I'd like a word with Dr. Napier, if I could …'

'Of course,' she said briskly. 'We are always at your disposal, Mr. Durris.' She rang the bell and sat expectantly at the parlour table, business-like. With a look from one of them to the other, Durris also sat, pulling out his notebook for support. Patrick took another seat as if he were afraid the table might bite him. He folded his hands tightly in front of him. Durris stared at his notebook – Hippolyta could see that the page was blank – then said to Patrick,

'Well, Dr. Napier, have you given any thought to what I asked you? Have you anything further to tell me?'

Patrick opened his mouth, but Hippolyta leapt in, her mind racing.

'Oh, yes, we do! Well, I do. Did you know, Mr. Durris, that Miss Verney has been meeting Mr. Brookes by night?'

'Has she?' Durris asked, and Patrick cried,

'She hasn't! Has she?'

'Hush!' Hippolyta made a little bit of a show of going to the parlour door, opening it suddenly on an empty hall, and shutting it again softly.

'What are you implying?' Patrick demanded. 'Miss Verney is a lady: she would not eavesdrop!'

'Perhaps not,' said Hippolyta, to Durris more than to Patrick. 'But she has definitely been going out at night on her own –'

'She was sleepwalking.'

'She told you she had sleepwalked as a child, and you believed her,' said Hippolyta patiently. 'But I'm convinced she only pretended to faint that night, because she unexpectedly came upon all of us in the hallway when she returned. I saw her eyes just before she fell.' She met Patrick's shocked gaze, and turned back firmly to Durris. She might have felt treacherous, telling of her friend's night time assignations like this, but Patrick's instant defence of Basilia irked her thoroughly, and the thought of Basilia's snakelike flirting with her husband – her husband! – wiped all other feelings of guilt from her heart. 'The other night I looked out and saw a man in our garden. I'm not sure who he was, but he very quietly let himself out through the front gate. Then last night I heard her go out again, and this time I followed her.'

Both men jumped.

'You did what?' asked Patrick.

'You really should not have put yourself in any position of danger, Mrs. Napier,' said Durris, looking alarmed.

'Danger? From Basilia? I hardly think so!' Hippolyta was dismissive.

'Never mind Miss Verney, there is still a murderer about the town!' cried Patrick. His hand hovered above hers, as if he should have liked to have taken it in his. What was stopping him? His feelings for that minx Basilia? 'If anything had happened to you …'

'Quite,' said Durris, slightly waspishly. 'Dr. Napier, may I ask, where were you when this was happening?'

'I … well, I … To tell the truth, I had been working late in my study. I must have fallen asleep: it was very late when I went to bed.'

'And it did not occur to you, Mrs. Napier, to fetch your husband rather than to wander the streets of Ballater on your own in the middle of the night?'

'Not at all,' said Hippolyta smoothly. 'When my husband is engaged in his – very important work, I am most unwilling to disturb him. This is not the middle of Edinburgh, surely, Mr. Durris: a lady may wander safely in Ballater at any time of the day or night!'

'My dear –' began Patrick, but Durris was more interested in the information Hippolyta might have obtained.

'Mrs. Napier, tell me what happened last night, then, since nothing we say now will have prevented you having gone.'

'Well, I went out a little after Miss Verney,' said Hippolyta quickly, before Patrick could intervene again. 'She was just about to turn in to the street down to the bridge and the river. I followed her and she went directly to the bridge, then about halfway across it. Then I could see another figure come to meet her, in a – well, colours are difficult at night, but I'm almost sure it was a brown coat. This time I could see the shape and the height of the man much more clearly: the man in the garden, whether it was the same one or not –'

'Surely you would not malign Miss Verney's reputation by insinuating that she meets various men by night?' asked Patrick, his head in his hands.

'Certainly not,' said Hippolyta acidly. 'I think it maligns her reputation quite enough to suggest that she meets with one man by night. But I imagine that neither of you will be gossiping about it, and nor, I suppose, will Miss Verney.'

'Please continue, Mrs. Napier,' said Durris with a sigh.

'They met about the middle of the bridge. He was a little above her height, but it was hard to say much about his build for his coat seemed thick, and I could not see his legs.' Patrick made a little groan. Hippolyta chose to misunderstand him. 'They were in the shadow of the bridge's parapet. Anyway, they embraced …' Patrick's groan this time was a little louder. Surely he was not jealous of this mysterious stranger? If he was, how dare he show it in front of her!

'I left then, for I did not want them to see me: the embrace was – was of a private and intimate nature,' she stopped, not quite sure what to say next. Durris seemed quite pink about the ears. 'But I was convinced that it was Mr. Brookes, my husband's patient at Pannanich Hotel.'

'Your patient, sir?' asked Durris, and Patrick lifted his head from his hands. His eyes were wide and hopeless.

'My patient,' he agreed, 'who is bedridden. He requires a servant to lift him and carry him, and goes about out of doors only in a wheeled chair, propelled by the same servant.'

'Then how was he walking over the bridge on his own,

embracing young ladies?' asked Durris, with a straight face. 'For you did at least imply that he was on his own, Mrs. Napier.'

'He was, as far as I could see. At least, he was walking unaided. And it must be Mr. Brookes, for he has been seen, you know. Lang, the night watchman, saw him out by the Strachans' house, on the night of the murder.'

'That has to be a ridiculous rumour,' said Patrick.

'No, it isn't, for Lang told me himself when I asked him what he had seen that night,' said Hippolyta, forgetting that Patrick had forbidden her to go to see Lang. There was a moment of silence, as each met the other's eye. Eventually Patrick's gaze slid back to Durris.

'Lang is a reliable man, I believe,' he said quietly.

'That's the impression I have of him too, sir,' said Durris. Neither mentioned the fact that it was Lang who claimed to have seen Patrick, too, that evening.

'Yet …'

'How well do you know Mr. Brookes' case, sir?'

Patrick shuffled in his seat, and held his head firmly in his hands, thinking.

'I have been attending him for two years, since he first came here. He asked for me by name …' The pride that had been in his voice when he had first told Hippolyta that seemed more like confusion now. 'I examined him, of course. He is desperately thin: he suffered from a number of diseases including, I believe, yellow fever, in the West Indies, where he made his fortune. He has never in my sight walked or made any great use of his legs, and he swore to me that they were useless. His servant, who is a local lad, carries him about without any great effort … His heart is not strong, and I should say that – I should have said that – he might die at any time.' He frowned, staring down at the cloth on the parlour table, clearly reviewing his association with Brookes and wondering how wrong he might have been. Durris cleared his throat.

'Might I suggest that we go and have a word with this gentleman at the hotel, then?'

'I'll fetch my bonnet,' said Hippolyta at once.

'I think you've had quite enough expeditions, my dear,' said Patrick.

'But I was the one who saw him!' said Hippolyta. 'If he's

going to try to deny it, I'm the one that can say no! I saw him!'

Patrick looked at Durris, who busied himself with his notebook.

'Well, then, I suppose you're right,' he conceded, with an attempt at good grace. Hippolyta scurried off and was back in an instant, ready to join them. At last she and Patrick were going to make some progress in the business of finding him innocent.

Chapter Eighteen

As soon as they were outside the garden gate, Hippolyta tucked her hand under Patrick's elbow, refusing to think he might pull away. After a moment, he squeezed her hand gently against his warm body, and they walked on. She glanced back irresistibly at the house, but Miss Verney's bedroom shutters were firmly closed: nevertheless she allowed herself a tiny smile.

The congregation of the parish church had already dispersed, as if they had dissolved like sugar sculptures in the damp air. At least the rain had stopped, but the streets and the green were Sunday midday quiet as they set off. All three of them walked abreast to the street that led down to the river, Hippolyta in the middle, not quite sure if she should feel protected or hemmed in by the two tall men. She had been thinking hard about Mr. Brookes and what they should say to him, but then a thought struck her.

'Mr. Durris,' she began, 'did you know that twenty years ago there was another murder – two, in fact – at Dinnet House?'

He glanced at her.

'Mr. Tranter and his manservant, a Rab Lattin? Yes, I was aware of that.'

Hippolyta was momentarily irritated that he seemed to know more of it than she did, but then she took in the information and added it to her mental notes. So Mrs. Strachan's maiden name was Tranter, then? And the manservant, yes.

'Don't you think it's an extraordinary coincidence?'

'Aye, maybe.' He walked on a few paces, and then seemed to think he needed to rouse himself to a more thorough response. 'It's not so strange, perhaps, to have a man and his servant killed, though to have nothing apparently stolen on either occasion is odd. Dinnet House is a wee bit lonely there at the edge of the village, and it looks large and wealthy: I would not have been surprised at burglary with violence there on any night.'

'But the coincidence of having a girl and her maid there at the same time, and no one else: doesn't it look odd to you?'

'Are you telling me you suspect the girl or her maid?' Durris asked, with a wry look. 'And do you mean for the present murders, or for both lots? I doubt Miss Verney is hardly old enough to have killed two grown men twenty years ago, nor her maid either.'

'There's the woman who was the girl in the first murders,' said Hippolyta, though at once she regretted it. She had been playing with pieces of a puzzle, and had momentarily forgotten that the girl twenty years ago was now the lovely Mrs. Strachan. She added quickly, 'And her maid: we know nothing about her, do we?'

'We do, as it happens,' said Durris mildly. 'Her name was Jean Cassie. She died of the typhus, ten years ago or more in Aberdeen.'

'Oh.' Hippolyta mentally crossed her off, this anonymous maid, Tabitha's predecessor. 'So you know then that the girl was – is now Mrs. Strachan.'

'Aye, we know. You'd be surprised at the records the sheriff keeps. We know that Mr. Strachan was questioned about the murders at the time, but he was thought not to have had anything to do with them in the end. There was – substantial evidence of the sheer quantity of alcohol he had consumed the night before, and we knew he had started before the men were killed.'

'Because Dr. Durward was able to vouch for him.'

'Aye, when he could stand upright himself,' agreed Durris, and Hippolyta felt Patrick chuckle quietly. 'They were young men then,' Durris said politely.

'He's still fond of a glass or two now,' Patrick grinned.

'Aye, but I think it was a bottle or two then,' said Durris, with a twitch of his eyebrow.

'Is it my imagination,' said Hippolyta, 'or is the river wider than it was before?'

They paused at the peak of the bridge, and stared downstream, to their left. The river, always broad, was draped over its bed like a grey eiderdown, bulging and overstuffed at the edges.

'It'll be all those heavy showers we've been having,' said

Durris, eyeing the waters in a calculating way. 'There's a fair bit of that pasture will be lost. Look at the sheep.'

The sheep, indeed, offwhite and thin after their shearing, were lining up at the upper end of their pasture, grazing determinedly as if they feared that grass too might be covered soon. A boy with them was trying to encourage them over the road out of the way of the encroaching water, but the sheep were reluctant to leave.

'It's flooded before,' said Patrick, nodding. 'That's why the bridge has been built so sturdily: there are often winter spates.'

'Aye, it can be bad enough,' nodded Durris. He gave the river a final analytical stare, then turned to continue on their way over to Pannanich.

The walk was not as pleasant today as it had been when Hippolyta and Patrick had meandered up arm in arm over a week ago. The skies were grey and heavy, the river noisy, the birds silent in the birch woods. Obscurely, Hippolyta blamed it all on the murders and on Basilia Verney: if they had never gone to visit Colonel Verney at Dinnet House, Basilia would never have invited her to paint last Monday morning, and she would not have discovered the bodies, and she would not have invited Basilia, that snake in the grass, to stay in their lovely little house. She shook herself, and told herself not to be ridiculous. The weather was heavy and weighing down on her, but all this rain would no doubt clear the air, and she would regard their poor bereaved guest much more charitably – particularly if they were able to sort out the matter of Mr. Brookes and the night time assignations. Perhaps he was imposing on Basilia in some way, and all she needed was their help to free herself from his demands? Yet she saw again in her mind's eye that passionate embrace: Basilia had certainly not looked very reluctant at the time. Hippolyta felt herself blush, and addressed her gaze to the landscape. How could she paint those dark trees, wreathed in the mist of rain that draped the valley down to their left? How could she show the birches wet and dripping, the colours of their trunks and of the lush blueberries cushioning the ground beneath them? Those were much more appropriate thoughts for a Sunday afternoon, along with a few suitable prayers for Mr. Durris' success, for ways to deal with Mrs. Riach, for Basilia's happy departure, for murderers successfully discovered: this was how she should be thinking.

They passed Pannanich Lodge, square and wet and much nearer the water's edge than it had been before. No one was sitting outside today, taking the air. The walk from there to the hotel seemed much longer than it had the last time, and Hippolyta found herself weighing on Patrick's arm as they reached the top of the rise where the hotel sat watching over the valley. They were dewy, all of them, the men's black Sunday coats grey, her own cloak sparkling as she let go of Patrick at last and led the way into the hallway of the hotel. Durris, last through the door, looked about. The parlour was full of fractious guests who wanted to be outside, and Brookes was not amongst them. Durris turned to find some servant, but Patrick waved his hat towards the stairs.

'I know his room: follow me,' he said, and led the way up to the first floor.

At the top of the stairs he turned left, and along the long corridor knocked on the last door on the left. In a moment a serving boy opened the door, surveyed them, and stopped in surprise.

'I know Mr. Brookes was not expecting me,' said Patrick at once, 'but I hope he might see us. We are not here on medical business,' he added in a louder voice, as the boy had already turned back into the room to announce them. They could easily hear Mr. Brookes receive the news of their arrival with pleasure, and he called them in, as the serving boy returned to open the door more widely in welcome.

'Go and fetch some tea for our visitors, Henry, will you, and some of the cook's delicious shortbread?' Brookes said to him, and the boy scurried off. 'Dr. Napier! This is a pleasant surprise on the Sabbath – and Mrs. Napier, too! And a stranger: more amusement for a poor invalid!'

'I hope you will not find it all too tiring,' said Patrick, slipping quickly into his professional role. 'This is Dod Durris, from the sheriff's office: he is looking into some incidents in the town and would like to ask you some questions.'

'By all means, Mr. Durris. Please take a seat.'

The room was a large and pleasant one, taking up a corner end of the front of the hotel with views in two directions over the valley and the road. It was to all intents both a bedroom and a sitting room, and though the curtained bed stood against one wall, there were chairs and a sofa clustered around a cheerful fireplace, where the guests were expected to sit in some comfort. Mr. Brookes himself was dressed as if for the Kirk and lying on a daybed in yellow silk, a little old-fashioned but still with some style, which could be said, Hippolyta thought, of Mr. Brookes, too. He had pushed himself up on to his elbows with some apparent effort in order to greet them, but the effort seemed to have exhausted him, and at last she was assailed by doubts. Could he really have been wandering on his own about the town? When she looked at him, she found herself gravely doubting the evidence of both the night watchman Lang and of her own eyes.

They exchanged some remarks on the weather and on their respective church services that morning: Mr. Brookes had been to the centrical church, he said, riding in splendour on the back of a cart as he had not asked for a more dignified form of transport in time.

'It's a tremendously busy church!' he said. 'One can slip in at the back quite unnoticed in the crowds. Mr. Douglas' sermons do not strain the intellect, I suspect, but they are nevertheless heartfelt, and leave me with a very tender feeling each week towards my fellow men. Ah, and here is more reason for tender feelings: the cook's shortbread here would melt the heart of any heathen. Thank you, Henry. I think you may leave us for a little: no doubt Mrs. Napier has a hand skilled at pouring tea, do you not, madam?'

The boy bowed awkwardly and left them by the fire. Hippolyta poured the tea and handed the shortbread around. It was crumbly and delicious, and so fresh she suspected the cook had been infringing the Sabbath just a little.

'Now, to business!' said Mr. Brookes with glee. 'What incident in the town could possibly require information from me? I am delighted to find I might be of use!'

'You'll have heard about the two murders at Dinnet House?' Durris began solemnly. He brushed shortbread crumbs from his coat front and took out his inevitable notebook.

'Yes, indeed! A gentleman I had not met, I think, and his manservant. I had not been to Dinnet House.'

'The gentleman, Colonel Verney, was an invalid: perhaps you might have met him at the Wells?'

'Oh! I had not realised. So he could have been coming up

here? I'm still not sure I ever was acquainted with him. Colonel Verney, you say?'

'That's right.' Durris surveyed Brookes, whose expression was as bland as his own. Hippolyta and Patrick made no sound. 'Richard Verney. He was a Waterloo veteran, and inclined to relate his experiences there.'

'Hm. It sounds faintly familiar, but the Wells are so busy these days. I am sorry I cannot help you. Had he served at all in the West Indies? Not that I should definitely have met him there, but there have been one or two with whom I have exchanged yarns about the places we've seen there.'

'No, he hadn't,' Hippolyta spoke up. 'Or not that he ever told his niece, anyway.'

'He has a niece? Poor lady: she will have had quite a shock.'

'She has had,' agreed Hippolyta, admiring his sangfroid. Had he not been consorting with the same niece only last night? Could the Colonel have objected to their association – after all, Brookes was much older than Basilia – and so Brookes murdered him? That had been the motive assigned to Strachan, for the first murders, had it not? But Brookes was a newcomer to the town: it would have been remarkable if he had carried out the same murder twenty years on.

'Mr. Brookes,' said Durris, watching the invalid closely, 'you have been seen in the village recently – specifically on the night of the murders.'

'Have I?' Brookes looked puzzled. 'Forgive me: when did the murders take place?'

'Last Sunday evening. A week ago today.'

'I was not in the town at all last Sunday.' Brookes shook his head sadly. 'I felt myself too frail even to go to the kirk in the morning. It is a miserable thing, this weakness.'

Durris looked at him.

'You were seen, by a most reliable witness, standing beneath a tree behind the house belonging to Mr. Strachan, the merchant.'

'I was?'

'You were.'

Mr. Brookes looked thoughtful, pressing his thin lips together.

'And I saw you myself last night!' Hippolyta plunged in. 'Standing on the bridge to the town!'

Durris and Patrick both lifted hands to hush her, their eyes on Brookes. He seemed hardly to have heard her.

'Who says they saw me at Strachan's house?' he asked slowly.

'Lang, the night watchman. He's observant and keen,' Durris added with conviction. Brookes looked at him for a long moment, staring out from under the loose yellow lids that hooded his eyes. Then he gently set down his teacup.

'Well, he's right,' he said, and Hippolyta heard Durris breathe out.

'He's right?' asked Patrick. 'But you told me you could not walk!'

'I'm weak, certainly,' said Brookes, with an apologetic glance at him. 'I'm not the man I was, and doubtless my heart will give up soon enough: you have seen that yourself, I know. But I can walk, most of the time.'

'Then why lie about it?' Patrick demanded. Hippolyta's heart went out to him: he looked so hurt that a patient could seek his sympathies, so readily given, falsely.

'Well, I've lied about a number of things,' said Brookes philosophically. 'My name, for example, is not Brookes.'

'Then what is it?' asked Durris, his notebook at the ready.

'It is Burns. A small pun, and a convenient one.'

'Burns?' asked Hippolyta. 'The Burns Mortification? That Burns?'

'That Burns,' the man agreed. 'I mortified that money to the parish some years ago. Now that my end is near, I wanted to make sure it was being properly administered before I would write my will to leave the rest of my money to it, too. I have no family, but I was born and brought up in this town before I travelled to the West Indies and made all that money. I always wanted to go to the King's College in Aberdeen: it's too late for me now, but at least I can help other young men to do it. Naturally if I went to ask Strachan or Durward or Mr. Strong whether the trust was being run properly, they would nod and tell me everything was fine. I needed to find out for myself.'

'But did you believe there was something wrong with the trust's administration?' Hippolyta asked, excited that her own suspicions might be shared.

'I have no concrete evidence,' Burns admitted with a shrug. 'I just had a feeling, if that does not seem too vague. And I wanted to come home, home to mild weather, healthy air, gentle rain …'

'So you were at Strachan's house to do what?' asked Durris, focussing on the practicalities.

'I knew the trust papers had been removed from the church,' said Burns. 'I could not examine them there: it went against the grain to break into church premises, but anyway,' he added with a grin, 'the door is very strong and the lock is large.'

'Could you not simply have asked the minister?' asked Patrick.

'What reason could I have given? He would not recognise me, it's true, for he was not here when I was young, but he might have mentioned me to the other trustees, and they would no doubt have been suspicious. I went to see if I could see into Strachan's business room or Durward's business room in case I could slip into either of them and look at the papers, but then I found that Colonel Verney had been sounded out as a new trustee, and that he had the papers at Dinnet House. I had heard about the murders, of course: the gossip is about little else at the moment, and I also heard that the Colonel's niece had sensibly left the house with her maid. Naturally I seized the opportunity to take a look for the papers – and there they were.'

'You broke in through the study window?'

'Yes, I confess all! But I stole nothing, of course. And I'll happily pay for any damage.'

'But did you find any irregularities in the trust?' Hippolyta pressed on.

Burns frowned.

'I'm not sure that I did. It all looks in order. I fear I shall have to travel to Aberdeen and make sure of matters at that end. I had planned to leave tomorrow, actually. There is a list in the papers – I have copied it – of the students who have received bursaries. I just want to make finally sure that they all exist – and are in receipt of the money.

'They won't be at the college at this time of the year,' said Durris astutely.

'No, but I'll talk to the teachers there and find out what they have to say.'

'I'm not sure I want you to leave Ballater just at the present time,' said Durris courteously. 'You still have not accounted for all your movements about the town.'

'I've confessed to breaking into Dinnet House!' said Burns in surprise. 'And I've agreed I was lingering around Strachan's house – done very well for himself too, I have to say. As has Durward: I wonder sometimes why I bothered going abroad to seek my fortune. My friends seem to have found theirs here.'

'You still haven't said what your connexion is with Miss Verney, the Colonel's niece. You met her on the bridge last night.'

'I did not!' Burns looked from one to the other of them, then focussed on Hippolyta. 'You said you'd seen me? You were mistaken, I'm afraid, my dear.'

Hippolyta opened her mouth to argue, but she had to admit to herself that she really was not sure any more. Burns, whether he could walk or not, was certainly terribly thin. Had the figure she had seen on the bridge been so emaciated? She closed her eyes, trying to picture him.

'Are you sure there's nothing you want to tell us about that assignation?'

'It was an assignation? I don't tend to arrange assignations with young ladies, particularly ones I've never even met,' said Burns. 'Look, I've been truthful with you – now, anyway. I solemnly swear to you that last night I was here, tucked up in that bed behind me. I have never had any assignation with Miss Verney or any other young lady on that bridge, or anywhere else in Ballater in the last two decades, and to my knowledge I have never met Miss Verney. Does that satisfy you?'

Durris turned to Hippolyta.

'I – I think I must have been mistaken,' she said. 'I'm sorry to have wasted your time.'

'That's quite all right, Mrs. Napier,' said Burns, settling back on his daybed. 'It has been a most entertaining interval, I assure you, for life here is not at all interesting. I have enjoyed my night time expeditions. Ballater has changed so much in my absence, though: sometimes I feel like a ghost, returning to haunt the scenes of my childhood.'

'When did you leave Ballater?' Durris asked casually.

'Eighteen years ago on the twentieth of next month,' said Burns, his eyes closing. 'Eighteen years ago. A lifetime.' His voice faded: he was slipping into sleep. Patrick rose and gently checked his pulse, rousing Burns to a grateful smile as his eyes briefly opened again. 'I am tired, you know.'

'I know,' said Patrick, drawing the rug up over his thin chest. 'Don't tire yourself further just now, eh?'

A lifetime, perhaps, but less than twenty years, Hippolyta thought, as they gathered themselves to go. He was here when the first murders happened, and he was friends with Strachan and Dr. Durward. Had he competed for the hand of the lovely Miss Tranter, later Mrs. Strachan?

She studied him discreetly for a moment. He looked ancient, yellowed and wrinkled like silk washed too hot. But as he relaxed you could see that his bones were fine and strong, his face showing some traces of a distinguished past. He had been a handsome man, perhaps, twenty years ago. What had he known of Dinnet House and that bloody night?

The dark skies had lifted a little outside, and the walk was downhill, so though Hippolyta was distinctly embarrassed at her mistake in identifying Mr. Burns as Basilia's lover, her mood was not altogether low. After all, they had solved a couple of mysteries: and in any case there remained the incontrovertible fact that Basilia had had an assignation with someone, even if it had not been Mr. Burns.

Further down the hill, past Pannanich Lodge, they caught up with a familiar figure: Julian Brown was strolling, if that word did not convey too much in the way of energy, down the hill towards the bridge. It was not difficult to overtake him.

'Good day!' he said, his hair confused as he removed his hat.

'Mr. Brown, Mr. Durris,' said Patrick, indicating them both. 'Mr. Brown is staying at Pannanich Lodge, I believe.'

'That's right.' Brown was affable. 'Thank you again for your hospitality this morning: I thought the service went exceeding well, didn't you?'

'A shame about the weather, perhaps,' said Patrick politely.

'That's certain.' Brown waved a hand towards himself. 'Had to change my coat when I came back here: I believe they're wringing several Scotch pints out of it even as we speak.' He was wearing a brown coat now, flecked, Hippolyta noticed absently, with white. She had not seen this detail from the back. 'To be honest, I need to look after that black coat: lost so much at cards recently it's the only decent one I have left. This one's far from smart.' He gave a rueful sigh, and Hippolyta felt herself wanting to sort out his hopeless neckcloth and feed him a good meal. He was quite pathetic.

'Well, enjoy your stroll!' said Patrick, as it was clear they intended to walk much faster than Brown. The three of them strode on: Brown was clearly relishing his meander, for he was whistling cheerfully to himself as they stretched the distance between them.

'Odd: that's the gavotte from *Colin's Kisses*,' said Patrick, slowing a little.

'From what?' asked Durris.

'A suite of music by James Oswald: not very fashionable just at present, but one of my favourites,' Patrick explained. 'He was a –'

'Cat hairs!' Hippolyta exclaimed.

'What?' asked Durris in surprise.

'Mr. Brown's coat is covered in white cat hairs.'

'Oh, heavens,' said Patrick. 'I suppose we all are by now.'

'But he wasn't wearing that coat this morning, dearest: he was wearing his black one, didn't you hear?'

'Then there must be another cat …'

'Wait, what are you saying, Mrs. Napier?' asked Durris. They stopped and looked back: some distance away, Julian Brown was contemplating the birch woods to his left, where a little path led up the steep slope of Pannanich Hill.

'My husband is not the only one who admires James Oswald's music: Miss Verney enjoys it, too. You were playing *Colin's Kisses* the other night, weren't you?' she asked, not quite sure.

'Well, parts of it, yes. You'd need more than two people to play most of it, though.'

'And Miss Verney has been living in our house: she is probably as thick with white cat hairs as anyone else in it.'

'You're suggesting that the man Miss Verney met last night was not Mr. Brookes - Mr. Burns, that is – at all, but Mr. Brown?'

'That's exactly it! I'm sure of it.'

'Then let us go and ask him about it,' said Durris, and turned to retrace their steps – but Julian Brown had vanished.

Chapter Nineteen

'You'd be better to stay here a moment, Mrs. Napier,' said Durris as they reached the bottom of the path they assumed Brown had taken.

'But –' Hippolyta began to protest, but then considered. Brown might of course have popped into the woods for private reasons: Durris was quite right. Durris stepped solidly up the path, turned a corner, and disappeared – but a second later, they heard him exclaim. Hippolyta and Patrick exchanged a look, and ran up the path after him.

Rounding the corner they found an odd little tableau: Durris standing in the middle of the path, one hand raised apologetically. Beyond him was Brown, hat in his hands and a bewildered expression on his face. To one side of him was Basilia Verney.

'Miss Verney!' Hippolyta cried out. 'Are you all right?'

'Oh, Mrs. Napier too! Yes, I am quite all right now.' Basilia was breathing heavily, and her hands extended to Patrick and Durris. 'I believe these gentlemen have saved me! This dreadful man – Oh! Thank goodness you arrived in time!'

'I'm afraid,' said Durris, as if he were quite stupid, 'you're going to have to be a little clearer than that, Miss Verney.' She glared at him.

'This person came upon me in the woods and – and insulted me! He put his hands upon my person!'

'Good heavens!' cried Patrick, turning to Brown for explanation.

Brown did not seem likely to give one. He was standing with his chin on his chest, eyes wide, as shocked as if he had met himself coming the other way.

'I – I – ' was all he could manage. Hippolyta felt she should slap him, for his own good.

'You're accusing this man – this stranger?' Durris queried, and Basilia nodded quickly. 'You're accusing this stranger of assaulting you?'

'I am, yes,' she said definitely.

'I see,' said Durris. 'But,' he added clearly, 'he is your cousin, is he not?'

There was an awkward little silence. Julian Brown gave Durris a look in which he seemed not yet sure whether to be grateful.

'Brown is a very common name,' said Basilia hesitantly.

'But Julian is not.'

She flashed Durris an odd little look, as if reassessing him.

'Of course Julian is my cousin. Even cousins can be arrested for assaulting cousins, can they not?'

'It is not within the degrees of affinity, no.' Durris agreed calmly. 'How long have you been staying up here, Mr. Brown? For I conclude you are an Englishman, by your voice.'

'Oh, yes indeed! Mr. … Durris, was it not? I have been here two and a half weeks, or thereabouts. The air, you know, very good for – for all kinds of things.'

'I believe Dr. Durward was attending him,' Patrick put in helpfully. Durris gave him a glance.

'You are, then, I take it, the nephew of Colonel Verney who is mentioned in the Colonel's will?'

'I believe so, sir,' said Brown, just short of gabbling. 'Most generous of the old fellow, I should say. I'm his sister's son: they had a bit of a spat before she died, and he and I … well, he seemed to think a fellow could easily keep control of his spending, you know? He never seemed to see a fellow needs the right clothes and needs to be seen in the right places, you know? But I came up here to see if I couldn't win the old boy over: well, to tell the truth, he sent me packing before, but I thought I might just be able to try again. But I left it too late.'

'Then perhaps you could say where you were last Sunday evening?'

'Sunday evening?' Brown was thrown: the look on his face said that it would have been rare for him to remember where he had been a day ago, let alone a week. 'Last Sunday evening … let me think …'

'Well,' said Miss Verney, folding her arms firmly, 'I have to admit that Julian has – has tricked me into meeting with him a few times. I didn't trust him in the least, but he was trying to talk me into bringing Uncle round to a reconciliation. Of course Uncle had more sense. And then … and then since Uncle died … he kept insisting on meeting me. I was terrified! I had to do as he said.'

'Basilia!' Julian's face was a tragedy. 'How could you … what are you saying?'

'You could have told us,' said Patrick sorrowfully. 'We would have protected you, of course.'

'I – I didn't want to cause you any more worry and trouble, Dr. Napier,' said Miss Verney, in a voice that made Hippolyta's skin crawl. 'How could I, after all you have done?'

'Nevertheless …'

'But last Sunday, that was one of the nights he wanted me to meet him,' she went on to Durris, barely looking at Julian. 'I know I said I went to bed early, but really – once Tabitha had gone downstairs, I slipped out, myself.'

'Did you, indeed?' Durris looked her up and down, and she gave the slightest of shivers. 'Which door did you leave by?'

'The front door,' said Basilia straightaway. 'I was sure that my uncle would still be in the parlour but Forman could have been there or in the kitchen, and I knew Tabitha had been going to the kitchen. The hall was in darkness – oh! Do you think I could have crept past Uncle's b … b … body?' She finished on a whisper, her face aghast.

'Very possibly,' said Durris. Hippolyta glanced at him. There was something in his tone that implied he was no longer very impressed by Miss Verney. Hippolyta wondered if Miss Verney had noticed it, too. Surely he did not suspect her of killing her own uncle? But if she had been meeting Mr. Brown, then she could not have killed him, presumably. 'What time would this have been?' Durris asked without expression.

'Well … the time I told you before I'd gone to bed.' It seemed to bother Basilia very little that she was admitting to having lied to Durris before. 'About eleven, I suppose.'

'And when did you return?'

She glanced at Julian Brown, who stared back at her blankly.

'I was not very long … now, why was that? I remember

thinking that I should be meeting Mrs. Napier in the morning for our little painting expedition, and that it was not a bad thing that I would be back early … why was that?' Slowly her eyes opened wide, and her pretty little mouth formed a stunned O. 'It was because you and I were due to meet at the gate, and you never appeared! That was it! I waited there for – oh, a quarter of an hour, perhaps? But it was growing chilly, and I thought one of those heavy showers was coming, so I thanked Providence and turned to go in! That was it!' She turned in triumph to Durris. 'I was hardly out of my room for more than half an hour altogether. There!'

'So now neither of you has an alibi for the time of your uncle's death,' said Durris quietly. 'You, madam, admit that you were not asleep as you previously told me, but were about the house. You, sir – can you account for yourself? For if you were not engaged in an assignation with this lady, then where were you?'

'I was – I was –' Julian's face was empty of any kind of wit. He stared from Basilia to Durris and back again, lost. 'I was – I was –'

'Oh, heavens, you were playing cards with Dr. Durward!' cried Hippolyta, unable to stand his uselessness any longer. 'He told me so himself!'

Basilia's jaw dropped. An expression of surprised delight illuminated Julian's dim face.

'Oh, so I was! That was Sunday, wasn't it? That's right!' He turned to Durris, brimming with cheerful confidence. 'There you have it, sir: Dr. Durward and I were playing cards. He came over to the lodge about dinner time, and stayed – well, pretty much all night, actually! He had brought some very fine brandy, and between that and the cards, he left here about dawn – with a good deal of my money, I have to say.' He made a face, but the cheerfulness lingered.

'You – you left me by the gate while you played cards?' Basilia demanded. Julian's face fell a little.

'Got a bit carried away, m'dear. Won quite a bit at first, thought I was on a lucky streak. Turned, of course: always does. But one day, you'll see!' He grinned stupidly at her. She glanced from the corner of her eye at Patrick and Hippolyta, and turned from him in disgust.

'You would have wasted Uncle's money in a month!' she

snapped. 'You and your cards! I'm glad he listened to me!'

Julian had a moment's misgiving at that, and his eyes registered something distant. Yet that cheerful smile was still clear on his face, the smile, she thought, of a perpetually unlucky person who comes up sharp against an unlooked for piece of very good fortune. For once his card playing had been to his advantage.

'I shall confirm that story with Dr. Durward,' Durris said, half to himself, as they continued down the road to the bridge. Some distance ahead of them Miss Verney was marching along on her own, and Julian had returned to the Lodge. 'Though I must say that I find the picture of Mr. Brown playing cards all night is more convincing than the one of him sneaking up to Dinnet House to meet Miss Verney against her uncle's will.'

'He doesn't seem to have the strength of character, does he?' Hippolyta agreed. She had tried to tuck her hand back under Patrick's arm but he seemed always to be at the wrong angle. 'But it seems to me that she persuaded him to love her. Did you see his face when she accused him of assault? He looked betrayed!'

'Surely there was some misunderstanding,' said Patrick. 'Perhaps he was not bright enough to understand that her kindness to him was not something more.'

'It's possible,' said Durris, avoiding Hippolyta's eye. She was glad. 'I'm not going to arrest him for assault, anyway. Are you more convinced now, Mrs. Napier? Do you think it was Mr. Brown she met last night?'

'I'm sure of it,' said Hippolyta firmly. Julian's plump figure and dejected posture fitted perfectly, and his height in comparison with Basilia. And whatever misgivings she had about Basilia, she doubted that their guest would be trysting with two different men in the course of twenty-four hours.

They crossed the bridge to return to the town. The river was no easier than before, and the sky was again grey, more swollen looking even than the waters below. Durris left them at the inn, where he had managed to take a room despite the heavy tourist traffic: Hippolyta took the opportunity to go and see that the Dinnet House pony was still comfortable. It was, despite having bitten the stable boy three times: it had a self-satisfied air when Hippolyta greeted it, as though it had always said the time would come when someone would take it away from all this. She fed it a few oats, and walked it around the yard, while Patrick found some coins to console the stable boy.

Patrick did not seem disposed to speak much, and when Miss Verney joined them for dinner – looking wistfully disconsolate – he clammed up altogether. Hippolyta did not find his silence either comfortable or comforting: what was going on in his head?

She tried instead to focus on what they had learned in the course of the day, as she exchanged desultory words with Basilia and tackled the tender consolation that was Mrs. Riach's roast beef. Mr. Brookes was in fact Mr. Burns, of the Burns Mortification, and had been sneaking around the village checking to see that his trustees were behaving themselves. He had found no evidence – or none that he would tell them – that there was anything amiss, but he was still investigating. He had examined the papers in Dinnet House and appeared to have no qualms about breaking into Colonel Verney's study. He had been acquainted with Mr. Strachan and with Dr. Durward, and more to the point had been living in Ballater twenty years ago, when Mrs. Strachan's father – Mr. Tranter – and their manservant, Rab … Lattin, wasn't it? … had been murdered. So if the first murderer was the same person as the second murderer, Mr. Burns had been added to the list of possible suspects, along with the Strachans, the Strongs, and Dr. Durward, but not the minister and his wife. And Mrs. Kynoch, if she stood on a chair. It was somehow, even with the addition of Mr. Burns – and how strong was he really? – an unsatisfactory list.

If it were not necessarily the same murderer in 1809 and now, she went on, clearing the last vestiges of gravy from her plate, then she had to say that Julian Brown had looked very likely until she remembered his fortunate night of gambling with Dr. Durward. If she had not, she suspected that Mr. Durris would have arrested him then and there on the little wooded path at Pannanich. But what about Basilia?

She tried not to look at her guest across the dinner table as she considered the case against her. She had admitted that she had persuaded her uncle not to leave his money to Julian Brown – and she had lied to all of them about Julian Brown, saying that they believed him to be dead - and she certainly gained financially by her uncle's death. Since she seemed to have persuaded Julian that she had some feelings for him, could she have been hoping for his help in murdering their uncle? She shook her head: she could not see Basilia trusting Julian to take any active part in their uncle's murder. He was the very image of untrustworthiness. If he could not even remember his own genuine alibi, how could he possibly be relied upon to remember any untruths they wanted to establish?

Basilia had been in the house that night: she could have slipped down after Tabitha and taken her by surprise. Basilia was of a slighter build than her maid, but that element of surprise could have made the difference. It would have been a simple matter to kill her uncle, for he would have trusted her, and then perhaps she found that Forman had seen her, or heard her? At any rate, of all the suspects she was the one most likely to get away with standing on a chair in the kitchen, for whatever reason she might have given. 'What is that strange thing on the ceiling, Forman? No, come here and look – up there!' and a quick slice with a sharp knife.

Hippolyta shivered. Had Basilia heard the stories of the old murders, after all? Could she have drawn her idea from them, even?

Perhaps, she thought, on a more mundane level, Miss Verney was so greedy to be her uncle's sole heir that her apparent charming of Patrick had been some kind of ploy to have Patrick make over to her the money that Colonel Verney had left him. Heavens, did any of this make any sense? She was tired and anxious, she told herself, and though she was not entirely happy at leaving Patrick and Basilia alone together after dinner, in the end she excused herself, blaming the heavy weather, and went to bed early. Despite her rambling thoughts, she fell asleep straightaway.

When she woke, it was completely dark. She felt cautiously across the bed to Patrick's side: it was empty, and cold, and neat. He had not yet come to bed. What time was it, anyway? She slid over to his side, found his old repeater watch and pressed it. The delicate little chime told her that the last strike had been for half past two. Where was he?

She half rose to go and look, and then hesitated. What if he were not in his study? What if he were not alone? She might imagine all kinds of things, but she was not quite sure that she was ready to find them, all the same. She lay still, head swirling again.

Did she really believe Basilia Verney had killed her uncle? With or without her cousin Julian's co-operation? She no longer liked or trusted Basilia as much as she had once hoped to, but it was a big step from that to suspecting her of murder.

No, she was much more tempted by the idea of linking the latest murders with the old ones, for the chain of coincidences was too much for her And while she could almost persuade herself that Basilia was capable of slipping poison into a cup of tea, she could not quite see her slicing someone's throat. No, it had to be someone who had been in Ballater in 1809, someone connected with the Tranters in Dinnet House. But who? If she was honest, the person she really wanted it to be was Mr. Strachan.

Mr. Strachan, with his unctuous shopkeeper's manner and his bad tempered snarls at the dinner table, made a much more desirable murderer than Miss Verney, whatever her faults. Only his wife, who may well have been frightened to deny him, had vouched for his being at home on the night of the murders. He looked perfectly capable of slitting anyone's throat if they so much as looked at him the wrong way. He had threatened Colonel Verney, in her very hearing, and of the trustees of the Burns Mortification was he not the one most likely to have embezzled some of the money? Dr. Durward had plenty of money and no interest in business, and the minister was an innocent, by all accounts. Mr. Strachan was surely the one most likely to have had something to hide and therefore the one most likely to want to prevent Colonel Verney becoming a trustee – or even just examining the trust's papers. But what about Mr. Strong, the lawyer? He seemed upright and sensible, and dutiful, too: he would pay attention to any changes to the trust's funds, surely, and to the possibility of any recipients of the bursaries being less than genuine. That was what Mr. Burns had been suggesting, she thought: either that students who did not exist were in receipt of bursaries – but surely that would be difficult to arrange in a small parish or group of parishes, where most people knew everyone else – or that real students were not in receipt of the bursaries they were thought to be receiving. Hippolyta considered, gazing at the dark ceiling. Either would be difficult to arrange in a country place: she was fairly sure that Mr. Burns was wrong, and in any case Mr.

Durris was not going to allow him to travel to Aberdeen to investigate until the murderer was caught. Could Mr. Burns be the murderer? Could he have been a suitor for the lovely Miss Tranter – Mrs. Strachan now – and murdered Mr. Tranter because he stood in their way? But then why would he not have married Miss Tranter? Perhaps she did not want him: that would have been ironic. Understandable, then, that he might leave the country. But he had not left for another two years, so it seemed his conscience was clear. But then, she thought, he had not been flustered at the idea of breaking into Dinnet House, so perhaps if he had killed someone he would indeed have been quite calm about it. And, for pity's sake, he was not Mr. Strachan. She wanted Mr. Strachan to be the murderer.

She knew it was petulant, and of course she knew that for Mrs. Strachan to find her husband was a murderer would be beyond devastating. Hippolyta would not wish that on her. But she felt in her heart that Strachan was as guilty as could be, and she was desperate to find the proof. How could she do that?

She considered hard. Strachan had been at home when Colonel Verney had been killed. He had apparently been in the cellar of his father's shop when Mr. Tranter had been killed, but both he and Dr. Durward had been drunk, so perhaps – if he had not drunk quite so much, and waited until Dr. Durward was unconscious, then slipped out and back again … If he were stealing money from the trust, would it be in his house or in the shop? Would he show it in his business account books? She almost laughed at herself for such a ridiculous idea. But she felt an urgent need to go and look at Mr. Strachan's shop again, and to see perhaps that cellar. Should she wait until the morning, go in on some pretext and wait until another customer distracted him before she slipped down there? But the shopboy would see her: they seemed to have eagle eyes for customers there. Could she go now?

Her heart flicked into a swift, steady beat. Why not? She knew she could slip out of the house without disturbing anyone, and she could take the key with her so that she was not accidentally locked out. What about the shop end of things? She had no idea what the back of the premises looked like, but she knew there was an archway between Strachan's shop and the next building, where presumably one could deliver goods to a yard – and perhaps even to an outside hatch to the cellar. She might be able to open it without having to go through a door at all.

She would stay in her nightgown, she thought, and add, as she had last night, her dark cloak: all her dresses, even if she had felt up to lacing herself in unaided at this hour of the night, were altogether too wide and rustling for a discreet night time visit. Boots, however, would be practical, for she could walk softly enough in them. What about light? She had managed last night, chasing Basilia and her useless cousin, but she had been out of doors and the sky had still been quite light. Tonight was much darker, and a cellar would not allow in much natural light anyway. A candle would be a dangerous thing, and potentially fiddly to light in a strange place, and she could hardly carry it lit all the way from the house to Strachan's shop. Either it would blow out or it would attract the attention of that observant night watchman, Lang. A lantern? There must be one around … she tried to remember where she had seen one. The most likely place was in one of those presses that lined the corridor in the servants' quarters. She took a deep breath and rose at last, excited, and slipped her bare feet into a pair of short wool stockings, letting them roll down just above her ankles. A shawl would be useful for all kinds of things, she thought, and wrapped an old one around her head to keep out the night air: if she needed to carry anything, she could easily use that. Her boots were in the corner, and she slipped them on, tying the laces with care. Her cloak felt strange again over her nightgown, like an unfamiliar arm about her shoulders. She should probably not make a habit of this night time wandering, she thought: but she had to see if there was anything, anything at all in Mr. Strachan's shop that could help to determine whether or not he was a murderer. Put it like that, and the whole thing seemed entirely reasonable.

Downstairs she crept to the servants' door and eased it open. All was quiet beyond it. She stepped to the corridor press and reached inside, and was rewarded by the feel of a heavy metal square lantern, with a windshield which would make it all but invisible as she crossed the green. She had brought a tinderbox downstairs with her, and quickly struck a light with steel and flint, her hands shaking just a little. The wick flared and she jumped, then adjusted it warily, checking to see that the lantern was all set to burn for a couple of hours, at least. The tinderbox rattled as she slipped it into a fold of her cloak, in case she needed it later. Then she tucked her cloak more firmly about her, twitched her toes in her shoes, and lifted the lantern, closing the press firmly again. The door back to the hall was ajar, and she slid quietly through, making for the front door.

She was almost there. Her free hand reached out for the key, for it was for once in the lock. When the voice came, she almost dropped the lantern.

'Where are you going, Hippolyta?'

Chapter Twenty

There was no fire in the study fireplace, and the room was cold. Patrick had moved the single lit candle from his desk to the hearth, where it gave a poor impression of a warm blaze amongst the shadows cast by the lantern. Hippolyta shivered, even in her cloak. Patrick did not seem to feel it: he looked as if he had started undressing for bed, and then lost interest. He sat opposite her, his coat off, his waistcoat hanging open, his neckcloth loose and his shirt undone. His face was tired, but his eyes glinted wide awake as he watched her. If he had been indulging overmuch in the decanter of brandy that sat beside him, there was little sign of it. She wriggled her toes in her boots, and huddled into her cloak, feeling dreadful.

'Where were you off to, then?' Patrick asked, as if it was of limited interest. He considered, and then added, for her information, 'It's rather late.'

'I know,' she said, but her voice did not emerge as strongly as she would have liked. She cleared her throat.

'Were you, perhaps, hoping to meet someone?' he enquired.

'To meet someone? Not at all!' she exclaimed, thinking of the night watchman and Strachan's presumably empty cellar. She had actively wished not to meet anyone at all.

'I only wondered,' he said, 'because of course this is the second night in a row you have gone – wandering – in the middle of the night, isn't it?'

'Oh! But last night I was following Miss Verney …'

'So you say. I note that you did not mention it to me, but only to Mr. Durris.' He eased the brandy glass off the table and took a long sip, scowling, as if there were a bitter taste in his mouth. He set the glass down soundlessly. 'If you discovered last night what

Miss Verney was doing, and that she was not – it seems – merely sleepwalking, then why did you feel the need to go out again tonight? Particularly as Miss Verney is, as far as I know, sound asleep upstairs.'

Hippolyta shuddered. How did he know that? She glanced at the fire. Had he really been sitting here in this cold room all night, or had he been somewhere else? Was he half-undressed, or half-dressed? She slapped a hand to her mouth, suddenly nauseous. She could not even form the words in her head, let alone ask him out loud. He watched her, expressionless.

'So then, Hippolyta,' he asked in a flat voice, 'who were you going to meet? Mr. Durris?'

'Mr. Durris? No.' She sat up straighter, suddenly angry. How could he accuse her of a liaison, when it was he …? 'No, I was not intending to meet anyone – indeed I was hoping very much not to. I intended to try to enter Mr. Strachan's shop cellars, and perhaps to see his ledgers, to see if I could find any clue that might prove him to be a murderer.'

'What?' Patrick's jaw dropped.

'I think – well, to be honest I sort of hope, because he seems so likely – that he might have killed Colonel Verney and Forman. I think he was embezzling money somehow from the Burns Mortification trust and he thought the Colonel would spot the irregularity when he looked at the trust papers. He would have known all about the murders twenty years ago: he might have been trying to divert suspicion by making them look so similar. He threatened the Colonel in my hearing, you know, and what if his business prosperity comes from money illegally obtained? He just seems so likely, and yet I have no proof!'

Patrick stared at her for so long she thought he must have forgotten she was there. At last he took up his brandy glass again and drained it, pouring another generous inch from the decanter.

'Hippolyta,' he said, 'why are you so determined to become involved in this? Is it – could it possibly be because you think that I am guilty?'

She stared at him. His voice had faded towards the end of his question, as if he feared the answer. He still stared at her, but now his expression was softer, almost pleading. She forgot her fears, and pulled herself quickly across to touch his knee.

'Of course I don't,' she said firmly. But she could not help adding, 'Not of murder, certainly.'

'Are you sure?' His hand hovered near to hers, but not quite touching it.

'How could you think I do?' she demanded. 'I know you were out that night, but why on earth would you kill Colonel Verney? He was your friend, almost your patron, I thought. And Forman … he was nice. He loved his cats.' She tailed away, watching him: he did not seem convinced by her assertion. 'Why on earth do you think I think you killed them?'

'Well, Miss Verney told me …' he began, then looked directly at her. 'Miss Verney told me that you had confided in her that you were very much afraid I had killed her uncle,' he said at last.

'I never did!' Hippolyta reeled back on to her heels.

'She also told me that you were growing very fond of Dod Durris,' said Patrick, his face reddening. 'You do seem very easy in his company.'

'He's an intelligent man – and I'm trying to convince him that you – my husband - are innocent of the murders.' She glared at him. 'It's ridiculous. How could you believe her?'

'Well, I've known her for more than two years,' said Patrick, 'and she's always been perfectly honest. Why should I suddenly think that she was lying?'

'Because I'm your wife! I'm the one you're supposed to believe!' Even as she said it she thought it sounded childish, but she had gone this far. 'I suppose you have always preferred her to me? I wonder you did not marry her.'

'Prefer Miss Verney? Of course I don't!' He frowned, surprised if anything. 'We have always enjoyed the same music, as you know: she is a fine musician. But I have never wanted anything more than that from her.'

Hippolyta stared into his eyes, thinking.

'I suspect she wanted something more than that,' she said. 'I didn't see it at first, but that's what it is. She must have wanted you before, but you went and married me instead … She's nowhere near as nice as I thought she was,' she finished sadly.

'I suspect several of us are thinking that – including her cousin,' said Patrick. 'She seems to have led him up the garden path, too.'

'Well, I think so.' Hippolyta followed that line of thought for a moment. Even if Julian Brown had an alibi for the night of the murder, Basilia Verney did not. Was she the person Hippolyta should be investigating? Or did she just want to think that because she no longer liked her? 'Dearest, do you promise me you have never entertained any thoughts about Miss Verney?'

'I promise you, my dear,' said Patrick, and he reached out to touch her cheek. 'She could be the most wonderful musician in the world, and I should still prefer you – particularly if she has lied to me.'

'If what you say she said is true, she has lied to you,' Hippolyta confirmed, and it felt as if her heart were growing strong within her. 'I never told her, or anyone, that I was afraid you had murdered anyone, and I have not grown fond of Mr. Durris, I promise you.'

The next few moments were taken up with the kind of embrace that ought to follow a young couple's first quarrel, and few words of any sense were exchanged. Eventually, Hippolyta sighed a happier sigh than she had for days.

'Do you think she murdered her uncle?' she asked.

'Surely not!' said Patrick. 'She may be a liar and a manipulative one, but I cannot believe she is a murderer. But one thing is certain: I look forward to the moment she moves out of this house, for she seems to have been nothing but trouble since she appeared.'

'I am sorry, my dear.' Hippolyta was contrite. 'I should not have asked her to stay with us.'

'Not at all,' said Patrick, 'you could do no other: and I have come to realise in our short time together that, if nothing else, you are the most determined hostess I have ever met. Since you came I have had to share my home not only with my new wife and servants, but with a bereaved murder suspect who sleepwalks, her maid, a sick coachman who might or might not have been a thief, and seven white cats!'

'Oh!' said Hippolyta. 'When you put it like that …'

'Never mind! The cats, at least, are mostly delightful.' He lifted the candle and showed her three of them, curled up cosily on his desk chair in the shadowy room. 'Now, I think it is time you and I went back to bed.'

Hippolyta allowed him to help her up, then twisted her fingers together, eyeing the lantern where it still sat lit on the bookcase.

'What?' he asked, with amused wariness.

'I suppose you'll never let me go and break into Mr. Strachan's shop cellar now,' she said in as small a voice as she could manage. Patrick gave a brief laugh.

'Oh, my, you're serious!' He raised the candle to look into her face. He thought for a moment. 'My dear, I cannot let you go out about the town at night on your own. It is neither respectable nor, in the current climate at any rate, safe.'

'I know,' she whispered, disappointed.

'But if you will allow me to come with you – as your junior accomplice, of course ...'

She looked up. His face was straight, but his eyes were laughing.

'You'd come?'

'I'll come,' he said. 'But please: think of my medical practice. Let us try our level best not to be caught!'

'Let us hope,' Patrick whispered as they skirted the green, fearing to cross the exposed space, 'that the night watchman does not take us up as a courting couple up to no good, and bring us before the Kirk Session!'

'That would be distinctly embarrassing, on several counts,' Hippolyta agreed, and felt an awful giggle rise from somewhere in her stomach. She clutched his hand but pinched her ear hard with her other hand, hoping to use the pain to quell the hysteria. It almost worked.

'We should sneak out together in the dark more often,' Patrick went on, apparently oblivious to her struggles. 'It reminds me of the old days of our wooing, though then we were permitting to go no further than the end of the terrace after dark, as I remember.'

'We're a little further than that now!' She squeezed his hand, then nodded across the street. 'But besides that – we're here.' Something about the dark bulk of the shop front above them sobered her, and she swallowed quietly. 'Do you think Mr. Strachan has a boy sleep in the shop overnight?'

'I shouldn't think so: this is not Edinburgh or Glasgow,' said Patrick confidently. 'Though I suppose it would be a useful alarm against fire … And there are so many strangers here in town these days, and they would know his shop well. Perhaps he has taken some precautions.'

'You are very reassuring, dear,' said Hippolyta solemnly.

'Well, we shall have to find out,' said Patrick, rather less confidently. He grasped her hand a little more tightly, nodded at the entrance to the lane down the side of the shop, and with a glance about for any movement in the vicinity, crossed the street, Hippolyta nimble in his wake.

The lane was very dark, and between them they tried to conceal the lantern light from anyone passing by or looking down on the street, while still making use of it to avoid anything unsavoury underfoot. In a moment, however, they emerged into a generous yard, with the shop building behind them, a kailyard on one side and what looked like the back of a privy on the other. Beyond was a long patch of open ground, the nature of which they could not quite determine in the dark. Turning their backs on it, they examined the back of the shop. There was space enough there to turn a middle-sized cart and horse, a back door to give access to it, three shuttered windows on the floor above, and at their feet, as Hippolyta had hoped, a rough wooden hatch with a looped iron handle, leading, inevitably, to the cellar. She had been right: the cellar door seemed much less sturdy and secure than the back door.

It seemed so, but as it turned out, the cellar hatch was very tightly fastened. Patrick pushed and pulled at the iron loop, but the hatch moved only very slightly, making it clear that it was barred on the inside.

'I suppose it has to be,' he said in a low voice. 'He'll have wines and spirits and teas and coffees down there: he wouldn't want just anyone walking off with them.'

'Wretched man,' Hippolyta muttered. She stamped very quietly on the hatch, just to show it how she felt about it. 'I suppose the back door is just as bad.' She stepped carefully around the hatch, and climbed the narrow step up to the back door. There was a latch, and she tried it, gently working it so that it would not rattle. The door swung open, so suddenly she almost fell off the step.

'Oh!' she squeaked. It sounded tremendously loud, and they both froze, and listened. The shop was silent, and no sound came from the houses on either side. They slipped in through the door, and eased it closed behind them. They were in.

What they were in was a little hallway, the width of the door and not much longer. There was a door ahead of them, and one to their right. Both were closed.

Patrick was holding the lantern, so Hippolyta tried the door ahead of them. It opened easily too, and they found themselves in a little business room, with a shuttered window almost behind them facing the back of the building. Shelves lined one wall, and on one of them was a series of tall, cloth-bound volumes of a healthy width, all with dates on the spine.

'Ledgers?' Hippolyta whispered.

'I'd say so. Lots of them, though.'

They moved more closely, and studied the volumes carefully. Some were indeed ledgers: others had handwritten words on the spines: 'Day book'; 'Stock book'; 'Correspondence'. All were well-worn, and when Hippolyta lifted one or two down they did indeed contain what they should contain. Mr. Strachan was clearly an organised businessman.

'See: deliveries from Aberdeen,' Hippolyta pointed her finger at a page in the stock book from the previous week. The list included fish of various kinds, some cutlery, Belfast and Dutch linen, rum, wine, and three kinds of tea, one of particularly fine quality. The price of the bulk items was listed beside each one, as well as the price per pound, or per yard, or per piece, which Strachan evidently intended to charge for it. His profits were not perilously low.

'Come on, I thought you wanted to look at the cellar,' said Patrick. 'I suspect it's the other door.'

'Just a minute: let me see an old ledger.' She scanned the shelf, and as all the sections were in neat chronological order she quickly found the ledger for 1809 to 1812. She drew it out, knocking a little dust off the top of the pages. 'Here: this must be his father's handwriting.'

Strachan's father's hand was less well formed than his son's, but the records were still kept clearly. Hippolyta scanned the pages quickly. The columns of income and expenditure, profit and loss, told a slightly different story from the one indicated by the stock book of last week: old Mr. Strachan had run a much more dicey business, often in the red, and handling produce and goods that were more local and of, as far as Hippolyta could judge, a lower quality. What had happened to make the difference? Was young Mr. Strachan simply a better businessman?

She skipped down the columns and flicked through the pages, while Patrick held the lamp steady. Then she hit what she wanted: on the fifteenth of May, 1810, there had been a massive sum on the income side. It had not been spent all at once: to judge by the following sheets, there had been some building work, a little investment in a better quality of stock, and one or two new lines of products. More significantly, perhaps, it was at this point that old Mr. Strachan's writing all but disappeared, and young Mr. Strachan's took over.

'A marriage settlement?' Patrick breathed in her ear.

'Maybe. It says 'per Mr. Strong'.'

'That would make sense.'

'But what I need to find out is whether there are odd sums coming in over the last few years, ones from the Burns Mortification.'

'You'll never have time to go through all those ledgers,' Patrick objected. 'And they're so tidy he would be sure to miss any you took away.'

'If only …'

'No, come on,' said Patrick. 'Is he likely to make a ledger entry that says 'Money embezzled from Burns Mortification, two pounds, ten shillings and fourpence? It would be better hidden than that: you'd never find it.'

She gave the ledger a last hard stare, and reluctantly slid it back into place on the shelf.

'I suppose I hoped it would be obvious,' she sighed. 'But if Mr. Burns finds something out, then there would have to be an investigation, wouldn't there? Someone could come in and examine the ledgers, someone who knows more about these things than I do.'

'I thought you looked very competent,' said Patrick, impressed.

'Father let me play in some of his deedboxes when I was small,' Hippolyta explained. 'I always liked old bits of paper, so when he wanted me to learn my numbers he did it with some old accounts. Not that I was ever terribly good at them. Well, what about the cellar, then?'

Patrick put an arm around her shoulders, and led the way back to the other door they had passed as they came in. This time, it was locked, but they returned to the business room and found a rack of keys over the tiny fireplace. It did not take long to identify the cellar door key, and they quickly opened the door and found themselves, much as they had expected, at the head of a set of stone steps leading down into a generous and well-kept cellar. Above their heads, as they stood surveying the room, was the hatch to the yard, bolted with a heavy bar, and a ladder leading to it.

'No paperwork down here,' said Patrick, slowly turning with the lantern.

'No, but they're fine stores, aren't they?'

The walls were lined with heavy shelving, on which, all clearly labelled, were rows and rows of bins and barrels and baskets, as clean and tidy as ever Hippolyta had seen a cellar. No mouse or spider would ever contemplate setting up home here: they would be out in an instant, and nowhere to hide. She walked slowly down the room, admiring a feat of organisation that even her mother would have been proud of.

Her mother … She stared at the barrel in front of her.

'Patrick.'

'Yes, my dear?'

'Does this look familiar?'

He stepped over, lifting the lantern. The barrel had been painted with white paint with the words 'French brandy', with an official air. But the foot of the barrel – quite a large one, but one that could be rolled, she thought, easily enough by one strong man – was coated in a fine layer of blue powdery paint.

A noise above them made them both leap. Footsteps.

Patrick seized Hippolyta's hand and looked wildly around the room. If a mouse had nowhere to hide, nor did they. He quickly blew out the lantern, and pulled her back towards the stairs. Their feet made no sound on the flagged floor, but they could hear the footsteps above them, moving slowly, as if checking the building. They approached very close, Hippolyta reckoned, to the door of the business room.

Patrick was reaching up above his head in the darkness,

moving something. The bar across the hatch to the yard, that was it. The ladder to the hatch was hidden very slightly round the corner from the stairs they had descended, and he pushed Hippolyta on to the lower rungs, bundling her cloak after her. The door of the business room opened over their heads, and there was an awful pause. Whoever it was, would they check the cellar, or open the back door to look in the yard?

The second they heard the cellar door move, they were out, though Hippolyta scarcely knew how. She had the dead lantern in one hand and Patrick's coat tails in the other, and they scrambled not for the lane, but back, away from the shop, into the darkness behind it. There was a thump, and Patrick stopped suddenly, then she could hear him feeling quickly around something, scuffling and swearing very quietly under his breath. A voice cried out from the shop.

'Tam!'

'Fit?'

'Did you no close the cellar hatch after yon eggs arrived?'

'I did.'

'You did not. That's the second time this month, Tam. Mr. Strachan'll skin you alive.'

'Och, dinna tell him, Al, please?'

The voices were young: the shopboys that Hippolyta had wondered about. She peered back: dimly she could see a white face at the hatch, looking in her general direction. She turned away quickly, aware that her face was just as white.

'I thought I heared something,' said Al faintly.

'Fit kind of a thing?'

'I dinna ken.'

There was a thump, and an explosion of sound which it took Hippolyta a moment to identify. Then she smelled the rich aroma in front of them: Patrick had bashed into the hen house, and set the hens squawking.

'It's likely a fox!' cried out Tam in excitement. 'Should we gang after it?'

'Ach, no,' said Al, and he began to haul the heavy hatch closed. 'Likely it's away by now, and yon henhouse is built like Crathes Castle: no fox is going to get into that yin.' There was a final thud and the sound of the bar being slammed back, and Tam and Al were seen no more. Hippolyta felt in the darkness for Patrick.

'Are you all right?' she whispered urgently.

'Oh, just fine.' There was a hint of irritation in Patrick's voice. 'Strachan's damned Crathes henhouse has given me a black eye, that's all.'

'Oh, heavens! We'd better think of a good story for that. No one is going to want an accident-prone physician, are they?'

She reached out around the solid henhouse and found Patrick's hand, and he slipped his arm around her waist. Holding each other, they managed to negotiate the lane again into the street, and after a moment to check that no night watchman was around, they made their way back, circumnavigating the green, to their own front door, and slipped quietly inside. They took their damp clothes upstairs and spread them out to dry before Mrs. Riach found them, and were cosy in bed before Patrick's old repeater watch was prepared to give them four o'clock.

'Well, you didn't find anything, really, to link Mr. Strachan with the murder, did you?' Patrick asked, already sleepy. He lay on his back with a wet flannel on his eye, and it trickled a little cooling path on to the pillow where Hippolyta held his hand.

'Not with the murder, perhaps, no,' Hippolyta admitted. 'But that brandy barrel – well, it has to have been on the cart with our belongings, doesn't it? So at the very least, Mr. Strachan is selling smuggled spirits!'

Chapter Twenty-One

'Ugh,' Patrick remarked when he opened one eye the following morning – or the following morning proper. Hippolyta, reluctantly, had staggered to the window and opened the shutters on a dripping wet day more suited to October than August, the skies leaden, the air heavy.

'It's foul, isn't it?' Hippolyta mumbled. She felt as if her head had been stuffed with sheep's wool, and it was tangled at the back of her throat. Her eyes seemed oversensitive to what daylight there was. She turned back to the bed. 'Oh, my.'

'It hurts.' Patrick touched his closed right eye cautiously. 'I'd better take a look at it, I suppose.' He levered himself out of bed, holding his head. Hippolyta gave a wary laugh.

'We look as if we've been to a riotous party in Edinburgh, and danced till dawn. Actually,' she reflected, 'I've felt much better than this after most parties like that.'

'Yes.' Patrick squinted at himself in his shaving mirror. 'No permanent damage, I think. I'd hate to have to tell our grandchildren I'd been blinded by a hen house.'

'And that's not a story we'd better tell anyway,' said Hippolyta, waking up a little. 'What shall we say?'

'That you caught me making eyes at Miss Verney and punched me?' Patrick asked. Hippolyta scowled.

'Not funny: not yet, anyway. Better to keep it simple: say you tried to get out of bed in the middle of the night, tripped on the eiderdown and hit your head on …' She scouted around the room for something likely. 'On the knop of the poker there. It looks about the right size and shape.'

Patrick turned round and eyed her with his good eye.

'You're rather clever at making up stories, my dear. Perhaps I should watch you more closely!'

'You just need to be careful of the details,' said Hippolyta briskly, pulling on her wrapper. 'Now, I should go and face Mrs. Riach before she starts wondering why so many of our clothes are wet. I'll tell her one of the cats brought in another bird and we had to try to chase it out, and were caught in a shower. All right?'

'Yes, yes, of course. I hope you don't expect me to remember which cat?'

She grinned.

'I wouldn't expect you to remember which cat even if it had actually happened, so no, don't trouble!'

Hippolyta and Patrick were quiet over breakfast, still trying to waken up fully, and Basilia Verney ate her food and drank her cocoa with a kind of self-righteously delicate silence and the slightest of smirks. Hippolyta felt almost strong enough to tell her she would help her to pack as soon as she liked, but not quite.

'What are your plans for the day, Miss Verney?' she asked instead. 'I'm afraid the weather is not conducive to much outdoor activity.

'No indeed,' said Miss Verney primly. 'I rather thought this morning I should practise my music, though.' She flashed a look at Patrick from beneath her dark lashes. Patrick ignored it.

'I must go and see Dr. Durward about one or two business matters,' he said, rubbing the half of his face that did not hurt. Basilia heroically refrained from asking him about the bruise, and he did not mention it, but the sight of it seemed to evoke another little twitch of satisfaction to the smirk.

Mrs. Riach entered and squatted into something like a curtsey, before starting to clear plates.

'Strachan's boy,' she began, and Hippolyta felt herself tense. She did not look at Patrick. After a dramatic pause Mrs. Riach finished, 'says the river's rising.'

'It looked high yesterday,' Hippolyta agreed, her voice steadier than she had expected. 'Do you think it will breach its banks?'

'It has done it plenty times afore,' pronounced Mrs. Riach darkly. 'I'll no be going to Pannanich the day – nor the inn, neither.'

'I wasn't aware you frequented the inn, Mrs. Riach,' said Hippolyta. 'Well, let us hope that it does no damage. It may well go down again before anything happens.'

'Aye, that'd be likely.' Mrs. Riach jerked her head towards the window, through which steady rain could be seen drenching the garden. She stalked out of the room with two plates and a sugar bowl, just as Patrick was about to spoon sugar into his last cup of tea. He shrugged, meeting Hippolyta's eye.

'I can't imagine the wet weather is doing much for her rheumatism,' Hippolyta remarked lightly.

'Is that what it is?' Basilia asked. 'I thought it was just insolence.'

'She's a very good cook,' Hippolyta found herself saying defensively, though whether she was defending Mrs. Riach or her own management of her it was hard to say. Patrick drained his teacup, lips pursed a little.

'Well, I must be going,' he said. 'I hope the day improves!'

Hippolyta went to the door to see him off, and returned smiling to herself. Patrick's farewell had been very satisfactory, and a thought had occurred to her: the rain should keep Basilia indoors, but there was nothing to stop her popping out for a little on her own, was there? She knew exactly where she wanted to go, and she particularly did not want Miss Verney with her.

Patrick had gone out in his wet coat, though it was going to make very little difference, and it meant that they had no need to spin their yarn about cats and birds for Mrs. Riach or anyone else. In a similar way, Hippolyta swung her cloak around her and hurried out before anyone saw that it was still heavy with damp from the night before. It was not pleasant, but it was tolerable, particularly as she darted up the road and away from Miss Verney's insistent piano practice. Once again there were few people in the street for a Monday morning, and no one was lingering to watch who was passing and who was not. She slid past Strachan's shop, trying not to pay it too much attention, and hurried on up the hill to the edge of the town. The gateway of Dinnet House stood open as usual, the driveway unwelcoming amongst dripping trees tumbling in the rising wind, and the house itself grey and miserable as though it knew well what had happened within its walls, and was helplessly sorry for it.

The gravel squelched wet under her feet but there was no sign of life about the place to be disturbed: not even birds flew on such a soaking day. The front door was locked, as she had expected: she circled the house with interest, having never seen the sides and back before except as glimpses through the windows. There was the summer house, collapsed in on itself, as Basilia had described (and had hinted at all kinds of goings on within it, too, she thought crossly). There were the vegetable gardens in which Forman had worked and his cats had no doubt played. She came to some lawns, rather ill-kept, the soggy grass silver with rain and flattened by the wind, and as she stepped carefully along the back of the house she checked each window she passed, to see which room she was next to. It did not take long before she reached the Colonel's library, with its broken window frame. She put out a hand to it, testing to see how easy it would be to open.

'Trying a little burglary yourself, Mrs. Napier?'

She jumped. Turning, she found Dod Durris rounding the corner of the house after her, a polite frown on his broad face.

'I was – just interested,' she said quickly. 'If Mr. Burns admits he broke in here, and climbed over the windowsill, he must be stronger than he looks.'

'That's true. Are you wanting to go inside?' he asked without emphasis, and she blushed.

'If I may,' she admitted. He led the way back to the kitchen door, pulled a small bunch of keys out of his pocket, and let them both in to a scullery, which in turn led to the main kitchen where Forman's body had been found.

'What did you want to see?' he asked.

'Where did you get the keys?' she asked in turn, ignoring his question. 'You had them before, didn't you? Miss Verney took her uncle's keys away, but she left her own upstairs, and we left you in the house alone!'

'That's right,' he nodded. 'It seemed more polite.'

'Polite?'

'I needed to take a look around on my own. I'm sure if Miss Verney had thought about it she would have realised.' There was a very slight twinkle in his grey eyes, Hippolyta suddenly noticed.

'You wanted to take a look at her uncle's papers without her there, didn't you?' she asked slowly. 'That was why you didn't seem to care that someone had broken in. You had already looked at everything!'

He shrugged very slightly.

'I did. I had. Fortuitously, as it happens,' he added.

'Because,' said Hippolyta, 'you knew that she removed something herself, that day when the three of us were here together.'

'You saw that, did you?' he asked. 'I missed it, I must confess. But I know what she took: she took her uncle's old will, the one that had been superseded. And then she told us the Colonel always destroyed old papers!' There was the least hint of admiration in his voice, and Hippolyta found herself quite annoyed by it.

'She's an untrustworthy little –' She stopped. Durris looked at her with interest. 'I found out one or two things she has been doing. Nothing to do with the murder, but still …'

'I see,' said Durris. 'Deceitful?' he asked.

'Yes.'

'Greedy?'

She considered.

'Not as such, no. But it did cross my mind that she might have been very interested in the contents of her uncle's will.'

'Yes, indeed. The old will split the bulk of the estate with Julian Brown, her cousin, you see, but the new one gives it all to her. That's how I knew what his name was when you pointed him out - I had seen it in the old will.'

'You don't suppose,' said Hippolyta, 'that she had been leading poor Mr. Brown on in the hopes of keeping the money together?'

'It would not surprise me in the slightest,' said Durris blandly.

Hippolyta remembered the convincing embrace on the bridge by night.

'Hm,' was all she trusted herself to say out loud.

'But anyway,' said Durris, 'what was your interest in the house?'

'I just wanted to see everything again,' she said. 'Not from some gruesome curiosity, I assure you: if I had my choice I'd never come to this house again. But I felt I needed to see the two places again, the hall and the kitchen. Something is not quite right in my head – if you see what I mean – and I need to settle it.'

'Then settle away. Do you need me?' he asked, taking a step towards the scullery again.

'No, I don't think so, thank you.'

'Then I have something I want to do in the garden, if you will excuse me.'

'Of course.'

He left, closing the back door gently behind him, and she went on into the house, to the hall where she had found Colonel Verney in his chair.

The difference – a difference – between this murder and those in 1809, she thought, was that presumably Mrs. Strachan's father, Mr. Tranter, had been able to move about of his own freewill, and Colonel Verney had not been able to move without Forman's – or somebody's – help. Mr. Tranter had been found outside in the garden, but Colonel Verney was inside, here. She sat on the stairs for a moment, considering, then rose and went back to the kitchen. She pulled out a chair, and sat down, staring at the stains on the floorboards where Forman's body had lain.

The attacker had come into the house – which would not have been difficult, because Forman would not have locked the front door, though he had already locked the kitchen door beyond the scullery – and what? Did the killer walk in the front door and find Colonel Verney in the hall? Did he chase Forman into the kitchen and attack him?

What was Colonel Verney doing in the hall on his own? Had Forman left him there for a moment while he fetched something? She pictured Forman's body lying there, on the floor. There had been something lying on the floor in front of him: what had it been? Whatever it was, Mrs. Kynoch and Martha had probably cleared it away when they tidied. She concentrated hard, trying to picture what she had seen when Forman had been lying there. There had been milk, she realised suddenly, remembering the coppery glow of a pan and the beginnings of a sour smell. There had been a pan of milk, spilt on the floor.

There, that was it. Forman could not have been running away from the killer, because he would not have been in the hall to see the Colonel's murder while leaving a pan on the fire unguarded. He must have come into the kitchen to fetch the milk for Colonel Verney's bedtime drink, knowing he would only be a moment, and leaving the Colonel in the hall. But there would no doubt have been enough time, then, for an intruder walking into the hall and unexpectedly or deliberately finding the Colonel there to kill him, in his chair, and leave again. He had locked up Tabitha. Why then had the murderer gone to the trouble of walking into the kitchen and killing Forman?

There was only one explanation that made sense to Hippolyta. The murderer had killed Forman because it was Forman he had come to kill. The Colonel had only been killed because he could identify the killer.

They had been looking in the wrong place: it had nothing to do with Colonel Verney's will, or Basilia's greed, or anything Mr. Strachan might have been doing with the Burns Mortification funds. Now they had to think about why someone would want to murder Forman.

And, she thought quickly, did that shed any more light on what had happened in 1809? When Mr. Tranter had been murdered, was it simply because he knew who had killed his manservant? What was the man's name: Rab something. Rab Lattin, that was it. Was the killer still following the pattern? Or could the latest murders have been more directly connected with Forman himself? She reflected: she knew almost nothing about him, except that he had been a soldier and that he liked cats. Oh, and Basilia Verney had said that she thought he had no relatives. But how reliable was that?

She had to tell Mr. Durris what she had worked out. She glanced outside. The wind was stronger now, and rain was lashing at the garden's lush, weedy greenery. She could just see Mr. Durris' hat somewhere near the summerhouse. The idea of going outside was not appealing, but it had to be done. She went to the kitchen door and called out to him, but he did not hear her over the wind. Instead she pulled her cloak tight, grabbed the wing of her sail-like bonnet, and slammed the door shut after her, making her way by what turned out to be a circuitous route to the collapsed summerhouse.

Mr. Durris was round the side of the structure, which looked like a badly-folded letter on a grand scale, covered in moss and lichen. He looked round at her voice.

'What are you looking for?' she half-shouted.

'Looking at,' he corrected. 'Just wondering about these holes.' He kicked at the rotting feet of the summerhouse's wooden walls. There were holes of various sizes dug into the earth there.

'Badgers?' asked Hippolyta. 'Foxes?'

'No smell. But I suppose they are old ones,' he added. 'Have you finished in the house?'

'Yes. Well, no. Can you come back inside? I want to tell you something, and I can't hear myself think out here.'

He nodded, and waved her on ahead of him back to the kitchen door. Once they were inside, the silence of the empty house shouted at them after the wind.

'What is it?' he asked, standing in the kitchen by the empty fireplace. She went through with him what she had concluded, and waited to see what he would think. It was a while before he answered.

'Aye,' he said slowly, nodding. 'It maybe makes sense.'

'Of course it does!' she exclaimed, though she was delighted to have him even acknowledge the possibility. She pointed down at his feet on the floorboards. 'The milk pan was there, with the milk spilled. He would have been fetching it for the Colonel, wouldn't he? He would not have stopped with the Colonel waiting in the hall to warm milk for himself or for Tabitha, and Miss Verney had already had hers. He –' She stopped, staring at the floor.

'What is it, Mrs. Napier? Are you all right?'

'The milk had run down between the floorboards. The kitten had got under the floorboards and he had lifted them to rescue it. He found it was all full up with rubbish underneath, and Miss Verney told him to clean it out … What if he found something under there?'

'What kind of something?' Durris did not look as if he quite followed her, but he was willing to try. 'Oh: something to do with the first murder?'

'They never found the blade, did they?' Hippolyta went on, her mind galloping. 'A very sharp knife, and they never found it.'

'Those boards have been moved already,' said Durris. 'Probably that was when Forman was tidying up.'

'No,' said Hippolyta quickly, 'no, it can't be. Not the last time. That stain there is spilt milk, even though someone has tried to clean it up, But look: it's only half of the stain. The other half is here.' She pointed under the table. 'Someone that night, after Forman was killed, lifted this floorboard and searched underneath it, but put it back the wrong way round.'

'But presumably,' said Durris, nodding, 'that means that whatever the murderer feared he would find, the murderer then recovered for himself and took away? And whatever it was, even now, it would link him to those murders in 1809.'

'Does that make sense?' Hippolyta looked anxiously at him.

'It does: why else would anyone come in here after Forman's death and lift a floorboard? But who was it, and what did they find – and do they still have it?

Hippolyta fought her way down the road back towards the town, the wind whipping the thoughts from her head. It all seemed to make sense, she was sure. But who could it have been? Mr. Strachan? No, he had an alibi, and so, therefore, did Dr. Durward. Mr. Burns? Would he have been strong enough?

She jumped back as a roof slate crashed in front of her on to the road, and her heart raced. This was no weather to be out. Was that thunder? It was hard to tell with the wind lashing about her ears. She stopped by a small house to catch her breath, and to her surprise the door opened and she was bundled inside.

'Mrs. Napier! What a day to be out in!'

It was Ada Strong, grinning up at her.

'Oh, thank you, Miss Strong! I had intended to pay a call on you and Miss Strong, but not quite like this!'

'Aye, well, you'll be wanting a dish of tea, I should think – if we can get the fire to draw.' Miss Ada led her into a cluttered parlour, and a maid removed her bonnet and cloak, scuttling off to try the fire. Miss Strong was beside the parlour fire wrapped in shawls, with a blanket over her lap.

'Forgive me for intruding, Miss Strong,' said Hippolyta, curtseying.

'I doubt you had no choice,' said Miss Strong. 'My sister just announced she had seen you in the street, and took off to snatch you inside. You were not going anywhere urgently, I hope?'

'Home, that is all,' Hippolyta admitted. 'But with the weather as it is, I am very pleased to stop for a little, if I am not disturbing you at all.'

'Not at all, my dear,' said Miss Ada with a twitch of her eyebrows. 'It's around this time of day that my brother crawls out from his bookroom and joins us in a weary cup of tea, and we're delighted to have some company to liven us up a little.'

'Ada!' cried Miss Strong, as if it was her response to anything her sister said. The maid must have been ready with the tea, however, for she brought it in quickly, and in a moment Hippolyta heard a door in the hallway open and close, and Mr. Strong appeared, rubbing his hands together, his eye on the plate of shortbread. He was taken aback to see Hippolyta in the parlour, too.

'Mrs. Napier! I had no idea you were here. Venturing out on a day like this!'

'I was passing, and Miss Ada very kindly invited me in,' Hippolyta explained.

'Dragged her in, more likely,' Miss Strong added with emphasis.

'I was very grateful to be dragged,' said Hippolyta with a smile. 'And I had hoped to call on you, anyway.'

'Is there gossip?' demanded Miss Ada, her mouth full of shortbread. 'Has anyone been arrested for killing the Colonel?'

'Not that I know of,' Hippolyta admitted: she was sure that Mr. Durris would have told her if anyone had. 'But I wanted to know a little more about those murders in Dinnet House twenty years ago. What an extraordinary story!'

'Isn't it just?' Miss Ada breathed, and even her siblings nodded agreement.

'What was Mr. Tranter like? Was it difficult to think of anyone who might have wanted to kill him?'

'You knew him best, brother, didn't you?' said Miss Strong, tutting a little as she turned to find Mr. Strong brushing shortbread crumbs from his waistcoat front over the carpet. 'They were at school together, weren't you?'

'He was a few years older than me, though,' said Mr. Strong. 'He was a quiet, bookish man, very strict in his religious observance even as boy. I doubt he kept a close rein on young Bella - Miss Tranter. Mrs. Strachan as she is now.'

'I never had the impression that she resented that, though, did you?' Miss Strong looked at her brother. 'She's always been a respectable girl, Bella.'

'And would he really have approved of Mr. Strachan as her husband?' Hippolyta asked tentatively, trying not to let her own suspicions of Mr. Strachan tint her voice.

'Old Strachan was a decent man, an elder of the Kirk,' said Miss Strong. 'There wasn't a great deal of money, I should have thought, in those days.'

'Would Dr. Durward not have been a better match?' asked Hippolyta. 'And just as handsome.'

'Well, beauty is in the eye of the beholder, of course,' said Miss Strong knowledgeably. 'And of course, he had no money then, either: just back from his medical studies and trying to set up his practice. Not so many people in Ballater in those days, either: he didn't have it easy. They were both braw lads.'

'And good friends, I gather,' said Hippolyta, as if the idea were an appealing one. 'It was a blessing for Mr. Strachan that Dr. Durward was able to confirm where Mr. Strachan had been on the night of those murders, wasn't it?'

'Oh, it wouldn't have been the only night they spent in that cellar!' cried Miss Ada.

'Ada!'

'Well, it wasn't. Young Strachan never had a good head for drink: he was the despair of his father in those days!'

'That can't have appealed to Mr. Tranter,' said Hippolyta, trying to sound concerned.

'I suppose he thought he would grow out of it before he ever made an offer for Bella,' said Miss Strong. 'And he had, really: he started working with his father and the shop grew. It's the young lad has the business head, of course. And there would have been plenty of money with Bella: Tranter was a gentleman, you know.'

'Aye, capital, capital: that's what that business needed,' said Mr. Strong contemplatively.

'Not that you would know much about such things, brother, eh?' said Miss Ada with a sharp little smile. 'My brother's never had a head for the figures, have you?'

'I manage well enough!' Mr. Strong defended himself. 'I could not have run my own business all these years if I could not manage the arithmetic, could I?'

Miss Ada pressed her lips together and raised an eyebrow at

Hippolyta.

'Ada!' cried her sister.

'In any case it must be very useful to have a successful businessman like Mr. Strachan amongst the trustees of the Burns Mortification,' said Hippolyta, with as innocent a look as she could muster.

'Oh, aye, it's tremendously useful,' Mr. Strong agreed. 'And Colonel Verney would have been an excellent addition, too. I've never been very happy with only the four trustees: I suppose we'll have to try to find someone else suitable now – someone that everyone will approve of,' he added, sourly.

Chapter Twenty-Two

It felt like a rather bad idea to leave the Strongs' moderately warm house, but the rain and wind had eased very slightly, and Hippolyta did not want to intrude on the Strongs any longer. The maid had done her best to dry at least the lining of Hippolyta's cloak, and though it smelled very smoky it had a lingering warmth about it that made the first few steps into the rainwashed street tolerable. The air was odd, neither warm nor cold, with that slight fizz that comes with a storm – perhaps she had indeed heard thunder earlier. Like her, others had scuttled out to deal with whatever business was most urgent in the lighter rain, skipping over deep puddles and dodging waterspouts from roofs and pipes, clutching hats to their heads and shawls around their shoulders, keeping their greetings concise. The ground was sodden and slippery, and the green sat like a great loch in the middle of the village, the grass beaten flat and dark.

Interesting, she thought as she darted and ducked with the rest: the Strongs seemed to be in some agreement that Mr. Strong could not really have been keeping a competent eye on the business side of the trust. Mr. Strachan, with his excellent business mind, could easily have tricked him. But could he have tricked Dr. Durward? It would be a very good thing to have a talk with Dr. Durward, but she could hardly go and call on a bachelor in his house on her own. She would have to apply her mind to the problem of seeking out a few private words with him.

And Mr. Burns: why had she not remembered to ask them about him? Though Mr. Burns himself had implied that he had not known Mr. Strong very well: he had been closer to contemporary with Mr. Strachan and Dr. Durward, with the Strongs somewhat older, and Mr. Tranter older again. Who else would have known him well? Mr. Douglas the minister was no use: he and his wife had only moved here since that time. The previous minister was dead.

But Mrs. Kynoch, the previous minister's widow – she was still alive. She knew Mrs. Strachan well, and presumably had known the others all that time, too. She might be the person to ask for more details about the old murders. It was possible she might have something useful to say.

She pulled out her little watch, and checked the time, not sure by the day's dreadful light what hour it might be. She was shocked to find out that it was dinner time. She skirted the soaking green, slithering on muddy paths, and hurried home, to find that Patrick was not to be there: he had sent a message saying he had been detained at Pannanich Lodge, but would try to be home before dusk.

Hippolyta glanced out of the window: it had been dusk all day. She sat gloomily with Basilia in the miserable dining room, doing her best to ignore Miss Verney's continued apparent delight at what she evidently thought was a rupture between her host and her hostess. The meal was not one of Mrs. Riach's best: there seemed to be water in everything, and a smokiness again from chimneys trying to draw in the brisk wind. They retired in virtual silence to the parlour where they had to light candles even to read the Aberdeen papers, until eventually Hippolyta could stand it no longer, claimed to be going out to fetch something from Strachan's shop, and shot out of the front door still wrapping her cloak around her – a mistake, in the circumstances, as the wind was now violent.

Mrs. Kynoch's little cottage, however, was just the other side of the green, visible from her own front gate. She stepped up to the door and knocked, before she could change her mind or the weather could send her running back across the green and home.

The cottage was tiny, when she looked at it, but possessed of an upper storey – well, half a one, anyway, the dormer windows low-set on the slated roof. Hippolyta was just wondering whether she herself would have been able to stand upright in it, when the door opened, and Mrs. Kynoch peered out. She was wearing an apron over one of her more vibrant printed gowns, and was clearly in the middle of something busy, but she greeted Hippolyta without hesitation and hurried her into the house, out of the rain.

'My dear Mrs. Napier! Out in this! Come in, come in quickly, and I'll pop the kettle on.'

They were in a very narrow hallway out of which a toy staircase ascended to the upper half floor. Mrs. Kynoch took her damp cloak and bonnet herself, and waved Hippolyta into one of the front rooms.

'The parlour is much smarter, my dear,' she squeaked, 'but the fire has not been lit all morning, and you might catch your death, and then what would I say to dear Dr. Napier? And the girls won't mind in the least.'

They were in a schoolroom, to Hippolyta's complete surprise. At a round table in the middle, three girls of around eight or nine were practising their handwriting, and as far as Hippolyta could see they were very competent at it. By the window were two smaller girls with their sewing, one with oversized glasses sliding down her little nose and her tongue sticking stiffly out in concentration. An older girl, perhaps closer to twelve, leapt up with a smile at their entrance and swung the kettle over the fire, setting down her book which turned out to be a French reader.

'Girls! What do we do when we have a visitor?' Mrs. Kynoch put a gentle hand on the back of one of the little ones, and the girls all rose to their feet, wobbling into curtseys.

'Good day, ma'am,' they chorused, and Hippolyta found herself curtseying back.

'Have a seat, do,' said Mrs. Kynoch. 'Just move Puss there, he won't mind as long as he can sit in your lap.'

Hippolyta offered a finger and thumb to the nose end of the enormous mound of fur embedded in the only armchair. A condescending sniff was forthcoming, and the cat angled his head for a reverent scratch, then allowed Hippolyta to pick him up. His weight was equivalent to all six white kittens put together, and she felt she had been pinned into the chair. The cat began an anticipatory purr and she obliged by stroking him.

'Some tea, Mrs. Napier?' Mrs. Kynoch offered her a cup, setting it on a little table beside her where she could reach it without disturbing the cat.

'Thank you. I had no idea you ran a school, Mrs. Kynoch.'

'Oh! Well, it's always good to keep active. And I took great pleasure in learning myself when I was young, and it does young women no harm at all to have their letters and numbers, as well as the more domestic tasks.'

'Not at all!' Hippolyta agreed. 'But French, too?'

The older girl with the French book looked up defensively.

'All learning is useful,' she said clearly.

'I agree,' said Hippolyta, as Mrs. Kynoch gave the girl a warning glance. 'I'm delighted to find it here.' She hoped she did not sound too much as if she had expected Ballater to be an illiterate backwater.

'We do a little German and Italian, too, just enough to be able to read easy forms of the classics,' Mrs. Kynoch continued. Hippolyta looked in astonishment about the room, which was lined with books. She had underestimated Mrs. Kynoch's education, clearly.

'I'm sorry to have interrupted your work,' she began, more optimistic than she had felt before, 'but I had wanted to ask you something.'

'Then ask, by all means!'

'I don't know if you will wish to answer in front of your pupils,' said Hippolyta, with an apologetic look at the girl reading French. 'It concerns – what Mrs. Strachan told Miss Verney and me on Saturday night. The events of 1809.'

'Oh yes.' Mrs. Kynoch was solemn. 'Girls? Those buns should be just about ready to come out of the oven, now. Why don't you all pop into the kitchen and have some? There's milk in the pantry. Cattie, don't be greedy, pet, and don't eat the buns too hot! Mary, will you make sure any spills are mopped up? No, you can leave the book here, dear.'

Mary reluctantly herded the other girls out of the room and Hippolyta listened to them skipping down the passage to the kitchen. Mrs. Kynoch waited until the sounds had faded, then smiled at Hippolyta.

'That was very considerate, my dear. Children make up quite enough ghost stories on their own without adding to their material. And little Annie is quite nervous enough with the thunderstorm.'

'The weather is dreadful, is it not?'

'It's hardly August, eh? But we'd best get along with whatever you want to know, before they come back full of buns!'

'Of course, forgive me. The parallels between the present

murders and the old ones is very striking, as we all agreed. I'm trying to find out if there's a deliberate link between them. What do you think? There are people here now who were in the village then, too. Do you think someone could have killed all four men?'

Mrs. Kynoch eyed her thoughtfully.

'I suppose you've been upset by finding the bodies, my dear. You feel responsible in some way for sorting it all out, is that it?'

'It's awful for Miss Verney to have it hanging over her like that.' Hippolyta was evasive. She was worried that she was simply suffering from an unnatural level of curiosity.

'Oh, yes, Miss Verney. Is she still staying with you?'

'For now, yes.'

Mrs. Kynoch's eyes looked somehow much more intelligent than they had before. Hippolyta was sure at once that she knew exactly what Basilia Verney was like, and possibly what she had been up to. Mrs. Kynoch adjusted her apron over her skirts. Puss rose stiffly, turned round, and settled again across Hippolyta's lap.

'Was there anyone in particular you wanted to know about?'

'Well, I suppose, Dr. Durward and Mr. Strachan, and maybe Mr. Strong though I don't think he was in the same circle, and Mr. Burns, perhaps?'

'Mr. Burns?'

'Yes, the one who set up the Burns Mortification.'

'Yes, yes, I remember him well. I was just a little surprised that you had thought to ask about him. He was indeed a friend of both Mr. Strachan and Dr. Durward. He's another one who must have done well for himself: all three of them are much more prosperous now than they were then.'

'They were all local? I know Mr. Strachan worked in his father's shop.'

'That's right, and a poor enough place it was then. Dr. Durward came in to the school from somewhere around the Pass of Tullich, and Mr. Burns – it's a long time since I thought of him! His father was a … what now? A squarewright, I believe, but he had an accident and couldn't work. They were all at the school together, and my husband taught them for a while when they were a bit older. They were all bright. Dr. Durward, now, he was the one wanted to go to the university: Marischal College, he went to, in Aberdeen, and did his medicine there, on a scholarship. I thought he would be off then to some big town to gather up a fancy fashionable practice, but I doubt young Durward was always that bit too lazy for such things. Instead he came back here, and the fancy fashionable practice gathered itself around him. I never knew such a lucky man! But there, he's living on his own and frittering his money away on cards and such. I wonder if he's really happy – though he does look it, I admit.

'Mr. Strachan was the one with the business head always, working out ways of improving his father's shop. Money was his main aim in life, and I think he's made it, though he's never seemed settled and happy. Worldly things never give you true happiness in the end. I wonder if Mr. Burns is any happier? He wrote to my husband, oh! five or six years ago, not long before my husband died, and asked him to set up the Burns Mortification. He had no family, no wife or anything out there in that dreadful country, and so much illness about. But he was generous with what he had, and wanted the boys in the school he had been to to be able to go to university, if they wanted and were clever enough. He was a practical sort of a man, though he was good at languages, I remember. My husband was delighted to help, and he brought in Mr. Strong to make sure it was all legal, and Mr. Strachan and Dr. Durward at Burns' own suggestion, I believe, as trustees. It's been a great success: Mary that you saw there reading the French, her two brothers are both at King's College on Burns money, and doing very well. Clever family,' she sighed happily.

'What about the Tranters?' Hippolyta asked. 'I take it Mr. Strachan visited there often?'

'Aye, he and Dr. Durward and Mr. Burns, to a lesser extent, too. Mr. Burns was always itching to be away out of the village, whereas Dr. Durward was too idle and Mr. Strachan had his mind very much focussed on his father's shop, and his dreams and his goals were all there. But yes, the three of them would visit Dinnet House together. Bella – that's Mrs. Strachan – she had a couple of friends who would spend time with her up there, and no one knew who was courting which or if anyone was.'

'I heard that Mr. Tranter was quite a strict man?'

'Oh, he was. There was nothing improper going on at all: walks in the garden together, reading, some music.'

'Are the other girls still in the village?'

Mrs. Kynoch thought for a moment.

'No, no, they've both moved away. Charlotte married a man that took her to Calcutta! But I think Sarah went to Glasgow: that's right. Her brother became a minister and she went down there to keep house for him, and married a man there. Oh, they're away this long time.'

'So if no one knew who was courting whom,' Hippolyta asked, 'why was Mr. Strachan chosen as a suspect?'

'I suppose because he'd been there on his own that evening. Or not exactly on his own, but he had gone into the house while Dr. Durward had taken a walk in the gardens.'

'That night? But I thought –'

'Oh, not late on! They must have been there in the early evening – now, let me see if I can remember, for it's a long time ago. It was a Sunday evening and they had gone to call on the Strachans, but for some reason Dr. Durward wanted to stay outside and Strachan went in on his own. But Bella and Mr. Tranter were both out, at a friend's house for supper, so he came away again and he never said why he had gone – I suppose he didn't need to, for they were always dropping in. And Bella, of course, was able to say that her father had been with her then, and their manservant would have been there when they came home, and that was after Mr. Strachan had been … Oh, dear, it's all coming back! We were all so terribly upset at the time, and yet now looking back I can scarcely remember Mr. Tranter's face. Sometimes I can't decide if time is a good thing or a bad one: did the Lord send it as a blessing or as a curse?'

She rearranged herself, rolling gently from side to side on her ample hips, thinking back, her mind long into the past now.

'And then, of course, poor dear Bella came to stay with us. I had cause to be grateful to Mr. Strachan, I have to say, for she was in a bad way. She and her father were very close, and whereas before she had been very lively and bright and happy, afterwards she became quite withdrawn. Well, you see how she is now: she's terribly shy. She hates going out into company. Mr. Strachan came and visited her every day, trying to draw her out of herself, and I think if it hadn't been for him she would never have married at all, for no other man would have had the patience to do all he did. It was heartwarming to watch him.'

So Mrs. Strachan was not aloof! All Hippolyta had been doing to try to impress her, and it was just that she was nervous of company.

There was a sound at the door, and Hippolyta looked up, ready to change the subject if the little girls were about to flood back. Instead it was Mrs. Strachan standing there, her mouth open in surprise to see Hippolyta sitting by the fire.

'Mrs. Strachan!' Hippolyta tried to rise, but the cat had other ideas.

'No, please,' said Mrs. Strachan quickly in her light voice. 'Puss will never forgive you. Please don't!'

Hippolyta sank back down.

'Mrs. Strachan was upstairs having a little lie-down,' said Mrs. Kynoch. 'She has not been feeling very well lately, have you, my dear?'

'Just a little tired,' agreed Mrs. Strachan. 'It's always so noisy at home, with the children and Mr. Strachan about.'

'Even the weather is noisy today,' Hippolyta added. The wind was rising again, and whistling in the chimney. The fire crouched and ducked as if whipped.

'My dear,' said Mrs. Kynoch to Mrs. Strachan, 'Mrs. Napier has been asking for more information about your father's death.'

Mrs. Strachan paled, but did not seem shocked. Hippolyta wondered at Mrs. Kynoch telling her.

'What else did you want to know?' she asked huskily.

'I suppose I want to know anything that will help us to find who killed Colonel Verney and Mr. Forman,' said Hippolyta.

'She is convinced the same person killed all four men,' put in Mrs. Kynoch.

'Well, either that, or someone heard of the old murders, and thought it would work again,' said Hippolyta. 'I am in a tangle over this!'

'Why not leave it to Mr. Durris?' asked Mrs. Strachan, puzzled.

'Well, the sheriff's man did not manage to find the first murderer, did he?' Hippolyta asked gently.

'But Mr. Durris seems a practical, sensible man,' Mrs. Strachan objected.

'A man of information, too,' agreed Mrs. Kynoch.

‘I am sure you are right,’ Hippolyta conceded. ‘But … But he has a notion that Patrick might have killed Colonel Verney, and I know he did not!’

The silence that followed was not a comforting one. Mrs. Kynoch and Mrs. Strachan stared at her, and she could tell that each of them was considering the possibility in their minds. She had made things worse: now rumours of Patrick’s guilt would spread, and even if he was never arrested for the murders people would always remember that he had been suspected. And who would call in a physician who had been suspected of murder?

‘Well, my dear Mrs. Napier,’ said Mrs. Kynoch at last, ‘that seems to me to be a perfectly good reason for you to try to find out who really killed them.’

‘You mean you don’t believe he did?’ Hippolyta’s voice was as squeaky as anything she had ever heard Mrs. Kynoch say.

‘I shouldn’t think so for a moment,’ said Mrs. Kynoch firmly. ‘Dr. Napier is a very good man, anyone can see that.’

‘But he wasn’t even in that evening! He was called to see a patient at the inn, and then they couldn’t find her, and he was there for ages only nobody remembers how long or quite when …’ All the stress of the past week fell upon her head in one deluge like the rain outside, and Hippolyta found herself sunk over the furry back of the huge cat on her lap, sobbing her eyes out.

‘There, there, dear! Have another cup of tea,’ said Mrs. Kynoch, and her squeaky voice seemed infinitely kind.

‘Mother,’ said Hippolyta breathlessly, trying to sit up, ‘would be so ashamed of me.’

‘Well, she isn’t here,’ said Mrs. Kynoch simply. ‘Cry all you like, my dear: Mrs. Strachan and I will never say.’

‘How nice you are!’ Hippolyta gasped, and once again fell to heavy sobbing. It seemed an age to her, but after a short time she managed to straighten up, sipped her tea, and accepted a clean handkerchief from Mrs. Strachan.

‘Mrs. Kynoch is splendid when anyone is feeling – well, second rate.’ Mrs. Strachan put out a tentative hand and took Hippolyta’s. ‘There is no one like her.’

‘Nonsense, Bella, dear,’ said Mrs. Kynoch, but there was a little blush on her gentle face. She filled a cup for Mrs. Strachan and refilled her own, cocking an ear to make sure that her pupils were still peacefully destroying buns and milk in the kitchen. 'But I think we might need to help you, if only by listening to what you're thinking about.'

'After all,' said Mrs. Strachan, 'just because you are trying to prove your husband didn't murder Colonel Verney, it doesn't necessarily mean that his murder is connected with my father's.'

'But there are so many coincidences!' cried Hippolyta, making the cat jump. 'Please, Mrs. Strachan, tell me something. Tell me about Rab Lattin.'

'Rab Lattin?' Mrs. Strachan was puzzled.

'Your father's manservant, wasn't he? The one who was murdered that night, just as Forman was last week.'

'Well ... yes, I suppose so.'

'Tell me about him.'

'I don't know what to say.' Mrs. Strachan was hesitant, confused by the question. 'He was … um … he had been in the household since he was a boy, I believe: I couldn't remember a time before that night when he had not been there. My father trusted him absolutely, I know that: Lattin had all the keys, locked everything up at night, witnessed legal documents for my father, all kinds of things.'

'What was he like?'

'He was a quiet enough man, I suppose. He was tall, and very thin, and his nose was very long. I remember laughing at it with my friends when I was small, but later I was sorry for it because he was a kindly man. He liked to read the paper – Father's paper, when he had finished with it - on a winter's evening, particularly the articles about books, though I don't remember him ever owning a book of his own. Oh, in the summer he liked to garden: we had a man who came to work the kitchen garden, a few days a week, but Father allowed Lattin a say in some of the borders, and he worked them very well. They were always very splendid, and if we took visitors out to see them you'd always find Lattin just quietly in attendance, though whether he wanted to overhear their praises or simply protect his plants we were never very sure! He loved his garden.'

She smiled, reminiscing. Hippolyta bit her lip. Rab Lattin sounded as inoffensive as Forman.

'Had he ever quarrelled with anyone? Would anyone have had

reason to kill him?'

'To kill Lattin? What on earth are you talking about? Rab Lattin was killed because he disturbed someone murdering my father!'

'Ah, well,' said Hippolyta. 'I thought that, too, but now I'm not absolutely sure. It really doesn't work, you see, for Colonel Verney and Forman, and that raises the question: was Mr. Tranter murdered, in fact, because he disturbed someone murdering Rab Lattin?'

Mrs. Strachan's jaw dropped. Then she stood up, set down her teacup carefully on the central table, and ran from the house.

Chapter Twenty-Three

'She has left without her cloak!' exclaimed Mrs. Kynoch, the moment that either of them could speak.

'She must have gone to warn him,' was Hippolyta's first response.

'To warn who, my dear?'

'Her husband, of course!' Hippolyta slipped her arms around the huge cat on her lap, and stood up, transferring it as dead weight to the warmed armchair. 'I must go after her. Where is her cloak?'

Mrs. Kynoch bustled off to fetch a long cloak and bonnet from the parlour, while Hippolyta found her own outdoor things and hurried into them. Where would Mr. Strachan be? The shop or at home? The shop was on the way to the house, so that would be the first place to look. Mrs. Kynoch returned and handed her Mrs. Strachan's things with an anxious look.

'It seems to have grown even wilder out there,' she said. 'Do take care, my dear! Come back if you need help: I need to see my girls safely to their homes, I think.'

Hippolyta impulsively hugged the little woman, and darted outside. The wind instantly threw her back in through the front door.

'Good gracious!' she exclaimed, and fought her way back out, hauling the door shut behind her. She waved through the window at Mrs. Kynoch, and turned to look about her.

Despite the rain and the wind, the town was much busier than it had been earlier. People seemed to be dashing from place to place, carrying bundles. After a moment she realised that a small steady stream of townspeople were walking, burdened with packs and kists on their backs and occasionally on hand carts, up the hill from the direction of the bridge. Mrs. Strachan was nowhere to be seen.

Amongst the people she spotted Mr. Morrisson, the elderly constable, with a younger man carrying a pack for him. She hurried over.

'Mr. Morrisson? Whatever is the matter?' She had to shout to make herself heard over the wind.

'Matter, Mrs. Napier?' He stopped, apparently glad to take a rest, though the man with him moved ahead as if encouraging him to keep going. Rain slapped them all. 'River's rising, ma'am. The cottages below the bridge are filling up wi' watter.'

'Good gracious! Where are you all going?'

'This is my lass's man, Mrs. Napier. I'm off to stay with them up the town,' Morrisson explained. 'The river could be up here soon enough, ken? You'd best be away home, ma'am, and see to your own household.'

He wiped rainwater from his eyes and reluctantly placed one foot in front of another again, following his son-in-law up the hill. Hippolyta looked about. Should she go home? Mrs. Riach was more than capable of dealing with anything there, and Miss Verney … Well, she would not mind if Miss Verney suffered wet feet for a little. She shook her head, slightly ashamed of this thought, and joined the people hurrying up the hill.

At Strachan's shop she was shocked to find the shutters down. What time was it? Even if she had wanted to pull her watch out into the rain there was scarcely enough light to read it by. She huddled in the shelter of the shopfront. Could Mrs. Strachan be inside? Should she try to check? The shutters on the front had all been fastened from the outside: with a feeling of inevitability she picked up her skirts and darted into the narrow lane that she and Patrick had ventured down early that morning – really only that morning?

The yard at the back was sheltered, and she took a moment to catch her breath. Then she went and hammered on the back door of the shop. There must be someone in: surely last night had not been the only one where the shopboys had slept in the shop. She hammered again. After a moment there was a cautious withdrawal of bolts, and one of the young lads she had glimpsed last night was peering through the crack of the door. He looked surprised to see her there.

'Shop's closed, ma'am,' he said, wiping what was probably some of his supper from his mouth.

'I know – it's Al, isn't it? I'm not here to buy something. I'm looking for Mrs. Strachan. Is she here?'

Al looked even more surprised.

'No, she's no. I've not seen her the day. What for would she be coming to the shop?'

'She was looking for Mr. Strachan.'

'Well, he's no here either. He left about noon to gang hame. He wasnae looking happy,' he added, in a moment of perception.

'You're sure that's where he went?'

'Aye. Sure enough,' he added, a hint of doubt in his eyes. It would not be up to him to interrogate his employer's movements.

'Thank you, Al.'

It would have to be the Strachans' house, then. Again she joined the people marching up the hill with their belongings. There seemed to be more, now, including one or two she was sure were visitors to the town. The waters must be threatening the houses on the main street already: or perhaps the visitors were simply nervous. She hurried through them, not so heavily burdened, using the wings of her bonnet to shield her face from the rain as much as she could. Her cloak was heavy with water again, Mrs. Strachan's cloak was long and weighty, too, and it seemed more of a struggle than usual to climb the hill to the Strachans' fine new house. She rattled ferociously at the risp. Once again, it took two rattles before anyone appeared to answer the door. The maid inside hurried her into the shelter of the hallway, and a second later Mr. Strachan bounded out from a room off the hall.

'Bella! Oh! Mrs. Napier. I beg your pardon.'

'Forgive my intrusion, Mr. Strachan,' Hippolyta began, wondering if this was unctuous shop Strachan or angry home Strachan. 'I was looking for Mrs. Strachan.'

'She's not home yet,' said Mr. Strachan, and his look was neither unctuous nor angry. 'She was visiting Mrs. Kynoch down the hill. We're expecting her back shortly, though whether or not she will come back in this weather ...'

'She left there a little while ago,' said Hippolyta. A little bead of worry began to fret inside her head. 'Here is her cloak. And her bonnet.'

'She went out without her cloak?' Mr. Strachan's brow folded instantly into a frown, but it was of anxiety, not anger.

'We thought she must have come here. Or gone to your shop,' Hippolyta added, 'but I checked there and she has not been there all day.'

'Then where on earth has she gone?' he demanded. Hippolyta shrugged, helpless.

'Is there someone else she would have taken shelter with? Once she had realised she had left her cloak behind?'

'Surely she would have realised that the moment she left the house?' Strachan pointed out, and Hippolyta could not but agree. 'Did you try the Strongs?'

'Well, no – '

'Or the manse?'

'I came here first, straight from the shop, Mr. Strachan, because I thought she was most likely to go home! I was in a hurry to find her and make sure she was safe: I did not intend a tour of every house she might visit in the village!'

Mr. Strachan looked at her. She had pulled herself up to her full height, and the tone she had used had come straight from her mother. He nodded.

'I apologise, Mrs. Napier,' he said. 'My wife has not been well lately, and I am anxious about her.'

'Well, so am I,' said Hippolyta tartly, not quite ready to let him off his rudeness yet. 'Perhaps she should consult a physician.'

'But she does,' he said, looking puzzled. 'She consults Dr. Durward.'

'Really?' Hippolyta thought back to her conversation with Dr. Durward, his challenge to her to acquire Mrs. Strachan as a patient for Patrick, his anxiety over her state of health. What had he been up to? Was he just teasing her?

'Perhaps that is where she has gone – if she was feeling unwell?' For once Mr. Strachan seemed a little uncertain. 'I'll go down there and see. Give me that cloak, will you?'

Hippolyta was grateful enough to be relieved of the burden, and handed it over.

'I'd better go home,' she said, not quite sure now why she was hunting for Mrs. Strachan. If she had been hurrying off to challenge her husband, Hippolyta wanted to be there, but now where had she gone?

'Wait there until I fetch my coat and hat,' said Mr. Strachan, 'and I'll walk down the hill with you.'

'Thank you.'

He vanished briskly through a door, still frowning. Hippolyta spun on her heel, thinking. Mr. Strachan had good motives for murdering Colonel Verney and probably Mr. Tranter, too, and she did not like the man. But he did have that alibi for Mr. Tranter's murder, and more importantly, now, she believed that Colonel Verney and Mr. Tranter had both been murdered just because they happened to be in the wrong place when, respectively, Mr. Forman and Rab Lattin had been murdered. She knew of no reason why Mr. Strachan should want to kill Forman unless it had been because Forman had discovered something under the kitchen floor which identified Strachan as Rab Lattin's murderer, and she knew of no reason why Mr. Strachan should have killed Rab Lattin, even if he had been able to. It was all very well thinking of Mr. Strachan as a murderer in the abstract, but she realised she did not feel in the least nervous of him.

But if Mrs. Strachan had not rushed out of Mrs. Kynoch's cottage to confront her husband, what was it that Hippolyta had said that had made her run from the house? She had not even mentioned the possibility of something distinctive under the floorboards, she had only mentioned the idea that Rab Lattin had been the intended victim, not Mr. Tranter.

What had Mrs. Strachan told her about Rab Lattin? He was a keen gardener, and he liked to read the articles on books in the newspapers, though he owned no books of his own. He was a quiet and kind man, she had said, and trusted by Mr. Tranter. Had he somehow betrayed that trust? Stolen a valuable book?

That seemed ridiculous, and there was no evidence for it at all. What else could it be?

She was still thinking when Mr. Strachan appeared, well wrapped up against the weather. He ushered Hippolyta out of the front door, and wincing at the rain they set off. It was nearly dark, and as they rounded the corner of the house Hippolyta was bowled almost off the path as the wind caught her skirts: Mr. Strachan seized her arm and dragged her back, steadying her before they walked on, heads down against the wind.

A second later they both leapt and stumbled, as a great stab of lightning cracked the sky. Hippolyta had never seen a lightning flash so bright, and it was followed almost instantly by a crash of thunder that seemed almost enough to shake buildings. Then the buildings did shake, and they snatched at each other to keep their balance.

'An earthquake! What is this?' cried Mr. Strachan, clutching his hat to his head as slates crashed and sliced off the roofs around them. Beside them a cottage window cracked sharply. He grasped Hippolyta's arm and dragged her along towards the middle of the town, against the general flow of traffic: there were still people with handcarts and bundles, slowly moving up the hill.

'Is the river still rising?' Hippolyta stopped and asked a man tugging a donkey behind him.

'Aye, ma'am, but not so fast now, I think.'

'Maybe we're seeing the end of it,' shouted Strachan. The wind surged as if in defiance of his words, and they staggered against a wall along with another man in a cloak.

'Hippolyta!' the man cried, clutching her other arm. 'You're safe!'

'Patrick!' She grabbed for his hand. 'Mrs. Strachan is missing, without her cloak!'

'Where was she going?' Patrick shouted. They ducked as another great swipe of lightning lit the sky, and the thunder rumbled fast behind it. 'I've never seen anything like this!'

'She might be at Durward's,' Strachan called out as they straightened again. The wind dipped and his words echoed oddly. 'She's not well.'

'I need to go back to Pannanich,' Patrick shouted. 'They're taking the people out of the Lodge: it was a foot deep with water when the messenger left it. I'll come down to Durward's with you, but I must see Hippolyta home first.'

'I'm staying with you!' cried Hippolyta. The idea of being cooped up at home with Mrs. Riach and Basilia Verney, worrying about Patrick, was appalling.

'You should go home, my dearest!'

'I shan't!' He looked at her, faces streaming with rainwater, squinting in the wind.

'No doubt you'll go out again if I take you home,' he

muttered. 'But if you come you must be careful! The river is rising fast.'

'Is Durward's still safe? Could he have moved up the hill?' Strachan interrupted them.

'I have no idea. Come on, then,' Patrick shouted. 'Let's go and see. There are still some people in the inn: the landlady is refusing to move while there are guests upstairs.'

The sky crashed with lightning and thunder again, the whole town lit up like a summer's day for three or four seconds, images burned into their eyes. A man was shouting up at a first floor window, where a lady in a nightcap clutched her shawl about her.

'I'm not moving, my good man!' she called down to him.

'You'll have to, madam! The waters are rising!'

'But I'm safe upstairs, and we're all the way up here!' the lady called back. 'Look: I can see four or five houses between here and any sign of the river!'

'Why won't you just come down, you daft quine?' the man demanded, frustrated. 'I'll carry your damned jewellery case for you, if that's what you want!'

'I am not dressed,' the lady retorted stiffly, and shut the window on him. Patrick led Hippolyta past the scene, Strachan following, and they made their way down towards the bridge.

Hippolyta gasped. The river was at the level of the bottom of the street, licking at the edges of the Aberdeen road, filling the lower rooms of the inn and making Dr. Durward's little house just beyond it seem to be sitting on an island in the black flow of river waters.

'He can't still be there,' Strachan shouted, gaping at it. There was a man at an upper window in the inn.

'Are you looking for the doctor?' he yelled down at them. 'He's away across the river this hour or more.'

'At Pannanich?' Patrick called back. The man nodded.

'Are the animals all right? The horses in the stables?' Hippolyta shouted to him. The man frowned, clutching at his ear, then nodded again. 'They're all up the town, except for that pony that bites everyone.'

'What?'

'No, Hippolyta!'

'We can't leave it there to drown!'

She broke free of Patrick and ran, splashing through six inches of water, into the inn yard. All the stable doors were open but one, and she made her way quickly to it. The pony stood crossly inside, and whinnied reproachfully. She grabbed a bridle and fastened it as quickly as she could: her hands were cold with the damp, and clumsy. Then she led the pony out into the street.

'For goodness' sake,' groaned Patrick. The pony made a lunge to nip him, and he skipped after Strachan who was already heading up over the brow of the bridge. Hippolyta and the pony followed at a half-trot. The pony seemed impervious to the weather and danced a little, happy to be out of its stable.

Tugged along by the pony, they walked quickly to Pannanich Lodge. The pasture beside the road had vanished completely, and the river lapped the side of the road. The great block of the Lodge loomed, stuck out into the water like some coastal fortification. A huddle of people waited at the road's edge, raising lanterns to see them as they heard footsteps approaching. Some were wrapped in blankets and waiting on chairs, and Patrick hurried forward to attend to the frailest. Hippolyta drew in behind him, gazing with awe at the Lodge. The gardens were completely covered, as if they had never been. She remembered them in the sunshine the day Dr. Durward had introduced poor Julian Brown to them. What would they look like when the waters went down – if the waters went down, she wondered. Gardens … Something connected in the back of her mind, but what was it?

'Will that pony take someone on his back?'

'What?' Patrick was leading forward a sickly-looking child wrapped in a quilt. Patrick looked worried, but the child seemed numb.

'She can't walk all the way up to the hotel. She's left her boots behind, and she's ill anyway.'

'I'll see.' Hippolyta soothed the pony for a moment, guiding the child round the animal with one arm. Then she held the pony's rein tightly near the bridle, and lifted the child – so light! – on to the pony's back. She waited for a second, her arm securely around the child's waist, in case of protest from the pony, but there was nothing. Patrick nodded.

'We'll go on ahead,' Hippolyta cried. It was almost noisier here than in the village, for the birch woods on either side tossed and cracked in the wind, and the surging rumble of the river was ever-present. Strachan beside her had taken an old man up on to his back and begun a slow, steady ascent of the road to the hotel. Hippolyta followed, still holding the child steady.

The lightning flashed every minute or so, showing them the road ahead. Patrick followed, supporting two men one on each side of him, walking as slowly as Strachan. Hippolyta eased ahead, letting the pony set the pace. By the time she reached the hotel, Patrick and Strachan were just out of sight, but the hotel door opened the moment they approached. The hotel keeper had been waiting, expecting more arrivals from the Lodge, and lifted the child straight off the pony's back. Beyond him, the candlelit parlour was warm and crowded and smelled of wet wool.

'Can you take the beast round the back, ma'am?' the hotel keeper asked, and Hippolyta stumbled off to the back of the building. There a boy fitted the pony into a stall with another horse and Hippolyta prayed it would cause no trouble, before hurrying in through the back door of the hotel. In the parlour Patrick had just arrived with his two patients, explaining that Strachan was not far behind. Hippolyta pushed through to him where he stood with the hotel keeper.

'Have you seen Dr. Durward, or Mrs. Strachan?' she asked.

'Mrs. Strachan – she was by the fire a whilie since,' said the hotel keeper, with an effort. 'I feel as if the hail world has come through yon door this night. Dr. Durward? He's about the place, I ken. Now who was he attending to?' He frowned, trying to remember.

'It wouldn't be Mr. Brookes, would it?' asked Patrick, out of interest.

'It could have been,' the hotel keeper conceded, not sure.

'You said Mrs. Strachan was by the fire?' Hippolyta asked, trying to see through the crowd.

'Aye, over yonder.' The hotel keeper waved. Hippolyta left Patrick with his various patients, and plunged into the crowd towards the fire. There was a woman sitting by the fire, but she was nursing a baby, and was no one Hippolyta had seen before. On the other side of the fireplace were four children bundled into the same chair. Hippolyta turned and stood on tiptoe, trying to see into the furthest reaches of the packed parlour. She could see no one remotely like Mrs. Strachan.

She wandered out of the parlour and back through the hall, where more refugees were trying to organise what belongings they had brought with them, and find room to dry them. There was still no sign of Mrs. Strachan, or Dr. Durward. She came to the stairs, and began to climb them, heading for Mr. Brookes' room. It was almost as busy up here as it had been downstairs: many of the doors to the rooms were open, and it seemed that the hotel staff were trying to double up the accommodation to take in their extra guests. She walked unchallenged along the passage, towards Mr. Brookes' door, then noticed that it, too, was open. She paused, listening. Was that Mrs. Strachan's voice?

'Who would have guessed that that was poor John Burns?' she was asking. Dr. Durward's smooth tones answered.

'It was quite a shock to me. His boy came running down the stairs to say his master was in distress, so I came up. He's Napier's patient, I believe.'

'But what is he doing here under another name?'

'He wanted to laugh when he told me,' Dr. Durward said, a chuckle in his own voice, 'but he had hardly the strength. I've given him some laudanum in brandy: he'll sleep for a little.'

There was a pause, as if they were both contemplating their old acquaintance.

'But what are you doing here, Mrs. Strachan?' the doctor asked at last.

'I came to find you,' said Mrs. Strachan.

'Oh, my dear Mrs. Strachan, are you unwell?' Dr. Durward suddenly sounded alarmed. 'You should have said! I wish you would see a doctor – if not me, then surely Dr. Napier would help you.'

'No, no, I am not unwell, not at all. And I pray you do not mention such a thing to my husband.'

'But you're shivering! Come closer to the fire.'

'No, it's only because – because I walked up here in all that rain.' Without a cloak, thought Hippolyta, but why? 'I've warmed up now.' She was still shivering, though: it was clear in her voice.

'Then what is it?' Dr. Durward asked. His voice was gentle, as it always seemed to be when he was talking to her. Had he been a suitor, too, all those years ago? Was that why he had not married?

But that evening when he and Strachan had gone to visit Dinnet House, only Strachan had gone inside: he had walked in the garden. Had he ceded the race to Strachan even then?

The garden … Rab Lattin loved his garden, and it was summertime. He would have been working in the garden, no doubt.

'I never asked you then: never had the nerve, I suppose,' Mrs. Strachan was saying. 'I've always been much too frightened of hearing the wrong answer. But now I have to know. All those years ago, the night Papa was – was killed. You swore that my husband – that Allan spent that night with you drinking in his father's cellar. Is that the truth?' Her voice faded with her nerves. There was an awful silence. Hippolyta found she was holding her breath. Then there was a heavy sigh.

'No, my dear, no. It is not the truth.'

A dreadful cry came from Mrs. Strachan, quickly stifled, as if she had put her hands to her face. Hippolyta could hear her sobbing. Dr. Durward drew breath audibly.

'We were together for part of the night, but I woke at one point – rather drunk, I admit – and he was not there.'

'Then you knew he had killed my father! You protected him!'

'He was my friend.'

'You let me marry him …'

'Ah, yes, I did. I knew you preferred him, you see,' said Dr. Durward softly. The tenderness of it made Hippolyta catch her breath – but then everything suddenly cleared in her head.

She knew what had happened at Dinnet House twenty years ago, and if she was right, then she was sure she knew too what had happened at Dinnet House last week.

But how was she going to prove it?

Chapter Twenty-Four

'Oh, Mrs. Napier?'

The voice behind her made her jump, but she was not sure it could have been heard inside the room. She spun round. In the middle of the passage, looking as useless as ever, was Julian Brown, Basilia Verney's cousin. She stepped quickly towards him to take their conversation away from the doorway, and he staggered back a couple of steps as if she had slapped him.

'Mr. Brown! Good evening. What are you doing here?' She had forgotten about the evacuation of Pannanich Lodge.

'Oh, I just followed everybody else up the hill,' he shrugged, with a weak grin. 'Then I thought I saw you in the parlour downstairs, and I wanted to know if Basilia was here with you. Are they evacuating the whole town?'

'No, no, we came looking for someone,' she murmured. 'As far as I know Miss Verney is still back in our house.'

'Oh! Good, good.' But he looked disappointed.

'Mr. Brown,' she began tentatively, seizing the opportunity, 'last Sunday night …'

'You mean yesterday?' He was eager, but confused.

'No, the previous Sunday. The one when your uncle Colonel Verney was murdered.'

'Oh. Yes, that one.' He toed the carpet anxiously. 'I did like my uncle, you know, Mrs. Napier. We just never seemed to … well, I never seemed quite to …'

To finish your sentences? thought Hippolyta impatiently. 'To live up to his expectations?' she suggested more kindly. He looked up, grateful.

'That's about it, yes!'

'And you certainly would never have murdered him, would

you?' she asked kindly. He shook his head at once.

'He would have been so shocked if I had,' he added. 'I mean – Well, you know.'

'Of course,' said Hippolyta, who thought she probably did. For some reason, an image of her own mother appeared briefly in her mind. 'But you were up there that evening, weren't you?' This was a stab in the dark, in the hope that she could come to her real question from an innocent angle.

'Well … yes, I was. But not to go into the house. Basilia was right: we had agreed to meet – it was her idea, though - but I got completely lost in the dark and I couldn't find the house. I'd only been there once before, and that was in the daylight. Shocking how dark it gets in the countryside, don't you think? Not sure I like it that much.'

'And when would that have been?'

'Well … I forgot to wind my watch, of course. When I got back here – well, to the Lodge, it was after midnight.'

'And when did Dr. Durward turn up?'

'Oh, it was after that, of course. I went up to my room and had a drink, you know, and then I heard a knock on the window, and he was outside tossing pebbles up to attract my attention.'

'So he came in – with a bottle of brandy – and you stayed playing cards for the rest of the night?'

'That's right. Or was he there much earlier?' He thought for a second, his face screwed up in concentration. 'No, that's right: he told me to say he was there much earlier, in return for letting me off my losses at cards, but it would have been after midnight.' His face cleared, pleased, then clouded again. 'I hope you weren't one of the people I was supposed to tell he was there much earlier. People really shouldn't rely on me to keep secrets and tell odd stories, you know. I'm afraid I'm not really very bright, you see.'

'That's quite all right,' said Hippolyta, patting him gently on the arm. 'It's not brains that count, but character.'

'Do you think?' He looked wistful.

'Now, do you think you could go back downstairs just now, and find my husband? Dr. Napier, remember: he'll be busy with patients, no doubt.'

'Oh, he was!'

'Could you find him, and say I need him urgently up here?'

'Find him and say you need him urgently up here: yes, I'm sure I could manage that.'

'I'd be terribly grateful,' she added, with an encouraging smile. He bowed like a knight to his lady, and set off back down the passage to the stairs, intent on his errand. Hippolyta watched him go, then tiptoed back to the door of Mr. Brookes' room, which was still open.

Inside, Mrs. Strachan was still sobbing, steadily and intently. Hippolyta could hear the occasional comforting murmur from Dr. Durward, and could picture him sitting by her, her hand perhaps in his, maybe even her head on his shoulder. Her head was spinning: she felt as if a large paintbrush were inside it, mixing colours on its palette. What colour was going to appear when the paints were mixed? She could not tell.

She waited, sure that Mrs. Strachan was at least safe, trying not to move though her wet skirts were heavy and cold. Inside the room the sobbing eased a little, and there was a rustling sound as if Mrs. Strachan were perhaps sitting up and wiping her eyes. Some women looked much prettier when they had been crying, somehow, Hippolyta reflected: she herself looked as if she had been smearing red paint over her face, but she was sure Mrs. Strachan simply glowed. She gave a little sigh, then straightened. Mrs. Strachan was speaking.

'But if you knew all along that Allan had murdered my father, why didn't you tell me before I married him? You must have known a day like this would come, that I would find out eventually. And if a man can murder two people,' she added quickly, as if blocking an interruption from Dr. Durward, 'then he can as easily murder three, I should have thought. How could you put me in such danger?'

'Ah,' said Dr. Durward, who must have been thinking fast, 'He was my friend, too,' he repeated helplessly.

There was a silence. Hippolyta strained her ears for voices from the room, and for the sound of Patrick's footsteps on the stair behind her. Neither was forthcoming. Then at last she heard Mrs. Strachan sigh.

'How do I know,' she said, warily, 'that I can believe you?'

'Believe me? You don't think I would lie about something like that!' Durward's voice was shocked.

'I don't think you would tell me that Allan had not been there in the cellar with you if you had both really been there all night, no,' said Mrs. Strachan with care. 'I mean, are you telling me the truth about which one of you left the cellar in the middle of the night?'

This time the silence was almost deafening. Hippolyta held her breath, her heart walloping in her breast. Where was Patrick?

'My dear,' said Dr. Durward softly, but his tone was strange. 'What are you saying? I think you may be tired and confused, are you not?'

'I don't think so …' Mrs. Strachan did not sound so sure. Her voice was shaky. 'Can you promise me that one of you left the cellar that night, and that it was the man who is now my husband?'

'Bella …'

Hippolyta did not like the sound of that word at all. She gave one desperate glance back down the empty passage at the stairs, straightened her spine, and strode into Mr. Brookes' chamber.

'That's quite enough, Dr. Durward,' she said, using her mother's voice once more. Why had she never realised how useful it was? 'You found the Jacobite silver, didn't you?'

'What?' Dr. Durward had his hands in his pockets, and was standing very close to Mrs. Strachan.

'Do move away from him, Mrs. Strachan, please. I'd like to be sure you were out of reach.' Hippolyta watched as Mrs. Strachan moved across the room, like an automaton. There was a snore from the large bed: Mr. Brookes / Burns was clearly still alive, too. Hippolyta breathed a temporary sigh of relief.

'What are you talking about, Mrs. Napier? I thought your husband said you were an intelligent, informed sort of woman, not a mad girl.'

'You found,' said Hippolyta clearly, refusing to be distracted, 'the Jacobite silver in the garden of Dinnet House, that night when you walked in the garden and Mr. Strachan went into the house to look for the Tranters. You went back for it that night, after dark, once you had ensured that Mr. Strachan was as drunk as could be in his father's cellar. But Rab Lattin, the manservant, was devoted to his garden, and he saw you digging around the summer house. You didn't want to share, did you? So you killed him. Greedy and lazy: that's the sum of you. Then Mr. Tranter unfortunately found you too, and you killed him. It might have been the other way round, I suppose,' she conceded, trying to sound much more confident than she was, 'but that's the general idea. But your knife, your blade, whatever it was, you must have dropped it. It slid between the floorboards in that odd kitchen, and you lost it in your hurry. It was only last week, when I said – foolish of me! But how was I to know? – that Forman had had to take the floorboards up to rescue the kitten, and that Miss Verney had suggested he clear out the mess underneath: that was when you realised the weapon might be found, and somehow linked to you. How was that, then? It must have been a slim knife to slip between the boards.'

Dr. Durward took two strides across the room, snatching his hand from his pocket.

'It was a scalpel, you little fool!' he cried. 'This one!'

He slashed out at her, but her hands flew up in front of her face and she stepped quickly backwards, only to crash into someone at the door. She felt a sting on her forearm as she spun to the ground, and heard Mrs. Strachan scream. Someone passed her, struck Dr. Durward's arm to one side, and punched him solidly in the stomach. He folded to the floor with a gasp like a bagpipe, and Patrick, for it was he, stooped and retrieved the fallen scalpel.

'Rusty,' he remarked, slipping it into his own pocket. 'Good heavens, my dearest,' he said, panting only a little, as he turned to help Hippolyta up, 'that was a little foolhardy of you!' Then he leaned over Dr. Durward, who was still gasping for breath. He tugged the doctor's close-fitting coat back down over his shoulders, and held it tight, effectively pinioning the man. 'I learned that on a difficult patient. Now,' he said, 'run and ask the hotel keeper if we can clear a room with a good lock on the door.'

'It doesn't have to be a particularly comfortable one,' Hippolyta called back as she ran for the door.

A room was found, a laundry cupboard on the same floor, and the hotel keeper, who was competent at dealing with disorderly guests, helped Patrick to manoeuvre Dr. Durward, larger than either of them, into it. The physician did a great deal of shouting, and a number of guests came out of their rooms to watch: the hotel keeper, not sure what to say to show his hotel in the best light, decided to tell the truth.

'He's a murderer!' he called back along the passage. 'We're

locking him up!'

They pushed him face first into the cupboard and the hotel keeper locked the door, then looked dubiously at Patrick.

'Now what?' he asked.

'We need to get Mr. Durris to come for him,' said Hippolyta.

'But the river's rising again,' said the man. 'If he's still yonder in the village, he'll no be here the night.'

'In that case I hope the door is strong!' said Hippolyta unsympathetically. 'After all, he locked poor Tabitha in that cupboard all night!'

'So he did,' said Patrick, 'and killed four men.'

'And tried to blame someone else,' added Hippolyta.

The hotel keeper shrugged.

'Aye, well, I suppose.'

'What about Mrs. Strachan?' Hippolyta asked. 'And I'm worried about Mr. Brookes. Burns.'

'Let's go and see, shall we?' Patrick took Hippolyta's hand and led the way back along the passage to Mr. Brookes' room. Mrs. Strachan was on a sofa, once again sobbing.

'Such a shock, dear Mrs. Napier,' she said when Hippolyta sat down beside her. 'We've known him for years – all our lives. And he would have let my husband take the blame for poor Papa's death …' She shuddered, but the tears were drying up at last. 'But what about you?' she added suddenly. Hippolyta looked down: her arm was bleeding freely where Durward had sliced it with the scalpel.

'My dear.' Patrick was at her side in a second. He had brought his medical bag upstairs at her summons, thinking she needed help for a patient, and he had carried it into the room before checking Mr. Burns' pulse and temperature. 'If you're lucky, all this bleeding will have washed out any rust. I hope so, anyway,' he added, as he smeared some substance over the cut and bound it neatly. Hippolyta wondered, as she often did, how a man who could not keep his study tidy managed to make such beautifully arranged dressings.

'Now, if you are better,' he said, tenderly laying her arm along her own lap, 'there is still much to be done downstairs to make the Lodge guests comfortable. Perhaps you could both help?'

It was a good idea: there was no sense in sitting around

waiting and worrying when there was work to be done. The next few hours were pleasantly busy, for there was plenty of comfort available to offer: there were warm blankets and hot teas and whisky, and gradually the invalids and visitors in the parlour were accommodated in as convenient a manner as possible about the building, though Mr. Burns might be surprised, on waking, to discover two other guests asleep on his armchairs. When the last guest disappeared to his room at last, and the hotel keeper sighed and stretched his back with his fists pressed into his waist, Hippolyta glanced at the parlour mantel clock and was astonished to find that it was three o'clock in the morning.

'I wonder what the river is doing?' she asked of no one in particular. Patrick went to the window and peered out.

'It's still raining, anyway.'

'No likely to have gone down any, then,' said the hotel keeper, as Mrs. Strachan flopped prettily into an armchair by the fire.

'Oh, this is very smoky!' she exclaimed.

'That's odd,' said the hotel keeper. 'I was noticing particularly earlier that that yin wasna smoking at all.' He sniffed. 'But you're right, I do smell smoke.'

'It's in the hall,' said Hippolyta, jumping up. 'Not much … coming from upstairs?'

She walked up the stairs, looking above her, and was nearly at the top when there was a great thump outside.

'More thunder?' demanded the hotel keeper, but Hippolyta shook her head fast.

'No, it's Dr. Durward! He must have had a tinderbox: the lock is burned off the door, and the landing window is open!'

'Then that was him jumping out!' cried Patrick. Hippolyta sprang down the stairs and the two of them sprinted for the door.

'Wait!' called Mrs. Strachan. 'I must come too! He will not escape!'

Outside it was just as horrible as it had been earlier, and for a moment none of them could see each other, let alone Dr. Durward. The rain lashed at them and the wind blew, and even up here on the hill they could hear the steady, rushing roar of the river below. Then lightning flashed, not quite as brightly as earlier, but bright enough for them to see a running figure, ahead of them on the road back to the bridge and the village. They set off after him as quickly as they could, holding hands and staggering on the path, now cluttered and dangerous with fallen branches. Mrs. Strachan was panting loudly, and Hippolyta's arm was aching. It seemed like hours before they reached the bottom of the hill, where the water surged around the bridge. They stopped, gasping.

'This is ridiculous,' Patrick shouted. 'He can't be trying to cross.'

'The bridge is strong,' Mrs. Strachan cried. 'He'll want to get home, find his things, take them with him. I know him: he'd try taking money into Heaven if he could, rather than leave it behind.'

'He might be trying it sooner than he expects,' said Patrick in amazement. 'Look!'

Out on the bridge a solitary figure clutched the pediment, buffeted by the wind.

'We need to stop him,' shouted Hippolyta.

'We can't!'

'You heard Mrs. Strachan: the bridge is strong. We don't want him to escape. What if he killed someone else?'

Patrick gave her a long, hard look. Then he drew a deep breath, and tucked her hand under his arm.

'Together, then,' he said.

'Together,' echoed Mrs. Strachan, seizing his other arm, and weighing each other down against the wind they waded through a few yards of water, and set out on to the bridge.

It was much more exposed than the woodland road they had just descended. The river, four times its normal width, was terrifying, swollen and huge, a great grey creature rising up to swallow the town in one mouthful. Borne on its gliding waters were whole trees, the thatch from a roof, a window frame. Hippolyta feared to think what else she might see, and looked ahead of her instead, focussing on the distant lights of the village. It seemed to be miles away.

They were closing on Dr. Durward, though: he was slowing, staring out at the river upstream, as if in a dream. He glanced back and Hippolyta was sure he saw them, but it did not make him move any more quickly. Had he given up? It seemed an odd place to do it. Perhaps he was exhausted.

But then, when they could almost reach out and touch him, he gave a cry, spun on his toes and ran for the village. They hesitated, then ran after, but it was not them that Dr. Durward was fleeing. He had seen what they had not: one great surging wave hurling itself down the river towards the bridge.

For the next ten minutes Hippolyta prayed, incoherently and possibly silently, though she could not be sure. The wave hit the bridge with a roar like nothing she had ever even imagined. The sound echoed up and down the valley, the masonry of the bridge fragmented like a child's building brick tower, the rocks spinning over their heads as light as bees. The ground beneath their feet, a moment ago so solid, shook and fell apart, and they were falling.

Her hand slipped out from under Patrick's arm. She heard Mrs. Strachan scream, and shouting she could not identify. Then she hit the water, hard. It made no sense that a thing so hard and solid could then sweep up around her, filling her mouth and nose, tearing at her and pushing her here and there as if she were a toy. She shot to the surface, blinking, face running with water, and grabbed a breath of something like air. Then she fell again, and as she did so she saw a pig rush past, its trotters in the air, squealing maniacally. There was an urgent yell, and she tried to turn, just missing a barrel spinning in the water as it shot by them. She saw it hit Mrs. Strachan, glance off Patrick's shoulder, and ram Dr. Durward, suddenly all of them there in front of her. More masonry fell, but somehow the pig and the barrel had cleared her mind, returned a human scale to her surroundings. She knew where the shore was, and she pushed towards it. When she glanced back, she saw Patrick and Mrs. Strachan following, as best they could.

Patrick overtook her in a moment, for skirts made the whole thing so much more difficult. Once they were holding on to each other, they reached back for Mrs. Strachan, grasping her outstretched hands and pulling her towards them. There was no sign of Dr. Durward. The three of them together pushed and pulled themselves to something like a bank, and Patrick grabbed the branch of a low tree that still stood at the edge of the water. For a few seconds they could draw breath again. Then, amazingly, hands reached out from the bank, and hauled them up, one by one, with words of encouragement and occasional shocked curses. It was Mr. Durris, breathless and soaked, and a few equally sodden helpers, pulling them to safety.

'Is that all of you?' he shouted.

'Dr. Durward, too,' Patrick shouted back.

'But I think he was hit by a barrel,' added Hippolyta. 'And he's the murderer.'

'What?' Durris peered at them through his streaming glasses.

'We'll tell you later,' said Hippolyta. 'Not urgent just now.'

Mrs. Strachan was leaning heavily on Lang, the night watchman who had helped Mr. Durris. He guided her through knee-deep water up to the street – though they realised quickly that what they had thought was river was in fact the lower part of the street. They were almost at the green now, and Hippolyta saw with relief that the waters had not quite reached their own house. Candles burned in the upstairs windows there, as if guiding them home. She almost cried.

The town, though, was in chaos. Light and shade dappled it, with candles or lamps in most of the inhabited windows and dozens of lanterns in the hands of those about in the middle of the village. Just outside the church, the Aberdeen mail coach, usually resting at the inn at this time of the night, was harnessed and laden with people, packed in at all angles and in a wide variety of undress: one of them Hippolyta recognised as the grand lady unwilling to leave her lodgings earlier. The door of the coach was open, and a man hung off it like a curtain, swaying as the driver tried to urge the reluctant horses to drag their burden up the hill, while several other men fell off the top as the coach jerked. Their spaces were quickly taken by others more nimble. As she stood watching in amazement, her feet almost too tired to take her the last few paces home, a plump man with an Edinburgh accent wobbled towards her, two girls hanging about his neck.

'Papa! Papa!' they were moaning, even after he set them down on the edge of a horse trough by the green, their bare toes almost out of the water. He wiped his brow, and addressed Hippolyta for want of other audience.

'I thought they would drown me afore I could get them somewhere dry. Call you this a watering-place?' he added, with a rueful grin. 'If you catch me coming a-watering again at this gate, I'll allow you to mak' a water-kelpie of me!'

'Papa! Papa!' the girls called, and with a sigh he picked them both up again and waddled on up the hill. Then there were cries from beyond the church, and a great stream of water surged down the hill, catching everyone unawares.

'River's broken its banks further upstream!' someone cried out. 'Coming down through the town!'

'Oh, for goodness' sake!' Hippolyta was growing tired of all this. The new wave of water was heading down the hill along the street: though it was washing over the green it was not going much further to each side. She tugged the father with his girls so that he turned around, and pulled Mrs. Strachan, too, and all of them made for the Napiers' little cottage with the candles in the window.

Patrick pushed the door open to be greeted by Mrs. Riach, perched halfway up the stairs with Ishbel on the step above. The cats watched the proceedings from the landing, wondering what strange things were happening now. Franklin appeared to have a fish.

'Fit time o' the morn div ye call this to be coming in again?' demanded the housekeeper. 'This is no a well-regulated household, no at all.'

Chapter Twenty-Five

Patrick toyed absently with the piano keys. He looked exhausted.

He was currently sharing the study as a bedchamber, with Mr. Durris and the father of the two girls, who had offered to become a kelpie. The daughters were in Basilia Verney's room. Basilia, with much mutual strained courtesy, was sharing Hippolyta's bed. Ishbel and Tabitha were in the second attic room, and a family of twelve, including one set of grandparents, twin babies in arms and a distant cousin, were in the two bedchambers in the servants' wing, along with their three terriers. No one else in the house had met any of them before, but the older girl children had proved clever at finding sources of food about the town, while the older boys broke several windows.

Mrs. Riach, in the confusion, had come to Hippolyta to explain why she herself could not share a room. The explanation was vague, and on any other day Hippolyta might have queried it, probably to no effect. However, she was tired, too, after several somewhat disturbed nights, and so she merely sat in silence, wondering what to say next. The silence seemed to stimulate some level of guilt in Mrs. Riach, and she finally confessed that her elderly aunt, who was to say the least confused, had been living in the servants' wing for several years undetected and was now sleeping in Mrs. Riach's own bed, driven out by the boys and the terriers. Hippolyta tried to look as if she had known all along, and nodded thoughtfully. Shame-faced, Mrs. Riach retreated, and turned out some of the best meals she had ever made for three solid days, despite the meagre supplies.

The village was battered and bruised, and the land around had been much bereft of both cattle and crops. Every house that could accommodate extra people had them: the place had been crowded already, but quite a number of visitors had called short their stay as soon as they could make their way out of the town, which eased the crowding a little. Every able-bodied person seemed to be involved in sweeping, draining, drying, tearing down where the water had done too much damage, scrubbing and airing: the variety of smells about the place, from midden to soap, was fascinating and occasionally more than overpowering.

Mrs. Strachan had stayed with them for a night, but in the morning the door had been almost battered in and Patrick, opening it mildly, found Mr. Strachan on the doorstep, demanding to know if his wife was safe. Being reassured that she was, he claimed her back, much to their satisfaction, and they went home. Strachan had left Pannanich earlier than any of them had thought, thinking that his wife was not there, and so had been in Ballater all along. Strachan's cellars had flooded, so the word went, and so any trace of blue paint that might or might not have marked any barrel of brandy had been washed away.

Another barrel, this time of whisky, had been found on a new island formed by the retreat of the river waters, a mile or so below the town. Accompanying the barrel, which was miraculously unbreached, was a heathy and happy pig, and the sodden corpse of one of the spa town's two noted physicians, Dr. Durward. Fortunately it was possible to cross to the island and remove the corpse before the pig grew hungry, though there was some debate amongst the boatmen as to which it would be proper to remove first: several argued for the corpse, others for the pig, and a few convincing voices opted for the barrel. It was a close thing, but Durris was on the bank, and the corpse was removed first and taken into the sheriff's custody.

'You're sure of your facts, Mrs. Napier?' he asked, sitting in the parlour as Patrick dozed at the piano.

'I think so,' said Hippolyta. 'And surely the most telling thing is that he went for me with the scalpel.'

'Is that healing all right?' Patrick roused himself to peer over at his wife's arm.

'I don't think the dip in the river did it much good, but it looks clean now,' said Hippolyta, though the cut was long enough to make movement in the arm painful. Luckily it was her left arm:

any spare time she had at present was employed in sketching scenes of the floods and the aftermath. She moved her sketchbook off her lap just now, and stroked two of the kittens - they were all hiding in the parlour in protest at the terriers.

'So Durward's wealth came from the Jacobite silver, and not from his practice?'

'Everyone said he was a lazy man, and there weren't so many visitors when he was starting out,' said Hippolyta, softly pulling a kitten's pink ear. 'And he had no family money. He spent a good deal of time in the garden, though. We don't know whether he refused to go halves with Rab Lattin, but my feeling, from the way Mrs. Strachan described him, is that Lattin told Dr. Durward that he would tell Mr. Tranter, who would of course claim the money as his own as the owner of the house.'

'Poor fellow,' Durris remarked, making a tiny note in his notebook.

'I feel even more sorry for Forman, though, and for Colonel Verney: they probably had no idea why Dr. Durward attacked them. Colonel Verney was simply in the way, in the hall when Dr. Durward arrived, for the back door was already locked. Forman of course had been instructed to tidy out under the floorboards: we don't know if he ever saw the scalpel, or whether he would have made any connexion with the old murders if he had.'

'And Durward had the scalpel? Why didn't he just throw it away?'

'I think he was waiting to be able to throw it somewhere where it would not be connected to him.'

'And this is it?'

Durris fingered the rusty item on the table.

'It's just an ordinary scalpel,' put in Patrick. 'Any doctor could have dropped it in the last fifty years.'

'Guilt, I suppose,' Durris observed. 'Well, he's beyond the reach of earthly justice now, anyway.'

Rumours of Dr. Durward's guilt circulated as quickly as the news of his death, and no one did anything to stop them. The Strachans, indeed, had a kind of glow about them over the matter, and Hippolyta wondered just how much the mystery of Mrs. Strachan's father's death had affected them over the years. She visited Mrs. Kynoch, who had the families of two of her pupils staying with her, and they shared a pot of tea in the kitchen.

'He's a different man,' Mrs. Kynoch confided in her. 'I've never seen him look so – well, relaxed.'

'An ill wind, then,' said Hippolyta, and they raised their cups to toast it.

When the waters receded a little more, boatmen started to ply a lucrative trade across the river where the bridge had been. One day when Hippolyta was making a sketch of the picturesque ruins, the south side now gone as well and a great spike of pillar surviving alone in the centre of the river, a familiar figure was landed nearby her on the shore. It was Julian Brown.

'Mrs. Napier, I'm very glad to see you!' he exclaimed, bowing.

'I'm glad to see you well,' said Hippolyta. 'How are matters at Pannanich?'

'Not too bad, considering,' he replied. 'The waters have gone down in the Lodge, but the whole place stinks like a midden.'

'The same could be said for much of the town,' said Hippolyta wryly. There was some worry about disease, and Patrick was being kept very busy.

'Is – ahem – is Basilia still staying with you?'

'Why?' she asked, warily.

'I had thought I might come and see her, see how she was doing in all this: maybe take her off somewhere?' He finished uncertainly. Hippolyta felt sorry for him.

'Miss Verney left yesterday, on the Aberdeen coach,' she said gently. 'I believe she had plans to go further, but she said she would write with an address and of course there has been no time.'

'Oh.' Julian screwed up his nose, dismayed. 'I don't suppose … did she mention me, at all? Perhaps?'

Hippolyta was not going to give him the precise message that Basilia Verney had left for him: she was not that unkind.

'She just said she wished you well, but hoped you would allow her to go her own way, and not pursue her.'

'Oh.' His amiable face fell.

'To tell you the truth, Mr. Brown, I think you are as well off without her,' said Hippolyta bluntly. 'If you will take some advice from a woman –'

'Oh, of course!' he said eagerly.

'Then find yourself an interest in life that is not cards, or other gambling, don't assume that you need to be at the height of fashion for anyone to like you, and live a useful life,' she said. How easily her mother's voice seemed to be coming to her these days!

'Oh. Yes, yes, I think you may be right,' he said, but he did not look entranced by the idea, and bidding her good day he wandered off into the town, stepping clear of the worst of the mud and debris. As she watched him, a familiar figure appeared, glasses on his nose, medical bag in his hand, absent look across his handsome features. Patrick looked up, focussed, and saw her, and in a few long strides was beside her on the shore.

'That's good,' he said, seeing her sketch book.

'Thank you, kind sir!' She curtseyed.

'Coming home to dinner, though?' he asked. 'If we're not there in the first rush, those children will eat everything.'

She slipped her arm into his with a grin, and they headed up the hill of the little battered town, home.

'So, my dear Charlotte, you may perhaps excuse my lapse in writing – besides that the carrier could not get through along the road to Aberdeen for several days! It has been exciting and distressing in equal measure. I pray you if you meet a Miss Basilia Verney you give her a wide berth. But we still do not know if anything is really wrong with Mrs. Strachan, or if she will ever turn to Patrick for help and lead the rest of Ballater society his way!'

About the Author:

Lexie Conyngham is a historian living in the shadow of the Highlands. Her Murray of Letho and Hippolyta Napier novels are born of a life amidst Scotland's old cities, ancient universities and hidden-away aristocratic estates, but she has written since the day she found out that people were allowed to do such a thing. Beyond teaching and research, her days are spent with wool, wild allotments and a wee bit of whisky.

The cover illustrator, Helen Braid, is lovely, and can be contacted at www.ellieillustrates.co.uk.

If you've enjoyed this, the first book in the Hippolyta Napier series, and perhaps been kind enough to leave a review, then you can go straight to the sequel, *Death of a False Physician*:

> The dreadful day is approaching for the Napiers in Ballater: Hippolyta Napier's mother is coming to stay.
>
> But Mrs. Fettes is not just in Aberdeenshire to visit her youngest daughter: she has other reasons, and one will draw the whole family in, with deadly results.

If you'd like the chance to follow Lexie Conyngham's meandering thoughts on writing, gardening and knitting, take a look at www.murrayofletho.blogspot.co.uk, or on Facebook or Pinterest (Lexie Conyngham).

Finally! If you'd like to be kept up to date with Hippolyta and Lexie, please join our mailing list at: contact@kellascatpress.co.uk. No details are passed to third parties, not even for ready money!

The Hippolyta Napier series:
A Knife in Darkness
Death of a False Physician

The Murray of Letho series:
Death in a Scarlet Gown
Knowledge of Sins Past
Service of the Heir: An Edinburgh Murder
An Abandoned Woman
Fellowship with Demons
The Tender Herb: A Murder in Mughal India
Death of an Officer's Lady
Out of a Dark Reflection
Slow Death by Quicksilver

Also by Lexie Conyngham:
Windhorse Burning
The War, The Bones and Dr. Cowie
Thrawn Thoughts and Blithe Bits (short stories)

64005191R00187

Made in the USA
Charleston, SC
19 November 2016